GOD OF THIEVES:

INITIATION

GOD OF THIEVES:

INITIATION

V
Vincto Publishing

ARCHE

V

Vincto Publishing

DEDICATION

For my mother. Without your unconditional love and support, and a million more reasons besides, this book would never have existed.

My deepest thanks to my relentless beta readers and supporters. In particular, special thanks to Caroline Collins, Claire Fletcher, and Matthew Webb, whose invaluable contributions guided and motivated me during production.

CONTENTS

PROLOGUE

The thief held his breath as crumbs of plaster pattered down from his narrow perch inside the fluted dome of the basilica. The tap-tap on a lone guard's conical helm caused him to look up sharply. He brought his lantern to bear, searching out the disturbance high above. Sleepy hoots from indignant doves answered his investigation, followed by a white splat on his sandalled foot; a curse, a frustrated shaking of the besmirched toes, and he stomped off muttering unhappily to himself.

The thief breathed out slowly. He waited for his heartbeat to settle and the bobbing light to fade before questing with his boot tip for a lower crevice. He stretched out his arms as his weight descended, and carefully, so quietly, climbed down the wall.

He'd been in the city a scant few months. A few months which had rocked the relative order historically maintained between the natural balance of the triumvirate of powers that ruled. The landed Byzantine gentry, wealthy beyond measure and wielding the military force such funding assured; the sacerdotal priesthood of the Goddess, beloved of the common folk and bearing the moral authority of divine providence; and the Oikos families of murderers, pickpockets, whore-masters and drug-peddlers, whose mandate was such that they took what they wanted, and provided what was most secretly desired. Wealth and military power made Byzantium strong, the holiest sanctum of the Goddess made an attack the grossest sacrilege while also uniting the common folk, and the Oikos dealt in their own manner with fifth-columnists, spies and traitors, for they enjoyed the way things were.

This easy alliance offended the thief to his core.

1

There was one thing all three factions held dear; a sacred relic called the Arcasantos—a reliquary so holy that its very presence in the city made open assault by foreign powers such a politically unpalatable option that Byzantium's security was all but assured. Mysteries surrounded the Arcasantos, not the least of which was reputed to be the enigmatic power of reincarnation bestowed upon its owner. Such a powerful and valuable object was naturally protected by devious devices and fantastical monsters that between myth and legend claimed the life of at least one intrepid burglar a month—something that the thief had discovered during his research to have a basis in reality. Those heard boasting they planned the feat never returned to brag about their victory.

Naturally, the thief felt it already belonged to him, and that its acquisition would cement his reputation, which itself was already reaching epic proportions.

Standing on the cool mosaic floor, shrouded in shadow, the thief allowed his awareness to seep out into the darkness. Feeling something similar to gentle vibrations at the limits of his senses. In some distant chamber holy men chanted in unison; a gentle swelling chorus. The sweet odour of charred incense lingered faintly in the air, and mingled with the mouldering of desiccated parchment. All that was typical of such a place, and the thief allowed them to pass from his consciousness. The ripples caused by the passing guard faded out, but a louder pulse—nearby—drew attention. Keeping his hand near the dagger at his belt he crept forward. Circling the room from within the deepest dark. Avoiding the pale, elongated rectangles cast from the moon gauzily peeking through clouds above and trickling through the high windows.

He froze. Four doors led from the great chamber, shaped like a fat square with four ornate pillars that supported the angel's gallery. Each door stood paired with a brace of candles mounted on brass sconces. Sweet-smelling from the finest beeswax, their dim pool of flickering light was little

2

more than an aid to night-time navigation in such pervasive gloom. The passing guard exited through the door to the right, and the thief crouched such that a pillar shielded him from the doors to the front and back. The final door to the thief's left drew his attention—an interest validated by the tall silhouette, standing erect with long spear in hand. It could only be one of the renowned Athanatoi that pledged their lives to the defence of such holy places, and the Arcasantos above all. The man's armoured bulk nearly blocked the width of the open door; surely no-one could slip past?

The thief felt within his pouch, and between forefinger and thumb counted four bent and misshapen copper coins into his palm. The first of these he flicked across the room to patter at the door furthest from him. The Athanatoi guard trod a half step forward and brought his spear-head down to target the disturbance, yet wouldn't quit his post.

Such discipline!

The Athanatoi waited, flexed and attentive, but after some moments his shoulders eased, and the spear returned to the vertical. Immediately the thief flicked the second coin in the same direction—the spear descended! The guard cast his head about, peered into the shadows, but there was nothing there. No movement or danger that would persuade one so steadfast as he to abandon his position, and so with a glacial reluctance the spear once more ascended.

And the thief waited, his greatest challenge at that very moment to ensure the grin he wore didn't develop into a full-blown snigger. Too much at stake this night to indulge in such childishness. The Athanatoi's attention drifted back to the source of the tiny noises. Only when his weight rocked back on his heels did the thief flick the third coin.

Instantly the Athanatoi leapt across the room. A mighty thrust of his broad-bladed spear into the dark. A huge leap as swift and powerful as a lion—but the spear drove only into dust dancing in the air. As his sandals hit the floor the thief cast the fourth coin; cast it high into the sleeping doves

3

that clustered in the carved balustrades. Such a commotion! Feathers and plaster dust and cracked screeches filled the air, and for a moment the guard stood perplexed. He patrolled the room, swinging his spear before him, slashing at the darkest alcoves that might conceal an intruder, but found none. After several minutes searching he conceded the room was definitely empty. Darting glances from side to side, he resumed his duty in the doorway.

The thief had already travelled many yards down the corridor with the Athanatoi to his back, and his attention quested ahead; thoughts of laughter replaced with that of treasure. He advanced with caution but encountered no more men, armed or otherwise. The information he'd extracted in preparation for this night's caper, information plied by the generous application of beers, wines and spirits to the garrulous mouths of the few survivors of similar raids, warned him that watchmen were expected to be very few. Swords and spears mattered little for the Arcasantos was guarded by a succession of devious and butcherous traps. The thief paused as the passageway ended and ahead of him lay the great pillared hall of worship. Votary candles burned to stumps provided scant illumination, and he ignored the sacristy entrance in the floor which he knew connected to the catacombs beneath.

To take the path that had brutally claimed the lives of so many men of his profession was futile. The traps presented little challenge to him, other than staying awake for such tedious and time-consuming digressions. Furthermore, the thief felt it a labour he need not engage in, should a shrewd and stylish alternative present itself. He squatted behind the altar which surmounted the anticipated path down, and there he listened, not for footsteps but for the passage of air. He sniffed about, seeking the scent of something cool and damp. Every man knows that rain falls from the sky, but few pause to think where it goes next when there is no soil to soak it away. In these fields of stone water still needed to find its path and the thief, forearmed as he was with the knowledge that the temple had caverns beneath, sought to imitate the rain. He followed the shallow channels carved into the flagstones at his feet until he spied a mundane iron grill; circular but wide enough to admit a slender man with extremely flexible shoulders.

A rope tied here would present an unacceptable risk of discovery so the thief pried the grille free with the tip of the blue-steel dagger he wore at his belt. He wriggled into the tight vertical shaft, bracing his back to the wall, and slowly descended, pulling the grille back in place over his head. His initial concern that the descent would be challenging without a rope proved unfounded as he found himself almost entirely wedged in place. But that presented its own difficulty—rising waves of anxiety overwhelmed him at this narrow confinement. What should happen if he became stuck? His breathing quickened, painfully shallow, and his heart raced bringing trembles to his hands and weakness to his knees. Only his pride kept him moving down into the darkness, the dread of the deeps so nearly mastering him. He fought a quiet screaming war in his own head, the coiled animal within screeching for light and open skies. Despite the shaking that came in irregular bursts he still moved down, knowing that he must not stop, not even for a moment, for he did not trust his own courage that he could ever start again.

Time counted in the shifting of palms against the wall of the shaft, of knees chafing and the deep cold of ancient stone sinking into his backbone. Finally, as one foot found no purchase and dangled in space, a surge of elation chattered through his body bringing fresh energy to tired sinews. In this absolute darkness, fighting a primitive fear that he'd gone blind, he felt for his dagger and pried a small chunk of mortar loose, then dropped it between his legs. Almost immediately came the faint clink of it hitting the ground, so the thief allowed himself to drop out of the shaft. He landed in a deep crouch, his dagger in a slashing grip should it be needed.

It was not. The silence and the darkness were absolute.

5

Wrapped in his gear he had a tiny clay lamp, though remained reticent to light it, betraying his invisibility to others for a little visibility of his own. As he mulled his options he turned his head, noticing an area of grey in his otherwise inscrutable field of view. With little other option, he crawled toward it. The grey proved a true thing, not a raving of his imagination, and it lightened as he approached until he grew sure some light source lay ahead. Getting closer he discovered that he was in a small chamber or cave, and that in front of him opened a massive space. Although the floor was visible, a natural stone roughly hewn, any walls or ceiling were beyond his sight and lost in the darkness.

Peeking into the great cave beyond filled him with both confusion and curiosity. It would have been a huge space; empty and featureless for as far as the light allowed. Save that the light within bloomed from a profusion of smoking lanterns adorning a massive iron cage; stout and looking much like an impenetrable portcullis before the gates of a mighty fortress. If the Arcasantos nested within—for surely he had penetrated further than any other thief—why place so many lights around it and yet no attendant detail of Athanatoi, replete with spear and sword and axe? Surely it must be a trap, for what else could it be?

He prowled the circumference of cave and quickly discovered even the faintest noises he made proved without doubt he was alone. Still staying out of the light he began another circumnavigation, this time somewhat closer in, with his full attention now on the cage. Its bars too close to allow even a street-child, skilled in crawling through narrow passages, never mind a grown man like him. It bore but one gate, if that would be the right word for it, made obvious by three large padlocks that secured it. Of greater interest to the thief, he now saw what the cage protected; for inside squatted a metal cube covered with engravings, its sides somewhat longer than his own height.

Pondering these mysteries he waited, for he considered himself a patient man. Eventually, when he grew tired of listening to nought but the steady beating of his own heart, he muttered a curse at his own cowardice and stepped into the light.

Nothing happened. No sudden hail of arrows, deluge of burning oil or attack of burly sword-wielding buffoons. A trap it still must be, and if no attempt was made to stop him then he might as well proceed. The locks would be the first place he'd fit traps if he was being fiendish. Out came his tool roll, and from within it a series of specifically crafted implements designed to poke, prod and wiggle pieces of machinery (or in dire situations: pieces of people), but after some diligent testing it appeared they simply were what they appeared; unusually robust and complex locks. The first took him scant moments to work loose and he placed it carefully on the ground at his feet. It would certainly have kept out any save masters of the art of lock persuasion.

The second took the challenge to a new level. The thief knew of two women and one man in Byzantium that would be able to best it; had they been at the peak of their powers and given sufficient time to work undisturbed throughout the night. Eleven heartbeats passed before the lock joined its partner on the floor.

Flipping out a slender brass jimmy from his tools the thief attacked the final lock. It resisted. Battle ensued. The tumblers had springs, and with his ear to the cold iron of his adversary, the thief fancied he heard the whisper of cantilevers, and the ticking of fractional gears meshing. A great admiration for the designer of this lock rose in his heart. He'd never encountered its like, nor heard whispers of half the techniques he was led to surmise lay within the impenetrable casing. He bit down on two different jimmies, each tweaking a pin of their own, while a hooked prod in one hand worked part of the puzzle, independent of his other hand. A beautiful pleasure grew within him as he learned that no other man in the world would be able to defeat this puzzle. He wanted to laugh indulgently as the last mechanism clicked into place and the shackle snapped open, then he wilted with a

7

moment's empty sadness—the challenge was gone.

Any disappointment forgotten, he swung open the gate and regarded the baffling object within. The cube stood taller than he, finely carved on every available surface with scenes of conflict and battle led by a woman of great beauty and strength. The writings all quotations from a theological liturgy, and spoke of the triumphs and gifts of the goddess they worshipped. He stalked around the cube, carefully looking for more hidden traps, and finding none he tackled the cube itself. What on a cursory inspection appeared to be a solid mass of metal now revealed itself to be many interlocking components, the text and pictures serving to hide their presence. The thief nodded to himself, seeking the next step in solving this mechanical riddle, and began to probe fine cracks and depressions with his tools.

So nearly forsaken by a sixth sense that caused him to flinch away when something clicked beneath the lock pick. A sudden spray of tiny darts exploded from a hidden port to miss his face by the barest of margins.

Night Mother protect me!

Heart racing, he retreated several paces, picking up one of the darts. He rolled its shaft between his fingertips, barely bothering to confirm the poison he already knew would coat the needle point. He tossed it aside and moved his investigation to another side of the cube.

The scything blade that only scratched his chin would have taken his head off if he hadn't already been throwing himself away when he felt the minute vibration in the metal's surface. He lay on the ground panting until irritation became his over-riding emotion. So this was what it would be then; his skill and agility to be set against the ingenuity of the cube's designer.

Blades of varying sizes and operating by slashing or thrusting, gouts of flame, and poisons in powdered puff or liquid spray; all were served to him and no progress made he. Dejected, scorched, and scraped he sat facing the cube, elbows on his knees and chin on his knuckles. Too much time had passed with no progress and the longer that a heist lasted, the greater the risk of failure. He knew in his heart he was well past that time and it was only the celestial height of his own pride keeping him there. All the effort tired him and slowed his reflexes; if the next trap did not catch him then surely the one after would.

Forcing the squirms of failure deep into his belly he turned with downcast face to leave—then heard laughter, dry and rasping, but laughter most assuredly and definitely close by. The realisation hit him as fast as the ground did. His panicked break-fall tumbled him out of the cage, past the light of the torches and into the deep dark of the cavern once more. He spun, searching for danger, heard nothing but the dry rasping mirth that continued unabated, then he saw a balcony upon the stone wall. A balcony that must have been there all the time in the dark but now lit from an open room beyond. Silhouetted above stood a hunched figure from which all this merriment issued forth.

The wheezing mockery faded away as the hunched figure turned and left, closing the door behind them and the balcony once more disappeared. That coincided with the sound of distant tramping feet, which as it drew nearer and was supplemented by the jingling of metal fittings, easily identified as a marching troop of legionnaires. The thief retreated into shadows, unwilling to meet them head-on. Escape became his priority, but how could he avoid detection when a simple uniform was enough to tell friend from foe? Moments later soldiers swarmed into the chamber amidst shouted orders, punctilious responses and general military mayhem.

The two barking the loudest commands converged on the great cage and argued about the locks on the floor, while the rank and file fanned out to search the cavern for any interlopers. They called updates to their compatriots, though each had nothing in their sector. Out of earshot of their officers, the infantry whispered fearfully about ghosts, djinn and other threats. For what other than a malevolent spectre would haunt such a sacred reliquary then fade like mist when investigated? The bravest explored the darkest recesses, passing from the sight of their fellows for no more than moments. Despite fierce exhortations from their centurion the soldiers eventually returned empty-handed to the light in the centre of the cavern, fidgeting with their gear and weaponry until the disgruntled leader ordered them back to the barracks. A final disapprobation at the scruffy legionnaire whose uniform looked as if it had been hastily donned.

They marched out at a steady pace. Up a smooth ascending rampway on the far side of the catacombs which after a short time opened directly into the walled exercise yard of the Athanatoi compound built adjacent to the basilica. Men whose alertness had been fuelled by excitement now found themselves longing to return to the beds they'd so recently been roused from. Boots tugged loose, spears racked, swords stowed, and they chuckled at the scruffy footman claiming he about burst his bladder holding it in during their underground expedition. He made his excuses and headed briskly toward the latrines.

Footsteps became slower and the pace changed from marching to sauntering as the soldier walked past the latrines, and doffed a casual salute to the trio of legionnaires clustered around a brazier at the entrance to their camp. Just as brazenly he wandered through the training grounds and into the town, following the path down gentle slopes to less salubrious neighbourhoods. As he passed into the narrow lanes, he wiped his sticky fingers on his tunic, ridding himself of the last traces of the poison dart. He eased off the goose-feather plumed helmet and tossed it underhand into a pile of stinking refuse from the previous day's vegetable market. The ceremonial sword unbuckled and dumped in a horse trough (most unceremoniously). Finally he pulled the white surcoat off over his head. He tossed it to a drowsy vagrant who gratefully accepted its warmth—no thought given to the bloodstains still sticky around the collar—heedless to the barking of his little mongrel dog.

Thus unencumbered, the thief pulled up his hood and drew his cloak around his shoulders. Despite the unsociable hours the streets he passed through teemed with opiate vendors of dubious quality, and flesh-mongers of brazenly-advertised virtues. Finally reaching the crossroads at the centre of this district he passed under the sign of *Hekate's House* and into that famous temple.

Inside; the fumes of poppy pipes wreathed the ceiling, and the steam of sweaty, beery bodies fogged the air. The chattering, bantering rabble fell silent on his entrance and they moved aside as the thief walked to a secluded booth, empty although every other chair in the place was occupied. A young man with an earring marking him as a scion of the Oikos Scylla scurried over to the booth, setting down a flask of Gaulish brandy with his murmured compliments. Formalities observed, the patrons returned to their conversations.

The thief stared at the flask for several minutes before he sighed and uncorked it. And so, Zarbenus the God of Thieves took a big swig and swirled the fiery liquid around his mouth before swallowing and letting it heat his belly. This was what failure felt like. The laughter and smiling faces in his peripheral senses taunted him as he chewed on his lip. He took another drink. But to admit his first defeat? Zarbenus growled—it was not a defeat. Instead, an admittedly ignominious setback.

Something must be done, but he knew not what. The reverence of the patrons of this den of thieves, whores and murderers reminded him; he was far better than they. He was the most devious and ruthless villain in the world. And above all things, the most subtle and rarest of virtues, he was patient.

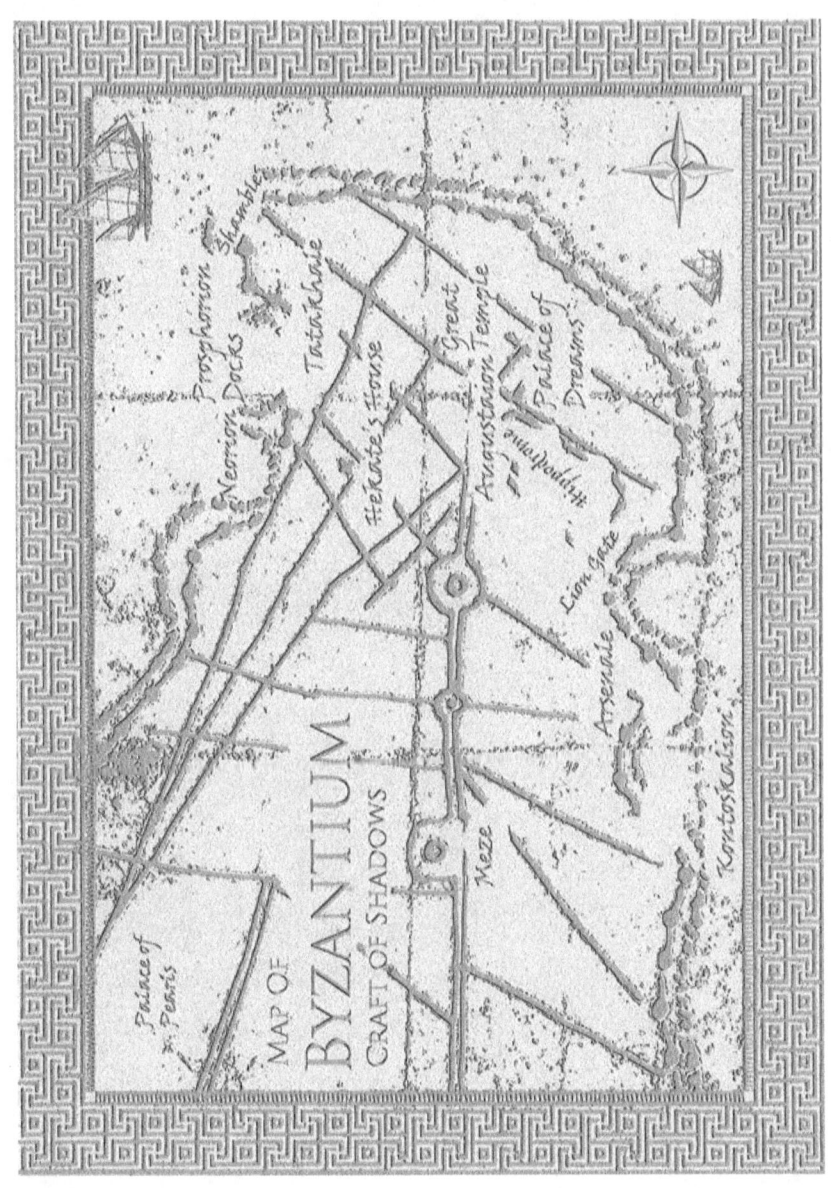

MAP OF
BYZANTIUM
CRAFT OF SHADOWS

Palace of Pearls

Neorion Docks

Prosphorion Shambles

TntrHouse

Hekate's House

A.L. Great

Anastasian Temple

Hippodrome

Palace of Dreams

Lion Gate

Arsenale

Meze

Kontoskalion

CHAPTER 1:

CATCHING A GHOST

Ten years later

Winter came in hard and cruel, and the ice in the air grew sharper by the hour. Zarbenus trudged in the lee of the trees as the mists of night shrouding the crescent moon choked away the evening's sparse grey light. Avoiding the war parties marauding across the hilly lands was trivial, but a landscape of slaughtered villagers, burned dwellings, cattle carcasses, wantonly hacked fruit trees, broken fences and poisoned wells left little of interest to a master thief. Little of interest to anyone living.

A stupid time of year to be out wandering at the best of times. But now, with the Horde's raiders devouring anything of value and destroying that which they could not take, was it even worth looking? Besides, he'd already rounded up a few that he'd selected to test. Ten years of careful machinations; flattering, threatening, and where necessary—terminal replacements. This was his great work. A noose he slowly tightened around the city's neck. This was only... an experiment. An indulgence of a whim. To satisfy his curiosity regarding certain far-fetched notions mentioned by the Hierarch of Byzantium. Why bother looking for any more candidates before seeing if the one he'd already selected would pass or fail? Doubts remained about their quality, and those inadequacies gnawed at him.

He sighed and shook his head.

Enough of this wasting time. Head for home and make do with what you have. Enough dreaming.

Zarbenus stopped and looked about to get a bearing on where his wandering had taken him. He pulled his cloak tight against the biting gusts and felt for the direction he'd seen the sun setting to. A footpath heading into the woods beyond some charred fields looked to be the right direction. He started to move then sank to one knee as a furtive shadow crept from the woods. It made swiftly to hide behind the wreck of an abandoned haywain, and so passed out of view.

Not a fox, too big, yet subtle. Movements harmonious with the elements that swelled rhythmically in the air and pressed against the ground. Unlike normal blundering people whose disturbing presence could be felt long before they showed themselves; crashing and jarring through the smooth intersecting ripples of the natural world.

Intrigued, he waited, until the small shadow left the shelter of the cart. It maintained its elegant, constrained, efficient progress across the field, sticking to the line of bushes that marked the boundary. All but invisible to anyone but he who could perceive the slightest movements and sounds, and had trained to hide even better. So, it was indeed a child. Very young, very small, moving with purpose; like a hunting animal. Thin, oh so thin, and only wrapped in rags despite the cold. Five or six summers at the most. Amazing that it had survived the onset of winter and—

A lone Horde marauder stomped at right-angles to the route of the child, spiked helmet clearly visible at this distance. The child had already stopped moving and all but melted into the bushes, but the marauder kept advancing. His head scanned slowly from side to side, then paused to sniff the air. A tracker, a hunter, or worse. The marauder shook out a heavy net laced with inch-long hooks; a slaver.

The little child was a good sneak, but he wasn't going to keep a seasoned hunter off his trail. Zarbenus watched as the marauder stalked closer to the child's hiding spot, sniffing. Always sniffing until at the last moment, already too late, the child bolted. Should have moved sooner, with more ground between them, but those that have learned to hide think that it will save them every time. Not this time. The net swirled from the marauder's hand, spinning weights and hooks and wire-strengthened cords wrapping around the child's flailing limbs. It crashed to the ground and the marauder bounded forward to collect his prize.

Interesting though; not a scream or even a yelp from the child as it was captured. Only those that learn that help is not coming stop calling out for father, mother, anyone. The silence of the utterly alone. Zarbenus felt... what was it he felt? Compassion? Recollection? Just as he'd decided to stop collecting the little brats and head home to sit out the winter by a cosy fire accompanied by some fine pilfered vintages to keep his company during the long nights.

The marauder probed his captive a few times with the butt of his spear then, receiving no response that interested him, delivered a solid kick into the bundle of child and rope. He heard a grunt, then administered two more kicks, each harder than the first and each precipitating a louder grunt.

Zarbenus' lip quirked and he stroked back his moustache to settle himself. The marauder kicked the bundle so hard it left the ground and crashed down a yard away. It rolled once then lay still, only a faint wheeze was heard. The enraged tormentor bellowed then hefted his spear, pointing it with shaking fist. The twitch in Zarbenus' lip moved to his hand; that involuntary spasm where the body knows there will be action before the mind has reached the same conclusion.

The marauder stood over the child; shouting at it. Gesticulating with the tip of the spear. Inches from the dirty face that lay on the ground. Staring up with neither fear nor rage nor any emotion at all. Eyes that had seen too much death to know the world had anything else in it. The marauder reached the crescendo of his furious babbling, drew back his spear arm with a sharp intake of breath to deliver a fatal blow. Then he dropped the spear on the ground. Patted his neck in blinking confusion as his lifeblood gushed from the incision across his throat. He opened his mouth and a gurgling whistle was the only noise he made before falling to his knees, slumping to the floor, then ceasing to move at all.

After some minutes of lying motionless, the child untangled the net. Never flinching as he pulled the barbs from his flesh. Freeing himself he stood cautiously, an arm comforting his ribs and looking around at the deepening shadows of the empty field. Eventually he stooped to tear the heavy cloak from the marauder's corpse, wrapping it over his own shoulders and then trailing away.

Silently, invisibly, and still wondering why he was doing it, Zarbenus followed; wiping the blood from his long knife.

Days passed and the boy moved through devastated towns. He avoided any sounds or signs of life, keeping to the shadows, sleeping in lofts and basements, creeping at night to collect scraps of food, wary of the daylight hours. Each day he grew stealthier, footfalls growing ever fainter until even Zarbenus struggled to keep up with him.

As he watched from a shadowed nook on a rooftop, knowing with years of experience that he was utterly hidden from even the most experienced seeker, Zarbenus' heart thrilled. The boy, passing from one house to another froze, tilted his head then stared straight at the chimney that concealed his secret watcher. The boy crouched there motionless before finally returning to his nocturnal expedition, and the grin unbidden drew across Zarbenus' cheek.

The Dark Mother blesses him! Such raw, unformed, untrained talent. Such potential!

In the days that followed the boy made his way down from the mountains and into the foothills below. The broken villages gave way to larger towns just as shattered, scorched and pillaged. Still stealthy of the few survivors, the boy hiding as warbands passed through, rooting in the rubble for any remaining loot they may have missed in their first destructive tempest through the region. As the night gave way to the grey half-light before dawn, the blush on the horizon painted the first colours of the day. The boy climbed the broken stone stairs of a once beautiful temple, his lair where superstitious locals would never tread. Zarbenus watched as the boy learned to pilfer more than food. Trinkets and shiny objects from cupboards and closets, nightstands and strongboxes; even from around the necks of sleeping victims while his skill and boldness grew.

The people in the town, already used to living in terror, now whispered about a ghost that haunted them, for nothing else could explain the mysterious presence that moved unseen amongst them. This amused Zarbenus, and he conceded that the epithet was appropriate. Each night the little ghost retreated before dawn and slept uneasily in his hidden place, surrounded by the treasures that meant to him a reclamation of power in his life, no matter how small. Each night he was so careful and so quiet that no-one saw where he went. Then came a time he failed to spot a solitary loping figure, clad in motley pieces of leather armour strapped around its war-seasoned form. A marauder with knife drawn, stealthily scaling the same steps to the broken temple.

Zarbenus hesitated; an enclosed place with no knowledge of what lay in wait. Unable to plan ahead, to scout, to weigh the danger against the reward, surely an unjustified risk? But these were the same risks that the ghost boy lived each day, without complaint. Never once breaking down and crying; crying for an adult to pick him up and shelter him. What would a child like that be capable of with the right guidance, training, and moulding? He moved forward, still questioning his own motivations. Still consumed by the odd fascination that had kept him shadowing this strange feral creature for the last two weeks.

The stairs turned through two sharp bends and Zarbenus smelt the sour rankness of the marauder lingering in the air. Ducking under fallen joists he reached the floor above and saw the man's armoured back. The dawn light filtered a pale straw yellow through dancing motes above broken stonework. And in the light, the glint of a blade.

The boy crouched on the ground. His back to the wall, limbs twisted tight, ready for flight. No possible escape save the stairwell blocked by the leering soldier. This was no slaver. Maybe he wanted sport, or to take his pleasure, or just some tender meat. The child would shortly die, and yet he still did not cry. He glared with bared teeth—the purest animal form of anger—at the armed man bearing down on him.

Fair? Zarbenus had no measure in his heart for the word. He took what he wanted because he could, and had never met a force that was sly enough or swift enough or utterly remorseless enough to stop him.

The knife drew back and the boy roared his challenge. He would meet his end in rage and hatred and defiance. Never be cowed no matter the insurmountable forces matched against him. Without thinking, without decision, without a pause, Zarbenus took the second throat he'd severed in defence of the boy. As the corpse fell between them, the child and the master thief looked at each other for the first time.

The child's lips twitched, his eyebrows bunched. Zarbenus slowly, very slowly, turned his palms upwards, showing them to be empty. The child's eyes flicked to them, darted to the now vacant escape route down the stairs, then back at this stranger who'd killed to protect him. He swallowed hard, his jaw moving and a sound somewhere between a whine and a grunt came out. Zarbenus wondered how long it had been since the child had spoken to anyone, and whether it still could.

Words were unexpected, but when it came there was only one. With no tremor in his voice, nor gratitude—or even any great interest—the boy said, "Why?"

Zarbenus looked down at him and wondered if he really knew the answer, if he would ever know.

"I saw something in your eyes that reminded me... of me." He spoke the

20

boy's own tongue, properly formed words and watched those eyes glisten at the familiarity of the sounds.

"Thank... you." The child's head inclined in the direction of the exsanguinated meat that was once a Horde marauder.

"Yes, yes. You are in my debt. Come, we must leave this place. It is not safe for you."

The ghost boy tumbled backward, arms and legs skidding across the floor as he propelled himself under the shelter of the fallen beams. He hissed, spat and yelped. Zarbenus crouched, never blinking, as the boy's gaze darted around, looking for an escape, then back to his rescuer, then away again. Eventually the boy fell silent and still, and yet he glared at Zarbenus.

"You're not an animal, boy. Not completely. Use your words. Remember."

The boy hissed again and tried to squeeze further under the debris. Zarbenus remained motionless and eventually the boy calmed. He gaped his mouth, whined, snapped his teeth, but still no reaction from Zarbenus. The boy shrieked, hammered his fists and feet against the ground, then froze in silence as a shiny coin appeared between Zarbenus' finger and thumb. The boy's eyes narrowed to slits, confused and yet intrigued by this blatant display of powerful magic.

Zarbenus moved the silver denarius from side to side, watching as the boy tracked it. "I know you understand me, boy. Show me your words, and this is yours."

First came grunts, then strangled vocalisations. Zarbenus nodded, and the boy tried again. "Wah... Where?"

"Somewhere safer. Come. No more questions."

Zarbenus flicked the denarius off his thumb, turned and made for the stairs. The boy snatched the coin out of the air then started to collect up his treasures, a handful of chains and charms.

"Leave that junk. Come. Now."

The boy let the trinkets slip through his fingers, keeping the silver piece clenched tight in his palm, then he followed the hooded man. Zarbenus stood at the bottom of the stairs, staring up at the boy through the tangled jumble of fallen beams.

"Hurry up."

"You quick."

"Aye. I am. Come now."

Zarbenus walked through the middle of the town. The skies were clear and bright, and the boy shaded his eyes and scowled. He watched as people ignored a strange man with his hood drawn up on a fine morning. As Zarbenus passed the people glanced up, but their interest never seemed to settle on him and they carried on with what they were doing. Their attention moved to the dirty vagrant boy, dressed in scraps and smelling worse. They turned up their noses and tutted and well-really'd; a skinny beggar child, barely reaching belt-height.

The lone sentry at the gate watched the hooded man arrive, stopped him and demanded his toll money. While Zarbenus searched in his tunic a call summoning the guards came from the market behind them.

"Wait here," said the guard through gritted teeth. He pointed his spear at the feet of the hooded man.

"Absolutely. I'm in no rush. You go see what the problem is." Zarbenus seemed diminished, more compliant, and more timid. He bobbed his head gently with each sentence, almost bowing to the guard.

The guard fired off another threatening glare then turned and hurried off to the market.

"Come." Zarbenus beckoned to the boy then strode through the gate.

"How do?" The boy hurried to keep up with the long steps. He kept holding up his hand as if hoping the hooded man would take it.

"Hmm?"

"How make noise behind?"

Zarbenus paused mid-stride and looked down at the boy. "You are uncommonly perceptive."

"What mean?"

The hooded man breathed in through his nose then puffed out. "It means, that amongst other things, we shall need to work on your vocabulary. Come now. There will be time enough for all these questions once I have you safely away from here. This is an unfortunate time to be a lonely *Kossak* boy."

"Why?"

The hooded man stamped his foot and loomed over the boy. "Enough! Come with me now if you want to live. Otherwise go where you please. Either way you shall not have another word from me until I am safe on the boat."

† † †

The hooded man who had rescued him walked away in long, loping strides and after a moment's pause the boy ran after him. The hooded man did not slacken his pace, but as a laden waggon clattered past them he swung up to sit on the backboard. He caught the boy by his outstretched hand and heaved him up to sit side by side.

The boy opened his mouth several times to ask questions, as interesting buildings or strangely garbed riders passed, but each time fell silent as he caught the look in the hooded man's eye. He dozed by measures but each time woken by a lurch of the waggon, only to nod slowly off and be awakened again. By late afternoon the boy smelt a salty tang in the air and the waggon descended a coiling path that took them out of the foothills. It was still cold, but milder than the biting chill of the mountains and without even a fleck of snow in the wind. As the ground levelled out they rolled into a noisy town filled with the shrill call of unfamiliar birds that swooped and spiralled above. Fish-hawkers put away their noisome catch as the market folded up for the day. The people had darker skin than those from the mountains, and many with rough, weather-worn faces, leathery and cracked.

The hooded man slid off the back of the waggon and pushed through the crowd, without looking behind him to see if the boy followed. The boy hurried after him, buffeted by big bodies and knocked from side to side. His chest tightened as he lost sight of the hooded man, and he wheezed in relief when he saw the dark cloak and cowl ahead of him, talking to a fat fellow with a beard that reached his paunchy waist.

Then he saw the sea.

The black glassiness stretched out the whole way to the horizon, wider than he had ever imagined the world could be. Spiky crests of white water rolled in a broken patchwork between the oily darker strands of deep currents. Ships with sails and ships with paddles bobbed industriously at sea, and more of them tied up at the long jetty. The breeze carried dampness in it, and the boy tasted salt as it speckled his lips.

He looked open-mouthed at the hooded man who seemed utterly unperturbed by the magnificent scene. The discussion between the two men appeared to be over. The fat one with the long beard smiled and held out his hand. The hooded man pulled a purse from his tunic, and after chinking within he deposited several coins in the proffered palm.

"Come. We catch the last boat."

He turned and loped off down the jetty, the boy scrambling after him. At the very end squatted a fat black boat; wooden rail high above their heads, and two rows of round glass windows beneath. Square sails dyed with wide yellow and blue horizontal stripes hung from three tall masts, and each side of the boat bore a huge circular waterwheel. Black smoke disgorged from a broad brass chimney that grew out of the decks between the fore- and mid-masts. The mid-mast was the largest and bore the mainsail, but its coloured stripes were mired with ash from the chimney.

"Quick steps now, little ghost."

24

Sailors cast off mooring lines and the walkway that descended from the paddleship to the jetty skidded noisily across the stones. The hooded man swept up the boy in his arms and ran up the bouncing and swaying walkway, though neither bounced nor swayed himself. He dropped the boy on the deck of the ship just as the walkway wheeled back in. Black smoke spewed and a high pitched whistle shrieked as the water wheels turned and the ship shuddered away from the docks.

The boy gripped the rail above his head and stuck his face over the edge, watching the frothy eddies in the stream reaching out behind them, and the town beyond that, and the dark shadow of the mountains beyond them.

Matir...

He felt the loss of his mother, but it seemed so strange, like something that had happened to someone else. Something someone had told him. Emptiness and sorrow lived inside him, the emotions more familiar than the fading memories.

The hooded man stood talking to a rugged woman; sword at her waist and a lantern swaying from her hand. She wore an eyepatch with scarring visible above and below the cloth strap, and broke off conversing with the hooded man to shout at the sailors working on deck. This command echoed up the rigging creating flurries of activity. The ship rolled from side to side, crawling forward to open water, but neither the hooded man nor the woman paid notice.

The hooded man nodded to the woman and motioned for the boy to follow. He descended steps leading to the belly of the boat, and with unsteady feet slipping and sliding on the spray-slicked deck the boy hurried to follow him.

Their cabin was narrow, the only furnishing a worn and stained cot with straw poking through where the cloth had frayed. Opposite the door was a round window, and frothy spray splashed it as the ship rose and fell in the swell. Beyond, just visible in the gloom, an outline of the waterwheel with a glistening stream of water falling from its edge. The hooded man put his back to the wall with the window and slid down until he sat on the edge of the cot, arms resting on his knees and his scarf-swaddled chin resting on his arms.

"Shut the door and sit down. The wind is poor so the crossing will be slow. Take your chance to rest, boy."

"No boy! I—huh?"

The hooded man pressed a finger hard into the boy's forehead. It hurt, but the boy did not flinch.

"You have no name until you have earned one. How could you possibly have a name when you don't know what you can do?"

"But..."

"You will have no name until I give you one, and then only when you have earned it. Until that time you are only Ghost."

"You no—"

"And I can take that name away with a snap of my fingers," said the hooded man.

The boy called Ghost crossed his arms over his chest and growled. After a few moments he looked up.

"What you name?"

"You have not earned that yet either. You may call me Magister for now. When I tell you to do something you say, 'Yes, Magister', and do it immediately."

The Magister withdrew his finger and, pulling his cowl closer about his face, hunched in the corner of the narrow room. Ghost still felt the impression of the fingertip, pulsing on his brow.

"What mean 'Magister'?"

"It means I am the master of moving without sound, passing without shadow. I whisper poetry to locks and lift bells from pockets. And at the end of things; the sweet dance of the long blade, and the goodnight of the short.

26

If you are worthy, and maybe not even then, you may learn these things from me." The Magister held up a hand to forestall any interruption. "In simple words, a thief, amongst other things."

A thief? A bad man?

Ghost continued to frown; so much to assimilate. "Magister?"

"What is it, Ghost?"

"Is ocean? Is big."

"It is just the sea, boy. The Black Sea. The ocean is far larger; that goes on and on until the ends of the world where it pours over into the endless void."

"I want go," said Ghost with a yawn.

The boy curled up on the edge of the cot with his back to the door. He felt the dulling need for sleep growing behind his eyes. A little light came through the round window but it cast scant illumination on the boy, and none on the hooded man collapsed in the corner under the window.

"He's too damn young..." The Magister continued to grumble to himself but the boy couldn't make out any more words, and was too scared to talk in case he did something wrong. Ghost sat in silence and worry crawled and skulked in his imagination, but eventually he heard a soft snoring from the darkest shadow in the corner of the room. Unhappy about the queasiness in his belly not just from the rolling of the ship, the boy listened to the snoring for some time before he too fell asleep.

He dreamed he was hiding in a barrel, but the barrel was rolling down the mountain. When it came to the end it would surely smash and kill him, but outside the barrel was a shadow and she was watching over him. He could smell the warmth of her skin, her fingertips stroking his hair, and slept deeper than he could remember for a very long time.

Watery sunlight tried to force its way in between tightly clenched eyelids, and he clapped his hands over his face as someone jostled him awake.

"Wake up boy. I've scrounged up food for us."

Half of a dried sausage dropped on the cot in front of the boy's face. He squinted out from between his fingers, and his mouth grew wet as the smell of the garlic overwhelmed him. Propping himself up on one elbow he picked up the half-sausage and took a large bite.

The Magister was back in the darkest corner again. He drew up his scarf so that his mouth and short-cropped black beard were visible as he ate. He stopped chewing as he saw the boy's intent gaze.

"What is it, Ghost?"

"Why no light? It hurt you?"

The Magister popped the last of the sausage into his mouth and then tucked the scarf back under his chin.

"It is just habit, little one. You will understand soon enough. Besides, I have the best view of the door from here."

"Why?"

"I always seat myself where I can be seen least and yet still watch the door. Better still if I can be seated somewhere I can make a discreet exit if I so chose."

The whine of the water wheels fell in pitch and the Magister tilted his head.

"We will be pulling into deep waters soon. Up you get. You'll want to see this."

The Magister coalesced upward and his tall shadow passed over the boy and out the door. Squashing the last of the sausage into his mouth the boy tumbled off the cot and followed him up the stairs.

For four days the paddleboat surged through heavy swells and brief squalls. Dark clouds formed over the land to the east drawing the captain's attention. She glanced at them and frowned time and again, but her fears were not realised and the storm passed many miles from them. Ghost had started his voyage with few words, preferring to sit on one of the benches that spanned the rear deck, watching the suntanned sailors at work with their

28

ropes, or sooty-faced compatriots splitting logs to feed the furnace in the heart of the ship. As time passed he began to ask questions in his own language, and receive answers in theirs, and by-and-by they managed to communicate.

The captain of the *Falaina* was more taciturn at first. She responded to the small voice chirping from beneath the height of her hand on the tiller with a grunt, or a shrug, or usually nothing. That was until he pointed to her eyepatch. A grin cracked her leathery face and she flashed him a quick glance underneath—an ugly mass of old scars that made the boy fall backward and yelp. She bellowed with laughter at his distress, but when he began to giggle she smiled back at him. Captain Callista quickly warmed to the inquisitive child and would sit him atop the con where she pointed out sights of interest as she steered with the other hand. Little consideration was given to whether he understood her language, yet all the same they got along fine.

The ship powered on steadily, frothing spume spraying from the waterwheels. At first light on the fifth day they left the swells of the sea, and entered the calm water of a rocky shoreline they could see on both sides. Woodland, farmland and diminutive villages came into view then slipped behind to be lost in the grey clouds that trailed the paddleboat's smokestack. After only a couple of hours Callista whistled for Ghost's attention. Ahead rose up a towering silhouette and as the morning light drew sharp edges he realised with a shock that it was not a mountain.

"Is house? They big big! Much lots people?"

"Houses and palaces, libraries and temples. Welcome to Byzantium, the city in the centre of the world. Home to kings and princes, priests and beggars, and of course the thieves that infest every alley, sewer, attic and crawl space between the walls," said the captain, glancing at the silent shadow of the Magister.

So many other ships, boats, rafts and other unidentifiable floating objects were intent on passing to and fro that the captain hollered for the paddlewheel to be stilled. With a grinding shudder and a volcanic plume of ash, the beast fell silent. The crew seized bailing hooks and long poles and between prods at other ships and the necessary lubricant of passionately exchanged sailors' curses they slowly made progress. To either side were dour and functional forts whose purpose, it was explained by Callista, was to guard the way against pirates or marauding armies. At night their vigilance continued by barring entrance to the whole strait with a giant chain that ran between the forts. To see this in operation became an insistent demand of the boy who became quite frenzied at all the activity around him. However, hastening nightfall was—as she wearily repeated—outside the conventional powers of a ship's captain, so he bit her hand. Her slap wasn't hard, but it was unexpected. Ghost yelped and scurried away. Callista didn't watch him go, her attention on the myriad of chores fighting for her attention. With all hands on deck there was barely a nook free for Ghost to hide in, buffeted by ropes and chains moving in every direction, kicks of frustration from barefoot sailors with the varied and creative curses that followed. He worked his way back to the con, wedged himself behind the pedestal and cabinet housing the *Falaina's* compass. After several minutes of studiously ignoring each other, Callista took a swig of water from a ladle passed to her by the chief engineer. She passed it to Ghost without glancing at him, he drank, passed it back and they continued in silence; friends again.

The morning light that first brought a yellow glow to the spires of the tallest buildings travelled down their heights; unveiling shining golden domes and tall white towers, as graceful and elegant as swan necks. Beneath the towers stood grand buildings with tall windows of coloured glass, and beneath them dignified townhouses in white marble. As the buildings ran down to the docks their height and splendour diminished to the lowest line of straw-thatched wooden shacks that crowded along the edge of the port. Vast walls of stone surrounded the city, but for all their immensity the hills of the city rose up taller. Tall conical cypresses and lofty spreading oaks thronged between the buildings so that the wild forest and noble metropolis seemed to live and breathe together seamlessly.

Battlements soared up both sides as they passed into the fortified harbour. Patrolling soldiers with spears to their shoulders glanced down from their lofty vigils. The whine of the engine that reverberated through the deck underfoot fell lower again and the waterwheels slowed as the paddleship coasted towards the docks. Gulls shrieked overhead, garrulous and shrill. The oily fishy odours of boats laden with twitching piles of massive spine-backed sturgeon and barrels of striped sardines overwhelmed the bituminous reek from the ship's smokestack. A tall sailing ship moored to a buoy passed by on one side and a flotilla of small rowing vessels scrambled to get clear of their passage. Callista stood at the prow of the ship, one foot stepped up on the barge board and her hand resting on the hilt of her sword. She barked orders to men on the jetty as harshly as she did to her own crew, busying themselves running the bow- and stern-lines to tie the *Falaina* fast in her mooring.

The Magister approached her as the ship bumped to a halt, and she turned to him with a wry smile. He bowed low and tugged his scarf aside long enough to kiss her hand. The scarf was replaced before Ghost could see any of his features. The woman flashed her teeth and let out a short laugh then waved the Magister away and returned to haranguing the dock workers.

A walkway hoisted into place and the Magister trotted down it without looking back. The boy wrinkled his nose and watched in annoyance as the hooded man walked down the jetty and started for the crowded dockside market. A stinking open sewer ran down the middle of the street and emptied straight into the harbour. With a flip in his heart Ghost realised the Magister wasn't stopping, and he scrambled down the walkway and sprinted across the jetty.

Chapter 2:

Byzantium

Ghost fell quiet as they carried on down the road; the towers of Byzantium tall above the city walls and the clusters of thatched dock buildings. To all sides crates and barrels and bundles of goods; wicker-caged chickens and pens of goats and sheep and cows with humped shoulders and long horns. Voices in a hundred tongues argued and sang and gossiped, while pied gulls screeched and dived and bickered as they fought over fiercely contested scraps.

"I have business to attend to in the city," said the Magister. "I need to meet someone. Someone I don't trust very much, so I want you to be outside keeping watch. Do you think you can do that?"

Ghost nodded. "Shout?"

"I want you to whistle for me. The sound will carry much better and you'll be harder to spot."

"Can whistle," said Ghost, nodding, then cupped a hand to his mouth and piped a reedy warble.

"A single hoot will suffice. Now, pull your hood back before we approach the Basilisks. Feel free to look awestruck and wide-eyed so they will think us simple pilgrims."

The Basilisks turned out to be a cadre of battle-scarred warriors. Kataphraktos, they called themselves after their heavy scale armour. They bristled with spears and spiked shields, all their gear cratered and scored with each man's history of warfare. To enter the city through the Neorion

Gates it was first necessary to pass them. Wordless they took turns to flick back traveller's cloaks with a javelin tip, pausing to thrust deeply into a waggon of straw. The boy had no need to act awed as the scene had him slack-jawed at the profusion of voices in different tongues; white Hellenic tunics worn by bearded men, Damascene jewelled finery around the necks of dark men with oiled hair, and even stranger tall lean-limbed men with skin as dark as the finest leather and exuberant curly hairstyles. Sweaty and spicy bodies pressed shoulder-to-shoulder as people toiled their way through the crowds.

A Basilisk *dekarchos* with shaven chin and long brown moustache turned his head to the Magister and his boy, beckoned them forward. His helmet bore a badge with an engraved 'X', marking his command over ten men. The officer idly scratched himself between the neck joint of his cuirass and iron gorget as the stoop-shouldered Magister drew near; his eyes downcast, holding a boy-child by his hand. The Magister mumbled something placating, but the Basilisk roared a challenge; stamping down with his studded boot to shower them with dust. The Magister fell to his knees, whimpering and holding his shaking hands above his head. Guffawing, the Basilisk *dekarchos* looked back at his fellows; they shared a grin, then he waved the trepidant travellers through, chuckling to himself.

Bowing nervously and whispering a stream of assorted apologies and gratitudes, the Magister collected the boy's hand and hurried them into the city.

The wide path through the gates led through a succession of broad plazas, each spreading further than the last. As they ascended the steep steps of the city the buildings that surrounded each square grew taller and more elaborate. Still, in between vines and marble colonnades, cool courtyards walled with azure tiles patterned with leaves and fruit, behind the wealth and splendour were signs that Byzantium had a more violent history than the peace it enjoyed now. Abandoned districts of burnt beams and collapsed stone; derelict parkland, decades-old, overgrown with brambles and the bobbing of dusty red poppies; quarrelling packs of dirty yellow dogs plagued by flies; fallen statues of ancient lords, their faces smooth and worn. To the west ran the great Mese, wider than a river, colonnaded by victorious sculptures, flowing with the trade of the city and the ding-dong-ding bells of the water carriers. They climbed the first great hill of the city, and as the buildings grew taller so the hunched and deferential Magister did also. His shortened scuffling steps lengthened, and soon as the boy started to ask the obvious question he found his hand abruptly released and needed to scurry to keep up.

All the chaos settled as they entered a plaza large enough to host an army. The Augustaion crowned the First Hill; its jewels the Hippodrome and Palace of Dreams to the south, and the Great Temple to the east. Monumental cedars spread welcome shade across a market of scribes and booksellers. Stalls piled with parchments and stacked pyramids of scrolls as advocates, doctors, philosophers and poets boasted the altitude of their abilities by castigating their competitors. The Magister paused outside the soaring purple-tiled and gold-domed temple and thumbed in its direction. The smoke of burning incense rolled out the door, down a short flight of broad steps, and wisped around the hooves of the animals. The vastness of the structure left the boy frozen in silence; entire towns of his short experience could have fitted under its curved roof.

"In that temple there is a solid gold box, but every side has so many rubies and emeralds and sapphires mounted in it that you can only see a flash of yellow if you squint at it from the right angle. A truly fabulous treasure."

Ghost whistled softly, and the Magister nodded.

"The box alone you'd think worth my time alone, but within lies the bones of some holy woman, long dead, and to the right buyer they would pay a thousand times the value of the gold and gems. These cities and temples vie with each other for prestige and power and for some reason the bones of martyrs make for rich currency."

"No take... tresha?"

The Magister waved a fly away from his face as he considered the temple door, and the two pike-bearing moustachioed Basilisks standing either side of it.

"Treasure, boy. Plenty of good thieves have died trying. Aye, even men I had a grudging respect for. No, that is not a job for a thief, but for a magician. Learn your limits and avoid an untimely death."

A row of proud, tall men clad in white tunics marched toward the temple. Each wore a sword on one hip and a long dagger on the other, and their white headscarves tied with a long trail that ran down their backs. Their bearing and the spotlessness of their attire glowed with pride in their role. In the middle of the row was a similarly white-robed old man on a padded chair carried on the shoulders of four broad-shouldered slaves with red hair and iron collars on their necks. The procession stopped at the bottom of the steps leading up to the temple and the slaves inched the chair to the ground. Slowly the clouds of dust settled.

The old man stood with some difficulty then adjusted his simple white robes. He cleared his throat and the murmurs of the crowd faded away. When he spoke his voice cracked with age yet carried a depth of love and devotion.

"When the world was young, and before men built their cities; when families farmed and hunted in small communities of close relatives, the wisest person in the tribe was the venerable grandmother. She had lived more years than any other, and she knew stories from her mother's mother's time; where to fish when the spawning failed on a dry year, or where meat might be found if the valley lay full of snow. She knew which herbs soothed a fevered brow, and which fungus would aid the painless passing of a gravely injured hunter.

"She was also the one to whom the Goddess spoke—for there were no gods of any stature in those days—and she brought forth the gifts that a mother brings; the birth of the sun in the morning, the birth of the spring after winter, the birth of the crops from the earth, and of course the gift of newborn children as were not all women her own mortal embodiment? Maiden, mother and crone was she all at once, but she needed no priests to explain her mysteries for all understood her word and her power—she was Life.

"And think ye not that the menfolk were unhappy, nay. They had small gods who guided the last arrows true as evening drew in when the hunting had been lean. Minor spirits they whispered to so they might spark a hearth-fire when all around was clammy and damp. But even the men carried with themselves carven icons of the Mother because she was the Why, and she was the How.

"Life was simple and life was good, but in the fullness of time men built towns and then they built cities. Many came to live there, not just families and kinfolk, but strangers of different colours of skin and hair, of languages strange and discordant, and all feared their neighbours. Into the cities came sickness from the filth of all the bodies pressed so close, desired by no other living thing save rats and fleas. So in the cities men were afraid, and as they could not hear the words of the Goddess amongst the rabble of so many voices they began to hear the hard and loud commands of the Gods. Terrible were they and wrathful to all, fear they wielded in one hand and a slaver's lash in the other. So confusing and contradictory were their voices that priests were needed to study these mysteries, interpret and instruct, but soon even the priests warred with each other and brother slew brother and the age of strife began.

"For a thousand years this continued, and might have for a thousand more had there not been born a simple shepherd girl. Great with child, alone in a cold cave protecting her flocks as a storm raged outside. She cried out for the Goddess, the stories her mother had told her, and her mother before that, that they were each the earthly embodiment of Her. And this time, She had not forgotten and She heard them. When the child was born strong and healthy there was a miracle laid upon her that would follow all of her days.

"All of you here know the deeds she performed and how she brought the message of the Goddess back into the cities. As the faith grew she was able to pass in peace and was gathered to the bosom of the Goddess. Her bones lie here, and about them the faithful built a temple to her glory where her work could be taught to others. Together we recognise her by one hundred names; in the east she is known as Ninmah, Asherah or many others. Many of you know her as Tanit, and far to the West they still call her Danu. Whatever name you use to honour her, know that all are united under her love and care. We swear, once this great city has been made pure we will turn our gaze of love to the rest of the world."

The assembled city-folk cheered and chanted to which the old priest smiled beneficently. He raised a withered and ancient hand on which a single large ruby was prominently displayed, and their clapping echoed off the surrounding walls. As he waved his hand to the crowd the faithful touched their fingers to their lips, shut their eyes and murmured prayers. The leader of the men in white tunics took the elbow of the old man and carefully supported him through each tentative and wobbling step. The pikesmen either side of the door readied themselves but before the heads of their weapons had moved more than an inch the man in white unslung his belt, sword and dagger still sheathed, and offered it to the guards.

The guards nodded as they took the belt from him and then took a step back allowing the old man to be escorted into the temple. The crowd moved off in twos and threes, their burbling conversations blending with the general hubbub of shopkeepers, stallholders and street vendors. The men in white eased their stiff-backed postures and swapped jokes with each other.

"Even the clerics are rich men, Ghost. So powerful they have their own guards. Aye, even their own armies. You'd think the worst dangers of a city were the cutthroats and vagabonds, but it is the nobles and politicians that dice with all our lives. They jostle and plot to gain influence and power and wealth, and the clerics are just as bad. They speak prettily but never be fooled to think other than our lives weigh less in their palms than a small copper coin. Temple to their goddess indeed. Twas the temple to Mithra when I was a boy, and the temple to the old emperor before that. So many lives thrown away for nothing more than a fleeting grasp of power."

"*Matir* gone." Ghost's head drooped as memories overwhelmed him.

"You and me, boy. I remember being small and powerless too; never again will I be ensnared by their machinations. We are just rats scurrying in the shadows in the corner of the room. It is better that way."

Ghost balled up his fists and his nails dug into his palms. "I kill."

"Idiot child." The Magister looked down at the scowling boy and wrinkled his nose. "I try to teach you but you never seem to learn."

Ghost's fists dropped to his lap, and he slouched forward. "Bad hurt hurt."

The Magister tugged the peak of his cowl forward so that only the tip of his nose could be seen. "Then seek for shadows, and in them find the coolness and calmness you need. Think of ripples on water and compose your mind. When you can do this you will be a master of the craft."

The boy bowed his head. "Yes, Magister."

The Magister walked onward. On the busiest streets the crowds moved imperceptibly apart as he flowed past them, but Ghost saw their gaze slip off the Magister like rainwater. The broad thoroughfares loud, hot and dusty, but every dozen paces sprouted a lane to the side packed with stalls and barely enough room to squeeze past on foot. A street given over to carpet sellers, turquoise and gold threads, geometric designs, stylised deer and antelopes; a lane full of spice vendors, brass scales, multicoloured piles of fragrant cinnamon, ground chillies, golden saffron; the twisting path of Songbird Street, alluring from afar, an enchanting dream of sibilant trilling as they passed. The Magister turned abruptly down narrow side streets, scaring gangs of feral cats, then doubled back to push through the flow of bodies down the central avenue in the direction he had just come from. Loops he described through the streets with Ghost running after him, buffeted by bodies and beasts of burden, until as the light was fading he turned into an alleyway with an overhead arch between the two facing buildings. At the end of the alley they found a tiny courtyard of grey flagstones, and an open door with the sound of merry voices and of chinking glass. Overhead hung a painted sign of a verdant apple and a tankard.

Loitering with intent beside the door was a pimple-faced youth with a mop of spikey black hair. His hand moved to grasp his dagger's hilt in a manner to make it obvious to the newcomers that the next portion of the greeting they could expect would have the taste of steel to it. Without raising his arm the Magister flashed the palm of his left hand, then touched his thumb to the tip of his ring finger. The signal was over in less than a second, and the youth immediately released his weapon as his head lolled back to rest against the wall.

The tiny room smelt of stale cider and staler sweat that the reek of the cheap tallow candles did little to mask. They entered and the Magister hoisted Ghost up by his shoulders and deposited him on a table by the door. Both other tables lay empty with just enough room left to squeeze between them.

"Wait here."

The Magister went to the bar, acknowledging the nods from a thin-faced man with a droopy moustache and his burly companion with a slight inclination of his own head. He spoke softly into the ear of the barman who, after eyeing his new guest for a few seconds, shrugged and led him into a back room. The barman returned after a moment and closed the door behind him.

"Is he training up a new pup then?"

The thin-faced man faced Ghost, but it was unclear if the man was addressing him, or the companion. He realised with surprise that the companion was in fact a heavily-muscled woman with a flat face, a nasty expression and hair shorn so short it was just a brown stubble.

Ghost said, "Me?"

"Aye, pup. It isn't often I see that one with company."

The boy swallowed weakly and his forehead sheened with sweat.

"Spit it out, are you his pup or not?"

Ghost opened his mouth just as the door to the back room opened and the Magister emerged.

"Your pup isn't very talkative," said the thin-faced man.

The Magister looked at him and grimaced, a short crease forming at the edge of his lip.

"You always talked too much, Karaman. I wager that when you die, be it by the hand of man or god, you'll have your yapping mouth open. I can't imagine you'll be able to go decently quiet."

Karaman scowled at the Magister as a slim figure in grey silks emerged from the back room and shut the door behind him. Handsome of face with nut-brown skin, the young noble's hand rested on the gold-wired hilt of a sabre. Karaman stood up and faced the young man.

"Hey you there, fancy pants! I'll do the job for half his commission. I bet he asked a princely sum."

"The assignment has been agreed. There will be no deviation unless he fails at which point the job will be available again. These are the rules of your own code, that is correct? I am content to follow your laws when I operate in your world." The young nobleman spoke very precisely, forming each syllable carefully as though each word had been planned long in advance,

Karaman leaned forward. "How many have you sent before him?"

"Oikos Scylla and Oikos Medea both dispatched representatives. Both have failed at this task, something which belittles the reputation of your order. I was gratified to learn that the matter had been... escalated." The young nobleman struggled with the last word before settling on his final choice with a sigh of regret.

The Magister dipped his head to the nobleman, but Karaman stepped between them.

"What were the fees for those that failed?"

"They were to have received one hundred coins, had any of them returned," said the nobleman.

"And him? What does our self-appointed leader demand?"

"One thousand. And I have agreed."

Karaman's moustache flecked with his own spittle as he spluttered and laughed. "A thousand? I tell you what. Tell me what you want and I'll return it to you tonight, and take only five hundred in return. Scylla and Medea aren't real thieves anymore—they're practically nobles these days. I'll show you what we Vlastos can do."

"I cannot change the assignment. These are the rules of your own kind."

Karaman spat at the feet of the young nobleman, who stepped back into a trained defensive stance, his sword arm pulling free an inch of steel.

"You're all idiots. You think too much of him and believe in legends and children's stories," said Karaman.

The Magister laid a hand on the young nobleman's wrist.

"I accept this challenge. If Karaman the Oaf can beat me in this task then I shall pay him myself."

The young nobleman nodded. "This is acceptable."

"Then the money's already mine." Karaman snorted.

He rubbed his hands together, but the Magister had already turned away and swept out of the tiny tavern. Ghost slipped off the table and chased his master's heels.

Streets with shallow steps every three or four paces led higher up into the city and the temples gave way to houses just as grand. The nobles favoured wide squares lined with trees, where the endless thrum of activity in the lower city was lost in the rustle of leaves. Marble-fronted buildings faced a plaza with a central garden of rose bushes and stone benches where the wealthy met in twos and threes to discuss business and politics. The shade of broad cedars during the day bought respite from the worst of the sun, but as evening drew in the squares fell into the darkness of midnight. The dusky gloom lifted only by the torches that servants set by the doors so that their masters could find their own homes, stumbling along the way after an evening's entertainment of cups. At the far side of the plaza a tall white mansion in the Ionic style impassively regarded its neighbours, a spearman serving silent vigil either side of the threshold.

With slight pressure on his shoulder the Magister guided Ghost to his knees amongst the flowers, the perfume of the petals rising as he crushed them. The Magister put his lips to the boy's ear.

"Here you have a good view of all that happens. Mind you stay low and still and be nothing more than a shadow yourself."

The Magister turned to leave but Ghost caught the edge of his cloak and tugged him back.

"Magister, look!"

He pointed to a neighbouring building and halfway up the wall, climbing without ropes, a lean figure spidered his way up.

"Karaman. Damn him."

"He quick?"

"He is a godsblast gecko, that's what he is. But he makes work for himself."

The Magister stooped to collect a small rock from the ground and tossed it clear across the square and through a glass lamp stood on the window ledge. The lamp fell backward and after a moment a glow could be seen as the fire caught. The Magister cupped his hands around his mouth and from the distant building the reedy, pleading voice of an old man could be heard.

"Thieves! Help me... someone!"

The spearmen at the Ionic mansion tilted their heads, then noticing the flames catching the curtains of the window that evidently the cry for help had come from, they hurried across the square.

The moment they had moved the Magister started walking to their prior station. When he was less than twenty paces from the door he whipped a bamboo pipe from under his cloak and put a spitwad through the oily flame of the clay torch that hung by the door. He reached the door, and with a backward glance to check his secrecy slipped into the building.

Ghost settled onto the ground and pulled his cloak around him as the last faint glow of the day's heat left the air and the stillness of night settled around him. He heard the crackle of the blaze in the building across the square as the spearmen banged the butts of their weapons against the door. They argued with the man inside who shouted that he wouldn't unbar the door at night to two men armed with spears, and how he believed nothing of their nonsense that his house was on fire.

Another voice called out from within the first house, and after that yet more voices and more shouting. The guards shook their heads and stomped back to their posts, puzzling over the darkened lamp and taking out flint and steel to relight it.

A shrill scream erupted from the stately house, and ice crusted up Ghost's spine as the scream ended abruptly. The guards huddled and after a few words the one with the saffron-stained beard went inside the house, muttering and slamming the door behind him. Then came a bellowed roar from inside and the door burst open. The Magister grappled with Yellow-beard, both of them trying to wrestle the spear free. The Magister cursed when he saw the second guard, and twisted the man he was fighting as a shield from incoming jabs. His heart pumping, Ghost's fingers closed about a pebble and he flung it at the fighting figures.

The stone dinged into the iron cap of the older guard, half knocking it from his head. He spun around, then sighting the boy, he charged at him.

Ghost yelped as the guard closed in, and he darted out of the flower bed, crushing delicate blooms underfoot. The older guard's pudgy face sheened with sweat as he panted heavily. Ghost jumped over the swinging tip of the weapon as Pudgy-face tried to trip him. Glancing over, he saw the Magister knock down Yellow-beard, then turn and run. The boy's heart sank as he saw his master fleeing, twisting into the street they had arrived from, then sprinting out of sight. Yellow-beard struggled to his feet, snatched up his spear and straightened his helmet. He glared at the empty street down which the Magister had disappeared, then turned his attention to Pudgy-face's prey.

They advanced from either side. Jabbing at him when he tried to dart past them, then whirling horizontal slashes with the edges of the long steel blades as he tried to run the other way. They forced him back into a corner of the square, then as he slowly held up the palms of his hands they both rested the tips of their weapons against his chest.

"Well if we can't have the thief then at least we have his rat." Pudgy-face seemed to find this very amusing, and he chuckled to himself.

The yellow-bearded guard tightened his grip on the spear, a thin and unpleasant sneer spreading across his face.

"We can still extract some information from this guttersnipe. Hold up your wrists, boy."

Ghost did as he was told though his fingers trembled. They drew the rope tight and he hissed under his breath as the hemp binding burned into his wrists. Pain ran up his arms and settled behind his eyes, driving away the fear and letting a little hate rise in his heart as the rope jerked and he stumbled after the guards.

They led him into the stately house, through half-darkened corridors and down wide stone-capped steps into a chilly basement. Past an open doorway behind which a fire burned and rose the scents of roasting ducks, hot vegetables and an unfamiliar heady spice.

They reached the guard room. By the scant light dribbling in from the hallway, Ghost saw two bunks, two chairs and a table with cards strewn on it. Yellow-beard stowed his spear in a weapon rack that stood against the wall, then lit the candle squatting between their playing cards. They forced Ghost into a chair and tied the rope around his body and the chair so that wriggle as he might he couldn't move his arms. Yellow-beard sneered at Ghost as he made sure each knot was fastened to his liking. Pudgy-face stood back a few paces and a frown grew on his brow as the knots cinched tight.

"What are you going to do, Khem?"

"I'm going to get a few answers to a few questions, then I'll let the poor wee lad be on his way... What did you think I mean to do?" He pulled a narrow knife from a sheath on his belt and peered closely at its edge. Turned it back and forth in the meagre light, and tested it with his thumb.

"He's just a little boy..." Pudgy-face's frown deepened.

Yellow-beard sighed and shook his head. "You know what our master will do when he finds out he has been burgled and we were on guard. If you were on your own I wouldn't want to be in your shoes, but I'm in this mess alongside you."

"There are other ways."

"Let's see, shall we. Whelp, what is the name of your master, and what did he steal? Where can we find him?"

Yellow-beard drew slow circles with the knife's tip near his captive's face. The bravery of Ghost's hate mixed with greasy fear that crawled up his throat and slimed his palms. He growled.

"Magister kill you."

Yellow-beard's back-handed slap split the boy's lip. Ghost's head lolled down and he gasped. His tongue touched the cut, and the taste fuelled the hate in him. When he raised his head to stare down Yellow-beard the fire burning there made his captor laugh.

"Such defiance! A stray rat without even an owner to come claim him."
He held the tip of the knife against the boy's cheek and drew a bright red
line across it with only the weight of the blade.

"You sure you got nothing else to say before I start?"

Ghost's cheek creased as he started to smile. "Where, yes."

"Good lad. Now spit it out; where can I find him?"

Ghost looked over Yellow-beard's shoulder. Pudgy-face toppled to his
knees, a pool of darkness deeper than shadow behind him. A thin black line
around his neck. His eyes bulged as he clawed at the garrote, scratching his
own flesh trying to get under the cord. Pudgy-face turned red, then white
and his tongue stuck out as the Magister rolled him onto the ground.

"Behind you."

Yellow-beard's head pulled back as he blinked at Ghost. Wide white eyes
with pin-prick pupils. The boy still grinning despite a trickle of blood
running down his cheek. Black eyes, hungry to see death. The Magister's
cloak curled and he was away from the corpse on the ground. A flutter of
black cloth then he had Yellow-beard's jaw in his hand. He wrenched it up
and brought his long blue-steel knife to the neck.

"Draw the blade deep across the windpipe; remember to lift the jaw
firmly with your left hand, lest they whimper."

The Magister twisted Yellow-beard as he made the incision and the side
wall drenched in the eruption from the neck wound. The corpse crumpled
to the ground and whistled for a moment before falling silent.

"Do you actually need me to untie you?"

Ghost wriggled and freed a hand. "I quick."

The Magister nodded as the rope fell loosely about the chair, and he
knelt to wipe his blade on Yellow-beard's tunic. His eyes were level with
Ghost's, accusation writ plain in the boy's scowl.

"You leave."

"I did nothing of the sort. I merely exercised discretion when the moment presented itself and returned at a more expeditious time."

"Two not many," growled Ghost.

The Magister drew himself up, receding into his hood.

"Your insolence continues unabated. Why tire myself fighting fat old men when I can easily run past them? I expected gratitude, and yet you seek to test my patience. Of course I could have ended these lives in any manner of ways, but I chose this one. You must look within yourself and decide which has the most style."

Ghost rolled his head to the side as he considered this.

"More funny."

"There you have it. Infinitely more elegant than brutish brawling oafs having at each other with lusty roar and sweating brow." The Magister turned for the door.

"Magister, has treasure?"

"Of course not, I hid it somewhere safe before I returned for you. After all; the job comes first."

† † †

The little cider house was still open despite the rapid approach of dawn. The young nobleman reclined gracefully with his legs crossed at his ankles behind the only occupied table. A clay flask and a pewter tankard lay on the table, and he rubbed the tip of a finger in circles around the lip of the drinking jar. He smiled when the two of them stepped in through the open door.

"Gentlemen. How nice to see you again. Is the thing done?"

The Magister set a cloth-wrapped flat box on the table. The young noble laid a hand on it, closed his eyes and sighed.

"Finally it is mine..." He seemed lost in a world of his own with a sleepy smile as he savoured the moment, then he blinked and coughed softly. "And Karaman Vlastos? What became of him?"

"Alas, as I had warned him, when his end came he did make rather a lot of noise. Surely boy, you must have heard the screaming from the street?"

"He scared scared. Then he stop," said Ghost.

The nobleman sat the box on his lap and stroked it. "That is, of course, your business. A man in your position must need to administer the ranks as he sees fit. Well, our business is concluded and I am eager to return home."

"In light of that," ventured the Magister. "Might I presume I'll not receive an inordinate amount of unwanted attention after burgling the personal office of the Pasha's private administrator?"

The nobleman chuckled to himself. "Many things will change after tonight, Sir Thief. My uncle will wake to find his authority to govern the council has melted completely away, and he'll decide to confine himself to traditional matters of state. He'll be nothing more than a figurehead. The noble courts are scheduled to convene first thing in the morning to be presented with information of the utmost urgency. My uncle will regretfully vacate his seat at the head of the Council of Courts."

"Leaving the empty seat to be filled by you?"

"Naturally. When it is offered to me I will be both surprised and flattered, but will of course accept with all humility."

"Then this may be the perfect time to remind you—"

The young nobleman raised a finger. "If this is a prelude to seek my favour, you may save your breath. I find your value to be inestimable and would that our relationship blossomed. Good night gentlemen, and once again you have my thanks."

As he rose with a bow, the Magister coughed and held out his palm.

"Of course." The nobleman tilted his brow. "How unforgivably rude of me. I was completely swept away with the excitement of the prize you have delivered to me. Here is your purse, as agreed."

The Magister weighed the pouch in his hand, then smiled at the young nobleman.

"Good night, Bey Izmir."

"Good night, thief-master."

Once Bey Izmir had left the Magister's smile twisted into something ugly, and he turned his gaze on Ghost.

"You were less than useless. You got caught and I had to waste time coming to get you—just to check you hadn't blabbed your mouth off." He shook his head. "You're no good to me and no-one will pay for such a scrawny baby that would cost more to feed than he could earn."

Ghost opened his mouth to protest as he felt his heart plummet in his chest, but only a piteous mewling sound came out.

"You're just a baby!" The Magister slapped his forehead with his palm. "What was I thinking, collecting a baby—fresh from his mother's teat? Night Mother protect me. I'm no wet-nurse."

The Magister shook his head then turned on his heel and stormed into a narrow lane that led away from the nobles' district.

Ghost's whole body trembled at the thought of being abandoned again. He waited just long enough to see that the Magister was leaving him behind, and then with a dry mouth ran after him.

† † †

Fireballs hurtled through the night sky; a sky thick with ash, the gagging stench of gore, and the screams of the dying. The Golden Horde smashed through the Athanatoi vanguard, their corpses lay thick on the ground, bristling with arrows. A knot of Basilisk legionnaires fought back to back with the remaining Athanatoi veterans, brothers in blood as they were hacked down to the last man. The Horde marauders ran screaming through the city, their axes splitting open men, women and children without pity as the civilians tried to flee and hide. Entrails, gore and the stench of death. Fire erupted in the temple of the Goddess, centuries-old scrolls tossed to the flames as the looters smashed their way through the archives searching for gold and silver. The roof joists smouldered, then the roar of an apocalyptic avalanche as the vaulted ceiling buckled, crumbled, and it crashed down.

The old man gasped as he shook himself awake; his veins cold as ice, bones seared with flames. Just like every time the Goddess used him as her oracle. His cheeks were wet and his eyes swollen; no memories of when he started crying and now he struggled to stem the flow. He clutched his blanket to his face—forcing himself to remember that it was not real.

It was not real yet.

The streets narrowed then widened at every turn they took without any pattern, save that the stones beneath their feet always sloped down, heading back down toward the docks. Ghost stumbled along. He rubbed away the sting of frustration in his eyes and tried to keep the Magister in sight; the Magister who never slackened his stride or looked back to see if he was being followed.

The cobbles gave way to an open section of broken flagstones and sand, bounded on one side by the city walls themselves. If there had been hawkers calling out to attract buyers then it might have been a market, instead there were many round tents with great numbers of horses hobbled together. Beyond the horses lurked shadowy animals of much greater size but the boy was so tired that even the first tinges of pink light dawning failed to whet his appetite for any excitement. As they passed the last few tents to enter the clearing in the plaza, they saw young men tossing black knives into the heads of straw dummies from a distance of many long paces. Their lean limbs went from an insouciant lazy swagger, through a moment of intense coiled energy, then the daggers flew like arrows unerringly into their targets. A chestnut-haired youth with an embroidered headband holding his locks away from his face glanced in their direction, then bowed his head to the Magister as the pair walked by. Ghost's weariness abated as he caught sight of boys and girls, just a few years older than him, corralling horses. Standing on the horses' backs and guiding them with a single hand on long reins, all the while tossing jokes and insults between themselves.

The Magister clapped the shoulder of a massive man with long black hair and a tumbling curly beard. The giant startled at the contact then broke into a grin.

"Welcome back, *effendi*! Please let me invite you inside, I have fresh bread and that Parthian wine you admire so much. Please, please, come inside."

His thickly muscled arm swept open the tent at such a height that the Magister didn't need to stoop to enter, and Ghost hurried in behind him.

Formalities were then exchanged; first cups of tea served with almonds, each action requiring praise from the visitor and gentle self-deprecation from the host. Then the presentation of bread with a bowl of fat olives to enfold in it, and mint-speckled yoghurt to dunk the assembled parcel. Ghost shoved a chunk of crust in his mouth, and while chewing it he hid another piece in his shirt. Praise, and denial of the worthiness of any gratitude, continued as the wine finally made an appearance. Finely engraved brass bowls held the dark liquid, and Bayezid began a heavily poetic description of the wonders they were about to savour. Ghost yawned, and finding a comfortable nook between two long cushions threw his tattered cloak over his head and shut his eyes.

"Where is Raseyda?" The Magister made a show of looking around the tent that clearly had no other occupants than the three of them.

Bayezid lowered his bowl and somehow couldn't seem to raise his gaze from it.

"She took a fall, didn't she? Broke her leg and cracked her ribs... I didn't know she had missed her monthlies for some time. I just thought... she'd put on a little weight—not that I minded! But... well she doesn't speak much anymore; she never smiles. Gods how I loved her smile. She was the best, such grace on the high line as if she didn't need it to stand on, as if she was just dancing in the sky. Now... her limp is very bad, she needs a cane to take a bit of the weight."

"That must be inconvenient... for your night-time endeavours," said the Magister lounging back on his elbows. "It interests me how you propose to continue with the tasks I have assigned you."

Bayezid spread his hands. "What can we do? I spoke with Curator Nicodemus, he was compassionate, but left our instructions nonetheless. I thought upon seeing you that you had come to offer help."

"I notice neither of you has visited Hekate's House of late," said the Magister. "Nor have your offerings been counted. Remember you only work for Nicodemus under my instructions, though he must remain under that illusion. Summon your wife."

Chewing his lip Bayezid nodded, then he bellowed for Raseyda.

A short woman, slightly built with plaited brown hair lifted the tent flap and slowly walked in. She kept her head high but her weight of step clearly favoured her left leg. She barely glanced at Bayezid, nodded to the Magister then seated herself on a cushion, her right leg stretched in front. Her expression was downcast, not demure, just filled with an empty sadness.

"My condolences for your loss, Raseyda," said the Magister.

She glared at him. "You feel sadness for no-one."

The Magister shrugged. He leant over to where the boy lay and turned down the cloak so his face was visible. "This child is an orphan. He will starve if I can't find someone to take him. Look how thin he is."

A frown crossed Raseyda's brow, then her whole face lit up. "He... he can be ours? Bayezid!" She moved next to the boy and she brushed his hair away from his eyes. He appeared to slumber, just small flutters of his eyelashes betraying him as he struggled to keep listening.

"*Effendi*, words fail me," said Bayezid, putting his hands together and bowing his head.

"Then let that be the final failure on your part." The Magister drained the last of his wine and stood up. "Set the child to the tasks at hand. I call him Ghost. He is nimble and has spirit, but has much to learn. Perhaps travelling with your troupe he may be able to make himself useful in some way. For now he is just a burden to me. You may not, however, change his name. Are we understood?"

Raseyda looked up, smiling with glistening eyes. She nodded then returned her gaze to the little boy lying beside her.

Listening through a drifting veil of sleep Ghost didn't understand all that was happening, but the gentle lady kept stroking his hair and he succumbed to the warmth and safety and fell deeply asleep. Once the Magister had left she returned her attention to the sleeping boy and didn't move from his side until she too fell asleep.

The murmur of voices beyond the tent woke Ghost early the next morning. Raseyda still slept close by and the boy wondered how he was supposed to feel about her. Did she want to be his mother? Half of him yearned for that to be true, the other hated her fiercely for trying to take his mother's place. *His real mother.*

He slipped out the tent, hoping to be unnoticed, but ran straight into the broad and round belly of Bayezid.

"Shush! Don't wake her. It's the first good sleep she's had in weeks." Bayezid's broad hand scooted the boy along and he led the way between the tents to the animal pens. "Come on, Ghost. Look; you'll like these for sure."

"Where's the Magister?"

Bayezid coughed, scratched his chin, then examined the hairy backs of his hands. "He's gone away—for now. But we're going to look after you. Just like you were our own."

He left me.

Ghost's head drooped, and all the energy gained from his long sleep drained out of him. The alone-empty ache in his chest was back. Dark and frightening. Stronger than ever.

"Be brave, little man. You'll find lots of fun things to do here," said

Bayezid. He swept Ghost into the air and settled him on his shoulder.

The boy sniffled, but he felt the view from up here might be worth it. Several babbling youths with lean muscular frames clustered around a pot hanging from a tripod over a cooking fire. Intriguing savoury scents made Ghost's stomach growl. An older lad with a tufted beard flashed white teeth at the strongman as he approached, then took a circular bread in one hand and ladled a scoop from the stewpot into it. The cook passed it to Bayezid, thence up to the boy; spiced aubergine and lentils mixed with fried onion. It disappeared quickly. Waving farewell to the young cook, Bayezid's long strides took them past more children about Ghost's age. They climbed a rope ladder that ran up the side of a small wooden fort, then jumped off while screaming, and rolled when they landed. It was higher than Ghost could ever remember jumping from, the challenge tugging at his pride. A couple of the children looked at him with naive curiosity, and one waved.

The young knife-thrower with the embroidered headband sat on a barrel, overlooking two young girls juggling knives. Ghost stared as they tossed the blades back and forth, oblivious to the danger. The youth in the headband suddenly slapped both hands against his barrel, and at this signal the two girls spun and hurled each of their daggers in rapid succession into a straw target. Ghost tugged on Bayezid's hand as the youth grinned and proffered a knife in his direction.

"Tomorrow," said Bayezid. "I promise! But there is still more to see."

A paddock of mottle-coated ponies took the boy's interest next, and Bayezid cut up an apple and showed Ghost how to feed the animals so they didn't nip his hand. Their velvety noses tickled his palm, and he quickly came to the opinion that Bayezid was a lot more fun than the Magister. Next, they stopped in front of a large pen wrought from iron bars that even covered the roof. Inside, an enclosure strewn with dirty straw, the shattered bones of some beast, and grubby piles of yellow fur. The stench was stronger than horses musk, but not unpleasant.

Ghost looked for anything of interest, and was about to complain when one of the piles of fur stretched out and yawned a foot-wide snarl of jagged teeth. Half a moment later Ghost discovered he was already standing behind Bayezid, clutching him and peeking around his thigh to watch the terrifying animal.

"Lions," said Bayezid, chuckling to himself. "If you like I can give you some meat to feed them. Don't get too close or they'll devour you!"

"Li-yons..." murmured Ghost. "Big big cat!"

Bayezid dragged Ghost out from behind him and knelt down. "The big one with the long hair? That's the man. He's the lazy one—all he does is make a lot of noise! The others are his wives, and listen boy; never, ever turn your back to them. Do you understand?"

Ghost nodded quietly, unable to take his eyes of the beasts as one by one they stretched out then began to languidly prowl the space allotted to them.

"Is most scariest animal! Ever ever."

Bayezid chuckled. "Then one day you must visit my homeland. We have an even bigger one we call tigers! They can be the size of horses. Ah, I miss my home. My brother would know what to do with you. He's the clever one, he teaches children. What do I know? I'm so stupid I just lift rocks and bend iron bars. My head is as thick as a rock!"

Ghost laughed aloud at that. "You stupid I say brother!"

"You'd tell my big brother?" Bayezid feigned a look of horror. "Well, if you do, tell him his little brother still loves him and I'm sure he'll look after you. In his school they learn *Gatka*—how to fight, but more importantly, how not to fight! But you are too small to worry about such things. Maybe you can visit him one day, little one, but in case that doesn't happen, we try to find you something to do around here. Agreed?"

He held out a sausage-sized finger for the little boy to shake, and with formalities concluded they set out to explore the rest of the camp.

Chapter 3:

First Amongst Equals

Six years later

"What a lovely morning! I find this view so peaceful at this time of day. I often come here to spend some quiet time in contemplation."

The old man in simple white robes sat on a crumbling stone bench, a relic of a bygone era. The gentle hill offered a panorama of the river estuary curving around its feet, the city spreading out in all directions, and a cool breeze rustled the shady acacia trees. Across the waters lay the rich farmlands of Galata, a stern tower guarding the northern approaches. A much younger man, handsome and dressed in a fine grey silk tunic and loose trousers, arrived and sat down beside him.

"I thank you for inviting me, it is so refreshing to be able to meet in less formal settings. The Council of Courts can be so wearisome, with all clamouring to have their voices heard," said the young nobleman in grey silk.

"And when so few voices are worth hearing?" The old man smiled at the younger.

"Ah, we are in a like mind about that for certain, most respected Hierarch."

Hierarch Pallas nodded, then his bushy eyebrows shot up. "I forget my courtesy! I gather congratulations are in order for a very happy event?"

The young Bey blushed and looked away. "My thanks indeed. Yes. After so long, and so many tears, my wife has blessed me—"

"The Goddess blesses," said Pallas as he drew Her symbol in the air with his bony finger.

"Of course. The Goddess has blessed my wife with a child. A beautiful boy. Healthy too judging by the vigour of his crying."

The Hierarch clasped his hands. "It is moments like these that bring us all together and remind us why it is we do what we do."

"Although I fancy we still differ on the threat posed by these Horde incursions. My sources confirm they are nothing more than raiding parties. We've seen them come and go, just as we've seen warchiefs rise and fall through their tribal squabbling."

Pallas frowned, his long eyebrows bunching together and quivering. He snorted then sighed. "What you call a raiding party I call a scouting force. The Horde is not organised like any army we are familiar with, yet do not let its barbaric trappings deceive you into thinking that they are chaotic savages. Even here, at the periphery of its forces, there is an animal cunning to the beast that we underestimate at our peril."

Bey Izmir, First Voice of the Council of Courts, breathed deeply as he surveyed the view across the river. Seagulls circled, lazily swooping, taking respite from the squabbles at the various docks that sprouted along the city's river walls. "I search for the right words, as I would fervently wish you to understand I mean no insult."

"There is no need for concern," said Pallas. "I am far too old to be bothered by insults even if harshly slung. A turn of phrase that might be misinterpreted matters even less. Words themselves are ephemeral. It is only the actions that do or do not follow them that are worthy of notice." The Hierarch patted the young man on the arm. "Continue, please. We are here today because yours is the only voice amongst all the courts I care to listen to. Your ascension was a coup I admired greatly, and your behaviour since has continued to be intelligent and subtle. Indulge this silly old man."

Bey Izmir chuckled and shook his head. "We both know *that* isn't true.

58

But what I wanted to say was; I understand what you are asking for."

"Full mobilisation of our joint forces and to take the battle to the Horde," said Pallas, inclining his head.

"It will never happen—and I do not speak of whether or not it should happen. It would destabilise all we have here and civil war would tear us to pieces faster than the Horde ever could. Then the savages will simply pick through our bones. Your plan leads directly to the outcome you dread most," said Bey Izmir.

Pallas combed his fingers through his long beard. "Unless we join forces. Two level-headed and intelligent men; surely reason must prevail?"

"Would the priesthood mandate the formation of an empire, with myself wearing the crown and all being at my command? For two men cannot share power long. Even the dullest of my compatriots—and of yours I'll wager—would see failure in anything less than an absolute monarch," said Bey Izmir.

Shaking his head, Pallas exhaled. "This is a holy city. It should never again bow to secular power."

"The alternative being... what? All power should be wielded by the temple? You already know even if I was to support such a move it would be laughed out by the noble courts."

"Not all power," said the Hierarch. "Just sufficient to control military forces necessary to wage the war."

"There is no need to veil your words, eminence. You mean a crusade."

"It is for our people! Tens of thousands have already been slain or driven from their lands on our borders—millions across all provinces since the Horde began its rampage. Women, children, the old and the infirm; butchered! I see their ruined, bloody and burned corpses in my dreams every night. Blessed Goddess, even the Parthian emperor has withdrawn his forces from his provinces. Abandoning them just to protect his heartland. If the King of Kings flees before the Horde, what chance have we?" The

Hierarch covered his face with his hands, breathing deeply.

"Hierarch, I know well that you make no grasp for power—"

"Mortal power is all too fleeting. Only that in the next life is of worth," muttered the Hierarch as he lowered his hands to his lap and stared at his palms as if he might find the answers he sought written there.

"—But power is all the nobles have ever sought, it would be unimaginable to them that was not your final goal. Even wise moderates like Bey Yilmaz could not agree. The same for the Oikos families; intrigue and betrayal runs in their blood. Neither faction will countenance it," said Bey Izmir. He stood and patted the Hierarch's bowed shoulder. "Another way must be found."

Bey Izmir paused as he sought other words, but finding them lacking he turned and walked away. The Hierarch watched the tiny figures unloading boats on the estuary docks below. The wisps of smoke from hearth fires, the people that thronged the streets; all simple lives, busy with their own tribulations and triumphs, unaware of the looming spectre of death. Fragile and fleeting and so easily snuffed out by the agents of destruction—and by good intentions gone astray.

The Hierarch rubbed his eyebrows and sighed. "Goddess protect me from men of morals."

The doom of his people was a burden he alone carried and it felt unbearably heavy on his hunched back. The old cravings came upon him their strongest at these times, but he ignored the ravenous demon that haunted his soul. The poppy tears called to him day and night, but their use was sacred and he swore to only draw upon them when absolutely necessary. His faith armoured him against the desires of the flesh, and he would not allow it to weaken his resolve. Izmir was a good man—too good—for he did not fully appreciate the darkness in men's souls. A failing shared with all young men. To know the evil that lay within others, one must first know the darkness that lives within oneself. Long had he walked that narrow thread with the abyss howling for him on both sides. Always drawing the strings of power ever closer. And the finest, most fragile, string led to the leader of the Oikos, and from him a net that swept the whole dark and bloody underbelly of the city. If he could but influence that great poisoner of minds and bodies, subtly, then some slim shred of hope might still remain.

Chapter 4:

Reclamation

The purpose of his visit to the Hippodrome—the city's great amphitheatre of entertainment—had been to make some observations on certain secretive relationships that were forming between two young nobles that were coming of age. Supporters of the Green faction sat opposite to those of the Blue, waving coloured pennants. Today's display of acrobatics left nothing to gamble on, unlike the fierce rivalries over the chariot teams. Despite this, taunts and threats echoed across the sands that separated them. The supporters came as much for the entertainment as the fighting afterward, and like as not several families would be mourning lost menfolk by the evening.

Zarbenus felt his attention waning even before he'd begun, as other matters left him uneasy. The Oikos families remained devoted to him; through either love or through terror—and Zarbenus didn't care which. However, that devotion to him had not erased centuries of bloody conflict. A complex tapestry of vendettas meant that directing the combined force of the Oikos with a single scheme was impossible. Without able lieutenants he could not command a grand strategy, and besides, he was disinclined to put sufficient power and trust in the hands of another; not when he did not own them body and soul. This circumspect approach made him simultaneously impossible to dislodge by his enemies, but also unable to expand his power and influence. Six years had proved this. He chewed on his knuckle as he glared at the illiterate, unwashed, and gullible city-folk around him. Let them hoot and shriek like wild geese, he had more lofty towers to assail.

It was traditional in his vocation that a master took an apprentice. They made a semblance of training them, but in reality relaxed into a flabby middle-aged senescence while the apprentice did all the work. Right up until the inevitable and usually terminal betrayal. That ultimate, unavoidable outcome made the waning years of the master-apprentice relationship understandably fraught. The imminent arrival of such a time was one of the problems that preoccupied Zarbenus, as was the status of his apprentice. His first selection, a youth who had already his name of Timan, but bore the taint of a growing streak of independence. In reaction to this threat it had become necessary to expand his list of alternative candidates. Additional lieutenants, forged with stronger bonds of blood-loyalty, would allow him to run multiple strands of his grand artifice in parallel. And the way Zarbenus had it planned, should his scheme be successful it was unlikely that anyone would ever forget it.

A gamble worth taking had high stakes for success or failure, and it was whilst considering exactly those variables that Zarbenus caught sight of a face he'd completely forgotten about. Memories returned of a child bearing sparkling promise—then but a babe and incapable of achieving the lofty ambitions of his master. The boy he'd sold six years ago now looked very interesting.

Perched astride the restless horse, his fingers curled loosely in its mane, Ghost sat calm and relaxed. The cheers of the crowd washed over him. By the fluttering of his eyelids Zarbenus recognised him entering the trance of performance. When reality and illusion merge into something fleeting and magical, and disbelief waits patiently outside the room. With some twelve summers under his belt he'd grown well, though less than the height of most of his friends of an age. His once emaciated features now bore a healthy glow, and his casual stance amidst the controlled chaos of the circus would have been unimaginable to the hunched feral child who hid from the sun and startled at every noise. The Tahtakale barkers promised today to be a special day. It was the boy's first in performance on the high rope; younger than any other who'd attempted it. The gleeful barkers warned it was far more dangerous than his usual performances with the knife throwers, and that young children and old women would do better to leave the amphitheatre.

A leopard skin across one shoulder and dark makeup smeared around his eyes, Bayezid stomped across the sands of the arena. He threw up his broad hands and flexed his great biceps as he taunted the crowd.

"You don't have the nerves to watch a display of real terror—it will freeze the blood in your veins!"

The crowd heaved as it jeered at him, throwing fruits and crusts.

He raised his massive arms and yelled, "Then begin!"

Ghost vaulted from his seated position to stand on the horse's back and just by subtly altering his weight distribution the horse whinnied and trotted forward. Two tightropes were strung high over a steel-barred enclosure built on the arena sands, with three snarling, pacing lions caged within. Bayezid turned from the crowd and bellowed a raw challenge at the lions. They hurled themselves furiously at the bars, dagger-long teeth gnashing and claws raking the steel between them and their tormentor. There was a smattering of soft, polite clapping from the people as Ghost came into view; unimpressed by the child's horse-riding skills, something they had seen too many times before. An attendant standing on the edge let down a rope. Ghost snatched it as his horse passed by and he quickly scaled to the top. The attendant passed a long pole which Ghost held horizontally for balance. He strolled along the rope until he stood in the middle of the crossed lines; right above the enraged lions as they reared up and slashed golden paws at him, tantalisingly out of reach.

Bayezid pumped his arms in the air and the crowd cheered. "Will this child negotiate a peace between these warring courts?"

Ghost crossed to the side of the Blues and plucked a corsage of orchids from a gaudy youth who spluttered red-faced at the affront (while allowing the folded letter that had been hidden under his shoulder sash to be palmed by Ghost). The youth was known to all as the oldest of the Ertegun boys, a noble family whose ancestry was nearly as old as the city itself. Despite his nobility, or maybe because of it, he wore a scarf of the Blue over his left shoulder. Flagrantly ignoring the Pasha's dictum than the Courts should distance themselves from the factions of the common people, even though the spire of the Palace of Dreams—the source of that authority—was visible from where he lounged.

The crowds on the Green side cackled at the indignity afforded to their enemies, and Ghost turned and began to cross back. As he reached halfway, directly above the lions again, the biggest male roared. Ghost swayed, red-faced as the tightrope vibrated. The crowd jeered, throwing sandals and wineskins (empty of course) and walking sticks and—the line was struck. Ghost wavered as the rope shook then the balance pole slipped from his hands—and down he tumbled. The lions savaged the balance pole into shards then roared their rage as the boy dangled above them, hanging from the tightrope by one hand. Women shrieked and fathers covering their bawling children's eyes from witnessing the gory carnage that surely must follow.

Circus folk armed with rakes and willow brushes leapt forward and beat the sides of the lion cage, clashing and thudding, drawing the beasts' ire. One black-maned lion broke away and hurled itself at the bars. The circus folk leapt back to avoid its raking talons, but the other predators circled beneath the boy. He gritted his teeth as the sinews in his hanging arm raged with flames. Ghost managed to get his other hand to the tightrope, sweaty fingers clutching at the rough hemp fibres. The crowd took a half-breath, and silence reigned. His chest bellowing with the effort he twisted one leg over the rope, then an elbow. He hung there panting. Small cries of encouragement came from the crowd and the boy flipped his body around so he sat astride the line. Spreading his arms he brought his feet up so they pressed the line from above—then he stood.

The crowd exhaled as one being, an impossible second of absolute silence, then they roared and stamped their feet. Carefully, wobbling, Ghost made his way to the end of the rope. An ivory-skinned maiden in a jewel-embroidered corset stood waiting for him, both hands over her mouth. Although she sat on the Green side of the Hippodrome she displayed her tact by showing neither colour in her dress, favouring instead white and yellow. Surely this was Celia Juventia, her family less ancient as the Erteguns, but known by all as the most beautiful girl in a thousand miles? Ghost swept a deep bow to her then removed the stolen corsage from his own jacket and pinned it carefully to her bodice (whilst simultaneously passing her the note sent by her apparent lover in the stands opposite). He grinned and quickly shimmied down a line to the arena floor, holding a basket he produced from somewhere, and attempting to catch the copper coins that hail out of the crowd towards him.

In a shadowy spot in the crowd, well out of sight of anyone who might be watching, Zarbenus allowed himself a smile. Maybe, he thought, this one may be the answer to all my problems with Timan. The boy he almost forgot about could well be the one he'd been looking for all this time. Desire became decision in a heartbeat. A sufficiently compelling lie would get him what he wanted, and he held himself to be a peerless master of that art.

As the crowd began to disperse Zarbenus made his way down to the circle of tents the Tahtakale called home. Raseyda sat cross-legged outside her tent with a pile of ropes across her lap. She looked up from her work and smiled when she saw the Magister arrive. He squinted to both sides before squatting beside her and keeping watch on the people coming and going.

"Curator Nicodemus saw the boy make the switch. I was observing him in the stands, and he gave orders to one of his thugs the moment it happened," said the Magister, his words only for her ears.

Raseyda was up into a low crouch in less than a moment. "Where is the assassin?"

"Steady, act as if nothing is wrong. I lost him in the crowd, but he could strike at any moment. We need to get the boy out of here," said the Magister. "I can take him somewhere safe."

"I won't give him up," said Raseyda. "We've dealt with problems worse than this ourselves, and we'll do it again."

The Magister gripped her wrist so hard she cried out. "If you do that, then the Oculus Dei will come for you too. Resulting in the destruction of many years of my work. Are you willing to risk my wrath as well as theirs? Think of the boy."

Raseyda breathed deeply staring at the sky. "Where will you take him?"

"That isn't your concern. Making sure the child doesn't run away from me and make his way back here; that is the problem. You must ensure he never wants to see you again. I can't protect him if he does that, and Nicodemus will have the boy's throat cut if we fail to act. You know as well as I; the old man to whom Nicodemus answers is brutally unforgiving."

Raseyda's shoulders shook as tears ran down her cheeks. "I can't... not to the boy..."

"If you want him to live then you must. And you must make him hate you." He shoved a coin-purse into her hand. "Tell him you sold him back to me."

She nodded her head as she sobbed. "Please keep him safe..." She turned to beg for more but the Magister had already gone.

†††

Zarbenus watched from a distance as Ghost arrived at the tent, bouncing with every step and grinning widely. The boy's head tilted as he listened to Raseyda speak. She stood tall and straight and wouldn't look directly at him.

Zarbenus saw Ghost's jaw drop, saw him reach out to hold her but be pushed away. She showed him the purse of coin, shrugged then waved him away. Ghost screamed and ran into the crowd and the Magister saw Raseyda fall to her knees wailing. More lies would need to be skilfully told before the day was through, though that didn't present a problem. There remained a chance that Ghost would try to come back, looking for Raseyda and Bayezid. An unacceptable risk, if even a small one. He would have to ensure that they were no longer here to find.

Ghost ran and ran, climbing buildings and fleeing over their roofs. Zarbenus chased him, sweating heavily just to keep up with the rage-filled child. Time and again the boy evaded the Magister so adroitly he couldn't be found until it almost appeared he allowed himself to be spotted; then he was off again. Pushing the Night Mother's art near its limits the Magister kept after him, muttering curses while a small admiration grew all the same. He ran across rooftops, slid down tiles. Leaping from one building across the street below to land precisely on the top of a narrow wall. Crouched to absorb the impact then sprinted along the high slender path. Alleys and passages thick with people and animals blurred beneath him and yet the boy kept his lead. Their route led higher through the city. Ascending higher walls and braving wider jumps until it became clear that the boy knew Zarbenus pursued him and chose the most challenging and dangerous ascents. Heart pounding, Zarbenus followed. The boy lazily vaulted a carved balustrade, slid with both feet down a slate roof, somersaulted from the edge to fly through the air over another alley and didn't look back until he'd landed on the building opposite. Their eyes met for an instant, then the boy jumped again and he was gone. Eventually, as evening breezes cooled the air, Zarbenus closed in on Ghost; hiding in a pergola, behind a huge clay urn. Covering his face in his hands, he'd been crying so long that wracked breathing punctuated by arid sobbing was all he had left inside.

The Magister squatted down in front of the sullen boy glaring at him.

"Remember me, boy?"

Ghost sniffed and nodded.

"I came for you before, when that Horde soldier was hunting you," said Zarbenus. "And now I come for you again."

Zarbenus held out his hand but Ghost slapped it away.

"You left me!"

Pulling his hood back the Magister stared at the boy, who turned his face away with a wet sniff.

"Twice already have I killed for you," said Zarbenus. "Can you say the same for any other in this world?"

Ghost glowered at the Magister, then after some time he shook his head.

The Magister held out his hand again, and he waited. Ghost looked at it, rubbed his nose with his knuckles then reached out and took the offered hand. He allowed himself to be helped to his feet and when he stood straight he reached just past the Magister's chest.

"You've put on height, and some much-needed flesh on your bones," said the Magister, appraising the boy's lean frame. "Are you ready to put this life behind, and to come into mine?"

Anger still flickered in the eyes of Ghost, but there was determination in his clenched jaw. He grunted a tentative agreement.

"Good," said Zarbenus. "Now we can begin."

† † †

The Magister led the boy through the streets of the city, at that quiet cool time as evening settled into night. Still and empty for a brief spell between the bustle of the day and the furtive oppression of the night. The rot of vegetables and the manure of beasts misted in the air, squelched underfoot. Descending the First Hill they left behind the wealthy neighbourhoods of broad streets and cool plazas, passing into a maze of lanes and alleys and narrow gaps between weary and battered buildings. Districts heaving with merchants by day became territories of more grim intent; the domains of warring gangs beneath the notice of the great factions. Although the hooded man in the black cloak felt himself justified to take any path he should choose—without paying respect or coin to their nocturnal denizens—it transpired that those parties firmly held other convictions.

"Why do you not carry a sword, Magister?"

"Hmm? What are you wittering on about now," grumbled the Magister, eyeing the aggrieved street enforcer approaching with blade drawn and pointed at them.

"You said you were an expert with both long and short blades." Ghost ignored the armed man, his face dark with rage, and instead inquisitively watched his mentor who stepped backward and appeared to be glancing about for avenues of escape.

"You carry it for me then. Swords are heavy. I couldn't be bothered to lug a great lump of steel around with me all the time on the off-chance I'd need it."

Just a few feet lay between the Magister and his assailant, and they circled each other. The tip of the sword jabbed tentatively, while the continuous tirade of gutter-born abuse was anything but.

"Well it would have been useful about now," said Ghost, biting his lip and looking vaguely disappointed in his master's lack of bold combat moves.

The real attack was swift and without warning; a slash to the neck that Zarbenus ducked under; a backhand swipe for his chest that he simply stepped away from, then—accompanied by a blood-curdling roar—a thrust like the charging of a bull, straight for his heart.

The Magister caught the wrist of the hand holding the sword as it passed him. Struck at its thumb with his other hand. Collected the weapon as it dropped from numbed fingers. Reversed it and let his attacker's momentum drive it deep through their own abdomen and out the other side.

The Magister let the body fall to the ground, oblivious to its twitching and groaning. He raised an instructive finger to the boy, wagging it slightly.

71

"I answer to no-one. If I want something I will simply take it."

Ghost grinned, feeling awe and pride and jealousy all at once. "Yes, Magister."

"Excellent, now collect his purse and we'll find somewhere to dine. I have an intense desire for something spicy."

His choice was the *Three Crows*, hard by the south-eastern Lion Gate to the city. At this hour, locked and guarded by the night-watch, overwatched by the bronze form of a great lion, the closed gates drew people's attention to the bright lights of the nearby taverna. Within, clamorous laughter vied with sweaty, garlic-fumed bodies and tendrils of hashish smoke to see which would be the first to overcome the newcomers. Surviving that initial assault they forced their way through the crowd, and by strength of shoulder alone the Magister reached the bar.

There he was greeted like an old friend by the innkeeper, a one-armed fellow with a hawk nose and red-veined cheeks, answering to the name of Savarus. The old legionnaire would lay his remaining hand with its blurry *aquila* tattoo on the table between any men whose raised voices passed a certain point. The simple illustration of his competency for violence superseded the need for verbal threats. Savarus worked the bar and the stove with equal gusto, tucking his dishrag under his stump as he stirred a spitting pan, and haggled with the Magister as he topped up tankards. Negotiations were carried out over a shared dish of sliced sausage and tiny red peppers, tackled with fingertips. The conversation broke off repeatedly as one of them would choke red-faced on a particularly fiery mouthful, the other chuckling and issuing a congratulation for such great fortune. Ghost didn't understand more than that as the conversation was carried out in a rapidly barked dialect that hovered on the very brink of violence before ending in laughter.

Eventually the Magister slapped a few coppers into the hand of Savarus and led the boy upstairs. Their room was little more than a cubicle; the only furnishings a chamber pot, a box bearing a basin and a jug of water, and two straw pallets. Wordlessly the Magister flopped onto one and wrapped himself up in his cloak, and after a pause the boy curled up on the other cot.

The normally familiar sounds of the city at night unsettled Ghost. Every time he felt himself drifting off to sleep a drunk cried out from the street or a cart rattled by. The Magister slouched on his bed, his back to the wall and a half-empty canteen of wine in his lap. He hiccupped then rolled across the bed pulling the sheet over him, and in a short time began to snore. Ghost sat in the darkened room, his brow furrowed and a determination growing inside that prickled his skin. Ghost slept only lightly, waking on the slightest sound and even creeping to the side of his master's bed with a fear that came to him in waves that he might be left behind, that he wouldn't be found good enough. When dawn came he rose, and hearing his master still deep in slumber, he slipped downstairs. Finding the stable yard empty save for some sleeping steeds that whispered and snorted softly in their slumbers, he began to practice with his little throwing knife.

CHAPTER 5:
THE GREY MOUSE

Ghost woke suddenly, forgetting that he had curled up in the yard to rest for a few moments. He heard the Magister's voice somewhere down the street and he bolted towards it. The Lion Gate that guarded the docks stood open, thronging streams of package-laden merchants and their animals shuffling their way in both directions. The Kontoscalion harbour was almost a town in its own right, a nexus of travellers and traders from across the world as galleys from Sparta bobbed and jostled shoulder to shoulder with fan-sailed junks from Han. A burst of reminiscence at the sight of a great paddleship tied up there took Ghost back to when he'd first arrived in Byzantium.

He caught up, and panting heavily he watched as the Magister talked to a gaunt bald man hunched over the reins of a waggon. The Magister turned to Ghost and motioned up to the back of the waggon where rough jute sacks had been piled into a mound with a waxed canvas sheet drawn over them.

"Get on. We'll ride from here."

"Can we explore the city?" Ghost looked up at the Magister.

"Too far to go before our next stop. We make our first camp before nightfall."

Ghost scuffed the ground with his toes then climbed up grumbling to himself. He wriggled against the canvas until he settled into a groove and looked up at the city. Rolling his head back he saw an inverted view of the sea, with the paddleship they had arrived on hanging from it. The Magister vaulted up to sit beside the driver and after a snapping of the reins they trundled off.

They followed the docks, skirting the city walls, and then came to a muddy lagoon surrounded by rickety piers. What Ghost first took to be some kind of violent conflict turned out to be traders negotiating passage for their goods. The vociferous crowd waited impatiently as casks and amphorae were hefted onto a wide flat-bottomed boat looking little more watertight than a raft. The waggon driver had some kind of privilege for he drove them down a ramp and straight onto the boat. Deckhands settled the horses then moved bales and crates around to keep them level in the water.

After an hour watching the traders curse, beg and threaten each other the whole squabble came to an abrupt end. As a final barrel of fish came aboard, the only member of the ship's crew who hadn't made a single sound suddenly blew a whistle. The deckhands immediately cast off the ropes making them fast to the pier and shoved away from the shore with long poles. The navvies trimmed the sail and caught the breeze, but they moved at little more than a drifting speed, heading to the east. Ghost gazed at the city, remembering exploring its routes and buildings, all gold and marble and tinted glass. It grew smaller as he lay there and was finally swallowed by the dusk.

When Ghost startled awake it was dark, and he couldn't recall falling asleep. The whole boat jolted, and with it the chattering and cursing of the deckhands. In the gloom he saw the silhouettes of trees and people throwing ropes and pulling them tight. By the time the waggon and the horses had been cajoled back onto land, dawn crept over them. Pinks then oranges dusted the leaves around them, and the driver urged his team forward.

The old road was well-made and straight, the stone slabs striking a rhythm with the wheels. The regular clattering and the weak sun on a clear winter's day lulled the boy back to sleep. He half-remembered the driver starting up conversations and the Magister fending him off monosyllabically. It wasn't until they started moving for higher ground and the jostling of the waggon increased, that he woke up properly, feeling more refreshed than he could remember being for days. He propped himself up on one elbow and surveyed the gentle hilly land they were travelling through.

Pine woodland covered the slopes, their canopies spread like huge mushrooms. Tilled in striped fields, chequered and draped across the hills, the earth a rich black speckled with brown and yellow stalks of the wintering crops. Where the chaff of the harvest had been left to rot over the fields the cloying scent caught on the breeze and squirmed in their noses. Clouds of sparrows rose and fell over the fields like waves on a beach as they quarrelled over the last grains. The sun passed its zenith and with each degree it descended Ghost was reminded more of winter. He sat up amongst the nest of sacks and tucked his cloak around his knees.

"Magister, where are we now?"

"Anatolia, boy. All the land west of Byzantium, as far as Parthia in the east and Akkadia to the south. We are many miles from your homeland and have left your enemies behind. Remember this lesson; you can always leave trouble behind if you are quick enough to jump on a horse and get moving."

"Why did the Horde kill my people?"

Ghost's voice cracked as he spoke, but he swallowed and held his head high. The Magister turned himself on the seating board at the front of the waggon and rested an arm on the canvas-covered sacks. He watched the boy's eyes glisten and his fingers clutched the canvas into knotted clumps. The Magister cuffed him across the back of his head and the incipient waterworks were replaced by a sullen scowl.

"Who knows?" The Magister shrugged. "Likely some wildly rich prince bickered with another wildly rich prince over something fatuous they both desired. Regular folk just get caught in the middle; like I say, run or die."

Ghost looked down at his white knuckles.

"I ran."

"I know. You're clever. That is one of the reasons I picked you up," said

77

the Magister.

"What's the other reason?"

The Magister turned his head back to the boy. Between the shaded peak of the cowl and the scarf swathed nose, grey-blue eyes narrowed and the creases of a smile appeared at their corners.

"I liked your eyes."

Ghost flopped back onto the sacks and stared at the sky with its diffuse veil of winter cloud that made everything feel dull and tired.

I won't run forever.

Pulling his hood even closer the Magister gave every appearance of going to sleep, and any murmured questions that Ghost raised went unanswered through the rest of the afternoon.

Three days passed as they travelled further inland. In lieu of conversation the Magister demonstrated how to conceal a coin in one palm, to pass it between hands unseen, and then to pluck it from the air. This rare magic entranced Ghost, and he spent hours practising as they rattled their way onward. By the fourth day he'd gained sufficient dexterity that his proud demonstration earned him a chuckled "*kudos*" from the Magister. The immediate rush of happiness took Ghost by surprise, and he daydreamed through the rest of balmy afternoon; wondering what else he could do to gain more praise.

As evening drew closer the road began to rise, and the breathing of the horses deepened. As their heat rose their musk rolled back over the waggon, until with the fading light all Ghost could hear was the rattling of the waggon, and only smell the steaming horses. He peered over the heads of the waggon driver and the Magister looking up the path; a grey strip between darker hedges in a moonless night with thickening clouds.

Further ahead, a light flickered between swaying branches, some way up the hill. As they rattled closer the light became a cluster of stars and then windows lit in a squat stone building that thrust from the very side of the hill itself. The bottom windows glowed of oil lamps and the flickering of open hearth-fires. Lights smouldered in the row of windows of the floor above; the dingy yellow of tallow candles, smoking up the glass, crackling sullenly.

They rolled up and went under the arch to a stable mew, passing under a painted wooden sign hanging from a post mounted in the wall. Illuminated by the windows above, it creaked when the wind shifted direction. Painted there was a mouse carrying a wheel of cheese, its features shaded by a black hood, tiptoeing past a fat sleeping cat. Ghost stared at the sign, his mouth open as they passed it by, and he fancied that despite the gloom he could make out a smirk on the mouse's face.

They rattled to a halt and the Magister clapped a hand on the shoulder of the waggon driver then leapt down. Mist clung to the horses' flanks and trailed from their nostrils as they fidgeted and snorted and champed at their bits. The Magister brushed aside two stable boys that emerged, leaving them to attend to the heaving horses, and pressed on through the open door.

Ghost looked around the doorway. The raised voices of dozens of people, punctuated by guffaws of men and squeals of women reverberated against the plain stone walls. He stepped inside and felt the glow of the fires lifting the evening's damp from his skin. Tiny panes of red, green, and blue glass cast coruscating light from dozens of lanterns strung across the ceiling, winking in the fog of pipe smoke and of lamb haunches roasting on a spit.

The Magister seated himself at a small table in the corner, a ginger tom-cat purring under it. The lamplight faded into the shadows and he lounged back in the chair, his arms dangling at his sides and his head tilted to the side as if he was listening. A slim older man, grey hair tied back and beard shot through with the last few strands of black, came up to the table. He wiped his hands on a yellow-stained cloth then thrust it into the front pocket of the apron tied around his waist. He frowned at the Magister and set his hands on his hips as if expecting something in return.

"I need a room for the night; a bed for me and a cot for the boy. Also while you are up and about, hot meat and a skin of wine," said the Magister.

"I bet you do, but you left last time without settling your tab," said the grey-haired man.

The Magister sighed and his head lolled forward.

"You of all people know that I always cover my debts. I was moving quickly and travelling light; just as I am now. I have little money on me, but I assure you when I next come this way I'll bring all that I owe and even a little more."

"And when will that be?"

"Kanesh, I made a promise to you that I would never inconvenience your patrons, at least not as long as they were under your roof. I have held to that promise; otherwise I would simply pay you everything I owe in the next few minutes."

The Magister lifted his head and held his hand over his heart. The slim old man glanced around the rowdy customers in his tavern, then back at the Magister.

"Aye, you could that. Very well you scoundrel, but this is the very last time. On your next visit you had better bring a weighty pouch of gold or we will stop being friends."

The Magister patted his heart again. "My grateful thanks for your boundless generosity, Kanesh. Now, hurry yourself to the fire and the cellar. I have a powerful thirst and appetite. Go, go now."

Kanesh rolled his eyes, but he obeyed the Magister's waving hands and retired to the bar. Some minutes later he returned with a wooden platter piled with slices of steaming meat, the dripping juices pooling in a groove at the platter's edge, and placed it under Ghost's rapt eyes. The Magister frowned when he leaned forward to smell the plate as a candle at the next table caught in his eyes. Without looking at the candle he pinched a globule of seared fat from a slice of meat and flicked it through the wick, extinguishing the flame. He grunted his approval and lowered his scarf to ferry chunks of meat on the tip of a knife to his mouth.

Ghost looked up at the Magister who nodded his assent without ceasing his mouthfuls. The boy picked apart the slices and crunched through the crackling, sucking greasy fingers and getting his cheeks and chin shiny with the juices. Kanesh returned with an earthenware pitcher of water, a black and white goatskin of wine, and two wooden tumblers.

"The wine is a bit sour. The summer was too short this year. Not enough heat to sweeten up the grapes. Oh, some letters for you. Timan, amongst others."

Kanesh pulled out a sheaf of folded parchments and laid them on the table. The Magister wiped the back of his hand across his lips then unstoppered the wineskin. He sniffed it, then tilted his head back and squirted a long stream of the purple liquid down his throat.

He coughed, then smacked his lips together. "It certainly is dry, but I've been on the road for a week and would sleep easy tonight. My thanks, Kanesh, you may attend your other clients now."

Kanesh tutted at the dismissal, but returned to the bar as other patrons clamoured for his attention.

Ghost mumbled with his mouth full. "Were you two friends?"

"That was many years ago. Eat your food."

The Magister settled back in his chair. Back into the darker shadow so that only the light glinting in his eyes could be seen beneath the peak of his cowl, cradling the wineskin in his lap and taking squirts from it every few minutes. The boy's ripping at the mutton slowed and he picked off favoured chunks of crackling while several thick slices of meat lay untouched.

"Finish the meal, boy. All of it; every last piece."

"Thank you Magister, but I'm really full now." Ghost groaned and rubbed his belly.

"Every last piece." The Magister tapped on the wooden platter with the flat of the small knife he had been eating with. "Do you know when your next meal is?"

"No Magister."

"And neither do I. Every last piece, boy. Eat it all up."

He sat in silence, his eyes skimming over the increasingly drunken crowd, flicking from one coin purse dangling on its strings from a belt around a portly waist, to another that was always tucked inside a jerkin and patted safely on its return. He sipped his wine, scowling at the patrons of the tavern.

"I feel sick."

"Finished up? Good. I can't stand to watch these cattle any longer. We retire early and hopefully we can be up before we miss that waggoneer getting on his way."

With a rising wave of nausea Ghost staggered after the Magister up the stairs to the lodging rooms. Their quarters looked out on the stable yard and the boy peeked over the window ledge before shuttering the window and flopping down on the cot. He rolled onto his back and groaned as he rubbed his belly, then after some time he grew quiet and his breathing slowed. As Ghost dozed, Zarbenus poured wine down his throat and gave the skin an encouraging squeeze as the stream turned into droplets, then he tossed it onto the ground. He belched and loosely fixed his bloodshot gaze on the boy.

"Ghost."

"Yes, Magister?" Ghost rubbed his eyes as the numbness of his slumber drifted away.

"Go get me some more wine."

"But I don't have any money, Magister."

"Neither do I. Just go and get some. You know what I mean. I've seen you work."

Ghost rolled from the cot onto his knees.

I am a thief.

He heard laughing downstairs, but also singing from beyond the stable, out in front of the tavern. The singing faded away and Ghost crept out of the room and along the hall to peek down the stairwell at the bar room.

Two hefty fellows still haunted the bar, clutching tankards and nodding their heads together, loose lips smacking as they slobbered at their cups. Their eyelids fluttered; their conversation little more than incoherent mumbles. Several more patrons lay under tables and beside overturned chairs, drooling onto the floor and snoring. A sleek grey cat padded between them, sniffing as it went. Kanesh moved from table to table; collecting cups and tumblers, pinching out candles and snuffing lamps.

Ghost stayed close to the wall and climbed down the stairs, careful to place his feet as close to the wall and the sturdy joist as he could, avoiding the creaking of the middle of each step. The taverna keeper had his back to the stairs and was taking a tray of empty cups out to a side room. Ghost slipped down the last few steps and crouched behind the corner of the bar. He could hear Kanesh in the next room; chinking cups and splashing water. Underneath the bar squatted two large casks with spigots driven into them for the refilling of the ale jugs. Two tall amphorae leaned against the wall, recent deliveries waiting to be decanted into more practical vessels. On top of the barrels, out of sight of anyone on the other side of the bar, rested a crossbow, a short hand-axe and a sheathed dagger. Behind the bar hung a shelf with variously shaped flasks, gourds, and urns, and on a shelf above them a row of wine jars, stoppers sealed with red wax.

The chinking and splashing continued from the other room and was joined by Kanesh's soft whistling of a song unfamiliar to the boy. Ghost crawled behind one of the bar stools but bumped it as he passed. He twisted to catch it with one hand then it went down with a knock that echoed around the room. His breath caught in his throat, his eyes darted to the open door to the kitchen, but Kanesh's whistled song did not skip a beat and the splashing continued.

Ghost shut his eyes as he felt the pounding in his ears subside, then he righted the stool and climbed up on top of it. He looked at the row of wine jars with their wax seals of authenticity stamped onto them.

Which one would the Magister want?

His hand moved from one to the other then he grasped one by the neck and dropped down from the stool.

"You sneak well, boy. I almost didn't hear you."

Ghost jumped back and clutched the jar to his chest, his heart hammering and his breathing ragged. Kanesh's face betrayed no emotion as he slung the cloth over his shoulder and squatted down until he was level with the hunched-up boy. He reached out and tugged the jar from the boy's grasp, then turned it around and frowned at the label.

"You have good taste. This is an excellent wine; however I'd have thought you rather young to appreciate a vintage like this."

"I'm... sorry." Ghost stared back when the taverna keeper held his gaze.

"You're sorry? Sorry for what? That you tried to steal from me, or that I caught you doing it?"

Ghost opened his mouth to reply, then shut it as he pondered his answer.

"Well, which one is it? Spit it out."

"How did I not hear you come up behind me when I was lifting the jar?"

Kanesh's cheek creased with a brief smile, then he coughed and ran his finger across his moustache and down his beard, as if he was trying to smooth the thought away. His eyebrows had the most black of any of his hair but longer grey strands bristled as he frowned at his captive.

"Answer my question, boy. What you say next will determine what I do with you."

Ghost's face darkened. "I don't care what you do with me! I'm sorry you caught me but I still want to know how you managed to creep up on me."

Kanesh's cheek twitched again and he coughed into his knuckles,

84

struggling to straighten his face.

"Did that scoundrel send you to do this?"

The boy's fierce scowl stayed resolutely fixed as he nodded to the taverna keeper.

"And he neglected to mention that he and I once shared the same career?"

Ghost felt his heartbeat returning to normal and his fists lowered.

"Well." Kanesh put his hand on the boy's shoulder and gripped it firmly. "That scoundrel is a thief and a liar. The less he has told you, the less he has had a chance to lie about."

Ghost squinted at the taverna keeper as he considered this new information. "How do I know that it is not you who is the liar? He rescued me—I don't trust you."

"Ah, trust." Kanesh released his grip on Ghost's shoulder, and settled down cross-legged on the floor. "You should give trust very, very carefully. That will be one of the lessons that scoundrel will teach you, if you are going where I think you are going. And if you are going where I think you are going, you may need to get away from time to time to talk."

Ghost held out his hand. "I still need that wine."

Kanesh held it out, but tightened his grasp when the boy's fingers closed around the neck and tugged at it.

"Here's my offer. You get the jar and I'll let you get away with trying to steal from me, but you have to do something for me. Drop in here every now and then. Tell me what you've been up to. Even more importantly, tell me what he's been up to; either what he says he is doing, or you know that he is doing."

"That doesn't sound so hard." Ghost tugged again at the jar and although the taverna keeper allowed him to pull it to his chest, he kept a firm grip on the bottom.

"One final thing. Never let him know that we have these little chats. It'll be our secret."

Their eyes locked for several moments until Kanesh smiled. His fingers slipped away from the jar and the boy wrapped both of his arms around it. He turned for the stairs, then looked back at the taverna keeper sitting on the floor behind his bar. They nodded to each other, then Ghost climbed quietly up the stairs.

A line of paler grey passing between the shutter panels ran across the floor of the sleeping room and across the boy's cot. The Magister's bed lay in absolute darkness, his snoring a slow rhythmic vibration in the air. Ghost stood beside the bed, half-holding his breath, but the snoring continued. He waited for some minutes, trying to decide if he should wake his master, or go to sleep himself, then he placed the jar on the ground near the head of the bed and returned to his cot.

"Did that grey old fox give you any trouble?"

Ghost sat up in his cot, but was fighting to stay awake and yawned widely. "No, Magister."

There was a chuckle from the darkest corner of the room and the pop of a wooden bung being pried loose. "Good work, boy. Off to sleep with you. We have a long way to go tomorrow."

† † †

The words of Kanesh swam in Ghost's head as he tried to sleep. Every snippet of half-truth he learned was accompanied by two more mysteries, and the threats and warnings only served to fire his imagination. The silence of the rural night eerie and oppressive after the comforting confusion of city sounds.

"Are you still awake, Magister?"

The bed opposite creaked and the Magister's arm patted the floor, moving around, stretching fingers. His fingers closed around the abandoned wine jar, jiggled it, and the resultant sloshing was enough to persuade him to roll onto one elbow.

"Is your hearing really that bad? I expect you to be able to tell the true sounds of sleeping from pretend."

"I know I am not ready for my own name yet, but I wondered... will you tell me yours?"

The Magister swirled the wine in his mouth, swallowed it then chuckled. "Would you believe that I am Shadestep?"

"That's a funny name!"

Instantly the Magister appeared over Ghost's cot, iron fingers digging into his shoulder. He shook Ghost violently and brought his face so close that they shared the stale wine breath.

"Funny? Do you think so? It makes you laugh?"

"Not funny like that. I mean strange," said Ghost.

"Then use the correct words. A silver tongue is one of your greatest tools. A master thief's lips can open more doors than the fingers of the nimblest expert at lockpick."

The Magister released Ghost and sat down on the edge of the bed. "Would you believe me if I told it to you?"

Ghost nodded his head. "I think I would know if you told me the truth."

"Then my name is Greywhisper," said the Magister.

"No, it isn't!"

The Magister flourished his fingers. "My name is Darkhand."

"Uh-uh."

"How about Bladeshadow?"

"Now you're just being silly."

The Magister looked intently at Ghost. Staring into the grey-blue eyes that were so much like his own.

"Names give power, do you know that? If I tell you my name it will bind our fates together in ways you cannot possibly understand. Is that what you want?"

Ghost held his master's gaze, unblinking. "Yes Magister, I want to be just like you."

The Magister fell silent, and with him every creak of the roof, every gust in the trees. "This cannot be undone, boy. A path that once taken has no return, only forward into darkness, danger and death. I ask again—for the final time—do you accept your peril and place your body, your mind and your life in my hands; to do with as I will?"

His mouth dry, he nodded, and his words were hushed. "Yes, Magister."

"Then bound we are until I name you in return, for I am Zarbenus, and I am the God of Thieves."

Ghost's heart beat so hard he was sure the Magister could hear it. Each pulse throbbed at his temples in time with his shallow breaths.

"Magister... what does that mean?"

"That I alone can do things other men only dream of, and I am the greatest of my kind; blessed by the Night Mother herself. One day I too will leave this plane of existence, and I search for the one who will inherit my power on that day." He broke away and stumbled back to his bed, drained the last of his wine and rolled the empty jar on the ground with a soft curse. "And boy..."

Ghost felt his heart pounding so hard his chest hurt. "Yes, Magister?"

"I still have not found the one I seek yet. Who knows? As for you, well. You have no past, you have no family. You are nothing until I say that you are."

Another, longer yawn from the boy curling up on the cot. "Yes, Magister."

✝ ✝ ✝

Ghost grumbled into the crook of his arm as the tip of a boot was periodically applied with increasing forcefulness to his rear end. Whinnies and the clattering of hooves drifted in through the shuttered window along with a whiff of fresh manure, but the room was still dark.

"That waggon driver is getting a very early start indeed, so that means the

88

same for us."

The Magister grabbed the end of the stuffed straw mattress and yanked it sideways, rolling Ghost across floorboards. He tossed it onto the cot and walked out of the room, oblivious to the accusatory squinting of the boy who sat scratching his head on the cold, hard floor.

The balding waggon driver looked up with blinks of surprise when the Magister stepped into the stable yard, clapped him cheerfully on the shoulder and then stepped up to the waggon and settled himself in his position of the previous day. The horses shuffled and the ghostly veil of their breath hung about their heads in the chilly air.

"Good idea, old man. A fine early start like this will have us well on our way."

Ghost stumbled into the dark yard, puffy eyes still half closed. He pulled his cloak lopsidedly across his shoulders.

"Jump up, boy. Let's not keep this diligent waggoneer from beginning the day."

The old man cocked his head at the Magister lounging on his waggon, then shrugged and climbed up beside him. He snapped the reins twice and with a snort the horses pulled the waggon out of the stable yard and off along the road. Ghost rolled his head to watch the sign of the mouse and sleeping cat pass overhead, then turned over under his cloak and settled back to sleep.

When he later yawned awake and stretched out his limbs, rolling back against the sacks, the sun was well risen. The still winter air, with no snow or sleet to dull it, boasted the sharp clarity of the distant hills, rising blue-tinted ahead of the road they slowly ascended.

"Where are we going, Magister?"

"Somewhere safe."

"Will I ever be able to go home?"

"Is there anything for you to go back for?"

Ghost's stomach lurched and his head fell. "I guess not."

The enigmatic hooded figure stayed silent after that, his lack of words continuing to raise questions in Ghost's mind. Kanesh had been more forthcoming—about the Magister—not about himself. Maybe that was the way of things. Maybe it was easier to tell a secret when all you did was reveal more secrets. Ghost had begged Kanesh for stories, hints or anything he could learn about the Magister. Before they'd left the *Grey Mouse* the old taverna keeper had relented, glanced around, then hunched forward with a mischievous grin.

"You want the truth? What do you say we make a promise, you and I. To always tell the truth to each other. You know lies have a life of their own. They take control and there's nothing you can do about it. When you start lying it's a curse you make yourself. From that point you can never believe what someone else tells you is the truth. So try this on for size. You and me we make a pact: we either tell each other the truth or we say nothing at all. How does that sound?"

"Tell me about him already!"

"What? Before you've held up your side? I'll tell you this. He was gone for years. He had good reason I admit, and truly I never expected to see him again. But when I had he'd changed. He came back better, faster, luckier I guess. I tried to get the truth from him but it was a different story each time. Let me remember some of them; there was the one about a legendary tonic to preserve him against poisons created by the great alchemical brothers from Baghdad, an indefatigable Eastern warrior who owed him a life-debt, a personal visitation from a goddess. He truly is the prince of lies, but whatever it was he no longer was just the second son of a disgraced noble, no longer a common cutpurse. He'd become something else. Something more."

And that left more questions than answers.

After an hour Ghost saw two hills ahead. Far beyond the hills, a jagged white-capped mountain peak, a giant on the horizon. The hills grew sharper-edged as they rolled closer and as midday passed the boy made out the individual features of each. Great slant slabs tumbled against shattered giant boulders, crusted over with creeping vegetation that trailed over ledges and crawled down slopes. The greatest hill stood proud for miles around, a craggy shard dominating the local area. Through the dark green waving fingers of the cypress trees that ringed its waist, the ruins of once-mighty walls could be seen. Atop the hill, seeming to grow from the base rock, a lonely tower with ruined walls falling away to the side. Once a forbidding fortification, it had been nearly totally destroyed in some ancient calamity. The sole tower summit shattered on one side, sunlight passing through the sockets of the highest windows. A skeletal glare, balefully regarding their approach.

The road headed to a small village tucked in the dell of two of the hills; one stumpy spire rising apologetically out of the middle, and a score of red-tiled roofs scattered each side of it.

The waggon driver tethered his horses at the fixing post beside a water trough in the sandy square in front of the villager's chapel and looked expectantly at the hooded man stretched out on the waggon's bench. The Magister stepped down and walked without a word into a shop on the opposite side of the square. Ghost jumped down and waved to the waggon driver.

The waggon driver nodded then returned to checking his horses.

In the shop Ghost found the Magister in front of a counter, two small sacks lying on it. He scribbled on a piece of paper then tossed down the stick of charcoal. A busty woman of middle-age watched him write then took the paper, folded it, then placed it inside a drawer in a cabinet with many such drawers. The Magister pulled a wrinkled fist-sized cheese from one of the sacks and chucked it over his shoulder. Ghost caught it and, after an exploratory sniff he bit into it. The shopkeeper smiled at the boy and crossed her arms in front of her chest.

"Such a lucky boy. The lord takes such care of you children himself, and never says a word, Goddess bless him, his father would be proud. I shudder to think what would have happened to all you little ones. Bless him, I say!"

She took a tin from her counter and extracted a large crystal of brown sugar from it and handed it to the Ghost. It moved from hand to mouth instantly, and the woman's benevolent smile was answered by the glow on Ghost's face. The Magister bowed to the lady then left the shop, and the boy, with one final look up at the beaming woman, tucked his half-cheese into his shirt and followed him.

"Not her Goddess. Not by any of her damned thousand names. Well then. From here we have a sharp climb, but we're nearly there." The Magister slung one of the sacks on his shoulder, and held out the larger one to Ghost. "Here, carry this. Time you did some work."

Ghost tried carrying it over his shoulder, but it was too big for him, Carrying it in front with both arms clasped around it made it hard for him to see where he was going as he followed the Magister up a footpath that led higher up the tallest hills. He tripped and landed on the sack, scraping his knee as he went down. The Magister kept walking, so with a twitching nose Ghost stood up and hauled the sack off the ground. After experimenting, he settled with balancing it on his head. His arms tired from holding it straight, but he would shake one out at a time when they grew too stiff and he doggedly followed the trail. Minutes dragged out interminably and eventually he stumbled and yelped aloud as he turned his ankle. Glancing ahead he saw no reaction from the Magister.

"I said 'ouch'."

"Be silent and pay attention."

Ghost threw down the pack at the Magister's feet. "I do everything you tell me to do."

Zarbenus' hand twitched for the dagger at his belt, then with white knuckles moved his fingers to his beard and began to scratch his chin. "Pick it up," he said.

"I hate you." Ghost turned away, covering his face with his arm, grinding his sleeve into his eyes as if that would stop the tears forming there.

The Magister glared at the cowering child. Still a baby, despite the years that had passed. The Tahtakale had taught him much that Zarbenus would find useful, but softened him too. Damn that Raseyda. Mothering him like a clucking hen. She had no right to ruin him like this and, by the Night Mother, he promised that she would pay for it. This whelp had once been as beautiful as a shard of broken glass; stained with blood, eager for more. It hadn't even known how to cry. It was ready to die with curses on its lips and torn fingernails. A child like that could have been moulded into something interesting. This snivelling adolescent... well, he was useless. Zarbenus spat on the grass. Unable to bear the rancid sourness of failure rising like a wicked miasma from the boy, he marched away without looking back.

Ghost looked up as he heard the footfalls fade away. Heart pounding and blood rushing to his pink face he rolled to his feet, grabbed the sack, and chased after the Magister with a fresh zeal.

"Get lost, brat," said Zarbenus as Ghost caught up with him.

"I'm sorry," said Ghost, choking down his pride and anger and doing his best to appear compliant.

The Magister shrugged and picked up his pace.

The boy's hurled pack collided with Zarbenus' legs from behind. He half-stumbled, then collapsed onto one knee as Ghost's weight hit him with force. Fingernails raked at his cheeks, tearing his hood aside. He dropped a shoulder, tugged one of Ghost's wrists, twisted the arm as he threw the boy across the path.

"I hate you!" Ghost's lips drew back, flecks of spit on his teeth. Insensate to the gravel burns across his cheek. His rage owned him and he flew at the Magister, clawing talons trying to shred flesh.

The black cloak swirled and the Magister disappeared from Ghost's view, appearing to the side a moment later. Zarbenus straightened two fingers and drove them into Ghost's throat. The boy collapsed, choking, heels thrashing against the ground. He retched then staggered to his feet, madness in his eyes and a shard of broken flint clenched in his fist. The assault was frenzied, slashing wildly, but the cloak swirled again and Zarbenus struck a cupped hand against Ghost's ear. The boy went down, clutching his head, blood seeping between his fingers, then he vomited.

The Magister stood silently above Ghost's body; no whimpers this time. Just laboured, painful breathing.

"At least this version of you is willing to die to take what it wants."

"I'll kill you," whispered Ghost.

"For what? I thought you wanted me to teach you?"

Ghost turned his face away, hiding his burning cheeks. "I do."

"And what if I gave you the choice? Kill someone else, and I'll teach you all my secrets."

Ghost stopped squirming, but didn't answer. Zarbenus shook his head and turned away.

"A waste of my time."

"I'll kill them!" Ghost glared at the Magister. He sat upright, still comforting his ear with his hand.

The Magister stared intently at the boy, fire and fury writ large on his face, the false subservience doing little to mask the truth.

"Then that's the first thing you've said I have any interest in. Will you stick to it, I wonder? Your appetite for slaughter piques my interest. It remains to be seen if you spout empty words or if you can deliver on those promises. Ahead of you lie mortal challenges, but not all appear at first as lethal as they really are. Can you trust no-one and betray everyone? I seek a blade in the dark; subtle, silent and swift. I care not for bawling babes." The Magister wiped his hand across his face, the intent fire leaving his eyes and the veil of indifference falling once again. "Yet I am not without my own disappointments. Already I've seen promising prospects stumble and fall, despite all I have done for them. Am I foolish to expect more from you, child?"

Ghost's sullen stare wavered, something deeper and darker hiding beneath the surface. Biding its time. Lying in wait.

The Magister took Ghost by the chin, turned his face from side to side, then grunted and shook his head.

"You're not special, you're trash. Irredeemable. No-one will ever trust you, and no-one will ever love you."

The boy's weight moved subtly, pressure building on the balls of his feet, fingers curling inward.

Zarbenus nodded, as if seeing the response he expected. "But I have uses for trash. If no-one is going to love you, then they may as well fear you."

Not waiting for an answer, the Magister turned away, arranging his cloak and hood.

"Your words are meaningless to me. But you have earned a chance—a brief one—to impress me. If you're not good enough then the others will do away with you soon enough. I don't have anything to lose at this point." He took a few steps then paused. "If you want a quiet life then crawl back down the hill. Crawl all the way back to Tahtakale and beg that limping brood-mare and dancing bear to take you back. A different fate lies in this direction. Cruel, bloody, and glorious." Then he carried on up the path in long, easy strides.

Ghost sat there, his pounding head hurting far less than his pride, and he watched the Magister disappear as the path curved around the hillside. Coughing and wobbling as waves of nausea lapped at him, he hoisted the sack onto his shoulders again and hurried forward.

Two men abreast might have followed the narrow path but no more. Littered with scree and fallen stones from the broken wall that once shielded travellers, the other side of the track nothing but the bare rock of the hillside. Where the way became too steep deep steps were cut into the rock. Ghost's thighs burned, and he loathed each twist in the path where he had to climb up. Once a line of statues had stood alongside the path, each broad-shouldered and bearing instruments of war. Now they lay tumbled and broken, their faces hacked away to crumble amongst the gravel underfoot. The Magister looked back after an hour's march and saw Ghost tramping after him, eyes narrowed on the path and his lips tight. A terse grunt came from under the scarf that wrapped the hooded man's face, then he turned and carried on walking.

The path wound higher, hemmed in by bushy stone pines. Their long rust-brown needles carpeted the ground, the footpath more sparsely covered and strewn with broken rocks that tumbled down the hillside. In the distance stood the great mountain, white shroud draping almost halfway down its slopes. A smaller peak off to its side. Their height, even from so far away, made him grudgingly grateful that he was on the route he followed and not toiling up their slopes. Twice Ghost spotted ancient waystones by the side of the path, waving blades of ragged yellow grass skirting their base, the inscriptions almost worn smooth by centuries of exposure to the elements. One looked as if it may have been a carving of a long-stemmed key, the other had a patination reminiscent of cobwebs. Their silent vigil seemed an oppressive presence; grim watchers whose warnings went unheeded. Underfoot, amidst the stones and crushed twigs, decaying leaves and rolling pine-cones, rusty chain links lay scattered. Sun-bleached and yellowing shards of bones grew in numbers as he followed the path onward. Long ago many had fallen here and had been left to rot where they lay. Chill tremored through Ghost as he realised he was walking on the remains of the dead. As the sun fell lower Ghost staggered forward, concentrating on the path for each footfall so that he would not stumble again. With a jolt he looked up as the sack he carried was jerked from his head.

They had reached the ruined castle at the top of the hill. Broken walls had left massive cascades of stone blocks around the remains of a once well-guarded bailey. The lone tower that yet stood now reinforced by tree trunks, roughly hewn and holding it up at angles. The tattered remains of the crenellations just the broken crown of a fallen king. Once it must have appeared that the fortifications grew directly from the earth, the boundaries between hill and castle hard to define. Now barring the lonely tower—itself a decaying monument to decrepitude—the rest of the fortress seemed to be melting back into the ground. Brown and white goats, ribs showing at their flanks, grazed on the meagre tufts that clung precariously to the near-vertical slope of shattered debris. Their piteous bleating claiming the ruins as their domain; too treacherous for clumsy two-legged humans.

Chapter 6:
The Vipers Nest

The Magister waved the sack at a ramshackle house built down the side of the tower in several stories. To the other side a sheer drop to the valley below. Dry stone walls gave way to wooden panels, red tile roofs mingled with grey slate ones. Dwarfed as it was by the remnants of the once-grand fort the house clung apologetically, looking as if it could crumble and slide down the mountain should the wind take an unexpected turn. The long shadows of the late afternoon sun hid corners and windows obscuring the overall shape, and poles held up precariously overhanging box windows that teetered over the edge of the cliff. Each story vied with its neighbour only to outdo each other with their dilapidation and squalor. Ghost's chest swelled and he wanted to jump from roof to roof as he explored the mysteries of each room. To make it his, to claim it as his birthright, and he wanted to deserve it. The Magister was right. Ghost's simmering anger turned inward, at the crying child inside. His own weakness disgraced him and he swore he'd learn to master it.

"Welcome to the Nidus," said Zarbenus with a dismissive wave at the building.

Children emerged from the house; one climbing the side of one level, one crawling through an open window and two more from around the back.

"Listen up, bratlets. Another worthless vagrant has attached himself to me. Make yourselves useful and relieve me of the burden."

A gangly blond boy, freckles across the brow of his nose, waved a lacklustre welcome after a clumsy exit from a ground-floor window. His ragged trousers barely covered his knees, the tip of his big toe sticking out of his well-worn shoes.

"Magister, you've been gone ages this time. Did you bring any food? We've eaten almost everything in the stores."

The Magister's brow furrowed as he tossed the sacks on the ground.

"You should have stolen some from the village, Crooked. If you can't manage a simple thing like that after being here a year, then maybe I should reconsider your future. The Night Mother blesses those who help themselves."

Crooked fiddled with his fingers. "I'm sorry, Magister. There'll be even less food now you've brought another. The villagers started a night watch... we were scared of getting caught."

"If you can't evade a fat, sleepy farmer then you deserve to be caught. And hung too. I won't be coming to rescue you."

The Magister cracked his knuckles and glared at Crooked. Weather-pitted boulders at the base of the crumbled tower sheltered a row of low stone cairns, most overgrown by nettles and moss but two stood out as freshly placed. The Magister regarded these with a sneer.

"In fact, my tolerance for your ineptitude is equal to your potential; that is to say—exceedingly small. Fortunately from what I have observed, your own capacity for failure will preserve me from having to put up with you for much longer, and you can join those that rot in the ground. Indeed, should some tidy and convenient misadventure befall you, I'd admire whichever of your fellow snakelings saved me the effort of dealing with you personally. Now, if you can provide some trivial service before your early but richly deserved demise, you are to make Ghost useful. Somewhere."

"Ghost?" Crooked looked at the new arrival who was pulling a grimace that wavered between fierce confidence and unobtrusiveness.

Zarbenus paused, his gaze wandering the horizon. After a moment's introspection, he shrugged. "He had a whole town of peasants thinking they were haunted, and he even managed to evade me—albeit briefly. But he will have to show me more than his shadows knack if he ever wants to earn a better name than that. Tell the others."

"Yes, Magister."

Crooked bowed his head again, receiving only a nod in reply before the Magister wandered into the house. Ghost rubbed his sore arms, trying to get the stiffness out. Crooked stared at him. Eventually his head lolled to the side, and he sighed.

"I remember when I first came here, it was all so strange I was pretty scared."

"I'm not scared," muttered Ghost.

"We'll ken soon enough. Anyway, this is Roach. The Magister calls him that because he's so bad at sneaking. You can hear the patter of his feet; just like a cockroach at night. He's even worse than a poor cripple." Crooked thumbed his chest.

"You want to be lame in both legs?" Roach glared at them, then turned away with a grunt. Shaggy hair hung about his shoulders, half-obscuring his grey-blue eyes. He looked to be a few years older than the others—not because he stood any taller than the rest, but his stocky figure held a shadow of the man he was growing into.

"Da mind him. Next up; these two are Dogan and Demir."

Ghost examined the pair. They were exactly the same height and had the same lopsided grin. Each had their pale brown hair tied back from their eyes which were exactly the same shade of brown.

"I can't tell you apart. How do I know who is who?"

Dogan and Demir grinned at each other. "Oh, you'll get used to it eventually. Until then though..." They laughed together and walked back into the house.

Crooked punched Ghost's shoulder. "Be careful, they back each other up fiercely. If you go against one of them, you'll get both. Times like that you should know who your friends are."

"They're bullies?"

"Well," Crooked twitched an uncomfortable half-grin. "It's just that... it's two of them against one, so you da stand a chance alone, you ken? I share a room with them and they da give me much trouble, but then I stay out of their way."

"How come they have real names?"

"Magister's favourites. All the tricks he can play with someone that can be in two places at once. Ask the Magister if you want, I da ken how long he's going to be around this time. When he's gone the rest of us look out for each other. Like a family."

Ghost's stomach flipped. "A family?"

"Guess you're just like the rest of us? Your family is gone and when you kenned you'd die alone then the Magister found you?" Crooked shrugged. "In a few days you'll get used to it. If no-one kills you first."

Ghost scrubbed away the dampness that had grown in his eyes. "I guess you're right."

"Of course I'm right. I'm always right! Except when we do weapon drills. Hmm. Watch someone else then. But apart from that. I'm always right."

"How long you been here?"

"He got me about a year ago. There was an older boy here when I first arrived, and it was just him and Timan, and me and Roach until the others got here. The older boy has gone though. I da know where, he just went on a job with the Magister and da come back. We asked Timan who told us to ask the Magister, but then he wouldn't tell us anything either. You'll get used to that, he can get pretty grumpy sometimes. I guess all grown-ups do that, don't they?"

"I guess so," said Ghost.

"When you can make yourself useful then the Magister takes you on trips," said Crooked. "Last week he took me to a fair, and while he argued with traders at their stalls I lifted purses from the crowd that gathered to listen to him."

Ghost frowned at him. "He makes you steal?"

"He says the more work we do, the less he has to. Come on. She'll have gotten some food ready, and you can meet the others, if they're all back."

Crooked walked with a long loping stride, but Ghost noticed the limp now that it had been pointed out. It didn't seem to slow him down so Ghost hurried his steps to keep pace. When they reached the front of the strange house they met a darkly tanned girl, some fifteen summers old with long black hair tied behind her neck. She wore boy's trousers and a multi-coloured jacket that was more patches than original material, and stood taller even than Roach. She peered intently at him with her own grey-blue eyes, sniffed, then wrinkled her nose.

"Another hungry mouth arrives. And this one hasn't washed for weeks." She played with an old key tied around her neck as she looked him up and down. "I'm older than you so that means you have to do what I tell you to, or else."

"Or else what?"

"Or... POW!" She held the knuckles of her balled fist up to Ghost's face and bared her teeth. "I'll knock your head off."

Ghost dug his nails into his palms. "I won't be told what to do by a girl."

The punch took him off his feet and he fell back, clutching a nose squirting hot blood.

She shook her fist at Crooked. "Did you have something to say, Crookey?"

He held up two placating palms. "*Pax!* You're in charge. Reckon Ghost will ken that now. I'll make sure, don't worry."

Temper lowered her tensed knuckles, but her glare that would have raised whimpers from a pack of wild dogs continued unabated. "Then you'll get the same as him if he keeps being cocky. He's your responsibility now, or you'll both get more smacks until he falls in line." She spun on her heel and her hair trailed after her as she marched into the house.

Crooked helped Ghost to his feet and handed him tattered scrap of cloth to dab his nose.

"Sorry about that. I should've warned you."

"What's her problem—and how can she hit like that? I'd didn't even see her move her hand."

"That's just Temper. She arrived in the summer and has been pushing us around since then. As dangerous as she is beautiful. She says that her people are warriors and that is all she will ever be."

Ghost glanced sideways at Crooked, continuing to smile despite the recent and future threats to his physical wellbeing. "Why did you do that? Stick up for me."

Crooked chuckled. "Just being friendly."

"What do you want for it?"

"It? I figured we can all be friends unless you do something really bad. Even then if you're sorry I'll give you a chance to make it up, deal?"

No-one ever did anything just to be nice, and Ghost wondered what Crooked's angle was. He could still taste his own blood in his mouth; bitter like his mood.

"You sound like a soft touch. I bet everyone walks all over you."

"You ken?"

Crooked's smile broadened until it reached his eyes; glittering like he had a secret surprise.

"I guess that could happen but I think people are more decent than they might first appear. Even if they look scary or angry I give them a chance, and the way I see it I can always prove my intentions by going first. And that's what I'm doing with you."

Ghost looked Crooked up and down, settling on the strapped leg. "Did you come up with this because you couldn't fight with a bad leg?"

"Who said I couldn't fight?" Crooked's hand slipped behind his body and Ghost tensed for the inevitable attack.

Crooked hand flashed into view, tossing something at Ghost's face. He flinched, hands covering his face and caught... an apple; small, green and unblemished.

Crooked laughed so hard his cheeks turned red. "A friend and a present in your first hour here? I think you'll be fine if you stick with me." He tapped his head. "I use this before my fists. Just you see, Temper isn't the only one I have a way with. The Magister mocks us if we team up but he never stops us. Never stops anything actually."

Ghost's nose twitched at first, then he exhaled. "That Temper girl. Her voice was strange, it sounded like singing..."

Crooked grinned. "Yeah it does sound a bit strange. Wait until she speaks her own language. We're all trying to learn each other's own speech. The Magister is very keen on that sort of thing."

"What does he say about pushing people around?" Ghost examined globules of black blood in the rag.

"Nothing. He leaves us to ourselves, which means we can play any way we like and for as long as we like, as long as we master our knacks. Besides, she looks after us and stuff." Crooked peered at the Ghost's blood-daubed nose and shrugged. "That's probably about as good as it is going to look for a few days. Come on, you must be hungry."

Most of the bottom floor was given over to a large room with a long row of windows; shutters thrown back and an expansive view of the valley below. Wisps of smoke rose out of the pine forest from the little village below. Facing the main entrance stood a solid wooden staircase that led up, beside it a single door. In the shadow of the staircase lay coils of rope and an untidy pile of rusty lanterns.

The twins sat cross-legged beside a low, wide table barely tall enough to accommodate the legs stretched under it. Roach carried in a tray from the next room and laid out cold meat and jars of vegetable preserves. Temper followed carrying two flat, circular breads. She tore them into portions and handed them out, pausing to nod curtly to each as they took their share. Roach got the largest piece. This formality concluded, everyone helped themselves to meat and vegetables, and rolled them inside the bread before ripping in. Ghost watched them, then made his own roll and set to it. They ate in silence and when he opened his mouth to ask a question Crooked shook his head. Ghost caught a flash of anger in Temper's eyes. They kept eating, and despite the odd groan or puffed cheeks, carried on until all the food was finished. The twins rolled back in unison and sighed as they laid on the floor.

"Well, that's over with." Temper rose from the table and went up the stairs.

Ghost raised his eyebrows to Crooked who said, "You can talk now. She always makes us eat the way the Magister told us to, but when he is away we do what we like."

"Why doesn't he eat with us?"

"He used to, but I da ken him doing it for ages. That's why we had the blowout meal tonight; he'd brought in new provisions. Usually it's just the stuff Temper gets us, and she's stingy with those rations."

"This is the second night in a row I've had to stuff myself like this," said Ghost.

"Hey! Don't complain. It will be soon enough we'll be back to short rations and you'll soon enough be dreaming of a feast," said Crooked.

"Why? What will happen?"

"The Magister will go away again. He always does," said Crooked. "Then it's up to us to look after ourselves. We practice our knacks. Lots of different things, ya yen?"

"I don't... *ken*... anything! Everything happened so fast!"

"This is a fight to the death; don't kid yourself it's anything else," said Roach, his voice low and creaky. He stared at Ghost, but then tossed his shaggy hair, discarding the idea, got to his feet and left the room.

Crooked pinched the brow of his nose. "It isn't that dramatic, though Roach has a point. The Magister's the greatest thief in the world and he's going to make us like him."

A thief.

Ghost glared at Crooked. "What... if we don't want to be... like that?"

"Why not? I reckon if we play it smart and stick together we'll do alright. Except that there were others who..."

Temper's voice sounded very loud even though she was upstairs. "Shut up, Crookey. I can still hear you!"

He froze, shoulders hunched.

"What don't we talk about, Crookey?" Temper dangled upside down from the top of the stairs so they could only see her head. Her expression convinced both of the boys they didn't want her coming any further down.

"We da talk about the dead," said Crooked loudly as he tapped his brow to Ghost.

"Good," said Temper, and her head disappeared, presumably to join the rest of her body.

Guilt welled in Ghost as he remembered standing in bedrooms with their mumbling, slumbering, innocent occupants. And he remembered the face of the wheat-haired child whose neck he had choked.

"He wanted us because we're already thieves?"

"Or so I ken," said Crooked. "But you can try asking Timan when he shows up. Get him at the right moment and he'll open up. Though get it wrong and he'll come down on you like a storm's wrath and make no mistake."

The staccato percussion of running feet rapidly approached and the door of the house flew open. Two boys shoved past each other then stood panting and sweating as they stared at the empty trays.

"We missed dinner again? Hekate's teats!"

The first was thin and pale with a dirty face and blackened fingernails. His partner almost half the height of any of the other children, and his tongue flicked out to lick a trail of mucus trickling out of his nose. A number of unpleasant smells emanated from the pair. Ghost held his nose and shuffled back on his knees, keen to get as much as possible of the table between himself and the newcomers.

The pale boy picked up what few crumbs and scraps remained on the table and deposited them in his upturned trout mouth, grumbling to himself. He glared at Ghost.

"Did you eat all of the food? You just got here and you've eaten my dinner. I don't think you're very nice."

Idly picking his nose he advanced as Ghost waved him away, turning his head from side to side and refusing to let go of his nose.

"Have you nothing to say for yourself?" The pale boy's cheeks flushed and he slapped Ghost's hand away from his face. At that moment the pale boy decided to release a particularly noisy new smell, delivered at close quarters. Ghost yelped and scrambled to escape, hanging off the door frame with his head in the evening air, choking and spluttering.

The pale boy and the tiny boy shrieked with laughter, pointing at Ghost. Then every time as their eyes met they started cackling all over again.

Crooked grinned from a safe distance. "Well, you were going to meet up sooner or later. Your smelly assailant is Foul, and his scrawny sidekick is Scab. They got here a couple of months ago. Boys, this is Ghost."

Ghost closed the door and faced them with a queasy expression, his eyes still watering. Foul and Scab's laughter softened to chortling, then as Scab resumed licking his dribbling nose they fell silent.

"Sorry I ate your dinner," said Ghost.

Foul shrugged and scratched at his shrunken belly. The last of his smile faded into his trout pout and he looked sadly at Ghost.

"We're used to going hungry. It happens to us all the time. He wants us to call you Ghost? That's his worst one yet."

"Worst one? At least all of the rest of you have real names," said Ghost.

"You can have mine." Scab chewed on the edge of his lip. "Scab's a rubbish name. He let me choose you know; Scab or Snot. Not much of a choice, huh?"

"Maybe I'll just stick with Ghost for now and see what he comes up with later."

"It'll probably just be Snot left." Scab crawled around the edges of the table picking up any remaining crumbs. Finding the area scoured clean he ambled, slope-shouldered, over to the stairs.

"G'night."

Foul picked his nose thoughtfully then sucked the finger before nodding to himself in internal agreement. "Me too. G'night lads."

"Come on. I'll show you to a spare bunk. If you stay in our room you won't have to smell those two. Everyone makes sure to be in a different room and..." Crooked pointed a warning finger at Ghost, wagging it with the seriousness of the situation. "And they fart while they sleep. All... night... long."

Ghost clasped his hands over his mouth while Crooked nodded sadly.

"That's why it is important to know who is in the room you choose," said Crooked.

"Where does the Magister sleep?"

"At the very highest floor, inside the tower. The only door to that floor is locked. Probably booby-trapped. Roach told me that once there was a boy who was dared to go there. He went there in the middle of the night, and all they heard from him was a terrible scream. They say his body was never found."

Ghost stared wide-eyed at Crooked.

"Come on. Let's get you that bunk. At least you won't have to stay with Foul and Scab. No-one ever goes in their room if they can possibly avoid it. It's... disgusting."

Crooked screwed his eyes shut and shivered as if ridding himself of a bad dream. Then he led them up a slanted stairway, up a ladder propped beneath a hatch in another room, and round a twisted staircase on poles that rocked with every step. He paused outside a door and looked around before drawing Ghost close by the shoulder.

"Look," he whispered. "You seem alright so... tell you what, you watch my back and I'll watch yours. Fair enough?"

Ghost frowned at him. "For what?"

"For anything," said Crooked dropping his voice even lower until he could be barely heard. "If someone comes for you, I'll stand by you, and you do the same for me—got it? No-one is tough enough to take on two of us, even Temper."

"Oh," said Ghost. "I get it, we're friends then?"

Crooked grinned and stuck his hand out. "Shake on it, and a demon take you if you break it!"

Ghost shook the offered hand then Crooked immediately turned away and opened the door. Beyond was a long rectangular room with a single small window opposite the door. He shared the room with Dogan and Demir, their beds swung out from hinges on the wall and held in place with ropes. The twins, one above the other, turned in unison, to greet Ghost as he entered.

"Hey."

"This is our side of the room."

"So just keep your mess on your side and there will be no problems."

"You have that half and stay with Crooked."

"If you dump any of your stuff on our side we'll chuck it in a fire."

Their sentences spilled out of alternate mouths in a practised stream, and

Ghost's head nodded up and down as he flicked from the twin in the upper bunk to the twin in the lower bunk. They had a wooden chest stowed under the bottom bunk. Demir, or at least Ghost thought it was Demir, reached down from his reclining position and patted the chest.

"Got it?"

"But I don't have any stuff," said Ghost.

The twins grinned back at his confusion.

"Then there is nothing to worry about!"

"And we can be best of friends!"

"Or at least not enemies."

"At least not now."

"But I don't want to be enemies," said Ghost.

"What Demir suggests," said the dominant twin, now identified as Dogan. "Is that we're not enemies now because you haven't done anything stupid and gotten in our way. In fact, because I'm in such a great mood today, I'll even make you a promise. If you run away tonight and never come back then we won't hunt you down and kill you."

Demir nodded. "It's a great offer, Ghost. Think it over," and with that he rolled over and turned his back to them.

Ghost saw Dogan's smile as more of a grimace; like a dog's face when it pulled back its lips to snarl. He had to be in charge of the pair. Crooked coughed and directed Ghost's attention to the two bunks that swung out from their side of the room.

"Which do you want; top or bottom? I've been using the bottom one as it's just been me, but I don't mind taking the top one now. I'm taller than you and it would probably be too much of a climb for you."

Ghost flushed and stared at Crooked, unsure if he was being made fun of again, or if the offer was genuine.

"I can climb fine. You stay in your bed, you don't have to move for me. I can take the top one."

Crooked nodded and threw Ghost a woollen blanket that had been patched and repaired and stained and bleached until it was a pilled and dry indistinct grey.

"Hey," said Crooked tossing himself onto the lower bunk and folding his hands behind his head. "So what do you think of Temper, then?"

"Think I'm going to keep out of her way."

Crooked smiled to himself. "That's probably best."

Ghost tucked the blanket under his arm, and treading on the edge of Crooked's bed, pulled himself up to the top bunk and curled up. Although the full dark of the night was only just settling outside their small window he felt the comfort of the blanket and the softness of his cot luxurious after days of travelling. When Crooked put out the lamp a few moments later Ghost managed to count three stars in the blackness before he slipped away.

✝ ✝ ✝

Back at the Grey Mouse, Kanesh had gotten around to sweeping out the lodging room. Another long day, and his back ached from all the amphorae he'd moved that afternoon. He grumbled under his breath. Times were he could have done that all day, spent the night drinking and dancing until dawn, and still had a spring in his step come morning. He bent to collect the discarded jar and saw a folded note on the bed. Kanesh took it nearer to the candle to read, saw the job requirements and was satisfied with the payment terms.

Why Zarbenus would want a couple of circus performers quietly killed was none of his business. Kanesh didn't ever ask, and doing jobs quietly was what his generous fee assured. For that kind of money he'd always be persuaded to come out of retirement, even for just one night. Time for him to spread his wings.

✝ ✝ ✝

The room at the top of the ruined tower in the wilderness lay quiet and still. Zarbenus sat hunched in the dark, his mind patiently assigning tasks to his agents, and receiving the fruits of their labours. That made them sound like farmers; the fruits he received were much more valuable tokens. He rose and stepped over to the ancient hearth that lay cold and abandoned in the opposite wall. Small logs lay across the fire-irons and the ashes had been swept away. These he stepped over and ducked inside, a dribble of light descending the chimney stack. Reaching up he depressed a brick, and the back wall of the fireplace slid noiselessly aside. Faint indeed was the click of the first trap arming, and this he disabled by toeing a lever mounted behind the laid wood in the fireplace. His way clear he entered the narrow passage and climbed down a series of iron rungs.

His descent took several minutes for the chimney was only an antechamber to a natural tunnel in the rock face. The remote location where the castle had been built was not by accident. Eventually his feet touched a smooth stone floor, and it was only then he felt around for a hanging lamp and sparked its wick into life.

The cave deep beneath the Nidus was poorly illuminated by the single lamp, yet he made his way to a table stacked with books and lit two candles there. Watching from the shadows; an ancient statue of a cowled woman. Her presence comforted him, guided and protected him, for this was her shrine from a time beyond reckoning. Occasionally, he remembered a small boy running in terror from a street gang. Fleeing through sewers in a city far away, finding—by accident or divine grace—a shrine to Hekate, and emerging without fear. The street gang submitted to him a short while after; he made them his. Now terror was something he wielded, not flinched from. He never forgot the feeling that came over him as he lay crying at the foot of her statue until he felt her gaze, and his tears were taken from him. He'd never again cried since that day.

He withdrew a scroll and a pouch from inside his tunic and laid them on the table, then drawing one of the great ledgers towards him he began to meticulously update his records. The Night Mother set this task before him, and he would not fail her. His enemies had centuries of tradition that constrained their actions; he had none. Their hierarchies of power, division of responsibilities, chains-of-command; all were exploitable weaknesses. Their actions, reactions, secrets and lies were so predictable they were almost tiresome, but he grinned to himself as he continued the inexorable finesse of his stratagem.

A letter, originally encoded in a cipher of Zarbenus' design.

Third day of Gorpiaios

Magister,

I have not received word from you for some time, therefore I continue upon the course you have plotted for me.

Oikos Vlastos remains unstable and has lost much of their territory, specifically around the Prosphorion docks. The young Doma has proven to show no lack of bloodthirst in consolidating her control over what remains, yet at present has too few faithful (or fearful) doing her bidding. Whether she will regain that what she has lost to Oikos Medea remains to be seen. Doma Medea rarely relinquishes anything or anyone she gains sway over.

I am pursuing another trail that is yielding much progress into the operations of the young Bey Izmir, an approach which I earnestly hope will garner your admiration when I describe its subtlety. That tale I will save for when we next meet.

I crave your indulgence for the length of my absence. May the Night Mother bless you.

Your dutiful son,

Timan

Chapter 7:

Village Burglary

A week passed and Ghost woke in a high bunk that felt safe and familiar as he rolled in his blanket, but a rhythmic rocking inched him out of his slumber. Ghost groaned and rolled his head over the edge. He peered through the gloom at his roommate. Crooked kept kicking the bunk from underneath and Ghost scowled at him.

"What is it? It's the middle of the night..."

"I'm hungry," said Crooked.

Ghost rubbed at his eyes with the heels of his palms. "I da ken what you want me to do about it."

"Aren't you hungry too? The Magister has been gone for days and there's nothing left."

"So?" Ghost squirmed and pulled his sheet over his head.

"So he said we should steal some if we were hungry," said Crooked.

"I ken," came the muffled voice from the bunk above.

"You da seem too excited about it."

"You just get hungry faster than me."

"That's true, you're pretty scrawny." Crooked chuckled. "But you said you were on your own for ages, you know, stealing food and stuff before the Magister found you, yeah?."

"I guess," said Ghost.

Dogan mumbled and rolled over onto his side. After waiting a moment to check the brothers weren't waking up, Crooked renewed his whispers.

"Well, I only managed a few scraps before I was caught. If it hadn't been for the Magister coming..."

"What's your point, or can I go back to sleep already?"

"I thought that if we went down to the village, well you could show me what to do, you know, so we da get caught. And plus, the twins will be sick with jealousy when they find out."

"You've been here a year longer than me," said Ghost from under his covers.

Crooked lolled his head back and rolled his eyes. "After all the help I've given you, I can't believe you won't help me. I thought we were friends. You heard the Magister, he'll let them catch and hang me."

Ghost grinned. It was true, Crooked had kept his word and introduced him to the special games they played, the ones that pleased the Magister when he watched them. The ones that he said would make them useful to him, someday. Chief amongst these was Chase-me, and success in this was the primary currency they used to judge each other's worth. Running after each other, escaping through windows by jumping and rolling; Ghost quickly found his time with the acrobats of the Tahtakale put him in a good stead to keep up even with the biggest children here, however it was his little throwing dart that earned him his first measure of respect. Killing a sparrow on the wing—a boastful display—yet it earned him a '*kudos*' from Temper. Everything seemed easier after that.

"I didn't say that," said Ghost. "Come on, get dressed and let's go."

The moon lit the cloudy sky in a broken grey pall that left their path only barely visible between the rustling dark of the trees on either side. The misty wisps of their whispered conversation trailed off as the dark peaks of the village houses came into view at the bottom of the trail. Their eyes met and Ghost nodded. He motioned, palm down, for Crooked to get lower then crept toward the nearest building to squat with his back to the wall. He heard no noises that were not simply the fretting of the sleeping forest around them so beckoned his companion forward.

Sections of palisade and rough woven withy fencing circled the village. No defence against intruders seeking to enter, rather nocturnal enclosures for their small livestock. In the middle of the houses, beside the well that drew these people to live so close together, a bonfire tended only by a heavy-bellied man with a lantern and a weighty polearm. The studs on his leather vest caught the firelight as he moved, dancing like sparks in the night. Ghost knew he'd made no noises, nothing to alert the watchman. Yet the fellow stoppered his wineskin, and peered into the darkness. He rose ponderously to his feet swinging the long chopping blade of his halberd in front of him as he paced toward the limits of the village.

Crooked tugged on Ghost's sleeve, thumbing in the direction of the guard heading in their direction. The watchman walked straight toward them. As if he could see them lying under the cover of the bushy brown ferns that grew in abundance around the feet of the birches encircling the village.

"Let's just go now," said Crooked.

"Don't be scared."

"I'm not—"

Ghost slapped his hand over Crooked's mouth. He waited until his friend had stopped moving; waited as the guard stood right beside them, holding up his lantern and casting the beam between the knotted web of branches and trunks. The watchman grunted to himself, put the lantern on the ground and leant his halberd against a tree. Then he bowed his head to fumble with the laces on his trews. His signs of relief were a good deal louder than were wise for a man guarding alone at night, standing in the only pool of light in a grim and gloomy forest. Crooked screwed up his face as the steaming spray landed beside him, and Ghost frantically hoped his friend could stay silent under such an assault. One hand restrained Crooked, the other searched on the ground. His fingers closed around a fallen branch, smooth and hard. A good hard strike to the watchman's head should put him down, but what if it only angered him?

A loud crash, twigs snapping, rustling, and then silence. The watchman's activities ceased as his head snapped around to the direction of the disturbance. He tied off his laces, picked up his halberd and lantern, and holding the light high and his blade in front he cautiously advanced into the dark. It might just be a fallen branch, but it could just as easily be a malevolent band of desperate cutthroats. A fearless guard ought to investigate.

Ghost crept from the bushes and keeping his head low pattered down the path to the village and vaulted over a chicken fence. A warm rush of relief coursed through him, glad he'd thrown the stick as a diversion. Peering over the edge he could just make out the swinging ball of light amidst the trees as the guard searched for anything hiding out there. Ghost waved for Crooked to follow then ducked back down to hide. Starlight glinting in the whites of his eyes, Crooked silently joined Ghost, who held a warning finger to his lips and received a slow nod in reply. His fingertips tracing the wall, Ghost moved around the side of the house. He rested his head against the back door as he listened for movement within. On hearing nothing he pushed gently, and proving unlatched it swung open.

The pair stepped into the house, Ghost alert and tilting his head as he strained to listen, Crooked biting his bottom lip. Wisps of hazy memories from when he was a little child came to him; creeping around other people's houses looking for food. The scent of wood smoke remained in the air but the embers long since fallen silent. Ghost pointed to a cloth-covered tray on the table in the centre of the room, the light from the open doorway falling across the abandoned meal. Crooked pulled back the cloth to reveal a half loaf of seed bread, a square block of a blue-veined cheese and some unappetising grey vegetables flopped over each other.

Ghost's hand shot out and grabbed the half loaf and Crooked snatched up the cheese. With a wink Ghost turned for the door with his partner a half step behind, but hurrying overmuch Crooked stepped too fast and tripped Ghost, sending him crashing against the door. It slammed shut, shaking the frame of the house and followed by the thud of the door bar falling into place. They froze as fast as their hearts did, icy tightness in their chests. It took only seconds for heavy footsteps to be heard clumping in the room above, then feet on the stairs and the wavering rose glow of a lamp.

"Who's there? I warn you I'm armed. Better not be those damned cats." The voice was deep and steady, not the tremulous quailing of a coward, but a man who knew how to look after himself.

Ghost struggled to push up the beam that locked the door, but lacked enough height to get it over its catches; Crooked just tall enough but fighting against the weight of the solid block of oak.

The villager stepped into the room, raising his flickering lamp high and showing it to each corner of the room. Tall and broad-shouldered, he hefted a short hatchet with ease and familiarity.

"Huh. Nobody here after all. Maybe the wind took it," he said.

Glancing at the disturbed cloth on the table, he paused and frowned. He placed the axe on the table then went to the door, taking a firm grip of the latch beam and shaking it to check it was firm in its catches. He grumbled as he did it and then stood there scratching the stubble on his chin, eventually drawing the cloth back over the remains of the meal. He didn't see the two small shadows creep from under the table behind him, into the next room and melt away through an open window.

Ghost and Crooked lay back in the damp grass, sweat running from their temples and puffing as their hearts raced. They'd run as fast as they could up the trail, until they were sure that no-one pursued them. The winding path only had the mountain and trees to one side now, the other a view over the infiltrated village. Ghost propped himself up on one elbow and looked down, trying to pick out the roof of the house they had just escaped from. A hunting owl called faintly amongst the trees.

"That was fun," said Ghost. "We should have done this ages ago."

"Fun? Are you crazy?" Crooked sat bolt upright and stared at Ghost.

"Sure it was exciting, and hiding from that lumbering oaf under his own table? I nearly burst out laughing!"

"I nearly burst too, and it wasn't for laughing." Crooked's tone was sour, but a smile started to creep across his face. "Well, maybe it was a little fun, now that I think about it."

Ghost laughed and tore the bread in two, passing a chunk to Crooked. "Here you go. The spoils of our first joint burglary. Gimmie some of that cheese and let's just enjoy it."

"One thing I don't get. How in seven hells did you stay calm enough to drag me under the table when we heard him coming?"

Ghost looked at the cluster of peaked roofs in the valley below and he wiped away crumbs from the corner of his mouth with his knuckle. The strange familiarity of a midnight intrusion, a bold theft, the heart-stopping terror of being discovered. He hadn't felt that vital, surging energy in a long time. Not since Zarbenus had found him. Now as the glow faded he realised he had missed it, yearned for it, somewhere deep in his guts.

"No other thing to do, ken? The door behind us was barred, ahead of us someone was coming, so we had to hide."

"We make a great team," said Crooked, nodding to himself.

"A team? I did everything," said Ghost.

"And I dealt with Temper and all sorts of things for you. Seems fair enough to me. It's tough here, Ghost. I promise I'll help you any time I can."

Ghost smiled wryly. "So I should leave anything to do with Temper to you?"

The punch to his shoulder wasn't meant to hurt. He rubbed it and giggled at Crooked's embarrassment.

Crooked gazed at the stars as they peeked between misty strands of clouds in the night's sky. As it cleared they could see Nimrud the Great Hunter in his celestial glory, loyal hound shining brightly at his heels. "My mam said that the stars were candles lit by the gods to spare us the utter blackness of the night. What was your mam like?"

The sadness swelled through him unexpectedly and Ghost stared at his feet. His eyes grew damp and he struggled to speak, knowing that his voice wavered. He closed his eyes and let the familiar emptiness take over, the hollow inside that never quite faded away. When the words came it felt like talking about someone else.

"She loved me and kept me warm. She fed me before she ate herself, and she told me how handsome and brave my father had been."

"You don't remember him?"

"Nah. Only my mother as far back as I can 'member. You 'member yours?"

"I remember he used to hit my mam and make her cry," said Crooked speaking slowly, choosing each word with care. "If I cried or made any noise he would hit her again. I swore when I got bigger I'd do the same to him, but when the village got sick both of them did too. People started coughing and said the water was cursed. My folks locked us inside our house, but their coughing kept getting worse. When I woke in the morning they were both cold and had blood around their mouths. I didn't realise they were dead for some time. I was just little then; I thought they were sleeping."

"I didn't mean to..."

Crooked gasped a deep breath, his shoulders shaking as a trail of silver ran down his cheeks. He sniffed and wiped his nose with the heel of his palm.

"That's alright. I'm sorry for you too... I mean for your mam."

A bell rang from the village below, its tones clear in the cool night air. Within a few minutes a handful of torch flames could be seen bobbing and

123

waving.

"If anyone back in the Nidus sees that we're going to get it in the neck tomorrow." Crooked slumped with his chin on his hands as he watched the activity in the valley. "Get it good."

Ghost shrugged, breaking off another lump of cheese and popping it in his mouth. The Magister had been right. The tears he'd shed were a weakness he'd never borne when he was alone. There was always someone in the Tahtakale to talk to, someone to help him. Someone to hold him and tell him everything would be fine. And that was a lie. They'd given him up for a purse of coins as the first opportunity and he swore he'd never let himself forget that. Cursed himself for remembering Raseyda's warmth and her false kindness. Never forget he was always alone and the tears of a baby were just a sign of weakness. It felt good to take what he wanted, and he felt powerful knowing grown-ups could be bested by his skill and his stealth.

"They didn't catch us. If no-one can prove we were there, then I already forgot about it."

They ate in silence, punctuated by the occasional chuckle. When the food was done they watched a few stars that could be seen when the clouds parted. As the sky turned darker still drops of rain fell on their faces and they made their way back to the Nidus.

A letter, originally encoded in a cipher of Zarbenus' design.

Twenty-third day of Hyperberetaios

Apprentice,

Your failure to adhere strictly to the terms of your deployment neither impresses nor surprises me. I did not instruct you to surveil or in any way tamper with the operations of Bey Izmir. Had I wished it, I would have commanded so. Interference with what I already have well in hand might lead to an irritating disruption.

Cease immediately.

I require that you complete the sole outstanding task you were dispatched for, then return with expediency. There are mundane issues you will now be responsible for, where I can better oversee your waywardness.

By Her Will,

Zarbenus

CHAPTER 8:
THE CRAFT

A sudden shock of fear woke him in the morning, as it did each day, but his panic melted as he remembered where he was. Safe in a warm bed, not alone, not hunted. Chill air loitered outside the shelter of his blanket, but restlessness and the pressure in his bladder quickly won out. He yawned then dropped off the bunk. Crooked only visible as a curled mound under his sheets; his appetite for sleeping inexhaustible, which left Ghost bored in the early hours.

He trotted downstairs, the creaking house an orchestra; motley groaning accompanied by whistles as the wind drafted through cracks between the planks. A quick brave dash outside to relieve himself, then into the kitchen to pilfer some dried apricots. These he took back into the main room that he had already passed through twice this morning, but pulled up short when he saw a hooded figure reclining against the cushions by the table. Had he walked past the Magister each time?

They'd been left alone for several days and Ghost was growing used to a house where the rules of their games governed the passing of the hours. Now the Magister was back Ghost felt another force exert itself, creeping along the floor and up the walls. Beds and floorboards rasped and scraped as the others responded to his presence.

The Magister held Ghost's stare without blinking and without a word until the others came down the stairs, yawning, rubbing puffy eyes and stretching stiff limbs.

"Good morning, noisome rabble. Have you practised your skills while I was gone?"

They chorused their assent and the Magister nodded.

"This next knack takes us outside." He walked them around to the back of the house where a low shed with a slanting roof had been erected to shelter the toilet. The wind stung their eyes and reddened their cheeks. Winter had long passed but oftentimes the chill gusts that ran through the hills didn't seem to remember. While the children blew into their hands and hugged themselves to keep warm the Magister stood motionless, the edge of his cloak flicking in the breeze.

"Jump up to the top of the shed. Ghost, you do it."

Roach snickered behind his hand and then fell silent at a look from the Magister. Ghost glared at the Magister then hurled himself at the wall of the shed and slid just as quickly to the ground.

"Again."

Ghost picked himself up, took a few steps back then ran and squatting into a deep crouch launched himself into the air clawing against the stone as he slid down the wall to land on his backside. There was a giggle from the others.

"Again. I expect more from a half-trained circus monkey."

He jumped as hard as he could and threw himself against the wall scrambling repeatedly to climb it then fell back and sucked his cracked nails in his mouth. He glared at the Magister again.

"You want to see us fail before you show us the trick. That's how it is?"

"Trick?" The easy smile the Magister had worn broke into a spittle-blowing snarl as he raised his hand to slap Ghost. "These are the techniques of our craft and you would do well to remember that." He lowered his hand slowly and wiped the flecks from his lips. "Roach. Show them how it is done."

Roach jumped away from the shed, planting his foot against the wall of the house, and then vaulted across to the shed. His heavy frame proved to be no hindrance, and he grabbed the edge of the roof with both hands then muscled himself up. Chest heaving, he stood up on the roof of the shed and waved down at the others. The Magister's eyelids drooped as he lost interest in his charges.

"There you have it. You have seen how to perform the Triangle Jump. The Plant. The Jump. The Catch. Now the rest of you, practice it. I have better things to do than watch you fumble, but remember; you will each show me that jump before you eat today."

The Magister turned then drifted around the edge of the house and was gone. Temper pushed Ghost aside, planted her foot high against the wall of the house. She leapt so lightly she landed her arm and shoulder over the edge before rolling onto the roof to join Roach. Crooked gave Ghost a wink, then mimed raising his knee to his chest. Ghost opened his mouth to speak but Crooked, despite his limp, ran at the wall and two steps later he pulled himself up onto the roof. The three of them looked over at the remaining children whose jaws hung open.

"We did this last year. Time for you babies to catch up."

Temper crossed her arms over her chest, and the wind whipped her long tail of black hair around her neck. She caught it and worked her fingers threw it, easing out the knots and tangles. Ghost scowled but pondered on Crooked's strange actions. He tried the jump after planting his foot on the wall but didn't push hard enough and fell awkwardly on the ground. He got up rubbing his shoulder and ignoring the sneer from Temper. He just felt glad that Raseyda was not there to watch his failure.

"I don't see why I have to stand around watching you babies flail about," said Temper. "The Magister knows full well that I can make the jump, so I'm off to find something more interesting to do."

She swung herself over the edge of the roof and dropped down. As she strutted back to the house, her head high, Roach clambered down to land with a thud and trotted after her.

"Same for me lads. See you later."

Demir looked at the rest of them. He smiled at Dogan, slinging an arm over his brother's shoulders.

"Here's what I ken."

"We make a line."

"And we each take one jump."

"And then go to the back of the line."

"That way we get to see mistakes each other make."

"So we can call them out."

"And help each other."

Ghost frowned, but even Foul and Scab agreed that it seemed like a good way to start. The twins went first, cheering each other as they ran to the wall and tried the jump and push that would thrust them back to the shed. They cheered with such energy that Ghost started to cheer for them as well. Soon even Foul and Scab joined in—albeit in a listless and dispirited fashion. While Ghost and the brothers applauded a near grasp of the edge of the roof, Foul and Scab blamed it on bad luck or pointed out it really was too far to make it. The chilly air was soon forgotten as they puffed their way through each attempt.

Ghost was the first to get a handhold on the edge of the roof but slid down the wall as he couldn't catch on with his other hand fast enough. His next jump, after feeling the frustration of having to stand in the queue watching the others take their turn, was better. He hung from both hands, his mouth gaping in a silent smile before pulling himself up onto the roof and jumping and waving.

Demir applauded him and whistled shrilly, his brother watching with a half-smile. They all then took their places again and redoubled their efforts under the encouragement of Ghost from the roof. Foul surprised them by being the next one to get up, his light and lanky frame easily elevated after his first successful grab. A few attempts later the twins arrived in predictable tight succession.

Only Scab remained on the ground and he muttered to himself.

"It's not fair. You're all bigger than me. It's too far to jump. I can't do it."

His foot plant was not much lower than the others as he vaulted at the wall, but as he pushed off to reach for the edge of the roof he fell well short each time. He sat on the ground and cried, his shoulders shaking as the sobs wracked him. Elbows and knees grazed and bleeding, his face smeared with dirt where he'd wiped away trails of snot and tears. Dogan and Demir looked at him, looked at each other, then they laughed. When Ghost glared at them they shrugged, climbed down and walked away.

Ghost dangled from the edge of the roof then dropped down to stand beside Scab. He looked at the distance from the wall of the house to the shed, and from the height of the shed to the sobbing child at his feet. Ghost walked around Scab and knelt on one knee, leaning against the wall of the house. He rested an elbow on his other knee as he squinted up at the edge of the shed roof. Puzzled faces gazed down at him.

"Scab," said Ghost, beckoning him over.

Accompanied by moist snuffling Scab rubbed his pink eyes dry.

"What?"

"Ken if you could make it jumping off my shoulder?"

Scab idly licked the wet trail from his nose as he glanced from Ghost to the roof. The faces on the roof smiled down at him.

"I'll try."

He turned to take a few steps back and then froze. The Magister stood there, watching them with a tight-lipped frown.

"Barely past your first week here and you're already cheating? Not a very auspicious start, is it Ghost?"

"I da ken what *ospishus* means," said Ghost.

"That irritating patois you toerags use is getting on my nerves.... It means you are in trouble," said the Magister.

"Why?"

The leather of the Magister's glove creaked as he flexed his fist. "I gave you a knack to practice, and I expect to be obeyed without question."

"We are, but the wall is too far away for Scab. He's too little, so this just makes it fair," said Ghost.

"I never said it was going to be fair. I just told you to do it."

Ghost's nostrils flared as anger built in his chest. "Come on Scab! You can do it!"

Scab glanced at the Magister then locked eyes with Ghost and nodded. He ran forward and jumped, one foot landing on Ghost's shoulder. Scab pushed off with a grunt and barely got a grip on the wall opposite then, with a small fart that made Foul giggle, he pulled himself up.

Ghost stood up and brushed off his shoulder as he pointed at the others on the roof of the shed.

"The Triangle Jump. The Plant. The Jump. The Catch. They all did it. They learned the knack. Isn't that what you wanted?"

The Magister stared darkly at Ghost, but at length his knotted eyebrows loosened and he exhaled heavily.

"Show me yours."

Ghost nodded and in two steps jumped against the wall of the house, pushed firmly off and caught the edge of the roof. He glanced back at the Magister before pulling himself up.

"*Kudos.* I am convinced. You all pass and may head in for feeding. Timan visited me last night, and has left out a box of honey cakes. I would have been sorry to deny them to you, had your practice not progressed so well. Down off that roof and go eat your cakes."

The prospect of honey cakes had the children off the roof faster than if it had been on fire. As they rushed past the Magister he stopped Ghost with a hand on the shoulder. He knelt to speak softly, his expression inscrutable.

"Tell me why you helped Scab. You had already accomplished the task; what did it matter if he did?"

"I da ken. He was trying so hard and only failing because he was too little. Crooked said we could work together, why not? And you were just being mean for no reason."

"No reason? I am trying to give you—to give you all—the tools to survive in a harsh world. Tell me, the soldiers who killed your family, who burned your village, who did the same to the families of all these others here; did they tell you why they were being mean?"

Ghost's head fell but the Magister lifted it up with a finger under his chin.

"The reason doesn't matter. You will either learn, or you will die. Do you understand?"

Ghost nodded slowly. "Yes, Magister."

The Magister closed his eyes and breathed slowly. "There is something else here that you should also learn. If this was the real world and he was alone, Scab would be dead today. The only way he could survive would be to rely on you. This means that if you ever need to rely on someone then *that* is the weakness that will kill you. They say a great general ensures his soldiers are fed and rested before himself, yet he does that so they are best prepared to spend their lives on his behalf—precisely where and when he wills it. Do you understand this as well?"

Ghost scratched his head and opened his mouth to speak, then closed it as he reconsidered. "Doesn't it mean we should help each other?"

The Magister sighed and stood up shaking his head. "You still have to learn the true meaning of that lesson, but that is enough for now. Inside now, boy. I'm sure they will be holding back one honey cake for you, but don't test the patience of hungry urchins with honey cakes. Friendship has its limits."

"Another lesson, Magister?"

Zarbenus tilted his head without reply; the discussion was over. Ghost trotted off to the house, eager to discover what a honey cake was and why the others were so excited about it. The Magister watched him go, and stood very still there a long time after the boy had gone inside.

† † †

The wind turned just before dawn and whistled through the small window. Dogan and Demir defiantly kept their heads under their blankets to eke out another hour, but Ghost woke up refreshed and sat cross-legged on the bed with the tatty blanket wrapped around his shoulders as he watched the orange daybreak.

Despite arriving with anxiety and deep uncertainties about both his new Magister and all the other children he'd been thrown in with, as the days passed without any new danger presenting itself he began to relax. Temper he gave a wide berth, Foul and Scab were best encountered outdoors, or at a pinch in a large room with wide-open windows and a good breeze.

Playing games was the best part of the day. The Magister seldom rose early, so the first hours could easily be whiled away playing rounds of Chase-me, or even better the newly discovered Hide-and-chase-me. The latter had been invented one morning when they were absorbed in a particularly noisy and shrill bout of Chase-me, and they noticed the Magister watching them sprint across the grass and mud in front of the house. He shook his head slowly as if that simple gesture could truly communicate the depth of disapproval he felt. Temper had been the first to fall silent and to pad gently over to him.

"It seems this is a game that would only interest little runts... babies even," he had announced to no-one in particular. "Whereas to chase and discover someone who had well-hidden themselves would be infinitely more rewarding and exciting. Then again, that may only be of interest to more developed... more mature individuals."

He stared at the ground for a moment, spat to the side and then dissolved into the shadows inside the house. The silence was palpable

134

before a tumultuous shriek was uttered in unison and they scattered on chaotic trajectories to explore this new variation to their game.

Games needed the others to be awake (and the Magister to be asleep) and Ghost found himself alone for the moment. Thinking that he might forage some treat from the kitchen before anyone else was up, he swung his legs over the edge of his bunk and dropped to the ground. He shivered as he took off the blanket and balled it up and tossed it up to his pallet. The house was quiet as he climbed down the swaying spiral staircase and through the hatch in the floor and down the ladder. When he reached the top of the stairwell he heard voices and instinctively knelt in the shadows.

"This is all you managed? Pitiful. It is as if you have learned nothing at all."

"There were more guards than usual, Magister. I think they were expecting me." The voice was deferential and that of a young man's, deepening as he grew into his first signs of beard.

"Ridiculous. No-one would know your target last night beside you and me. Your incompetence is finding excuses in its own paranoia."

"Magister, please! Are you not being a bit cruel? I brought all this back for you, not a guard saw me, nor will anyone know anything is missing until they unlock their chests themselves. I had been proud of the night's work until you scolded me so. I hoped you'd be proud of me."

Ghost lay down at the top of the stairs and tilted his head over the edge so that he had a sliver view of the room below. A cloaked and hooded figure knelt at the feet of the Magister who held a pouch in his hand and stirred its contents with a long pale finger. The kneeling figure had his head bowed and was slightly built, just like the Magister. By their similarities in dress Ghost found it hard to tell them apart, had he not heard them speaking.

"I'll be proud of you, Timan, when you have earned more than just your name. Survival, whilst an essential trait, is not a characteristic meritorious of praise. Let that be a lesson to you, Ghost, hiding there—oh so still—but breathing so hard you would wake a corpse. Strive for excellence every day, and eventually you will receive your reward."

Ghost froze, but the Magister did not turn around, or look up to the top of the stairs. The kneeling figure lowered his hood and smiled up at the one wide eye fixed on him. The young man had long black hair and the grey-blue eyes that were so common amongst the Magister's companions. His jawline was darkened with stubble, and his cheeks creased with mirth as he peeked up the stairs.

Ghost stood up and stepped down the stairs, slowly and one at a time, expecting rebuke.

"I'm sorry Magister, I wasn't trying to overhear you. I just didn't want to intrude."

The Magister tied the pouch he held and tossed it up and down in his palm as he looked down at Timan. Ghost heard metal clinking against metal.

"You may be right, Timan. Sometimes I may be too harsh on you, but it is only to get the best out of you. Soon will come your reckoning. Tell me, do you think you will be ready, or will you join the ghosts of all those that came before you and shared the same confidence?"

Timan stared up at the Magister, his jaw set firmly. He made a fist in front of his chest.

"I will be ready Magister, and I will accomplish what those before me have tried and failed. By Her Will."

"We will see," said Zarbenus. "For now round up the rabble. Send them down to me before seeking your pillow."

"I see you have found another one," said Timan. "The prize is still undecided?"

Ghost wondered whether the terse tone was amusement or displeasure.

"You have no-one to blame but yourself, Timan. If you had progressed as fast as your talent promised then not a one of them would have been necessary," said Zarbenus folding his arms across his chest.

Timan bowed his head, stood before the Magister then bowed again before melting silently up the stairs. The Magister turned to Ghost. He resembled Timan in many ways, but his close-cropped black beard was thicker and more extensive; his forehead lined with deep creases and a few grey hairs at his temples.

"For good or for ill, that is the path you must tread," said the Magister, then he fell quiet as footsteps drummed on the stairs. Crooked jostled with Temper to arrive first and the others fell in close behind.

"Temper, take a tally and write up tonight's score." The Magister tossed the pouch he'd received from Timan to her.

"She can write?" whispered Ghost to Crooked, but immediately regretted it upon seeing the look of smug satisfaction she gave him.

"The rest of you make yourselves useful," said the Magister. "There is far too little firewood stacked, and the water urns are depleted. You are old enough that I should not need to ask for such things to be taken care off. Roach, it falls to you to control such matters. And when he speaks you should all hear my voice."

The Magister faded up the stairs and Roach clapped his hands together. As physically imposing as ever, now he bore the Magister's authority as well.

"No games today until everything is in order, ya ken?"

The others groaned but didn't argue and they filed outside, dragging their feet.

Chapter 9:
Destiny

On the coldest morning he could remember Ghost unshuttered the window and looked north at the distant mountains, white snow reaching almost to their bases. The taller of the two peaks had a haze of cloud strands caught on it and the clarity of the still winter air made him feel as if he could almost touch them. He held up his hands and framed them between his fingers and thumbs.

"Planning a heist, boy? That would impress even me—stealing a mountain would be a job worthy of its own songs."

Ghost laughed and turned to his master.

"Can we climb the big one, Magister? Please? I can't wait to see what the world looks like from the top! Can you see the whole world from there?"

Zarbenus rested his elbows on the window frame, sharing Ghost's view of the great peaks.

"They are as dangerous as they are beautiful, and for good reason are called the Great Sadness. They have taken more lives than the greatest assassin. Ravines and gullies so deep that even if you saw a friend fall you would never be able to retrieve his body for burial. As you walk up its slopes, strewn with loose rocks and boulders, you move from the baking heat of a summer's day to the harsh, frozen torment of the worst winter storms you could imagine. It is said that any man who makes it to the summit will find his destiny there."

"But have you climbed it yourself?"

The Magister stared impassively into the distance, then slowly nodded his head.

"Once. I was paid to kill a man, and he ran—oh how he ran. I chased him all the way from Byzantium to the very peak of the biggest one right there. He thought his gods would save him in that place, a place they hold sacred. I know not the names of his gods, but there was no-one there for him. We circled, knives drawn. He was a better runner than he was a fighter. At the very summit I slew him and cast him off a precipice. The crows surely made a feast of his corpse."

Ghost swallowed and peered at the mountain, straining to make out any circling black dots that could be a flight of crows.

"Why not search for his body, Magister? Maybe he had something on him that would be worth selling?"

Zarbenus hawked a glob of phlegm out the window. "Risk my own neck? No, someone goes over an edge like that you toss them a coin for the ferryman if they deserve it, or spit on them if they don't."

Ghost pondered this in silence for a moment. "How hard was it, Magister? The climb I mean."

The Magister shrugged. "I had a fair day for it, a summer's day that burned my skin until I was halfway up, then the snow which was a relief until I got so cold I couldn't feel my feet."

"So can we go? Is that where you found your destiny, Magister?"

"My destiny had already been decided before I ever took a step on those frigid slopes. Maybe you can go someday when you are older. Me? Not unless I was paid as much as I was the last time. The mountain curses with a sickness anyone who defiles its stones. Every step saps your strength, poisons your mind. It is a terrible predator. You wouldn't go into a lion's den, would you? Not unless you held your own life to mean nothing."

The Magister looked down and saw the boy wasn't listening. Entranced eyes fixed on the distant peak, young mind full of dreams. "Nevermind, I have something for you to show your friends." His two empty palms clapped together, then out of the air he plucked a wrinkled brown globe of a walnut in its shell. "What do you call that game you play? The one with all the screaming?"

Ghost took the proffered walnut and examined it closely, finding nothing unusual save only the faintest chime when shaken vigorously.

"Hide-and-chase-me?"

The Magister nodded. "What fun it would be if one of you had that nut tucked in your pocket, and while they all tried to hide you were able to pluck it away from them without them noticing."

He stepped back from the window and skulked away. Ghost stared at the walnut, ignoring the cold that streamed in the windows and all thoughts of setting foot on the mountain forgotten, for the moment.

†　†　†

Snow had not fallen for several days, but it still lay thick about the house, brilliant and blinding as the shallow winter sun rose on a clear morning. The Magister appeared at the bottom of the stairs and sorted through some of the sacks that were stored there. Presently he slung several coils of rope over his shoulder and, taking a cloth wrapped hook that looked like an evil bent dagger in his hand, he went outside. Crooked glanced at Ghost who raised his shoulders in reply before stuffing the last of his breakfast into his mouth and following their master out the door.

The others followed suit, the frozen crust of snow crunching beneath their feet and breath-mists hanging in front of their faces. As the last to arrive Foul and Scab saw the Magister knotting the end of a length of rope to the padded hook. He held the knot out to his students and ran his finger around it to trace the path he'd worked to secure it.

"How would you best reach where Timan now stands? Which method would be the fastest and the most silent?"

They followed the Magister's gaze up the side of the house and saw

Timan perched alone on the steepled roof above the forbidden room at the top. He waved down to them and seemed very small, framed against the steep mountainside where only the wild goats perilously climbed.

Temper tossed her hair and opened her mouth, but the Magister stared past her.

"Someone else, someone who has not been asked the question before."

She looked away, muttering under her breath.

Roach nodded to the hook in the Magister's hand. "I guess you throw that to catch on something then climb up the rope."

"Quite so. This is the grapple. It is a rather ponderous object and it does tend to raise awkward questions—if people see you carrying it about—but in many situations it can give you a speed that the most skilful climber cannot match, and as well you take less risk in the process."

The Magister let a short length of rope slip between his fingers as the grapple dropped from his grasp, then he closed his fist and span the padded hook around in a rapid blur. The rope whistled softly before he cast it high, up the side of the house. The grapple clattered across the roof tiles, inches from the stationary Timan, and caught tight against a joist when the Magister tugged the rope.

"If you don't pad it you make quite a racket at night, but now all you have to worry is about how softly you step," said the Magister, looking pointedly at Roach.

Holding the rope with both hands the Magister set a foot to the wall, then in only a minute ran to the top of the house, ignoring Timan's outstretched hand and swinging onto the roof with ease. He stood and placed a foot against the grapple so that it did not come loose from its point.

The Magister straightened his cloak, then called down to them. "Keep the rope taut so that it does not slip, then try it yourself."

Temper pushed away Roach who was reaching for the end of the rope, then she started climbing immediately. If anything she was faster than the

Magister to reach the top and he patted her on the head when she arrived. Timan cheered at her but she turned quickly away, not meeting his smiling gaze. She tilted her head, staring at the scree and debris that sloped up the side of the ruined tower, then she frowned pensively.

"Next," said the Magister.

Roach didn't need to be asked twice, and his stocky frame belied his rapid ascent. Timan clapped him on the shoulder with a few words of praise. Foul made a great show of standing on the loose end of the rope as he fussed with the strings that wrapped his foot-coverings, apparently oblivious to Scab taking the opportunity to scale the tense line. Despite the apparent assist from his companion, Scab went up like a spider and shrugged his shoulders when he reached the summit. Foul himself ascended at a moderate pace, muttering phrases in his native dialect that could only be interpreted as curses. Nonetheless, a minute later Scab grabbed him by the wrist and hauled him onto the roof.

Crooked shaded his eyes as he looked up at them.

"I'm going to call in some favours here, Ghost."

"I owe you favours?"

"Sure you do. This is an easy one for you and I need you to keep that line tight as I go up."

"You're scared of falling," said Ghost.

Crooked waved a finger at him. "Scared of failing you mean. Do your part and it'll be fine."

Irritated at having to go last, Ghost grabbed the end of the rope, looped it around his waist then took a good grip and nodded at Crooked.

"Here I go," said Crooked as he dragged himself upward. Despite looking awkward he still managed to walk up the wall, though he took longer than any of the others and gained the summit flushed and sweaty.

Eager to make amends Ghost fairly trotted up the wall. A trivial challenge compared to familiar stunts he'd practised in the Tahtakale, and he had visions of a hero's welcome—graced by the Magister's admiring greeting. However, applause was not waiting for him when he arrived. The Magister's scowl failed to hide his distaste bordering on revulsion. Behind him, Timan shook his head slowly. The only person who looked happy was Demir, smirking at Ghost and whispering to his brother.

The Magister cleared his throat and hawked off the rooftop. "For those of you endeavouring to actually be of value to me; practice tossing the grapple until you can put it where you want it, first time. There are few things more embarrassing than watching a burglar fluff his cast time and again, besides, you'll end up pulling off a tile and waking the whole household."

The bleating of a isolated goat kid on the rocky slope that the house leaned against caught his attention and he stared at it with his head tilted.

"It occurs to me that you have a natural game here that will challenge your climbing skill as well as your stealth. Very well, a competition it shall be. None of you are good enough now, but if you practice enough and are brave enough I'll warrant that one of you could catch a poor lost kid on the rocks and bring it back down unharmed. Whoever of you is the first to do that will win a very special prize."

The chatter between them exploded as they variously declared that they would be the first to do it, or that the others lacked the talent to accomplish the task. The Magister grunted as if hearing an answer he'd expected.

"Your enthusiasm is infectious and most endearing, but remember your life should be more valuable to you than the whims of your clients. Do not reach beyond what you can grasp when attempting this. It would be an irritating waste of all the time I have spent on you if I have to collect your broken bones from the bottom of the mountain."

Crooked nudged Ghost in the back. "We should do it together. You'll need to show me how to get past the tough parts, but I've got a clever idea how to catch the goat that no-one else will have thought of. What do you think?"

Ghost watched the kid bleating in fear, marooned on a rocky outcrop and separated from its mother. Weakling, he thought. *I never made a noise, why should you?* Feeling Crooked's stare he turned his head with a half-smile and nodded.

The Magister placed a hand on Timan's shoulder.

"Timan will supervise you for the rest of the morning, and if he is satisfied with your progress he may let you practice on the rocks in the afternoon. Hopefully the weaklings will then fall to their death, and will cease to waste my time."

With that he turned his back on them, dropped off the side of the roof and swung through the window of his room.

If they hadn't have climbed the roof Temper would never have noticed it. If there hadn't been a storm the day before it would have stayed buried in the fortress. The torrential rains had flooded the remaining enclosed areas, open to the sky through burnt-out joists. Dirt and debris sluiced through the cracked remains, arcing waterfalls erupted from vacuations in the crumpled and compacted stories. The glint of polished metal in the sunlight of the following day, sunlight without warmth on such a cold morning, and a flash of yellow metal saying: here I am, find me.

Why she pretended she had seen nothing, why she mentioned nothing to her friends, and why she waited to scale the tumbledown cascade of stone blocks, there were no formed answers in her mind. Only a fierce fascination, a call she couldn't resist. Something whispering to her; alluring, exciting, like a secret assignation with a lover.

She waited until nightfall, until the sounds of feet on floorboards, closing doors and creaking bed frames had all passed away. The Nidus had its own daily cycle, a life of its own. The mismatched tiles and slates creaked as their joists languorously stretched out in the sunshine, shivered and shrunk in the cold. The ticking, moaning and groaning faded into the background after

living there for months, but if she closed her eyes and listened she could feel
its rhythms and knew no-one was wandering around in the dark. Long
before she'd woven ropes between the vines beneath her window, and
having used it frequently enough this route was as easy—and quieter—than
creeping down the old stairs.

The night was cool and damp, the moon all but obscured by swift dark
clouds, pale silver glowing as they passed. The wet mulch underfoot
breathed its sweet and sour vapours as a tracery of mist snaked around her
ankles. A last self-conscious glance back at the house showed no suspicious
lights in windows, no furtive silhouettes, so she knelt and began to search.

Brushing back the dirt revealed a disappointment. It was only a travel
case for scrolls, no doubt once expensive, with a filigree of silver worked into
the carved ivory. She waited until she was back in her room before prying it
open, crestfallen it wasn't more exciting, yet still curious to see what might
have survived within. Only parchments. Different qualities and in different
states of decay, some were obviously ancient and others looking less than a
score of years old. The youngest squares of vellum bore densely scribbled
words in a fine, fluid style. The same script adorned the oldest fragments;
notes in margins and on the reverso. Much of the writing was tightly packed
Hellenic letters, groups of five then a tiny gap and another group of five.
Staring at these she couldn't divine their meaning, other than that they
represented some kind of code. The rest of the writing was a diary of sorts.
One man's journal of his passage from sin to salvation, his dreams and
aspirations, and his adoration of the personification of the divine that lit his
path. Temper had read religious works before, witnessed sermons and
rituals of a myriad of deities. Interesting, stimulating, but ultimately the
passions of others. She needed not the guidance of a supernatural force and
never doubted the deep well of conviction within her, the abiding rightness
of her course. She closed the scroll case slowly, regret tinged with envy. The
words of rapture and fierce burning faith from a man long dead continued to

whisper to her as she lay in bed seeking her sleep. The temptation to fall into the embrace of his goddess—dark and terrible and beautiful—pulled at her soul. Then the feeling of loss and emptiness because he had felt it, not her. She curled up her fist, looked at her knuckles, remembered that she alone chose her destiny. She chose to be her own guiding light. She would never bow, never prostrate herself, never allow anyone to tell her what to do.

All that changed the same night. Dreams came to her, and they awoke a hunger in her so strong she felt like she had been starving her whole life. A new Temper awoke the next morning. She no longer needed to trust in faith, for with absolute certainty she *knew*.

CHAPTER 10:
PROPHECY

Zarbenus fidgeted in his chair, facing the old man who had summoned him; the sole person in the world who could compel him to attend. And yet, how did he do it? There were never any threats, no repercussions if he failed to arrive; it was always phrased so well as to be solely for his own personal interest. At least he was always greeted quickly, ushered past any waiting supplicants or followers.

"Zarbenus, do you wonder how the gods came into being? How was it for millennia only the Goddess existed, and then in the ages of strife Gods began to walk the earth? Your brethren call you the God of Thieves, a prescience that I prophesy will come to pass; for I have seen it. Zarbenus, do you not wonder how it is done? It will not be long now before you see me in another form, but when you look in my eyes and we speak you will know that the heavenly power is real."

Zarbenus snorted as he adjusted his seat but the old man had to control his mirth when he began to speak again as the thief's gaze narrowed perceptibly.

"Let me speak plainly to one who knows these mysteries to be true, but yet feigns that only trickery rules; even over he who is the master of tricks and lies? The Arcasantos, Zarbenus. It is not just a relic that has brought peace to this city after centuries of war. It contains the mortal remains of the Goddess, all that was left behind as the greater part of her ascended to a higher plane. This allows the most devout of her adherents, dedicated to her words and deeds, to have a lesser transcendence, a purely mortal one. A perfect vessel is chosen and willingly accepts the blessed role to take within themselves the patrician soul. So have I chosen and so have I been reborn a score of times, thus has my wisdom and power grown. You know something of what I speak, for does not Hekate—your Night Mother—grace you with gifts of her own?"

A long bone pipe, finely carved with silver fittings, rested on a stand by the old man's right hand. Sitting as close as he was, Zarbenus saw the sheen of black residue within the small metal bowl. The old man did not leave things to chance. If he'd left it there then he clearly wanted Zarbenus to notice it.

Zarbenus did not care to play the old man's game. "What's this to me then?"

"There is a unique destiny awaiting you that I do not fully understand, but the Goddess has revealed it to me. As her will, it therefor becomes my purpose," said the old man.

"So the services you would have me deliver—they are for her ineffable will, not your own?"

"I find it difficult to understand why you do not embrace such a wonderful fate. I know that you have your own faith, but if you would just open your mind and listen then the Goddess would speak to you directly." The old man tapped a finger on the pipe that lay on the desk.

Zarbenus grimaced. "That filth melts the mind and rapes the will. The dreams bring only madness."

The old man smiled as he picked up the pipe and rolled it between his fingers, admiring its craftsmanship. "As with all things, there is a price to pay. Would you not willingly allow the restless dragon to live within your veins—for the gift of prescience? The feeble-minded cannot bear the visions; it is a thing too powerful for their ken. But for the strong-willed, the revelations are quite illuminating. You should seek the words of the Goddess and see for

150

yourself."

"I'll take that under advisement," said Zarbenus. "What have you really brought me here for? Surely not these fairy tales. I grow weary of your company."

The old man's smile faded as he laid the pipe back on its stand. "Your sire understood the importance of these mysteries. It is not something you have inherited from him. How many years ago was it that you first came to me? Your position amongst the Oikos was still fragile, and to be fair I was not faring particularly well with the courts. Should I have expected more from you, more than just another poisoner and backstabber living in the shadows? When you failed to steal the Arcasantos you spared this city from destruction that would have been wrought in the inevitable chaotic aftermath. But you gained as well, for I recognised you as the one that the Goddess willed be granted a rebirth. Our working relationship was to have been one of shared information, yet of late I've received very little of use from you. I prefer to think that you've merely been busy with... your other projects, and not that you had formed another alliance. With Bey Izmir, for example?"

Zarbenus eased himself out of the chair and stood. He brushed down his cuffs and glanced around the room. "The quality of what I provide is reliant on events transpiring that require my intervention. No such happenings have transpired of late, but rest assured I am as vigilant as ever for the important matters. You have your lick-spittle Nicodemus to handle the other trivialities. If in return all you have to offer me is this prattle about the will of your Goddess then I will take my leave. As for my father's faith, we both know the dark road that it led him down. I suffer no such illusions; he deserved his fate. As did all the fools who followed him to their deaths."

"I've had a recurring dream ever since you came to Byzantium," said the old man. "The clarity and peace I feel when I wake assures me that it is prophecy sent by the Goddess. I believe it concerns you, Zarbenus, and the aspirations of your father as well. Would you like to know what I vision I am sent?"

"I have absolutely no doubt that if I continue to stand here you will tell me, whether I beg to hear your tale or not—O wise and wrinkled one," said Zarbenus.

"In my dream, there is a man on the highest spire of a stone city. He is cowled in shadows, but in the pale moonlight his eyes glitter like sapphires. His hands are drenched in the blood of children, and one day empires will bow at his feet."

Zarbenus threw his head back and laughed. "By the gods small and large; you tell a tale with gusto! You should ply your talents around the alehouses— you'd be showered in silver."

The old man inclined his head with a mirthless smile. "I am not a king, Zarbenus, but I am a kingmaker. And for many years each time that dream has come to me I have wondered on the spire behind me."

The God of Thieves looked past the old man and through the open window beyond. Framed like a romantic painting; the city at night, starlight gleaming on golden steeples, and highest amongst them the sky-scratching pinnacle of the Palace of Dreams. Once it was an emperor's glorious boast, now the pride of the Pasha.

"That is a near-suicidal climb with nothing to be gained. I can think of no reason I would wish to attempt it."

"Then do it because I wish it. I require it as a reassurance of your affiliations, and I require it to break the spirit of Bey Izmir; a man whose position is a little too secure. He is young and that makes him over-confident, and that is a trait that places this city in peril. He must learn what the young do not appreciate, that death is but a moment away."

"I fail to see how my climbing to the top of his palace will inspire such mortal dread," said Zarbenus.

"In the morning the white spire will be streaked with blood, impaled at the top will be the head of his little son—just sent to him from the women's court. It was the boy's birthday last week and now he begins the lessons of a man. Izmir's new princeling. His legacy. This will destroy Izmir, and you will fulfil the prophecy. Then you might seek the favour of the Goddess, and thereby your resurrection." He shook his head and winced. "The letting of the blood of an innocent pains me greatly, but if the loss of this one life will save thousands of others I fear it must be done."

"It has melodramatic flair, I'll give you that, and as such, it appeals to me. Being the hand that changes history. I might even consider it, if only to prove your dreams are nonsense."

Without waiting for an answer Zarbenus stalked out the room. Hierarch Pallas picked up the pipe again and he tapped it against his lips. As he scented the aroma of the poppy tears there, a smile returned to his face. Possibilities and probabilities weighed themselves, outcomes and influences made battle, and the old man felt very pleased indeed. He knew that depending on which way Zarbenus chose, there the future of the city lay at stake. Only the Goddess in her wisdom could understand—for he could not—why the lives of so many good and innocent rested in the actions of such an irredeemably stained soul.

† † †

Zarbenus walked through the city. Stones underfoot worn smooth by centuries of feet and hooves and wheels. Old buildings with new plaster, cracked and fading all the same, and he could smell the taint of decay all around. Weariness enveloped him like a shroud. Buffeted by shoulders, he was too tired to practice the art, yet it irked him all the same. Miserable creatures, mundane lives. It would matter not at all if they were erased from existence. What had they accomplished in their lives? Worse, what yet could he achieve if his time was without end? In a hundred years no-one would remember the deeds of Zarbenus.

It was the faces of the young that angered him. Smooth, unblemished

153

skin taut, plump and rosy, looking like immortal babes. Pallas was right about one thing: he craved the immortality he was being offered, even as he knew it had to be a deception. Hekate, the Night Mother—he had served her well, and she had given him so much. Would she take it all away if he pledged himself to the old man's Goddess? Did he risk so much if he were simply to sacrifice Timan? But the apprentice had to give himself willingly, so Pallas said. Therein lay the unanswered question, or more accurately, the question unasked.

Timan must be put to the test, sooner rather than later. Zarbenus ground his teeth. Before the year was out.

† † †

As he had explained in the barrel room of the vintner's house in his village that doubled up as local tavern and countryside courthouse when required, it was worth taking the long route to market, just to avoid the easier road that ran near the haunted castle. Once the headquarters of an evil and bloody cult that had terrorised good folks for miles around until it was utterly wiped out by the wrath of the gods. Even seeing it during the day gave him the shivers, so Edip the farmer made camp in a grove of ancient, twisted and gnarled olives. Everyone knew that the sacred trees protected you from djinns and all sorts of evil spirits. He unhitched his plodding old mare. Rubbed her down with a chequered woollen blanket, checked her hooves for stones, then tethered her to his two-wheeled cart with a long line so she could graze at her leisure. His yellow-furred one-eyed bitch crouched nearby, watching him. She was well aware of the order of business; her dinner was coming once he'd made everything ready, so there was no point in whining for attention until then.

Edip turned back the oilcloth that protected the barrels he transported in his cart. Between the casks of couscous, rice and wheat, lying on top of a tall jar of choicest honey, nestled a stained and battered satchel. He took this out, tucked it under his arm then shook out a bedroll across the grass.

The yellow bitch whimpered and wagged her tail. It was nearly time.

Edip smiled at her, then sat cross-legged on his bedroll. From the satchel he produced two bundles wrapped in cloth, and a leather flask—almost full as he'd only had a few sips of the rich red wine at midday, just to sustain him.

Her tail thumping the ground, the bitch whined again, at a higher pitch. Edip opened the greasy parcel and tossed the mess of fat, bones and entrails he had set aside over to her. She pounced forward, almost choking herself trying to eat it all in one bite. The farmer opened the remaining package and took a bite of the roast lamb and vegetables wrapped in flatbread. A celebration in his mouth! His wife was ugly, true. And frequently angry (for why else would he always volunteer to be the one to drive two days to market on behalf of all three farms in their little hamlet?), but no-one could deny that she was a sublime cook. She'd even pasted the bread with houmous before adding the meat! Yes, his ugly, angry wife was quite the catch and Edip blessed the gods—none of them in particular because it was hard enough being a small, unimportant man without angering any capricious and vindictive celestial forces—or any benevolent deity that may listen to a simple farmer like him, for sending her to him when truth be told he barely deserved her.

Once the food was done, Edip started on the wine. Spending an evening under the stars and telling your favourite tales to someone (the bitch) who never interrupted, or said they'd heard it before; what could be better?

After another philosophic observation on the nature of man, and a good half of the flask consumed, the dog's ears pricked up. It growled, and Edip stoppered the wine. He looked around, the hairs rising on the back of his neck as his tipsy mind wandered back to the idea of djinn manifesting themselves in the gloom. If some apparently-innocent traveller arrived, he wouldn't be easily fooled. No! He'd demand they took off their shoes to prove they didn't have cloven hooves, and turn around so he could check them for a forked tail. Edip knew he lacked the reading of his letters and others might think him deficient in wits, but he brimmed over with common sense and wasn't going to be easily fooled by any supernatural shenanigans.

The bitch snarled at the darkness then burst forth, teeth bared. She landed, rolled and stood up all in one movement, a bloody rat dangling limp from her jaws. It didn't even wriggle, she must have killed it in a single bite. Edip slapped his knee and chuckled. Getting all worked up over nothing! The dog lay down and began to tear and crunch through the second course of her dinner. The pressure in his bladder, not to mention the jolt of fear, had reached a point it needed answer, so Edip stood behind his little cart and dealt with that business.

Much relieved, and also a little thirsty, he returned to his bedroll and reached for his flask. Funny that, because he thought he'd stoppered it. Lucky then he hadn't knocked it over and spilled it! That would have spoiled the evening and no doubt about it. This happy thought in mind he worked his way through the wine, always more enjoyable knowing that his wife wasn't going to sneak up on him and castigate him for indulging such simple pleasures. Sleepiness came much easier than usual. He yawned, poured in the last mouthful, and smacked his lips. He could barely keep his eyes open. The bitch had finally stopped worrying and gnawing her rat, and was lying peacefully as well. He put his head down and was snoring a moment later.

Temper stepped into the grove of humped and twisted olive trees. She folded away the parchment twist she'd kept the mixture of ground white poppy seed and a touch of henbane leaves. The dog and the farmer should recover by the next day, though she couldn't guarantee pleasant dreams. Killing and poisoning a rat, then moving swiftly and quietly enough to salt a common farmer's booze were not things to be particularly proud of. That didn't bother Temper, as the outcome of a simple night's work was the thing in question.

As she hitched the old mare, who whinnied her disapproval at being disturbed in the middle of the night, she wondered if the Magister knew or cared about her nocturnal banditry. He left them alone long enough and so frequently she'd decided to deal with matters herself. Daughter of warriors indeed. She chuckled to herself. This was what she was becoming instead, ever since the dreams started. Ever since she started feeling protected and special, and ever since she started to understand her mission. Ever since she'd found the journal she knew things had changed forever—she had changed forever. It would be midday before she reached the path up to the Nidus, but driving a cart at night was so peaceful. She relaxed and let the reins lie loose in her lap; safe in the knowledge that she was the reason the simple folk were scared of the dark.

CHAPTER 11:
THE WARRIOR

The spring passed into summer and with it came the sultry heat. The pine trees creaked their complaints, shedding sweetly scented golden tears that glistened in the sunlight. The ebbing and flowing but ever-present whine of the cicadas throbbed in the dense air. A procession of ants trailed around the tree trunk, solemnly plucking droplets of the sticky amber to carry back to their nest. Zarbenus sat in the shade with his back to the tree, more interested in the industrious insects than anything else going on. Timan stood shirtless with his hair tied back, on the grass outside the Magister's house, the children facing him expectantly. His muscles tightly strapped over his lean and wiry frame, every move smooth and supple.

"Watch my feet; the solid steps, the regular pacing. See my shoulders, relaxed and pulled back, my chest naturally rising and spreading. Notice my face, relaxed and calmly scanning from side to side. I look over the heads of those who are no threat, holding without blinking the eyes of any who catch my gaze. My arms swing in time with my legs, and my fists are unclenched. This is the Warrior Stance. It is the most simple to master, after all it needs to be; they have to teach it to soldiers in only a few weeks."

He smiled as the children tittered, then tossed his hair back and straightened his jaw.

"Follow me, little assassins, and we will march back and forth like soldiers. You only look to the front, never behind. You are confident and powerful, if you heard pounding feet behind you, stop on the spot and turn your whole body. They will not be a threat. You are the Warrior."

Temper stood with folded arms and a scowl wrinkling her lips. An observant witness would have noticed that, despite her fierce demeanour, her cheeks were tinged with pink and she wouldn't meet Timan's gaze as he stood there, bare-chested, sweating, hands on his hips and smiling at her.

"Warriors don't train like this. I remember them practising in my village. There was a lot more red-faced screaming, and a lot more clashing of steel."

"We are not here to learn how to fight like a warrior. The stances you will master will allow you to blend into different situations. You will be able to march through a crowd and have people part in your way, their eyes to the ground lest they receive your wrath. You will learn other stances as well, but this is the first one. Show me; let me see you perform the stance."

Temper scanned the scene, her jaw jutting out, then with measured, steady steps she paced past Timan, stopped then turned slowly around, one fist at her hip.

Timan clapped and pointed to her as he addressed the rest of them.

"She takes to this stance naturally. If she were but a few years older you could put a soldier's uniform on her and she could walk through an armed camp with not a single hand raised to stop her. Imagine the power, to pass unnoticed. It is almost a mastery of invisibility."

"She'd use that invisibility to slip into his bedchamber, I'll warrant," whispered Crooked out the corner of his mouth.

Temper's head snapped around to incinerate him with the ferocity of her disdain. She held up her forefinger to him.

"One what?" Crooked chuckled at her. "Is this an advanced technique called the finger of death?"

Ghost and Scab giggled until Temper shook her head.

"I've decided I'm going to break one of your bones, not sure when, but I'm putting it on your account. I'm thinking about your good leg. At least that way you'll finally walk straight."

Timan drilled them for many days before he was satisfied they had understood the basics. Letting Temper bruise both their skins and their egos proved an effective motivation for progress.

"You are improving, all of you, but it will take many years before you perfect this stance. But that is not a problem, as you have many years before you may need to use it. Keep the principles of the Warrior's Stance in your mind while I teach you the next form."

Timan's eyes widened and his head moved sharply, looking to one side and then the other, then twisting to look behind him. His shoulders hunched and his hands clutched together in front of his body. He took short scurried steps and it seemed as if he favoured his left leg, the right foot only touching the ground lightly on his heel before being picked up again. He turned, one shoulder raised as he held his arm in front of his face, shielding it from the children. His voice trembled as he spoke.

"This is the Victim's Stance. *Excuse me.* With it you can pass by powerful people, secure behind their armour and heavy weapons. *Don't mind me.* An alert city guard warned of brigands would never notice you hurrying through the main gates, clutching a tattered bag of scraps. *Sorry. You first, my lord.* Better than being overlooked, you are never even remembered."

He smiled and straightened himself, brushing imaginary dust from his sleeves as the illusion faded.

"It has other uses too. I was hunting recently for someone who had beaten me to a prize that I was adamant that I would reclaim. Failure is another word for insufficient effort."

From his shaded resting place, Zarbenus barked a mocking laugh. Timan ignored him, keeping his attention front and centre. "The man was a craven brute and preyed on the weak," he said. "I used the Victim's Stance to lure him away from his compatriots and deal with him in private."

"You killed him?" Ghost watched intently as Timan paused the tale and inclined his head in thought.

"Yes, that is often the way of it. We each take our path differently so it may not be the same for you, or it may be more so. I cannot say how much gore will wet your blades; be you a spotless master burglar or an assassin whose sleeves are stained black with the blood of your victims. The Magister does not force you to choose; these choices are yours alone. Some you can make at your leisure, but others will be forced upon you and your path will determine itself by the actions you take at that time. Once I trained alongside friends as you do, now they are just memories." His head turned to regard the cairns old and new at the foot of the dark tower. His smile had faded.

The children fell quiet, and Ghost recalled the feeling of a cold child's neck between his fingers, and of how his guilt seemed more distant with the passing days.

"Enough of the sad faces! You have so much to learn and are years from choosing your paths. Today it is summer and I want to see a field full of victims scuttling away from me as if they would beg mercy from an overaggressive mouse!"

The younger ones brows wrinkled with worry. It played into their performances, and in short order they were whimpering and stumbling around as Timan judged, cajoled and complimented them.

"Keep it subtle. You're not supposed to be drawing attention to yourselves!"

Enjoying their limping and whimpering alter-egos, they moaned and whined as they got into the role, rising to melodrama as they swooned in fear.

"You are supposed to be cautious and timid, not some overplayed street-beggar imploring for pity."

They giggled then returned to their practice.

Timan grunted. "Better. Much better."

162

He looked over to Zarbenus who rose slowly from the ground. The Magister stretched out with a feline yawn and muttered, "But will it be good enough?"

Timan's knuckles whitened around his dagger's hilt and did not relax until the Magister sloped away into the house. Once they were alone he turned to the children, rubbing his brow with one hand.

"You are not the Magister's pets or his servants, nor is he the sole conduit to the Night Mother. She favours him for sure, but not he alone. You do not display faith through words alone, but through your actions. If you find yourself put to the test, then think on my words. Seek to be worthy of her blessings, which surely all of you have." He laughed, turning his grim countenance once more to a more handsome aspect. "But that is such serious talk for such a lovely afternoon. I am many things, be they noble or malign, but I am not the Magister. I still remember being a child. Go! Play in the sunshine!"

Such an order need never be told twice. With screams and laughter they charged across the grass to touch the old cedar, the winner of the race would get to start the first round of Hide-and-chase-me.

† † †

Autumn brought with it relief from the summer's swarms of insects, and at the same time the bounty of fruits and berries. The Magister appeared by the fire that evening, his hood thrown back. He poured chestnuts into a copper pan which he nestled against the glowing embers. Kneeling with his back to the fire he looked at each of the children, one by one, as the aroma of roasting chestnuts wafted from the fireplace. Eager, expectant faces met his gaze and held it without blinking. At length, he retrieved the copper pan and tossed a smoking chestnut to each child. They squealed as they rolled it from hand to hand and blew on it before cracking open the shell and enjoying the crumbly treat within.

"There are things we need to share, and I felt that now was the time to tell you more about the origins of our little family."

He only received half attention, heads that tilted up to him then back to their chestnuts as they chewed the last morsels. Zarbenus settled back on his heels, his hands resting on his thighs and beaming at his charges.

"The reason I use the word—family—is because in truth, that is what you are. You are all half-brothers and half-sister to each other. As well as your master, I am also your father."

The chewing stopped and the children stared at the Magister. Temper threw pieces of chestnut shell into the fire, raising a splutter of indignation from the coals.

"That doesn't make any sense," she said. "My father was much bigger and he dandled me on his knee. He was always laughing and telling me stories about great warriors to put me to sleep. He died in battle defending the lands of our people weeks before you found me. I will always honour his memory."

The Magister's nose twitched and he scratched his jaw through his long stubble.

"He wasn't your real father. I am," said Zarbenus.

Crooked squinted at the Magister. "I don't even look like you. The others have dark hair but mine is light."

"You take after your mother; that is all."

Crooked lolled his head back and puffed out his cheeks. "Magister, we're grateful to you for rescuing us and teaching us the craft and all that, but sometimes you say things that sound silly."

"Enough!" The Magister's fingers drew up from resting on his thighs. "Children, do not test my patience. I think sometimes I am overindulgent. It is no random coincidence that I found you and brought you here."

Temper stood, her arms crossed over her chest. She fixed the Magister with the narrow gaze she always held when she was likely to give someone a thump. "My mother wouldn't betray my father. They loved each other, and they loved me much more than you do."

The Magister sighed. He unclenched his fists, and lowering his eyes from the children he raised his hood.

"Your mothers would not have known. It was the same for each of them. I would come in the night and I would take the face of their husbands and I would lie with them. They would never know I was not their man, and then I would leave them. I have watched over each of you, when I've had the time. That is how I came to you when your need was the greatest."

Foul snorted. "Doesn't it seem odd that each of us lost our parents in a tragedy, and you were secretly our father after all?"

The Magister tilted his shadowed visage to Foul. "Odd? How so?"

Foul took a deep breath. "You told us to look for motive before intent, intent before action. Then you say you rescued us because you're actually our father."

The Magister stood still; nothing more than a cowled statue.

"If it's true then I can't understand your motive." Foul spread his hands. "Why did you want to secretly father a bunch of children from different places?"

"Do you think that will answer the tragedies that were visited upon your parents, your families, and your villages?"

"He's just questioning, as you have taught us to do Magister," said Roach.

The statue came to life as the Magister raised his arms. "There is no why as to the death of those dearest to you, when you are powerless to protect them. The world is a dangerous place and wars roll across the land like thunderstorms. When the storms abate there is peace for a short while. Then brigands and pirates and a hundred other terrors arise and take the place of the soldiers and the war machines. Nowhere remains untouched, at least not for long."

"Then what do we do?"

"You do as I teach you. You learn how to depend on no-one but yourself and how to take what you want."

Dogan smirked at that. "So you aren't expecting us to behave like a happy family and all work together then?"

"Certainly not. We are always alone in this world. The faster you learn that, the longer you will survive. You will, of course, use others for a while. Maybe even work together to achieve a goal; but never trust them. Expect the betrayal that must inevitably come."

"If everyone betrays everyone else that means only one of us here will be left," said Demir, looking at his brother.

"That too is inevitable. There is only one winner in life. If two thieves make a magnificent haul, then the first will plunge in his dagger as the other turns his back to count the gold."

Temper had kept quiet throughout the exchange but loudly interrupted. "So it's a competition then; you just want to see which one of us is best?" She froze and looked apprehensively at the Magister.

His steady tone of voice didn't change. "If you choose to see it as such. I can see why a child might think this all some elaborate game with rules and a prize at the end. That, however, would be an inaccurate view. This is simply life as it truly is; life with all the petty lies stripped away. You should thank me for this lesson, for only a father would take the time to teach it to such talentless, ungrateful wretches."

Ghost looked up at the Magister, unsure of the emotion he felt growing in his chest until he realised that the grief he carried felt a little bit less and for the first time he was experiencing the vertigo of hope.

"Magister... do we still call you that, or... what do we call you?"

The Magister's hood tilted back and his smile emerged from the shadows.

"I wondered who would be first to understand. Well done, Ghost. You may still call me Magister for now. You are all still a long way from claiming your names. Maybe on that day we will discuss this again."

He rocked back and stood up in one fluid motion. From under his cloak he pulled out the paper bag of chestnuts and tossed it to Ghost. "There are plenty more in there. Enjoy them with your brothers and sister. Goodnight children."

The bottom step of the stairs flexed silently under his weight as he slipped upstairs. As soon as they were sure he was gone the children examined each other with renewed interest.

"I don't think I look anything like you, Crookey." Temper squinted closely at Crooked, peering at his nose and his chin.

"That," said Dogan, "Is the most insane thing he's come up with yet. I'm finally convinced he has no grip on reality."

"Definitely," said Demir, nodding.

Foul waved a finger between Scab and Ghost. "We have the same colour eyes as him."

"We don't," chorused the twins.

"Me either," said Crooked.

"Well I have the same eyes as him, but I don't look anything like him," said Temper. "Everyone used to say how much I looked like my father but had my mother's eyes." She paced from side to side chewing on her bottom lip.

"People said the same thing to me," said Foul. "But I think they say that to all children. He's definitely nutty."

Ghost stood in front of the fire and the other voices trailed off.

"I believe him. I know I look a bit like him, but each of you does in some way too. Besides, even if he is wrong why not let him think you believe him? After all, he did do all these things to help us."

Scab sat quietly the whole time, hugging his knees to his chest. He raised his head slowly.

"I'd... I'd rather believe him, even if it wasn't true, just to pretend I still had someone."

Each of them felt his pain as he spoke the words, even the twins who still had each other and they watched Scab screw up his eyes as he struggled to speak.

"Can't we just believe him?"

Dogan snorted. "If you believe someone clearly irrational what does that make you? As daft as him, I'd say."

Temper laid a hand on Scab's shoulder, and he forced a weak smile for her. "I think we will each need to come to our own decision on that," she said. "All I know is that he'll get angry if I challenge him again. I'm going to let him think that I believe him, no matter what I finally decide is the truth."

Scab sniffed liquidly and removed a questing finger from his nostril. "That assumes we ever find out what the truth is."

The awkward glances between them all proved too much to bear. As the last surviving log rolled apart in glowing chunks they raked the embers into a pile for the night and went upstairs to their rooms.

CHAPTER 12:
TELL ME A TALE

They trained every day with Timan from then on. He worked them hard in the roasting sun, sharply critical of their failings, but ever easy to praise their progress. After some weeks he called a halt in the middle of their session.

"Your stances are improving. You know the key points and what each stance embodies. You'll always be learning, and the best way to learn is by observing. The next time you see a bold soldier, watch the exact degree of swagger in their hips, how long they will hold someone's stare before shrugging it off. Watch the fearful ones who are the first to scamper away when horse hoofs thunder along the street. Watch how they turn their faces away and tilt their foreheads to the ground, almost bowing in supplication to those around them."

Timan stood relaxed with his hands clasped together as they chorused their agreement. He held up a hand that silenced them.

"Today you will learn another stance, and you will not master it so quickly. It will be your life's work and it will define your worth in the craft. It is the Thief's Stance that will first allow you to pass unnoticed by night, and then eventually by day. I have seen the Magister pass unnoticed through a crowded marketplace. People stepping aside for him though they have no memory of it, their gazes slipping off his shoulders like so much spring meltwater."

Each shiny sweaty face, flushed with the summer's heat turned to him as flowers to the sun. They noticed how bright the sky was and how the nearby trees shimmered in the haze. The scent of their own bodies and the sweat of those around them. Especially Foul and Scab. They took steps to spread out, wrinkling their noses and wiping away perspiration on their brows. All these things seemed to have interesting qualities and their minds wandered on them. Everything seemed more interesting than before. More interesting until a man coughed.

Ghost blinked. Timan stood right in front of him, hands clasped and his head at a slight tilt.

"Did you not see me?"

Ghost shook his head. "I guess I must have, it just didn't... I da ken. It didn't seem to matter much. There seemed to be other things that were much more interesting."

Timan nodded.

"That is part of it, but there are many elements which work together. The essence of the stance is to reach out and feel the pace of a place, the layer underneath the human behaviour. At night it can be the creaking of the roof as the winds blow against it, or the snoring of a woman that sets a vibration in the air. By day it can be the swirling of dry leaves in a courtyard, dancing unremarkably around the ankles of people passing through."

"But you were just standing there! How does that work?"

"Have patience. It will come to you with time. First, you must work on the basics, and that starts with listening. Close your eyes and listen. Can you hear the ebb and flow of the wind as it coils through the tree branches? Further out, the mountain stream, not even there until you concentrate and pick it out of the background layers. All the time there are sounds like that, background sounds so faint you forget you even hear them."

The children swayed gently as they stood in silence, eyes firmly shut, and the sounds of the mountainside growing larger in their minds.

"The background sounds are the key to it all. If no-one hears them and they are the only sounds you make, how will anyone ever hear you?"

Eyes snapped open as they spun around. Timan stood behind them grinning merrily.

"You didn't hear me walk right through the middle of you? None of you heard a thing?"

Ghost furrowed his brow and thought about the flowing sounds he had been concentrating on.

"I heard the wind, catching in the grass and whispering as it went."

Timan inclined his head to Ghost.

"*Kudos.* Your concentration is impressive. I was wind-walking; making only the same noises that the wind does."

He stepped forward sinuously drawing his toe through the grass, making it hush and sigh and grow quiet. Then he stepped with the other leg and the wind ruffled through the grass.

Even as Ghost nodded his understanding, Dogan stamped his foot. "I da see how he got it so fast! There was just so much to listen to, how could he have heard the wind?"

Demir reached out and touched his brother on the shoulder but Dogan shrugged it off angrily.

"This is just a first day," said Timan. "You will have many years to learn and practice. The noises that the normal people hear take a long time to filter out. The shrill of a mosquito as it circles your neck, the rough voice of a stallholder calling out his trade. All these things take our present attention, and might they well as your survival could depend on it, but we must be able to hear past that; to feel past that. Come with me and I will show you something that the Magister showed me many years ago. I keep it within me, always."

Temper happened to be standing closest to him so he took her by the hand and, with the others trailing behind, led them down the path that led off the side of the mountain. After a few minutes the path kinked around the stream that trickled beside it. A small pool had formed, only big enough to

171

drink from, but greeted happily by the hot children. Dozing mottled frogs, until then safe in the mud and mulching leaves, hopped to safety with high-pitched croaks. The largest was too slow, Scab's hand struck faster than a cobra and the unfortunate amphibian disappeared like a conjurer's trick.

Timan squatted beside the pool.

"Wait now, and watch. Let the pool grow calm. See the flat water? This needs to be your mind in the Thief's Stance; not empty but calm and receptive. Now watch what happens as I drop a tiny stone into the water. See the rings grow and spread out and then die away? Now watch what happens when a second stone is dropped in the water. More rings, intersecting with each other but still following the purity of its path."

The children remained silent as they followed each concentric circle that pulsed out from each stone Timan dropped in the water.

"Circles. Keep them in your mind at all times. Let the sounds come and go, ebb and flow. Feel your breathing grow easy and breathe in time with what you sense. Flow into the background, be part of it, then you will understand this stance, and by measures, the essence of our craft."

† † †

The leaves first hinted at reds and golds but faded to brown as they fell and the wind stirred them in eddies on the flat ground in front of the Nidus. The autumn mulch smelt fresh and damp as the trees prepared for their winter sleep, but it was the coolness of the air after such a warm summer that prickled their attention as the children stood silently in a row. Timan walked slowly around, ghostly when he was behind them. The frown on his face gave each of them pangs of failure as they knew he never criticised unjustly.

"The Magister watched last week's weapon's drill."

Their stomachs churned as they remembered getting silly and sharing their laughter and giggles with Timan.

"It was only a few years ago that I stood where you do now, maybe I was lucky that when he trained me he was stricter than I have been with you."

He stopped pacing and his head slumped. His shoulders rose and fell slowly as he breathed.

"I take on this burden as well; there will be no more foolishness during lessons."

"Yes, Timan," said the children as one voice.

"Take up your practice knives."

They each pulled from their belt the sticks they had whittled; a chunky end for the haft and a tapered length for the blade.

"Temper. Come at me from the front."

She advanced on him in short cross-steps, her left hand bunched in a fist as if she held a cloak out, obscuring her knife hand. Timan did not move as she whirled back her invisible cloak and thrust her wooden blade at his belly, the point pressed against his jerkin.

"Good. Now come at me from behind."

He knelt and seemed oblivious to her presence as she circled around, drawing her toes through the dead leaves so that it sounded like the playing of a breeze. Teeth clenched she leapt forward and grabbed Timan under the chin. Wrenched his jaw up and drew her wooden blade slowly and deliberately across his throat. She relinquished the grip on his jaw, and stood back as he rose from the ground. Crooked turned a mottled shade of grey and green, and swayed as he watched.

"Which of you can tell me why Temper twisted my neck so harshly before cutting my throat?"

Dogan and Demir called out at the same time.

"So you can't cry out."

"So the blade cuts deep."

Timan nodded. "Both correct. The cut from behind must always be final. Deliver it instantly, without remorse, and without emotion. Any thought other than the perfection of the movement will make your hands tremble and become slow. The cut from behind is the great equaliser. There may be a guard. Imagine that he is a big man, strong, hearty, and seasoned with the experience of many battles. Imagine that he wears excellent mail; a good chain vest over a padded leather coat. Give him a shield, helmet and longsword. Does he not seem like a mighty adversary?"

They were unanimous in their nodding.

Timan grew in stature and power as he took the warrior's stance. His shoulders broadened and his chest deepened. He loomed over the row of children, his voice deep and nasty.

"I could crush each one of you weakling babes with my bare hands and all of you together couldn't stop me."

His glare fixed on Crooked who took a half-step away. Timan sneered and took a pace forward, his fingers clawing at the air between them.

"You will be first—"

Timan choked as Temper landed on his back. Locked her elbow under his chin, hissing with the effort of forcing up his jaw. Swept the practice knife from one side of his throat to the other; not lifting the blade until it had passed his ear. Roach grunted, whispering *kudos* to her. Timan slumped to his knees and Temper slid back from him, the tightness leaving her face and her composure returning.

His eyes remained closed for a few moments, then he rubbed the red line on his throat with a dry chuckle.

"I wish it had been this week the Magister chose to spy on us. If you would master these lessons and earn your Magister's respect, you need do little more than observe Temper."

He stood and motioned for Temper to stand beside him, and placed a hand on her shoulder. "There is nothing more I can teach you until you grasp these basics of the knife. Temper will drill you for the next few hours, and if you all work as hard as she has maybe we will have time to play with swords for a while this afternoon." He smiled at Temper who wore the supercilious slant of her eyebrows that she used every time she was placed in charge, then he went into the house.

Ghost watched as Temper's gaze trailed after Timan sauntering away from her. Crooked glanced at her, glared at Timan, then stared at his own feet. After a plaintive sigh, he leaned close to Ghost and whispered into his ear.

"Temper for the morning, then swords for the afternoon? Just kill me now."

"Thought you wanted more time with her?"

"Ah," said Crooked as his fair skin took a decidedly rosy glow to his cheeks. "Problem being she only has eyes for him, and it's pretty hard for me to catch her eye when he's... well... Timan. All muscles and charm and chest hair."

Temper cleared her throat. "So, I think I know where we need to start. At the bottom of the pile, as usual. Crookey, no doubt you've analysed the situation and dreamed up a clever strategy. Please show me how well you paid attention to the attack from the front."

He groaned but readied his wooden dagger and prepared to engage her. She held out a hand and he paused, looking from her to anyone that might give him a word of encouragement.

"And Crookey—Night Mother give me strength—if your attack is sloppy or slow I'm going to knock you off your feet." She tucked her wooden knife into her belt and balled up her fists.

† † †

The Magister had taken to lounging in the living room in the evenings. The first time he materialised on his couch in the corner furthest from the fireplace, a slender flask of wine uncorked on the floor beside him and a pewter drinking jar in his hand, the children fell silent, waiting expectantly. He watched them without an air of any particular interest and sipped his wine. When he reached down to refill his jar the tense atmosphere melted and the children resumed their conversations, first in hushed tones, then rising in volume and merriment.

The fire was lit out of habit, but the evening was mild enough that all the shutters had been tied back from the windows. Amidst the twining smoke of the pine logs and of the honeysuckle wafting from the slopes below, Temper held her nightly court.

If she was satisfied that all was in order and their duties faithfully discharged, she would kneel with her back to the fire and the other children would cluster around her. She was proud of her gift for languages and would tell them in the short and accurate tones of Ghost's own language, or in the melodious flow of her own tongue, or any of the other languages the children taught each other as they passed their days and nights in the Nidus.

Starting in a soft voice she lamented the poor world a hero found himself in, and how he battled demons or dragons or the gods themselves to rescue a hapless maiden. She normally reserved disdainful remarks for the kinds of maidens that needed rescuing—and how they ought to be rescuing people themselves—but after digressing she returned to the tale. At the height of the dramatic moment when the hero proved his worth or was defeated by his fate, she took on strident tones and shook her fists. The children leaned forward—their lips parted and the flickering of the fire dancing in their eyes—anticipating a heroic finale.

Temper knew hundreds of tales of epic heroes and legends of older times. Many of them she said were tales of her people who were known across many lands as warriors of great renown. She said that one day she would be named in tales just as dramatic, even if she had to rescue poor unfortunate men who had gotten themselves into difficulties with demons, dragons, or gods, as the situation demanded it.

Zarbenus sometimes chuckled at a humorous episode or a particularly outrageous escapade, but normally he sat in silence until he had finished the whole jar of wine, and then as smoothly and silently as ever, he would drift up the stairs and leave the children to their tales. One night as Temper acted

176

out a dragon having its head hacked off with a great axe by a particularly plucky plunderer, the Magister placed his jar on the ground with an indignant snort and swung his legs off the couch. He placed his elbows on his knees and cupped his chin in his hands. The children, who had been cheering the hero on, fell silent. Temper stared at the Magister, managing as always to appear as if she was standing at a great height and looking down.

"Yes, Magister?"

"Why didn't he just steal the diamond when the dragon was sleeping?"

"Well... because that's not how it happened."

"How do you know? Does this exuberant fellow bring the dragon's head back with the treasure, as well as the diamond, or does he return with just the diamond? I imagine a dragon's head is quite heavy, and of course, there is the issue of all that other treasure lying around. Would you want to carry back a smelly heavy dragon's head, or as much gold and gems as you could fit into a couple of well-sewn sacks? I know what I would do. And, more's to the case, I have actually done, many times over."

Ghost tripped up over his own feet as he struggled to untangle himself from the knot he'd been sitting in as he was entranced by Temper's tale. He fell half the distance to the Magister, landed on the ground and stared up with eyes even wider than they'd been during the storytelling.

"You've killed a dragon?"

"Of course not, idiot child. They are mythological creatures, and are only found in tales and nightmares," said Zarbenus.

Ghost wrinkled his nose. "Does *mithy-golicol* mean they are dangerous?"

"No, you silly boy. It means they are made-up creatures and do not exist in the real world."

"They do so exist!"

"And your proof are these lurid tales? The dragons are at least more realistic than the heroes in these stories. If you are hoping to grow up to be just like them I'm afraid you will be horribly disappointed by what the world

177

actually has in store for you. What I am teaching you will help you in the world we actually live in. Not one filled with dragons and admittedly pleasantly scantily-clad young ladies who have inadvertently gotten themselves captured and find themselves with large rewards attached. These warriors of yours are a fantasy as well. Any decently entrepreneurial adventurer would skip past as much fighting as they possibly could and make straight for the treasure."

Temper stood and dusted off the knees of her trousers.

"I will become a warrior."

The Magister growled and stamped his foot as he rose from the couch, tipping his drinking jar which rolled away in an arc, bleeding a trail of the last of the wine across the floor. Both fists clenched tight, he extended an accusing finger at her.

"Then what are you doing here? Why I am I wasting my time? Get out! Get out now! Any of you, you are free to leave any day. I'm giving you the greatest gift anyone could receive. To be the master of your own destiny; to dream the greatest dreams and simply reach out and take them. Isn't that magnificently greater than being a loincloth-clad barbarian, log-chopping a mythical creature to pieces?"

Temper held her head high, but her bottom lip quivered. When she spoke her voice wavered then grew forceful.

"I will not fail in any lessons you set me and I will prove equal to every challenge you set me, but I will remember my people and one day I will be a warrior. Even if I am the last of my tribe," she said.

The Magister withdrew his hand, but Temper kept her gaze locked until he looked away, fetching up his jar and settling back on his couch to refill it.

"You'll have no help from me in that regard, and should you fall below the standard I require of you, I'll have you out that door myself sooner than you can blink."

"Yes, Magister," she said.

"Enough of these stories," said Zarbenus.

A chorused groan of disappointment rose up from the children clustered around the fire and their shoulders slumped. The Magister held up a hand that silenced them.

"For now maybe, tell us one about the bold burglar who was smart enough to take the diamonds while the dragon slept. In fact..."

The Magister knocked back the whole jar of wine, chuckled to himself, then rolled onto one elbow. He grinned at the children, smacking his lips together as he savoured the draught.

"Let's play a game, shall we? Temper will resume her storytelling. The winner will be the one who comes up with a better way to end the tale; without resorting to enchanted axes or swords with the soul of a demon trapped within. What do you say?"

Temper plucked at the folds in her trousers, her cheeks growing pink.

"You're mocking me, Magister."

"I think this is just the opportunity I've been waiting for; to find out which of you is the kind of fiendishly clever plotter and schemer. Who amongst you will plan the great heists, rather than simply carrying out the orders of another? Go ahead, Temper, resume your tale. Children, speak up if you can think of an alternative sneaky approach that you might employ if you found yourself in such a scenario."

Temper held her chin high and slowly scanned the arc of wide-mouthed children, before coldly resuming her tale at the point she'd been interrupted. She said no more than a few words before each of her audience became an excited fountain of voices gushing forth.

"He slips sleeping dust in a sheep carcase and leaves it outside the dragon's cave, returning to rob the place as the dragon snores!"

"No! He climbs above the cave mouth then drops down as the dragon leaves and stabs it in the back of its neck!"

"Mine's better! He tells a villager that the dragon can be transfixed by a sweet lullaby, and then he steals the treasure while the dragon is eating the villager!"

Temper stood with a sharp glare at the Magister. She wrinkled her nose in distaste then walked up the stairs and left them to their excited jostling. The laughing of the Magister, slapping his thigh in glee, echoed above the squealing voices. Hours later she could still hear it in her mind as shame kept her from sleeping.

Chapter 13:
Terminal Inevitable

The front door swung open and hit the wall. Sharp air drove through the room, carrying with it clumps of snow. The sound of the wood colliding with the wall shook the room and the children froze, holding the trays and plates from their breakfast. The Magister fell against the doorpost, his head drooping low and his left arm folded tight to his chest.

"Magister!"

Ghost moved first and was at the door seconds later. He reached out to take the Magister's elbow but was swept aside. Zarbenus staggered forward and pulled his cloak tighter, concealing the bloody tear on his sleeve. He slammed the door shut, breathing heavily. His hand paused over the latch for a moment, then withdrew without barring the door.

"Back to whatever you were doing. I want to sleep."

Shaking steps favouring his right leg, his voice strained and hoarse. The Magister put his foot on the first stair, then looked down as Ghost pulled at his cloak.

"Where's Timan?"

The Magister's eyelids fluttered as he scanned their faces. "He has taken his final trial and his time here is complete. You will not see him again."

He snatched the edge of his cloak out of Ghost's grasp and clumped heavily up the stairs. The children watched in silence as the Magister disappeared from view and remained quiet until the last of his footsteps had faded away.

Crooked let out a low whistle. "He's dead, isn't he?"

Ghost whirled around. Crooked backed away, holding his hands up to ward off the balled fists.

"He didn't come back for his things," said Crooked. "And the Magister looks injured. I've never seen him like that."

Ghost bit his lip and looked up the stairs. He turned to the others who clustered around.

"I da ken the Magister would lie to us," said Foul. "If Timan was dead he could just tell us straight out, couldn't he?"

Roach shook his fringe away from his eyes. "The Magister's reasons are his own, but for what it's worth I agree with Foul. We've each got enough on our hands to deal with without worrying about stuff like that. You should all forget about him and get on with your own things."

Crooked raised an eyebrow, and Scab looked back at both of them with an equal degree of suspicion. All the colour leeched from Temper's cheeks as she listened to Roach.

Unease grew inside Ghost's chest, about things they never spoke about. "What about the others that went away with the Magister and never returned?"

"Of course they're dead," said Roach. "And that means we da talk about them."

"So we shouldn't talk about Timan then," said Ghost.

As his words faded away, he realised what it meant and the other children stared at him, open-mouthed. Temper whimpered a half-stifled wail then ran upstairs sobbing. The sight of her reduced to frail helplessness seared itself into Ghost's memory.

† † †

Zarbenus sunk onto his bed, rolled onto his back and closed his eyes. Weary, so weary in every bone. Eyes dry, head throbbing like the aftermath of a long night, hard at the cups in a Thracian slopshop. So many years wasted. Wasted on the fragile futility of searching for his equal. His successor. His rebirth. Ungrateful, worthless, bloody-minded... Timan.

Why would Timan betray him?

He twisted in his sheets, knotting them in his fists, the disappointment and frustration billowing through him like waves of guilt and doubt. But Zarbenus did not feel guilt or doubt, and the strange emotions soured and rotted and left him with a deep and seething anger. Ten years since his first triumphant assault on everything that was Byzantium. How quickly all his enemies fell before him! But then this priest, this irksome, meddling, conniving, scheming, manipulative priest; Pallas had beaten him at every step, and now? He was as good as the Hierarch's own man now—a pet assassin.

Pallas must die. He will die, but not before Zarbenus unravelled the complex knots that have been placed around him. So subtly had the priest made his moves that even the God of Thieves had been snared before he knew any better. Pallas must be lying about the rebirth rituals, mustn't he? Such tales Zarbenus had always laughed off, gullible fools willing to pander to fantasies just to enlighten their mean, dreary existences. As his anger cooled, sluggish frozen rivers in his veins, he admitted he may have over-reached—a confession that would never leave his lips—and underestimated the frail, old priest. They now played with dice together, laughing as each toss meant an accidental death here, or an unexplained disappearance there. He would slowly, with bad grace and much bitter complaining, slowly, slowly accede to the Hierarch. Zarbenus could lie and mislead as easily as he could breathe. On this he knew he was the master between them, then on this alone he would triumph.

Let Pallas manipulate him. Appear to wriggle and then be forced to accept. If there was but one in a hundred chance that the Goddess of Pallas could grant this ascension, something the blessed Night Mother could not, then he would steal the sun out of the sky to achieve it. But either way, when the truth was revealed Pallas would shortly draw his last breath.

With one hand he would draw the priest in, ever closer, waiting for his chance to grasp the gift that Pallas held high, sparkling like the dawn star. With the other hand he would forge his own counter-measures; a fist full of vipers. Already Temper had proven to be a useful asset, and Dogan... His merit had been most ruthlessly demonstrated this very night, the sole bright light in the darkness. Ghost's promise, a tantalising prospect but yet unfulfilled. Roach similarly untested. Crooked, Foul and Scab? Fast approaching a time when they must transform into weapons or be discarded. With the Night Mother's favour, the children themselves would prove their own worth. And between them, remove the unworthy.

Letter received from unknown courier, somehow included in the diplomatic messages sent to the Palace of Pearls, the generational home of the Firat lineage; twelfth day of summer.

Original message:

> *Dearest Bey Firat,*
>
> *It fills me with joy to watch your grandson and grand-nephew play together. With such strong boys, your bloodline will certainly boast another generation of triumph! It is wonderful that they have so many friends watching over them, friends that are deeply appreciative of the trust you place in them with delicate whispers of political intrigue. Our joint interests are well served!*
>
> *My heartfelt thanks for the warm welcome you will no doubt extend to my family when they visit you.*
>
> *Your obedient servant; in Hekate's name.*

Translated message:

> *I can snuff out your bloodline at any time or place of my choosing. Provide me with regular information sufficiently engaging that my threats remain nothing more than that. Deliver intelligence on your enemies and I shall deal with them. A mutually beneficial arrangement.*
>
> *Expect my Vipers; obey them.*
>
> *Zarbenus, God of Thieves*

CHAPTER 14:
COME TO THE TABLE

"Come, my Vipers. Come, my agents of ruin and retribution. Come to the table."

After the harshness of the winter, the early spring brought mellow sunlight and a sweet wind that carried with it the carefree song of the thrushes. The Magister sat cross-legged by the low table with his back to the windows. On the table lay a small tin medicine spoon beside a rounded glass bottle sealed with a waxed bung.

Temper sighed when she saw the bottle, and both Roach and Crooked retched. The younger children watched them with puzzled interest, while the brothers sat a little way apart; close enough to have answered the Magister's summons, but far enough so they could whisper to each other without interruption. They'd returned from some expedition—questions about which they answered only with mocking snickers—several days after the loss of Timan. On hearing the news they said nothing and smirked a great deal. Dogan now bore a kukuri knife in a battered scabbard on his hip. Its origins were both a source of amusement and of few answers when he was questioned. Questions went unanswered between all of them. Just days ago every danger seemed to be part of a magnificent adventure; the possibility of their own deaths a ludicrous fantasy. Now a pall of mortality hung over every interaction. Games once so enthralling now frivolous, puerile. The memory of every warning the Magister had ever told them now felt like a precise prediction.

"Enough of that. I expect you to receive this trial as any of your others."
The Magister glared at the older ones.

Temper bowed her head and clasped her hands together as she sat
down.

"I'm sorry Magister. It won't happen again. Timan says... said..." She
trailed off at the unspoken shift of Zarbenus' shoulders. "...I once heard
whatever you hate most is your biggest challenge and should be attempted
before anything else. Shall I go first?"

The Magister grunted his assent as Temper unstoppered the bottle and
poured a measure of a thick green goo onto the small spoon. Her hand
trembled for a moment but she quickly put the spoon in her mouth, and
with eyes tightly screwed shut she swallowed the mixture. As she put her
hand down her fingers unclenched and the spoon rattled onto the table. The
colour drained from her cheeks and her eyes rolled up. She moaned softly,
collapsed backward and lay motionless on the ground. The brothers
smirked as Ghost jumped to his feet, but the Magister held up his hand.
Temper wheezed faintly, and her normally plum red lips grey and sickly.

"Back to your places. Each of you will take your turn. I am teaching you
to build up your tolerances. It will take many years and must be a habit you
cultivate even if, ahem, even after you have left here. It will not kill you as I
have greatly reduced the potency of each, nonetheless, you will feel unwell
for several days. It is perfectly normal, and you are excused your other
obligations for two days after each dosage."

Roach gritted his teeth and reached for the bottle. He screwed up his
face, took his spoonful, then blanched and slumped to the floor.

Crooked threw up his hands in resignation. "Whatever you hate most?"
Scowling and grumbling to himself, he glanced at Temper's supine form and
grabbed the medicine spoon. Moments later he laid ashen-faced and still
beside the others.

"And who of you who have not taken this journey will go first; maybe you

Ghost?"

"I'm not scared," said Ghost.

"I never said you were."

"Then I'll take two spoons!" Ghost sneered at the Magister, confident of his victory.

"Then you will die, and I will have wasted a good deal of time on you."

"Oh." Ghost's face fell and his cheeks pinked. He poured himself a spoonful, and after squirming at the bitter taste, slumped unconscious to the ground.

Ghost awoke with a throbbing head, his tongue thick and dry. He tried to swallow but just coughed painfully and rolled onto his side as he retched. His puffy eyelids hurt to crack them open. When he did, the carrot-glow of the dusk pierced his vision with swirling black spots.

"How interesting. You are the first to wake. You've been stirring for some hours. Sip this. While you slept I gathered mint, and made tea with a little honey for you."

The Magister helped Ghost close his stiff fingers around a small wooden bowl. The steam was sweet and fresh and he sipped it through stinging cracked lips. Eventually, he swallowed enough to clear his throat and moisten his tongue.

"Have I really slept all day?"

"Almost two days. I had calculated the dosage for three, and as you can see, the others are still dreaming."

The Magister gestured to the supine forms laid in a neat row under the window, their heads on pillows and blankets pulled up to their chins. They all had the pallor of death with yellow swathes under their eyes. Other than Scab, who managed some occasional twitching, the rest of them all lay still as corpses.

"Will they be alright, I mean; they'll wake up won't they?"

"It would be somewhat of a waste if they didn't pull through. Children, I have discovered, are frequently more resilient than you may first observe. Look at Scab—half the size of the rest of you—yet making a faster recovery than most. In any event, the dosage was weak enough that they all ought to survive it. If they do not it is likely they bore a congenital weakness and I would be relieving their future suffering."

"I da ken all that, Magister."

Ghost's vision blurred. He struggled to concentrate on the Magister's words but they kept slipping away from him in the ripples and reflections on the surface of the bowl of tea.

"And you don't have to, boy. You only have to obey me, and you will become so powerful that you need only dream of something and it could be yours. Does that not seem like a prize worth struggling to achieve?"

"Dreaming... I think I need to sleep some more..."

Ghost took a last sip from the bowl and set it wobbling on the floor. He laid his head on the pillow and closed his eyes. Zarbenus reached out and moved Ghost's hair away from his face with a fingertip. He sat back on his heels and watched the sleeping boy; the orange glow of the dusk daubing a hint of colour back to his cheeks.

"Very well done again. How interesting."

CHAPTER 15:

SORAYA ASCENDANT

Months passed with only brief visits from the Magister, a hard winter with little to do but bicker amongst themselves. Now the only snow that fell on the coldest nights melted within an hour of the dawn, and Ghost watched as the Magister trudged up the narrow path to the Nidus. Even at distance, he saw Temper laughing and jumping, tugging on the Magister's sleeve to urge him forward at a quicker pace. Joy lit her face, torn between looking up at the shadowed hood of the Magister, then up to the Nidus. The Magister tugged on reins, dragging forward a horse that steamed and sweated, its head wearily held low with bulging saddlebags across its back.

Ghost pushed open the front door and whistled sharply. Several pairs of quick footsteps answered his summons.

"Something's wrong. I've never seen her that happy. Ever since Timan."

Temper had spent most of her time alone since then, appearing only for mealtimes, then disappearing for days on end. She barely spoke to the others unless forced to.

Crooked shaded his eyes to squint at Temper. "Yikes. That can't be a good sign. Who do you think she thumped to be that happy?"

The twins exchanged glances, and Scab carefully manoeuvred himself so that the imposing body of Roach stood between him and the oncomers. Foul let out a weak squeaky fart. "Err... sorry. That happens when I'm scared."

Temper drew herself up, composing her features and stroking her hair back from her face. Her usually haughty expression lasted only a moment before it broke with a wild smile and an uncontrollable laugh. She stopped just short of the waiting group and nodded to them, still grinning broadly, and she waited in silence as Zarbenus ambled the last few steps to join them.

"Welcome back, Magister," said Ghost. "How was your trip?"

The Magister opened his mouth to speak, but Temper caught him by the wrist. "May I tell them the tale tonight, Magister?"

He raised an eyebrow at her, and a twitch of a grin played around the corner of his mouth. "Very well. On this occasion, you may do so... Soraya."

The children gasped and Scab slumped to the ground, sitting with his legs sticking out.

Ghost pulled up his jaw, staring jealously at the laughing young woman in front of him. "Soraya?"

"It's a beautiful name..." Crooked's words trailed off, his cheeks flushed hot and red.

She fluttered her eyelashes closed and tipped her forehead to him. "That's very kind of you, Crookey. I would have been content with any name the Magister chose for me, but I love this one."

The Magister patted her on the head, then shoved her toward the house.

"Enough chatter for now, Soraya. You are to unpack all our things and take care of the tools before any more nonsense. Only you are to handle the saddlebags. When the horse is unloaded have one of the brats take it down the mountain, dispose of the saddle in some gully, and scare the beast away."

He swung his pack off his shoulder and dropped it at her feet. Unable to do anything but beam at him, she hauled it up and struggled to get it over her shoulder, crowded as it was with her own gear.

"Yes, Magister. What shall I do with the..."

"Wash them and weigh them, then bring them to my room."

"Immediately, Magister." She bobbed her head to him then staggered into the house.

Desperate pangs of urgent envy swirled in Ghost's chest. He looked at the rest of the Vipers and knew they felt it too.

"Now, back to your studies. If you wish that to be you someday, then practice, practice. Get to it." The Magister went into the house as the children exchanged glances, their foreheads creased.

"I thought it would have made her unbearable, but she hardly seems to notice us," said Roach, rubbing the back of his neck.

"I know," said Crooked. "When I told her that her name was... it just came out wrong—"

Ghost punched him on the arm. "Are you still soft for her?"

"No! You're just making me more embarrassed!" His cheeks flushed again yet he glowered at Ghost. "I just stumbled over my words at the shock of her being given a name by the Magister."

"Well, if you aren't interested, then I might try my luck..." Ghost backed away, still giggling at Crooked until the threat of a raised fist silenced him.

Foul gazed at the house, lost in his own thoughts. "Guess we'll find out how she did it tonight."

† † †

The meal was eaten faster than it had ever been. Chunks of bread choked down and loaded forkfuls hovered in front of frantically chewing jaws, ready to deposit the next load. When their plates were clear, Soraya who had eaten slowly and calmly, stayed seated alongside the Magister, just as Timan had done when he had eaten with them. She did not look up at the children collecting the plates and carrying them to the kitchen. Ghost felt his squirt of envy again and knew that she was now different from the rest of them.

With new logs on the fire and the shutters drawn against the night, Soraya knelt with her back to the fire and smiled at the others. Her shoulders relaxed and her smile more genuine than the imperious sneer they were accustomed to. The Magister draped himself over his corner chair and settled his wine jar against his chest.

Soraya cleared her throat. "Tonight's tale is not about warriors or mighty battles, but the daring adventures of a wily thief and his assistant."

The children whistled and clapped loudly, and the Magister chuckled from the shadows. Soraya's glance flicked to his corner then back to the bright faces clustered around her.

"A rumour came to an astute thief that a merchant had recently made a deal with a famed lapidarist for the creation of some master-crafted jewellery that he planned to take to another city and sell for a profit. The jeweller's reputation was such that anything he created was much esteemed in those parts, and the merchant felt sure he would be able to sell the items for a significant profit. An experienced trader, he also knew the difficulties in moving such a cargo safely so he made subtle enquiries as to where he might purchase some security.

"Sitting at his cups in the pleasantly well-commissioned local tavern, the fubsy merchant heard the approach of solid footsteps, and looking up from his wine found the steely gaze of a deadly warrior; a man a little into his middle age, with streaks of grey at his temples, but tall and powerfully built with broad shoulders. As the trader took the offered handshake—wincing as the iron grip nearly crushed his own—he decided that this seasoned soldier was not the sort of person that anyone would trifle with. Not even the most hardened brigands that prowled the long roads that ran from the city to the village."

The children looked over to the Magister's slouched form at the description of the wandering mercenary, and under their gaze he shook back his hood. As he leaned forward his expression hardened, brows knotted and eyes narrowed. He grew in stature and purpose, and the children shrank back at the swiftness of the transformation, recognising him only by the colour of his eyes. He held the face of the warrior for a moment then fell back into shadows and sipped at his wine.

"And so, sharing a flask of honey mead that the warrior selected and the merchant paid for, they agreed a mutually beneficial solution. The merchant was impressed by the equanimity of the warrior, who insisted that he be paid only one-twentieth of the value of the cargo as his salary, for anything else would be tantamount to the very robbery he was being engaged to prevent.

"It took a few days for the master jeweller to complete his works, during which time the merchant entertained the warrior at the tavern, raising an eyebrow at the warrior's fondness for the more expensive wines and his rapacious appetite for choice cuts of venison, but satisfied himself that he should consider it an investment in his new business partner.

"Eventually the master jeweller completed his work. The warrior accompanied the merchant to the jewellers, but was content to wait outside the shop, after an explanation that the final haggling on price was something that the merchant would accomplish best if left alone. The warrior demurred and it apparently never crossed his mind that the merchant might be collecting items worth a great deal more than the figure initially described—a figure which would have resulted in his one twentieth cut being so much greater.

"After some minutes of raised voices the merchant emerged, smiling toothily and carrying a padlocked chest. He assured the warrior that he could manage it on his own, but he puffed and sweated the short walk down the street to where their waggon awaited. He struggled to push the chest up onto the front seat, then climbed up and draped his cloak over it. The warrior joined him and taking the reins he urged the horses onward, out of the village and toward the city.

"The sun rode high in the sky and their journey halfway done, they first heard harsh voices when on the loneliest stretch of the road. Then came the keening wail of a child abruptly cut short. The warrior urged the horses to make a burst of better speed, lashing the reins and bellowing at them to pick up their hooves. Within moments he pulled on the reins to bring the team to a stop lest they trample the child lying motionless in the road, clutching a small sack to her breast.

"The warrior leapt off the waggon, his sword in his hand and protectively straddled the small body. He shouted bold and angry threats into the woods, but after a minute of listening intently no voices answered him. He sheathed his sword and knelt by the child, concern writ plain on his brow. He held his ear close to the child's mouth and with a sigh informed the merchant that, praise to all the gods, the child yet lived.

"Cradling the body in his arms he saw the child was a young girl who had taken a blow to the temple, blood matted in her hair. However, as he lifted her up to rest her in the waggon, she cried out in piteous tones for the return of her sack. The warrior passed the girl to the merchant who blushed uncomfortably as she fell into his arms and sniffled against his shoulder. The warrior snatched up the girl's sack, but exclaimed his surprise to the merchant for it was merely filled with stones and pebbles. Yet the girl begged for it so much that he laid it beside her and she mumbled her way into a fitful sleep.

"The journey continued peacefully after that and the merchant and the warrior shared some travelling food and another one of the expensive wines that had somehow managed to come from the taverna with them. When the city limits drew within sight the merchant breathed easily. He clapped the warrior on his shoulder, thanked him for his protection, and told him what an excellent fellow he was. The wine working its way through their system persuaded them take the briefest break, pausing to pass water together over an indignant bush and swap bawdy jokes. The waggon soon rolled on again and with the darkening of the evening sky they entered the city.

"The young girl seemed quite recovered after her long sleep. She thanked her rescuers with tears in her eyes, and promised she would say prayers for them this very night, safe in her own home that at one point she feared she would never see again. Calling out repeated blessings she disappeared off into the throng of the closing marketplace, clutching her childish bag of rocks to her bosom. The warrior and the merchant shook hands, with the merchant insisting that he felt perfectly safe in the city to make his way from there. The delivery to the palm of the warrior of a reassuringly heavy pouch of chinking coin concluded their business, and thus they parted company.

"It was not until some hours later that the merchant unslung from his neck the keychain that he wore under his fine garments and opened the stiff padlock of his heavy chest. Imagine his consternation and rage when he discovered within only common rocks and pebbles and not a single one of the fine items he had commissioned at such expense in the village. Meanwhile, the warrior seemed to have melted into the night and elsewhere a lean thief and his student, cowls drawn against the chill in the air, acquired a horse inadvisably tied near the city gates, and rode off with saddlebags bulging."

Soraya bowed her head as they cheered and clapped. Scab crept around behind Roach who mimed a pompous merchant, belly sticking out and oblivious to the clever finger on the purse dangling so temptingly from his belt. Dogan sat with his face screwed up, scratching his forehead.

"How did you lock the chest again? I can see you had time to charm it open, but lock it again?"

Zarbenus tilted his head to Soraya, waiting. She glanced briefly at Crooked who whispered with Roach. Her lips parted then she smiled.

"I think a lady should be permitted her secrets, don't you?"

A chuckle came from the Magister. "Enough prying, my little Vipers. Secrets and lies are the currency of our trade."

"That was wonderfully told Soraya, *kudos*." Ghost still surged with jealousy that it had not been him, and he had not received a name, but he was also proud of her.

"I was worried that, well some of you may be envious of me, but I have been here the longest so it just means your day could come soon as well," said Soraya.

"Maybe, maybe not. I've never felt one as young as you has been deserving of a name," said the Magister. "Timan was many years older when I decided him worthy. You others should not dwell on this one aspect of your training. Push yourselves to exceed what you can do today, and each day you will be better than the last. Do not measure yourselves by the failings or accomplishments of another, for when they are gone what does it mean then? Nothing. Only your performance should be in your mind, and only I shall judge it.

"Soraya, you have done well and I am very proud of you. I hope the others can learn from your example. Now I am tired. You may stay up retelling the tale if you wish, but I would sleep now." The Magister rose, and at the base of the stairs he paused. "And don't forget the little memento of your day's success."

When the small creak of the ladder that led to his room sounded they all turned to Soraya, pleading to hear the story one more time. With relief in her heart that they did not grudge her this day, this special day, she told the story again. And when that was done, and the children lay back staring at the ceiling and dreaming of themselves on an adventure with the Magister. They were distracted by a musical tinkling noise. When they looked up they saw Soraya shaking a tiny silver bell.

"It's been so long that we've played at stealing that old walnut from each other. I think I've grown quite bored with the game. The Magister brought it to mind when we found this in our haul and he said I could keep it. In fact, he said it would be pretty hard to lift out of someone's pocket without it making a noise, and that even he'd agree I had some talent if I could take it from any of you."

This resulted in a cacophony of clamouring voices begging to go first—amidst remonstration from Soraya that if they disturbed the Magister they'd probably have the bell taken away—so it was in whispers it was agreed that henceforth that the game which started as Chase-me many months before (which became Chase-and-find-me after some time, then later still Filch-the-nut) would henceforth be known as Filch-the-bell. Adopting it formally as their official game, Soraya led the inaugural bout.

Some hours later, very tired, and sporting a black eye, bloody nose, sprained ankle and multiple bruised egos between them, they finally made it back to their cribs to dream about future triumphs and peer recognition as the undisputed champion of Filch-the-bell.

† † †

Alone in his room, Zarbenus sat on the edge of his bed, very still in the darkness. Pallas would never know how his secret bribe shipment was waylaid. The plan was gently unfolding, like blossom in the morning, but like a blossom it was still very delicate. A general marshalled his forces to protect his vulnerable yet strategically important resources. A politician rallied public support to ensure their gambit would thrive. Zarbenus chuckled.

Idiots, all of them.

Give your pawn a goal, motivate them appropriately. Judge them harshly, and always have a replacement or two near at hand. For what are pawns other than to be expendable?

Chapter 16:

A Kid Must Die

The bleating goat stared down the cliff face, slant pupils in golden eyes contemptuous of the figures that toiled clumsily below, crawling higher and breathing heavily. It jumped to an outcrop of rock then picked its way toward an agreeable looking clump of grasses; yellow seed heads swaying in the chilly breeze.

"I think he's getting better." Demir glanced down at Ghost as he negotiated an awkward section of the cliff, taking a two-handed grip and swinging his legs across to the next hold, barely within his reach.

Dogan nodded then flashed his teeth at his brother. "That he is, but so are we." He wedged his toes in firmly then stretched out his hand for Demir who grasped it as a free handhold and stepped up to a higher position.

Beneath them, Ghost cursed as his footing came loose and stones tumbled to the base of the cliff. He looked up at the twins and tried to pick out the path they'd used to get ahead of him. He heard the door of the Nidus open and shut and looked back to see the Magister wandering toward them. As their races intensified the Magister had started to come out and watch them, studying them intently as they worked their way across and up the treacherous face. Then he would walk away shaking his head as the last of the goats grazing amongst the rocks clambered out of reach and the game would be lost again. The Magister never cried out in fear if one of them struggled, if their hands slipped. The ever-present spectre of a child tumbling down the rock face. Bouncing off boulders to lie broken, bleeding and dead at the foot of the cliff. Crinkled brown leaves swirled around his feet, and he watched with arms crossed over his chest.

Dogan drove his fingers between the roots of a tenacious scrub pine that grimly clung to the bare rock, took a firm grip and smiled as he reached for his brother to help him up. As their fingers locked the stubby tree came loose amidst clods of dry soil. Dogan swayed away from the rock face, letting the pine fall from his grasp and steadying himself with his brother's hand.

"Careful brother!" Demir's brow creased as his other hand tightened in the crevice hold.

"Where would I be without you?" Dogan winked at him.

They looked down as the debris fell past Ghost, showering him in dead pine needles and gravel. He spat out the soil that landed in his mouth.

"Idiots. I'll show them."

The brothers scanned the rock above them and to the sides, looking for another route. Off to their left grazed a black and white goat kid, its jaw rolling from side to side as it chewed, just a few feet from Ghost. They froze as they saw him stop climbing and look across to the same spot.

Ghost watched the goat, and it regarded him impassively. There were no easy grips between him and the goat, but the edge it perched on terminated in a scree slope then slid back down the cliff. His pulse quickened and he glanced up at the twins. Their worried expressions made him chuckle, and he felt a touch of relief that he hadn't waited for Crooked. The climb already tested the limits of his ability. Trying to help Crooked would have crushed his chances of winning.

He took a breath and jumped. His heart dropped away as his feet pumped in the air. The breath knocked out of him as he collided with the goat kid. He wrapped his arms around it and locking his fingers tight. The goat brayed and struggled, and the pair of them went tumbling down the slope. His head smacked a boulder. Sparks flashed in his vision as they rolled over. The goat's cries in his ears and its musky fur in his face; gravel burning against elbows and knees.

They slid off the slope and came to a rest at the feet of the Magister. He clapped slowly.

"An interesting descent, but you held onto the prize which I suppose is what matters. *Kudos*, Ghost."

Ghost wrestled the goat kid until it was underneath him, then got up onto his knees, never relinquishing his twisting and wriggling package. His scrapes and bruises burned hot but the excitement washed his pain into a background swirl of emotions. The twins climbed down and glared at him with deep frowns before shaking their heads and walking back to the Nidus.

Dogan opened the door and rapped his knuckles against it. "Ghost won the goat contest. Come on."

He slammed the door shut so hard that it shook in its frame then he stalked back to stand beside his brother, their arms crossed over their chests. Moments later Roach and Crooked were joined by Soraya and they formed a half-circle around the Magister.

"A champion has emerged from the fray. Not in a particularly elegant fashion, I have to say, but I did not stipulate that in advance. He has one final task to do before I declare him victorious."

He pulled his blue-steel dagger from his belt, flipped it in the air and caught it by the blade, proffering it to Ghost.

"The noise of that animal is starting to get on my nerves. Make it quiet," said Zarbenus.

In the grim silence that followed, Roach held out his hand, palm up. "I'll do it, if you haven't the stomach."

Ghost's pulse had just started to settle but it now raced again as he realised what was being asked of him. He stretched the goat kid's jaw upward and it fell silent and still. His hand shook as he reached out and closed his fingers around the wire-wound hilt of the Magister's dagger.

"Good technique, Ghost. Now make it quiet, permanently."

Zarbenus leapt back from the spray of blood, and he watched as the goat spasmed and struggled. Ghost's knife arm slowly lowered until he held it by his side. The others stood mute save Roach who nodded his approval.

The Magister plucked his dagger from Ghost's unresisting fingers and wiped it on the grass before sheathing it. Then he turned to walk away.

"What's my prize?" Ghost stood up and let the limp body of the goat fall to the grass.

Zarbenus scratched his beard as he studied Ghost's face. "What if I were to allow you to choose your name? What would you say to that?"

Ghost's mind spun. *A real name?* Then he scowled—it had to be a test. The others watched him in silence. Would he be the first to join Soraya?

"I only want what you choose for me, and when you know I deserve it."

"And this is not sufficient?"

Ghost looked at his bloody hands, then back at the Magister. "It should be something magnificent."

Zarbenus stared at him. "Very well, we shall await that day. In the meantime take that fresh meat into the kitchen. I rather fancy that dish Soraya makes with apricots, in the tagine."

He breezed away and for the first time Ghost met the stares of the others. Crooked's face a bilious mask with his hand over his mouth. The others looked at him with expressions moving between grimaces of disgust and frowns of envy.

"I should have been the first, but will instead be the first to give my congratulations. *Kudos*, Ghost." Soraya nodded to him, but Crooked looked like he was sucking on a lemon.

"You did it on your own," said Crooked. "So much for sticking together."

Ghost's elation sucked out of his body leaving nothing but a sudden awareness of a full bladder. "I just—"

"Hey, it's not important, really," Crooked shrugged, looked up at the perilous cliff face then shrugged again. "I'm not likely to impress the Magister here, on my own. Thought we'd have a great chance together, but well, you made your decision."

He turned to walk away. Ghost reached for him but Crooked shrugged him off and kept walking.

"A tidy kill, Ghost," said Roach and clapped him on the shoulder. "You proved you didn't need anyone else's help. And that you didn't need to help your friends either."

An empty consolation as his guilt consumed his glory. Roach moved away without looking back and said, "Soraya, walk with me. We should talk."

The brothers glared at him too, albeit for different reasons, then they left leaving Ghost alone with the goat's carcass. He stared at it for a long time, then grabbed hold of its legs and dragged it back to the house. Whatever he did someone was going to be angry with him and not for the first time he wished they would all forget about him and leave him alone.

Soraya's Goat & Apricot Tagine

Quantities for a grown man, a young woman, and seven hungry boys.

Start with a shoulder and leg of young goat, cut in generous chunks (give the rest of the animal to the boys and tell them to slice it into strips for salting and smoking. It will keep them out of your way while you do the real work). Boning the goat is good knife practice for all of us.

Pour some olive oil into a big pot, heat it, and add a finely chopped bulb of garlic and four sliced onions.

Add the goat meat and a big spoon of turmeric.

Throw in a handful of dried apricots sliced in strips and let them caramelise (fresh apricots just aren't the same).

Once it starts to brown add a small amount of stock, along with two curls of cinnamon, then two very finely chopped harissa peppers (for Crooked!).

If it's a celebration add some saffron.

Grind in salt and add a spoonful of honey.

Pop on the tagine lid and let it simmer for an hour or so, adding more stock as needed.

Grate some ginger in near the end, along with the juice of two lemons.

Serve with rice or bread. Don't expect any leftovers, those boys are like wolves!

CHAPTER 17:

RETRIBUTION

Suddenly a heavy weight landed on his chest, crushing him. The darkness churned and someone forced a rag into his mouth. He struggled, the shock and fear cutting through his sleepiness as he realised it wasn't a nightmare. He heard a soft chuckling and then a white flare as a lamp was lit.

Ghost squinted as his eyes adjusted to the light. Dogan's face just inches away, grinning and showing teeth.

"You made us look bad, Ghost. We'd have won if we'd cheated like you," said Dogan.

Demir sitting astride Ghost's was the weight on his chest that made breathing hard. Bigger and stronger, he gripped Ghost's wrists like manacles. Ghost struggled, cursing and snapping his teeth, but couldn't break free. Dogan slapped him across the face. His cheek burned more from the shame than the pain, and his heart pounded erratically.

"But what will it take to make ya ken?"

Dogan punched Ghost in the shoulder, then after a moment's pause once more much harder in the side of the head. Louder than the slamming of a door. Ghost choked as he tried to spit out the rag. Dogan hit him across his jaw; a flash of blackness followed by sickness before the pain came.

"Hit him, brother," said Dogan fiercely.

Ghost blinked against the spots dancing in his vision to see Demir's face soften, then snarl. Demir abruptly rolled his body off Ghost's chest, then yanked on the wrists he still held and tossed Ghost off the bunk.

Crushing impact on his shoulder. A pain flare that suddenly ceased as his head bounced off the floor. He lay there unmoving only dimly aware of those around him, sounds muffled like he'd fallen to the bottom of a well.

"You too. Kick him," said Dogan. Someone else was there, arguing, protesting—Crooked. "Either you kick him or we'll do you next. Do it now. Now."

Ghost could hear Crooked crying even as a foot drove into his belly. He gagged, choking on the rag in his mouth. All the breath driven out of him. He tried to curl up but his limbs so heavy and slow, his head swimming. Another kick hammered in, then another. Ghost didn't know who kept doing it. Everything fading distant and foggy. Seconds, minutes; it all collapsed into a maelstrom of agony and terrifying helplessness.

Through the assault a sensation sharply asserted itself. A knife pressed against his throat. A sting—so sweet and fine compared to the dull reverberations echoing in his battered limbs—as the skin on his neck parted under the weight of the blade.

"Enough." Which one of them said that?

"I'll say when it's enough," said Dogan. "He needs to learn his lesson. This kukuri has already ended one failure. Long past time due for another. "

"Enough," said Demir. He sounded tired. "Put that damned knife away. It's enough. Crooked, get him out of here. Both of you. We don't want you in our room anymore."

Crooked tried to lift Ghost up. His legs wobbled under him and ribs screamed each time he breathed. Taking short pants he managed to stagger out the room, Crooked propping him up. The door slammed behind them. The return to darkness disorientating, his thoughts sleepy and distant. He wanted to lie down and rest again, but Crooked kept pulling him along. Why was Crooked crying? Soon he was lying on the floor again, it was cold but he didn't need to fight to stay awake. Someone put a blanket over him. Then he slept.

† † †

Light came in the window and Ghost woke suddenly. Everything hurt and he couldn't open one eye. He touched his cheek to find it puffy and swollen. Crooked had pushed open the shutters and stood with his elbows on the windowsill looking out. Ghost didn't recognise the room he was in. The narrow window admitted enough sunlight to see a pile of broken chairs, cracked ceramic wine jars and old boxes. He lay on a pile of torn burlap sacks, and the stained, oil-spotted jute sheets they nailed over ill-fitting shutters during the winter.

"It's sunny today," said Crooked to no-one in particular.

Ghost gently probed his ribs. He was bruised down one side but it was bearable if he didn't lie on it. There was dried blood on his lips and he could taste the metal in his dry mouth. Thinking about last night made him queasy, the pain so fresh in his memory as he relived it. Knowing the twins had overpowered him so easily and he'd been stupid enough to have not seen it coming. It was too easy to relax in this place, despite the challenges, when he played games with the others every day.

I'm not a baby any more.

But what was he? The master's boy. Just a ghost. A memory of what he'd have been like in a normal life, or just a nightmare of what he'd become. A murderer, a thief. He'd tried to make up for it. He'd tried to help the others.

But I steal the moment the Magister tells me to.

Then it wasn't worth fighting. It only made him weak, sick to his stomach. Tears formed in his eyes and he angrily rubbed them away. Where had those come from? Trusting other people and then being let down. Only the worst kind of idiot would do that. Hating himself for what he'd become and how helpless he was; it was easier than hating the twins. They'd just been better than him.

Because they don't fight it. They know what we really are.

He lay broken on the floor; body and spirit. With no name, no idea who he really was when he looked inside. Seeing his own weakness sickened him. Self-loathing then swallowed by rage, an intolerable desire to smash and rip and burn. Anything to rid him of the shame of a child's tears.

Crooked turned away from the window and he coughed to get Ghost's attention. "I thought you'd like your own room now, I mean we're not little anymore. Well then. How are you feeling?"

Ghost squinted at his betrayer, his ex-friend. Crooked forced a smile but couldn't look Ghost in the eye. Faking the smile to cover his own guilt.

"Bruised but I'll mend," said Ghost, putting on a false grin of his own.

"About last night," said Crooked. "I mean... well you see..."

"It's nothing. Forget about it," said Ghost.

Crooked's frown eased and his awkward smile finally reached his eyes. "Really? We're still friends then?"

"Sure," said Ghost. "Best friends."

I can pretend too.

Chapter 18:
Fan's Triumph

It rained for three days straight. The first day Crooked left a jug of water and a cloth bundle of bread and some crumbly white cheese. He talked softly, as much to himself as to Ghost who drifted in and out of a deep sleep. Something about the Magister taking him away, and his anxiety that he would fail to meet expectations. Ghost didn't care. The dreamtime called to him with a woman's voice. She watched over him, he just needed to sleep, safe in her arms. No-one else came to visit him that day or the next, and hunger drove him to venture out the second evening. Conversations stilled as he moved through the house, everyone suddenly too occupied to greet him. He preferred to lie alone in his new sleeping place, rather than bear the weight of their rejection. Late afternoon of the third day his spirits lifted as he spied the Magister and Crooked toiling up the mountain path towards the Nidus. Crooked returned with slumped shoulders; he glanced repeatedly at the Magister who brushed past him, muttering a variety of barely intelligible deprecations. Crooked took one look at Ghost's face, still bruised and swollen, mouthed a silent 'sorry', then never mentioned it again. It wasn't difficult for him to avoid the subject; he avoided Ghost entirely which achieved the same result.

The following day the Magister left with Roach, who carried both their packs as if they weighed nothing at all. For the next week Ghost spent most of his time outside the Nidus, climbing the ruins of the castle. The blocks were easy to scale, but every stretch up with his right hand stabbed him in the side as his cracked rib protested. Still, he found a clarity to his thoughts knowing that a chance tremor or wince of pain might send him tumbling to his death. Only once did his path cross with the twins; they returned from a few days away and paused to watch him climbing. Ghost felt them staring and his palms grew sweaty. The next grip he half-fumbled, gravel falling away, then clung to the rock. Demir chuckled to himself then went inside, Dogan continued to observe the rest of the ascent. At the top Ghost sat with his legs slung over the edge, the glow inside comforting him. Half-shrouded by clouds, the white mountain to the north beckoned him. *Come climb me,* the half-forgotten nocturnal whisper said, *then you will feel true glory.*

The next morning the hoarse laughter of the Magister percolated through the Nidus; such an unusual sound that everyone who heard it felt compelled to investigate. Ghost beat Crooked to the bottom of the stairs but found Soraya already there, wrinkling her nose at the scene.

Roach sat cross-legged on the floor sorting gold, silver and bronze coins from a sack in his lap, and stacking them into little wonky towers as he counted them. He looked oddly larger and mature if such a thing were possible. The Magister sat in a chair behind him, head bowed and face in his hands, his shoulders quivering. When the stairs creaked with Crooked's arrival he looked up, red-eyed, noticed them, but looked straight back at Roach and started laughing again.

"Tell them! I want to hear it again!"

"Well," said Roach, not pausing in his calculations. "We followed a few snippets of information that a caravan of Han dancers would be leaving the city after a very successful run of performances. A rumour from a credible source suggested they would be covertly transporting more than just their usual takings."

"Elaborate! Enunciate! Elucidate!" The Magister slapped his thigh. "You're taking all the fun out of it."

Roach looked up and raised an eyebrow. "I'm not a storyteller, and in any event, I'll tell my tale in any way I see fit."

The air left Ghost and Crooked's lungs at the same time. They stared at the Magister, awaiting his inevitable violent retribution.

The Magister leaned back and waved a hand. "Don't leave out the good bits though."

"As I was saying," said Roach. "The caravan had already received a visit by a couple of Gavras goons. As far as we can ken they failed to get into the treasure chest in the lady dancers' caravan. Upon attempting to retreat were met by an angry—and apparently effective—bodyguard who dispatched them both."

"Now the good bit," cried the Magister.

The corner of Roach's mouth quirked although he was clearly trying not to smile. He composed himself. "Entering the caravan undetected was so trivial I won't mention it."

"The unassailable chest that the best of Oikos Gavras failed to penetrate!"

Roach wagged a finger to the Magister. "The chest had a vaguely interesting mechanism, but only for a few moments."

"The guard!" The Magister leapt to his feet and began to dance around the room with an invisible partner, humming a rural melody.

Roach now failed to keep his own grin under control. "I had forgotten to bring a dagger, focused as I was on the supposedly unbreachable chest. So it was necessary to improvise in order to dispatch the brutal Han warrior."

"A fan!" shouted Zarbenus, throwing his arms wide. "He killed the guard with a lady's painted fan!"

Ghost stared at Roach, then at Soraya whose own icy nonchalance had melted perceptibly, and she chewed on her lip to avoid laughing.

"Roach no more!" The Magister dragged the hero of the day to his feet. "Fan! Fan! Henceforth you shall be known as Fan!"

Fan—once the apprentice thief known as Roach—swept a bow. Then was nearly knocked off his feet as Ghost and Crooked wrestled to be the first to embrace his success.

"My earnest congratulations, Fan," said Soraya. She tipped her head to him, and then left the boys alone.

"Wine," shouted Zarbenus. "And lots of it! Tomorrow we shall nurse hangovers to match this epic tale."

And they did.

† † †

More weeks passed and the winter days seemed so short. They rose in the dark, woken by their bellies, struck flint to steel for their lamps and shuffled bleary-eyed downstairs to breakfast in silence. There seemed little else to do but practice the knacks they had been given. Sometimes Fan gave the younger thieves a word or two of advice. Soraya provided impromptu lectures if politely asked—her stipulation being that they call her "Miss" when they addressed her. Periodically the Magister took one of them away for a few days. When they returned they refused to discuss what had happened, but when their eyes were bright the others knew some thieving had been done and they had earned some praise, no matter how faint. Soraya and Fan seemed immune from the Magister's criticisms, at least in front of the others. Crooked and Foul increasingly took the brunt of his wrath. The last time Crooked had returned with bandages on his hands. Everyone knew what that meant. Failure was disciplined by a thrashing to the palms. It wasn't the pain that they feared, it was the disappointment in his face when he meted out the punishment. The pain faded faster than the guilt of letting him down. Since then Crooked turned quiet and withdrawn, even his glances at Ghost were tinged with sadness rather than disappointment.

Scab returned bearing a sack flecked with brown stains and an ebullient attitude. If anything he was more at ease than the Magister who watched him from a distance, face inscrutable in the shadows.

"Cakes for everyone." He emptied the sack and tipped glazed rolls across

214

the table. The motion made the significant blood-splatter that ran up his sleeves and across the front of his jerkin abundantly evident.

Foul snatched one up, sniffed it, then began to devour it. "You robbed a bakery? Wish I got such easy jobs."

"Actually," said Scab. "The job was to persuade a notoriously civic-minded baker to forget any significant details of a murder he happened to witness."

"He gave you cakes? You must have been very persuasive," said Foul between mouthfuls.

Scab shrugged and offered a double-baked cinnamon apple tartlet to Soraya. "He's permanently forgotten everything, including how to breathe, so I thought these little fancies shouldn't go to waste."

The half-chewed pastry fell out of Foul's mouth and rolled apologetically across the table. "A dead man touched these?"

Ghost snatched it up before it could bounce onto the floor. "Not something that bothers me. If you don't want it I do."

Scab's knife buried itself in the wooden table beside Ghost, freezing him in place. "I didn't offer them to you. They're what I call friendship cakes. And you don't have any friends."

No-one else met Ghost's gaze. He turned his head looking for support. Fan beckoned Soraya and the pair left in silence, Crooked stared out the window, Foul turned over each of the pastries until one appealed to him and he ate it with an artificial air of concentration. Scab continued to glare, unblinking, until the anger bubbling in Ghost's belly forced him to walk away before he started something that could only end with blood.

From then on Ghost stopped trying to fit in. If no-one wanted him then it was just like old times. No need to let anyone disappoint you if you didn't trust them in the first place. The tiny store-room he now slept in was never disturbed by any of the others. During the brief daylight hours he kept himself to his own plans, only returning to the company of the others on mornings that the Magister was expected to appear. A week of total ostracisation. His isolation moving him in stages through depression, irritation and finally into a simmering state of tempered aggression. As the late dawn struggled to warm the grey, the Magister emerged from the shrinking shadows.

"And now we practice true lock-craft. These mechanical locks are like nothing you've seen so far. You can only practice on the same mechanism so many times before you know the positions of the tumblers by heart and the skill is taken out if it. And what fun is that? I've had these locks specially made for you by a genius toymaker to the kings of the east. Consider yourselves very fortunate indeed. All you need to do is spin the cog at the top and it will jumble the tumblers so each time you work a new configuration."

Zarbenus tipped up a bag over the table and out tumbled brass cubes a palm's width on each side. They scattered the empty plates and bowls and each of the children reached for one, their faces bright with excitement. The cubes looked to be deeply engraved but on closer inspection tiny screws could be seen fixing the different parts into place. On the top a fat brass cog with a familiar iron-lipped keyhole on one side.

Ghost twisted the cog on the top of his cube and it ticked and clicked before the cog stopped moving. He looked up at the Magister.

"Get practising my thieflets. My indulgence for your inadequacies runs like the last trickle of blood from a dying man's chest. Soraya and Fan have shown you what you must strive to achieve."

He paused to glare at Foul and Scab, then a sneer reserved for the attention of Ghost, sitting alone and apart. Finally, and most cutting, he glanced at Crooked, then shook his head and walked away.

† † †

Shutters drawn against the night, the almost empty room at the bottom of the house lay cool and silent. The light from the stump of a single candle

216

danced with each soft breath taken by Ghost hunched over the lockbox, tense concentration on his face and tools poised.

"What are you doing up so late?"

The metal cube clattered on the table as Ghost startled. How quickly he'd become accustomed to no-one speaking to him, or simply leaving the room whenever he entered. "I da hear you come in, Magister."

Zarbenus scratched the side of his nose. "It will be many years, if ever, that you'll manage that. But you did not answer the question; aren't the activities of the day tiring enough for you?"

Ghost looked back at the mechanical lockbox, spun the cog on top and then picked up his tools.

"I want to be as good as you, Magister. Watch this."

He paused for a moment, his eyes closed. Breathing slowly and deeply he leant forward and delved into the lock; fingertip pressure and deft twitches. The mechanism clicked and the lock sprung open.

Ghost grinned at his master. "What do you say to that, Magister—pretty good, huh?"

Zarbenus pursed his lips. He picked up a coil of climbing rope and tied Ghost's ankles together. He tossed the other end of the rope over a roof beam, and then puffed as he hauled the weight until the silent boy dangled head down in front of the lockbox. The Magister tied off the rope and knelt down so his face was level with Ghost.

"Keep practising." He blew out the candle and drifted with the smoke out of the darkened room.

† † †

He is being chased, he can't see who, he's just running and can hear them behind them; his fear makes him angry. He gets ready to fight then he trips over the body of a small cold child with livid marks on its neck. The flesh yielding under his fingers as he choked the life out. *Hush,* She said. *It's our secret.*

Ghost woke shivering and clammy. As he lay in the dark, knowing it was just a nightmare he still felt sick. Fear that they'd find out what he's really like. Sleep eluded him and when dawn came it was a relief that he didn't have to lie in bed anymore. He needed someone to talk to, but how could he trust anyone in the Nidus with his deepest fears? Someone came to mind; someone who'd asked to share his secrets, and as far as Ghost could see, had no agenda of his own.

CHAPTER 19:
SOME WORDS OF ADVICE

Early that morning Ghost slipped out of the Nidus, his only company the song of a robin greeting the new day. He took a light pack and felt confident he could make his way down the mountain in only a few hours if he hurried, thanks to a hidden shortcut.

He tried to sort out his thoughts as he walked, the cool air soon melting away and a sheen forming on his face as the sun rose. Zarbenus had no rules about his wards wandering where they fancied, so he wouldn't be missed or cause an alarm even if he was absent for a few days. And the days out wandering on his own had started to outnumber those he spent in the Nidus. The others didn't like his company? He'd repeated to himself how little he cared so many times that eventually he believed it. Most of the time.

I'm big enough to do what I want. I'm not a baby anymore.

She had whispered he shouldn't go. That he didn't need anyone else. No-one wanted him, except Her. She would be his only friend. Weeks passed, rejected by the others. Days without speaking to anyone; backs turned when he tried, giggled conversations that stilled when he walked in. Of course, he didn't trust Her, not a hair's breadth. She was just someone else who wanted to use him, but the lonelier he got the louder came the voice. A voice that spoke to him from the darkest corners of his room at night, deep in the recesses of his dreams.

He passed through the village that he so frequently haunted for food or for frolics, waving to familiar faces as he passed, amused by their obliviousness. The path grew more level from here so he picked up his pace until he breathed deeply, enjoying the fresh air, the smell of the pines and the feeling of the way shortening under every stride. After an hour's brisk walk Ghost heard the faint hiss of rushing water, and he veered toward it. He snatched up a handful of pine needles and crushed them in his palms. The path turned and coiled as it crawled down the mountainside, but a stream had cut through the bedrock over the centuries forming a narrow ravine that the water trickled down; tiny glistening arcs as it fell down the natural steps. The channel descended into a mist of spray and twilight, the bottom lost in the mist. Ghost went down as easily as if it were a ladder. He emerged at the other end with his hair plastered to his face but invigorated.

Pride bubbled in him that his private shortcut pared the best part of a day's boring hike from the journey. It felt good to be the master of his own... what? Destiny? Those musings were cut short after a few hours when he passed through the fields that lay on the route to the *Grey Mouse*. He pushed open the door carefully, hoping to surprise the old innkeeper. The main room lay empty, neatly swept with all the chairs and tables set in an orderly fashion. The hearth was stacked with fresh wood, and in front a tabby and a tortoiseshell cat curled companionably. They regarded him with glinting amber eyes. He took another step and fairly jumped out of his skin when a pair of hands grabbed him from behind.

"Got you! You'll never sneak up on me," said Kanesh, chuckling with pride.

Ghost wriggled out of his grip, grinning broadly. "I've come to steal a cup of ale from you!"

"Splendid. I'd worked up something of a thirst myself. Here, take a pew at the bar and I'll fix us up."

Kanesh busied himself with the taps and soon laid out a foaming pitcher and two wooden jars. He poured, tapped his rim to Ghost's and took a long draught. Wiping the froth from his moustache he raised an eyebrow to

Ghost. "Well, go on then."

Ghost picked up his jar, touched it to his lips, then put it back down. "I've been trying to work out what Magister wants. And if I want the same thing. I da ken he'd care if we killed each other."

"Listen up, young man. You're just too young to make judgements about a man's character when you've known so few. Me? I've been a thief, a mercenary, a corsair, even a taverna keeper."

He barked a short laugh at his own joke.

"I've fought for money, for love, and for hatred. I've buried brothers, enemies, lovers and more than one loyal dog. I'm not saying you'll live a life like mine, but be sure to know that you'll do things that you are too ashamed to remember later, aye, and ones that you wouldn't believe yourself brave enough to do either."

Ghost stared blankly past the taverna keeper's shoulder.

"How do you forget the bad things?"

"You never forget. But you cope, and it slowly gets easier. What did you do?"

Ghost looked away. "Something unforgivable."

Kanesh nodded, familiar with the glassy look in Ghost's face. "Ah, that. No, that one never gets easier. It does different things to different men. Some it turns their very core to blackened evil, yet others fight to redeem themselves their whole life. Some just go mad with the grief."

"What will happen to me?"

"Only you can find out, lad. You're on your own on this one," said Kanesh.

"The Magister says we're always alone." Ghost thought about the twins, and about Crooked's weakness. How could he call someone a friend when they weren't there for him?

Kanesh wiped his dishrag absentmindedly across the surface of the bar. "Trust is hard, I'll give you that, but that one, your master; he never trusted as much as a dog. Maybe you could start there. I've had some powerful strong friendships with dogs, and remember them better than men I fought alongside a dozen times. Try it sometime; but remember, trust is earned, day by day. Put yourself in their shoes, think about how things look like from their side."

Ghost frowned. Crooked was just scared, why blame him for that? He knew what it felt like. He forced a smile.

"I'll try it sometime," said Ghost.

"Good man." Kanesh squinted at him. "That wasn't the whole thing. Spit it out."

Ghost rubbed his palms together, fears and desires all jumbled up inside him. "Everyone hates me."

"I don't. So not everybody. I reckon you need to work out them that you care about hating you, and them that you just don't. Some problems can be fixed with a simple shrug."

"I hate it there. Can I stay here with you? Just for a bit?"

Kanesh screwed up his face, then rubbed at his wrinkled brow. "I've got nothing for you, nothing to offer. Best you stick where you are—for now—just until you're a bit older and have some kind of idea what it is you've been put here to do with your life. Until then, well, probably best if you see what you can get out of that disreputable rogue."

"But you can teach me instead!"

"No!" Kanesh pounded his fist on the bartop, then shook his head as he relaxed his fingers. "I got nothing to teach you save the pouring of tankards and rolling drunks out of the door. Go back to your Magister. I'm sure he has a plan for you, even if you don't see it."

"I'm sick of other people deciding what happens to me. I want to make my own choices. I don't know what I'm supposed to do... Do I have a destiny? People say things like it's the will of the gods."

Kanesh rolled his eyes to the ceiling. "The will of the priests you mean."

222

"That's blasphemy!"

"Only if the gods are real," said Kanesh.

Ghost chewed his lip as he pondered. "You ken they aren't?"

"Well, I've seen many a strange thing in my time, but nothing stranger than folk themselves. Even your master believes the Night Mother grants him supernatural abilities," said Kanesh, smirking.

"I liked the idea that the Goddess watches over us. A goddess I mean," added Ghost, tripping up over the words.

Kanesh looked sideways at Ghost. "A goddess? There's a few to choose from, but I digress."

He topped up his cup, took a sip, then placed it on the table, sliding it forward and back as if seeking for the correct spot to rest it. "Maybe she does and maybe she doesn't. Seems to me I don't hear much about what she wants from us, only what her priests want. And I've always found it funny that the goddess who ruled before the age of strife we poor mortals live in, was driven out by gods and priests. And now she has a priesthood. Tell me boy, how many women priests have you seen, eh?"

"I... well..."

"Funny the way these things work. I never quite understand them, myself," said Kanesh. "Though if something doesn't make sense to me, well, I question if it's real."

Ghost frowned at him. "You're telling me it's all lies? But what... what about destiny?"

"Destiny? Well, that's a hard one. I reckon destiny is something you make for yourself, by your actions and your choices. Like the great legends, all of them had to fight 'till their last breath and still they weren't beaten— that's what makes them a legend. They earned their destiny, gods or no."

"But if the gods aren't real..."

Kanesh held up a hand. "Wait up. I never said that... not exactly. It's not up to me to say they are real—are they real to you? They sure are real to some folks. Real enough that they'd die for them. How much more real do you need than that?"

"So if the Goddess told me to find my destiny, told me where to find it and I went and looked, and sure enough it was there; what then?"

"Well I reckon," said Kanesh, draining his mug and wiping his moustache slowly with his fingertips. "I reckon then you'd know a great deal more about such matters than I do. I'm just an old taverna keeper trying to eke out a simple life in my waning years."

Tentative knuckles rapped on the taverna door. It creaked open to admit Orhan, the headsman of the local village, accompanied by two elderly women dressed in black save the brightly embroidered shawls across their hunched shoulders. Orhan snatched the tasselled crimson cap from his head and fiddled with it as he waited. When Kanesh looked up the headsman cleared his throat.

"*Karga*, might we beg some advice? The northern farms were burned and looted last night, but our lord has yet to reply to our messenger," he said.

"I ken you're more than that Kanesh. Much more," said Ghost.

"Am I really?" Kanesh laughed. He beckoned the headsman and his retinue to come in and take seats. "Now off to the prince of rogues before he misses you. I have more dreary tasks to attend to than the fun of jousting with your inquiring mind."

Ghost said his goodbyes then took the walk back through the fields, past the village and up the mountain much slower. He spent a long time sitting under the shade of an old apple tree, eating so much of the fruit it left him feeling queasy. He thought about the injustice of other people making plans for him, or plotting against him. Maybe it was time for him to make his own decisions.

† † †

Drinking a jar of water before he lay down to sleep was Ghost's trick for waking early, a bit of hedge magic common enough amongst the Tahtakale performers. He screwed up his eyes trying to decide if he could manage another ten minutes curled under his blanket, but as usual his bladder betrayed him. Stifling a yawn he sat up, feeling with his toes for the much repaired and still falling-apart bundles he creatively referred to as his shoes. The holes in the wall let through Crooked's somnolent sighs and half-murmured words from the next room. No longer friends, but Ghost's initial anger and betrayal had faded to a dull sense of injustice which he forced from his mind as he stepped around the creakiest floorboards and out the door.

From the top of the stairs he heard the tap-tap-tap of the bubbling pot Soraya had going over the fire, simmering the oats until they were soft enough to make a meagre, but welcome breakfast. For all her bravado Ghost could picture her right now; nose wrinkled as she stirred the pot, all her attention on her work. Unless he made a stupid mistake she'd never hear him. But he heard another sound. Someone was also stirring in the twins' room; the groan of a floorboard then the indistinct mumble of whispered words.

† † †

Dogan stepped out onto the hallway, running his fingers through his hair, smoothing it away from his eyes. Other than Soraya clattering away downstairs he seemed to be the only one up and about as Demir had rolled straight over into a second slumber. This morning breeze was chilly though. That stupid window above the stairs, the frame warped so that even when pulled tight the wind whistled around it. Simply an invitation to every insect for miles around to bother him as he slept.

Dogan pulled it closed, frowning as he did so. Barbarians. It was like living with barbarians who couldn't even shut doors and windows behind them. He wasn't going to miss any of them when they were all gone. All of them.

The window didn't even let in much light during the day as it was mostly obscured by the dark rock of the ruined fortress the Nidus slumped against. Dogan's grumbles receded as his stomach took precedence and rumbled. He decided to follow his nose downstairs and see if Soraya was in a good mood, and if he could get something to eat from her with a few flattering words.

† † †

Ghost kept his teeth firmly clenched against his bottom lip as he hung from the knotted fingers of the wisteria. His giggles spasmed against his lower belly. Sneaking past any of the others was fun, doing it to one of the twins was... like twirling in circles in a sunny field; dizzying, spiralling elation. Not that he expected to get away with it much longer. Last night lying awake he'd made the decision that had been creeping in his mind for weeks. Creeping, growing more malevolent. No longer would he run from those that threatened his life. Better to act first, without mercy. And the consequences? Don't get caught.

Vines were easy to grasp, but in this pre-dawn gloom he risked a slip with every grip. Reaching to the side his fingers clutched for the grooves between the great blocks of stone. The weak grey light faded away as he looked for his next hold. He'd been sneaking out to practice when no-one had been watching for weeks now and his route was almost perfectly memorised. First, the section that seemed to be an impossible start; dangle down as far as you can, toes slipping against smooth stone. Then release your fingertips for the heart-dropping moment of falling free, just to collide with the narrow ledge hidden under the overgrowth. Weeks of practice and it was so familiar he could have walked it in complete darkness. He panted for a moment, settling himself and rubbing his damp palms through his hair to dry them.

Ghost slid his foot to the side to begin the horizontal traverse and nearly fell to a bloody death on the boulders below as his sole slipped off a ledge that suddenly ceased to exist. Pulse throbbing in his temples he centred his awareness. Pushed out all external thoughts or distractions, willed his world to be about grip and balance and the confidence he would not fail. When his breathing slowed he opened his eyes and stared at the ledge.

It wasn't there anymore. Crude chisel marks and torn vines proved abundant evidence—someone had purposefully hacked away at the stone. Somebody knew.

Without the ledge it would be nearly impossible to make it to the flinty boulders that clustered above the scree slope. If he landed on the loose gravel he'd slide all the way down. Bumps and scrapes would be the worst he'd suffer physically, but a lot of noise and being spotted wasn't a desirable part of this particular endeavour. Sizing up the distance to the boulders he knew it wasn't too far, but the trick would be the landing. Ghost knew how to do it without failing. The problem was it was going to hurt.

Not allowing his fear time to present its case against such reckless abandon, he jumped. Trying so hard to keep his eyes open for the impact. He crumpled against the rocks, sternum burning as the air whacked out of his lungs. Nearly losing the tip of his tongue as he cracked his chin. He grinned as he clung there, finding the smear of his own blood on the stone vaguely amusing. Whoever had tampered with the ledge in an effort to stop him was going to be very disappointed, assuming they ever found out. When the last tremors of shock faded from his body, and he felt he could trust his fingers again, he began to climb up and veer to the side.

The limestone overhang was draped with long-dead strands of creeping ivy and sad, dishevelled clumps of yellow sawgrass. Ants filed along highways of activity, oblivious to the predations of the lizards that basked there on brighter days. There wasn't much more than a glimmer of morning now, but the memory of the translucent-bodied geckos feasting, sunbathing and fleeing for safety was large in his mind. It was over a year ago he'd been fired by the idea of capturing one of the little beasts and keeping it in his room to devour moths and other wrigglies that dared to disturb his nights. He'd pursued a fat one with determination, braving the unknown darkness as he thrust his arm into the cavity it had scurried into. Swallowing a trepidant shiver and imagining snakes and spiders sinking their fangs into his unprotected fingers, he quested within—the space behind the narrow cavity cavernous and cool. No sudden sharp pain and phantom jaws biting down. Nothing much of anything. He stuck his face up to the opening, grasses parting as he turned his head about, squinting. The gecko was to be a consolation prize of sorts. Something only he would have and a distraction from the perpetual worries of failing the Magister, or falling for a trap set by the twins. At least something living to talk to, even if it never talked back and just sat there, sticky tongue wiping bulbous eyes. If it thought that retreating to the furthest recesses of a narrow, dark hold would deter him... well, the fear was there. The conviction that the stones that had lain sleeping for a thousand years would creak and crumble and crush him the moment he trusted to their false air of solidity. Dogan would sneer at Ghost's childish terror if he ever found out, the barbs and insults (words, just words) cutting more deeply than a knife.

His head followed his arm and, wriggling like the reptile he pursued, he crawled inside.

Weeks of coming and going by this route had dulled his fears. He didn't like it but every time felt the sick annoyance at his own weakness, and the imagining of what the others would do if they knew his paranoia. Keeping that picture in his mind gave him enough courage to enter each time. He inched forward on elbows and knees, counting each breath until he reached one hundred, and knowing that at any moment he'd hear the faint drip of water as he drew close to his goal.

He moved aside the stones he'd placed to obscure the tunnel. Each time he'd gone through he'd kicked back any that had come loose and had used them to hide his route should anyone try to follow him. The crawlspace was narrow, the weight of the hillside above him a tangible, palpable, force of terror. It came in waves, his hands trembling and weak, breath short and tight until his self-disgust bolstered his courage and he could move forward. Each visit made the traversal more bearable; the conviction of his survival grew stronger and the imaginary endlessness grew shorter. There! The pale and fluttering glow that became cut stone blocks with flakes of candlelight glinting against them. Finally, he pulled his body out of the hole and lay on the smooth rock balustrade running high above the secret room.

An expansive space, a table laden with massive tomes, surrounded by chests, barrels and piles of bound and bulging sacks. The middle of the table bore a riveted and iron-plated chest with three hasp-locks holding it shut. Very nearly level with his hidden entrance, a chain thicker than his arm stretched across the ceiling, supporting an incongruous chandelier, all hooks and spirals and the stumps of melted candles.

To one side, nearly hidden by deeply layered shadows that never appeared to lessen no matter how many lights burned, an ancient statue of a woman, both palms raised—in supplication or in warning, he could not say. Her sculptor's passion was evident, her thin robe provocatively flaunting her full breasts and engorged nipples. Ghost's helpless adolescent arousal insufficient to quell the eldritch horror she instilled in him. With her broken keys lying in her lap and the cobwebs that obscured half her face, she'd terrified him during his first encounter; more so when the nightmares came, night after night.

† † †

"Kneel before me child, and pledge your soul to me," she said, words redolent with the love and the discipline of a strict mother. The others often mentioned their mothers before falling silent, lost in their own thoughts. Ghost could only draw on the faintest memories of warmth and security, no longer even sure if what he felt was a dream.

"I'm not your child!" He tried to turn, tried to run, but his legs stuck to each other. Stuck to the floor, webs binding him, choking him, restraining him.

"Give me your heart and I will give you the treasures of a thousand nations." Her thoughts reverberated in his skull, slicing and stabbing at him as he struggled to force them out.

"I don't want your treasures." His tongue laboured to move in a mouth filling up with sticky strands of silk.

"Give me your blood and I will make you the king of every land you can see from the highest mountain."

"A prisoner in a golden castle? Never!" Tiny spiders swarmed over him, climbing into his ears, up his nose, spinning silver strings across his eyes.

"Give me everything you have and everything you will be. I will make you my consort, and together we will rule the night. Serve me alone, and everything you desire will be but an arms-reach away. Dream it, and you shall have it."

Ghost wriggled his arms, leaden and dull, but the webs bound him and a thousand tiny spiders drew on their chains, dragging him to the base of the statue.

"Love me and you shall be free," said Hekate, mistress of the left-hand path, Queen of the Night.

"I hate you!" His tears burned his cheeks, the ignominy of his captivity worse than the helplessness. His flesh seared and melted, a pure agony one step from bliss.

"Love me!" Her words of command struck him like clubs. "Love me or die!"

✝ ✝ ✝

And every morning he woke twisted in his bedsheet, hair plastered across his face, damp and shaking. Finally, when his self-loathing overcame his fear he went down to the stream and turned over slick brown leaves, pungent with decay, and flipped smooth stones until he found what he was looking for. He stuffed a wriggling frog in his pocket and went to visit her. Palpable apprehension squatted in the clammy fetid air of the cave. Pulling out his throwing knife Ghost slit the head off the wriggling amphibian. He waited for a reaction from the stone woman, his palm wet with the creature's blood, then he laid it at her feet, and watched her lidless gaze intently. When the corpse of the frog finally stopped kicking Ghost felt sure the corners of the statue's mouth moved the tiniest fraction and the death-chill in the room receded.

Weeks had passed since his last nightmare and his regular offerings to the statue of Hekate kept them at bay. Today only a stout pillar of amber wax spluttered and smoked on the table. He knew it meant there had been a visitor recently and he had to trust this meant he had some time to work before they might return. The candle was regularly refreshed, a sign the chamber's usual denizen visited regularly, but he'd never encountered them during his daytime visits. He knew whom he suspected but dared not come during the night to spy on them for fear of being discovered. His eyes moved across the room, deliberately indexing every object. The chair in front of the table had been tipped forward giving an air of impermanence. The faintest trace of a thread led from the chair to a squat wooden cannister nearby. A new trap. And the flagstone for the first step of the stairs that conventionally gave access to the chamber looked to have been recently replaced, its layer of dust betraying faint brush marks. Another trap. The others looked familiar, but he knew it would be the single one he failed to spot that would kill him, spying new ones did little to calm his nerves.

As he focused on breathing regularly he unshanked the rope tied around his waist. The loose end he held between his teeth then he tested the strength of the chandelier chain; nearly perfectly rigid. He inched forward, one leg hooking the chain behind him, the other dangling free for balance. Ghost made his way along the gently swaying bridge until he'd reached the chandelier and the centre of the room. He tied his rope with a good fisherman's hitch, twisted loops around his arm then lowered himself headfirst down the rope. Inverted face hanging in front of the armoured chest he pulled a wire probe from his jerkin and lightly touched the keyhole of the first lock. Vague stickiness as the wire moved against wrought iron. He brought the probe close to his face and sniffed it. A faint aromatic pine scent, nothing else, but he knew what an effective base for all sorts of lethal poisons the tacky gum made. The tension in his brow responsible for his headache pulsed as he mentally listed off the toxic agents that applied well from skin contact or inhalation. He touched the second lock, recoiling instinctively as he heard the chirr of a spring taking on tension. Physical trap of some kind, either blades or darts most likely. Gently tapping of the housing of the third lock revealed a similar response, the wire of his probe vibrating in sympathy with the hidden mechanism.

Then as he paused, planning his next move, something unexpected and new from his repeated exploration of this mysterious cavern—voices burbling and indistinct coming from whatever space lay beyond the stairs that led down here. Without a thought he pinched out the light of the single candle, followed instantly by a pang of regret and self-loathing for the first time he'd left a trace of his presence, and the black swallowed him.

In the darkness Ghost heard two people whispering, insistently, arguing, drawing closer. Just the echoes of human tones, yet he knew who they would turn out to be. Although no shred of light reached him, he shut his eyes. Breathing, concentrating, shutting out the fear he would be discovered. His fingertips grazed the locks one after another, anticipating, preparing. The slightest wobble of the left-most lock, the one with the sticky residue, when he touched either of the other two. So, wired together for a special surprise from the owner of the secret cavern. Three locks, two hands, and only moments left to act. He took a deep breath.

† † †

Ghost had been the first to fight the sickening swoon, recovering faster after each monthly dosage until that morning, dizzy and nauseous he realised the others had all fallen unconscious and he alone was fighting to keep awake.

Zarbenus leaned closer, taking in the wavering lips and the fluttering eyelids that covered rolling crescents of bloodshot white.

"Did you take the whole dose, boy?"

Ghost's head lolled forward then jerked up before falling down again. His lips rubbed together, then pursed, then his jaw fell slack. His blinking slowed as he centred on the Magister, the sole steady object in a room that wouldn't stop spinning. He wheezed a cough and as his vision steadied he nodded.

"Yes... Magister."

Zarbenus sat back and scratched his chin through his scruffy beard.

"Well done, boy. Lie back and rest now. You've done enough for today."

Ghost slowly shook his head and when his voice came it was weak and strained.

"No..."

"Hmm? There is no need to push any harder. You have already excelled all your compatriots."

Ghost dragged his arms from his lap and rested them on the edge of the table. Panting unevenly, a whistling in his throat as he forced each pained breath, he forced himself up onto one knee. Then swaying wildly, he pushed himself up onto his feet, hands gripping on the table.

The Magister steepled his fingers. Ghost looked at him, a twitching starting to form at the side of his mouth, then collapsed his knees and heaved up on the floor. The Magister watched him until the retching had stopped and Ghost wiped his mouth against his sleeve.

"Progress is one thing, boy, but push too hard and you will kill yourself. Remember, we all have limitations. Recognising them and avoiding those situations is one of the skills that will save your life."

Zarbenus flowed upright and left through the front door. Ghost wrinkled his nose at the hot acid fumes of his own vomit and turned his head to look at the door the Magister had left through. His hands spasmed with cramp and the stabbing headache that threatened to split his skull throbbed just as hard, but the twitching at the corner of his mouth had become a one-sided grin.

I'll be better than you.

† † †

Each second drew into an infinity of indecision, and the absolute surety that through the black veil that draped his senses, She—that stone figure—was watching him. *Impress me, awe me, love me.* Hairs prickled on his forearms. He inhaled deeply, screwing eyelids shut, palming tools from inside his jerkin. Unerringly he reached for the middle and right-hand locks simultaneously.

Soft steps sounded somewhere above. The other way in, the stairs, the route the master of this domain used. Ghost never climbed those stairs, no matter how many times he visited the apothecary shrine. His route was his alone and the thought of something that belonged only to him, a secret of his very own, filled his chest with a fierce glow. The voices, recognisable now for certain, urging caution, and a sickly jaundiced glow, bobbing erratically and casting leaping, writhing shadows. The twins entered, stopped when they saw the ransacked chest on the table, and Demir groaned.

"You promised it would be here," said Demir.

Dogan, carrying the lantern, approached the table, peered at the open chest with surprisingly few vials in such a large container. Most of the remaining jars were clearly labelled with their useful but mundane contents; apple vinegar, two-needle pine resin, fiery Hellenic liquor. He shoved them aside and swore.

"Someone beat us to it," he said. "Maybe Zarbs left it like this, or maybe... Damn it, who am I kidding? I know it was him. That irritating whoreson. He's doing too well. We're going to need to do something about him. Soon."

Demir tilted his head to his brother. "Ghost?"

"No, I mean Scab... Who do you think I mean, you idiot? Of course it was Ghost. No-one else would try something like this on their own."

Dogan leaned close to the sprung locks. The poison trap had erupted and a glistening ichor still oozed from it. He sniffed the residue then flinched back, rubbing his nose.

"If he took a blast of this to the face, though, we won't need to worry about him. Ever again."

Demir nodded, a smile forming on his lips. "You really think so?"

Dogan shrugged. "Who knows? We might get lucky. For now, let's scarper. These will have to do." A faint tinkling sound like vials chinking against each other. "Scab is always messing with the poisons. No-one will think twice if he has a little bad luck and doesn't wake up."

"Except Ghost. He never accepts anything," said Demir, his voice growing fainter as he moved away. "Maybe he'll help Scab?"

His brother cleared his throat and spat noisily. "I'll have to come up with something else to deal with him if by some chance he survives, and isn't blinded or crippled, or something good like that."

"Have you prayed to her? She comes in your dreams with answers."

Dogan turned his head to look at his brother who nodded toward the statue of Hekate. "Your faith in her unsettles me. I don't need to trust anyone else. Me and you. That's it."

"Baba trusts her and so do I," said Demir.

Dogan rubbed his brow with his knuckles, inhaling deeply. "Stop calling him that you imbecile. I told you he's trying to twist your mind. Just pretend to believe him like I do and you'll be fine."

"There's nothing pretend about Her! Everything she promises comes true. I trust her with my life," said Demir.

"Then take care that trust doesn't betray you, brother."

Their words faded as they climbed the stairs out, taking the only light with them. Ghost sprawled on the narrow balustrade, fighting to control his convulsions, but as soon as he couldn't hear the twins he laboriously crawled back into his secret tunnel. If he was to die he preferred to expire alone and undiscovered. No-one would find his corpse until the stench grew too much to miss. The sickness rolled in, irrepressible like a storm at sea. All his confidence swept away. Crumbling as the breath stills in his throat. Ribs flexing then locking wide in reflexive spasm. The screaming of the sea in his ears as the shrill siren of asphyxia wailed at him. His eyes burned and the knuckles of his hands felt like they were being flayed from his bones. Vomit churned in his throat, he fought to control it but it surged out, splattering his clothes, filling him with shame, then panic and weakness. The moment's relief from expelling the toxins all too brief as another wave sloshed inside him, red splodges wobbled in the dark periphery of his mind, and with a last horrified thought that this time he wouldn't make it, everything sunk away into death.

Ghost woke cold, clammy and shivering, his mouth crusted with bile. The deep, wearying, frailty that made each breath dry and painful enveloped him. So he'd survived again. His hands twisted and knotted and each attempt to flex them was greeted by a thousand burning needles running up his forearms. Hands could wait. He sucked at fetid, dusty air to heave some oxygen into weary lungs that just wanted to stop fighting and slide back into the crypt's embrace. Ghost forced his elbows against the ground, and inch by inch dragged himself down the tunnel. A golden glow formed ahead of him and as he drew nearer he could hear a crow scolding its neighbours. Life burgeoned outside as a troubadour-cricket merrily serenaded prospective lady-crickets. Just a few more yards and he'd make it out of this black and chilling netherworld. It felt like an hour passed as he fought to push aside the sickness, demanded another few inches from the dull, lifeless appendages that propelled him, vain promises to himself that this would be the very last time he endured this self-inflicted contrition of weakness. When his fingers made it to the opening and the sun's rays teased, stroked and caressed them. He laid his head down in the grit and strands of dead moss, and without a single thought he slept again.

The shadows had grown long and in the skies above a cloud of starlings chattered through their evening symphonic society. Ghost's parched throat hurt to swallow, but he'd regained some clumsy control over his fingers again and breathing no longer felt like his ribs were splintering into his lungs. He wiped his lips as flakes of noxious, cracked vomit fell away, then he patted his jerkin. The vials he'd thrust there as he fled the chamber were intact. The faint chink as they moved against each other rang as loud to him as a clarion trumpet of victory. He started to chuckle but it was quickly overcome by dry retching. When that passed—despite the nausea and lethargy—he grinned. He laid out the collection of tubes and miniature flasks, examining the scrawls and symbols that marked each one. Reading was for him more of a matter of recognising swirls and twists than following an alphabet, but it was good enough for his needs. He moved three of them to one side, a satisfied glow in his belly growing stronger than the bone-weary sickness of the toxins in his system. The first, a tiny glass jar sealed with wax and containing a white powder, its label in a strange and unfamiliar script but the fragments of dried seeds within were enough to identify its contents. Zarbenus must have paid handsomely for something that had travelled so far from the Indies. The second prize, a copper tube wrapped in goatskin held sliced sections of mandrake root—the smell so distinct Ghost did not need any help identifying it. Either the scent of cat's piddle was recognisable, or Kanesh had secret stashes of mandrake hidden around his tavern. A derisive snort at childish memories; here was the treasure worth more to him than a purse of jewels and gold. The final vial, smaller than a pea, and hidden in a secret cavity beneath a green soapstone mounted in a cheap silver ring, was the prize of the collection. He knew what he wanted to find as he pried over the compartment. As if, by pure force of will, he could create a tiny stash of Dead Man's Coins—the flat, circular fruits that when dried looked just like the ferryman's fare on the closed eyes of a corpse. Just a few grains of the painstakingly prepared red berries would put a man to sleep. A few more grains would ensure that man never woke up again.

Ghost's head drooped when he saw the faintly sparkling dust within. Not the lethal poison he sought, and with that realisation he felt himself falling, his plans for revenge disintegrating around him. Anger followed, the cruel injustice of it all. His hand closed on the ring, then his arm drew back to throw the hateful signet of failure as far away as he could.

Sparkling like the tiniest flecks of gold and fragments of ground pearl.

He shook his head. Ridiculous. If it truly was that legendary concoction then his luck had turned to some kind of celestial benediction. Kingdoms had changed hands for the possession of notes simply rumoured to hint at its formula. Emperors had flooded fields with the blood of their armies to gain even a single dose. Hope rose in him, he shoved it aside, and yet it sang to him.

Looking at the ring in the palm of his hand, he eased it open again with his thumbnail. Tiny stars winked up from the soft grey powder within. If he'd been told an hour before he might find this treasure he'd have killed to get it, without remorse or pity. All those times Zarbenus dosed them with toxins, carefully building their resistances. That was all you did for soldiers, expendable if they fail. This was what you did for emperors. This was why the Magister's hand was so steady when he measured out the treatments, no fear that a careless mistake would send him to his grave. This was true power. But the glorious swirling dreams growing in his mind kept glancing down to the muttering, nagging wretch at their side. His conscience, quiet but insistent, tugging at his sleeve.

He came here for revenge, he found instead a restitution for all he had suffered. Without even time to savour the serendipity, he realised that something else mattered even more. He needed to stop a murder.

Chapter 20:
Tolerance

A sense of dread filled the children on the mornings they came down the
stairs and found the Magister waiting for them, a single glazed bottle and the
tin medicine spoon on the table. The days of sickness that followed grew
shorter and the after-effects—the sudden attacks of dizziness, the weakness
that made their legs melt, and the dry throats that no amount of water
appeased—all these grew less with time. It became a chore and the Magister
tolerated their grumbles as they sat down at the table, muttering to
themselves, but passing the bottle and the spoon from hand to hand.

Now he sat behind the table, a satchel in his lap, arranging several potion
bottles side by side. The bottles variously bore engravings of skulls or of
serpents, or yellowed labels in the dense curving script the Magister
favoured. Their breaths came short and shallow, and they darted glances
between them, none daring to speak as the Magister set out his scales and
measuring spoons; laying each in a row according to size.

"Some of you are adapting marvellously quickly to your dosages, others,
less so," said Zarbenus.

He decanted a tiny volume of clear fluid from one vial into a miniature
clay cup, once a child's plaything, now a harbinger of pain and sickness. Two
drops pipetted from a bottle of milky fluid labelled "Venenum nux". A
pinch of grains from a calf's leather pouch. He frowned at these, tilting the
palm that held them to the light, squinting. Then he shrugged and tipped
them into the cup.

"You will be ecstatic to learn I've designed individual toxins for each of you. Scab, as you are all probably aware, has a wonderful tolerance to sanguine-targeting toxins. No doubt an artifact of his overly choleric disposition. Although this dosage would slay most adults, I believe you will find the effects most interesting."

Scab gnawed on the knuckle of his thumb. If he noticed Dogan's maniacal grinning he didn't say anything. But Ghost saw it. He saw Dogan's eyebrows raise when Zarbenus opened the leather pouch. He saw Dogan flinch when the Magister paused to examine the contents carefully, and he saw Dogan smirk when the grains were tipped into the cup for mixing. Understanding flooded into him fully formed. Recollections of the twins' words, unbeknownst to them when he lay hidden and listening in the shrine to Hekate. They were going to kill Scab in front of everyone and get away with it.

Cramping cold started in his groin, then coiled up through his guts like an ice wyrm. Dogan's, lips pulled back to show a rictus of bared teeth, gleeful, ravenous for death. Demir just watching Scab lean forward, anxiety written clear on both faces. Moments later the poison would go into Scab's throat. He would swallow, wince, cough, then choke. The twitching would be followed fast by spasms, each harder than the last, paralysing breathing, locking the jaw as his face turned red then blue and his eyes rolled up for the last time.

"I can take anything he can!"

Ghost pushed the Magister's hand away as Scab reached for the cup. He snatched it to his mouth and swallowed the contents in the same movement. A shadow passed across Zarbenus' face as it twisted into a malevolent wolf's maw. He slapped both palms against the table then dragged his nails down his face. He shouted, but the words were caught in the wind that whistled through Ghost's ears. The faces around him blurred as all the colours in his vision blended, swirled like grey smoke, then faded into black.

Birdsong and sunlight. Somewhere nearby meat roasted over a fire, spitting, crackling. The pain. Deep, cold, aching pain that flayed his flesh open from the bones out.

"I think he moved! He's not dead after all!" An excited young voice, almost shrill. Is that Scab?

A snort, deeper and older. Slow footsteps coming closer. "So it would appear. He really doesn't understand how to die."

Ghost tried to open his eyes but they wouldn't respond, lips muscles twitched without words forming. Please just end the pain. A hand daubed his brow, gentle and kind. It felt like his skin was being torn off with rusty steel. He tried to cry out, he tried to move as the torment in his flesh possessed him entirely.

"Drink, careful now. Just sip it." The deeper voice dribbled something sticky and sweet into Ghost's mouth. It burned and numbed at the same time, but the cool nothing slipped down his throat and his thoughts drifted away.

"Should keep him quiet for a few days as he heals. We'll see what's left of him then." That was the last thing Ghost heard.

✝ ✝ ✝

The door creaked in the dark and Ghost's eyes snapped open. Deep sleep into cold awareness in a moment, despite the onslaught of nausea. He rolled to his feet and crouched, fists clenched.

"Crooked?"

The pale grey light filtering through the slats of the shutters picked out two figures entering his room, softly closing the door behind them.

"No such luck," said Dogan. He twisted an old blanket in his hands. Twisted it tight like a hangman's rope. "Don't think he'll be back for a couple of days. We came to keep you company. Heard you were at death's door."

Ghost's heart thumped against his ribcage. "What do you want?"

"We told you before. If you make us look bad in front of the Magister, we need to punish you. Why would you interfere with us doing away with that little snot? Its nothing personal; all of you will face a reckoning, soon enough. Tonight's your turn."

Dogan walked past Ghost, turning his back on him. He paused by the shutters, then pushed them open. The night was cloudy but Ghost could see Dogan's grin when he turned his head.

"Brother, watch the door," said Dogan, and Demir grunted.

That was enough for Ghost. He launched himself at Dogan, headbutting him in the face, knocking the twisted blanket out of his hands. A yelp of pain, then a cough as Ghost hammered his knuckles into Demir's belly. Then something hard hit him on the side of his head and he went down, the world spinning and bile rising from his gut. Dogan grabbed Ghost's hair, wrenched his head around, spat in his face.

"You think I'm scared to hurt you?"

Dogan slammed Ghost's head against the floorboards. Darkness swallowed him. Then the tempest of pain began, blow followed by blow. His head, his chest, his arms. Something cracked, the sound startlingly loud inside his head. He vomited, choking and coughing on chunks, and the beatings stopped abruptly.

"We got to go," said Demir. "I think I hear Fan. Hurry."

The world swayed, ebbed and rolled. Footsteps. The door creaked once more.

"Next time," said Dogan. "Next time I'll kill you."

There was silence after that, only his own ragged breathing that hurt with every inhalation. And the shame, a palpable thing, squatting beside him and leering at his weakness. Whispering horrible truths in his ear. Alone. Helpless. Worthless. No sleep came for him that night.

Many hours passed, and with them eventually came the dawn. Sometime later he heard the banging of doors, of footsteps on stairs. The others going about their morning, no-one missing him, worrying about him. He didn't want to move, couldn't find a reason to, learning the language of the different pains in his body. His ribs and the side of his head spoke the loudest. At first, he listened, then he tired of paying any attention. That would be like letting Dogan win. He would ignore it all, and he tried to, little by little.

Early in the afternoon came a light tapping at his door, and he realised he must have dozed for a while. The door cracked open and Soraya peeked in, wrinkling her nose at the partly digested pool on the floor. She shook her head, then came in and sat on the bed beside him. From a bowl in her lap she cleaned most of the blood off Ghost's face. It didn't really hurt that much any more, just the dizziness if he tilted his head.

As she started to rise he grabbed her by the wrist.

"Don't tell anyone," said Ghost.

Soraya stared at him before replying. "It doesn't matter, they've been laughing about it downstairs for hours. Better get used to it."

She shook her arm loose from his grasp, collected the bowl and the bloody cloth, then left him alone.

✝ ✝ ✝

Soraya mounted the stairs, her thumbnail between her teeth. Since she'd received her name she'd been allowed into the Magister's room a few times; a privilege that marked her as different from the others. She reached the highest level within the Nidus, and faced the stone walls of the remainder of the castle's keep. Some ancient violence had smashed through the stone walls. Beyond lay the circular steps that rose up inside the ruined tower where the Magister spent so many hours alone. The cold and emptiness were physical forces, and her heart fluttered as she stepped into the gloom. Each step higher felt instead like a descent into the underworld, her padding feet silent on the worn and slippery stones. Her fears chewed at her throat, her breathing shallow. A single scuffed toe could send her tumbling down the staircase, bones smashing as she fell, to lie amongst the broken stones piled at the bottom. After an unnerving minute, she reached the top. Just a glimmer shone through an arrow slit at the summit; illuminating the single entrance there. The door stood slightly ajar. She knocked, but receiving no answer she pushed it open and stepped inside.

The room lay in near-total darkness, faintly smelling of dust, mould and the still thick air of a cave. Soraya felt the Magister's gaze on her even though she couldn't see him. An air of tense expectation loitered in the darkest corners. Every time she'd been summoned to his room she had broken the silence after losing her nerve. The memories rankled her deeply and she clenched her jaw tight.

Nothing happened. The intensity of a stare that she couldn't see chipped away at her confidence. Could he see her in the dark? As she waited she found the minuscule glow that nervously crept between cracks in the boards nailed over the single window. Using the edges of her vision, like looking for the pole star during the day, she made out the outline of the Magister. Sitting there motionless, anticipatory, predatory.

He spoke first. She felt no elation that she'd beaten him, but her shoulders loosened a smidgen.

"You are to observe the operations of Oikos Medea, from a discreet distance. The Doma will of course be aware of you; you're simply not in her class... yet. Regardless, you should endeavour to quietly learn about their conspirators and informants, their safe-houses and where they cache their valuables. See who gives orders and see who follows them, and most importantly learn who betrays whom and for what price."

"And the other Oikos, Magister?"

"They are not your concern. Any other questions?"

Soraya chewed her lip as she thought. She understood that the Magister desired both independence as well as subservience. It wasn't easy to walk that line.

"No Magister, I can begin at once but will return should I need direction."

"Events are moving apace in the city. My enemies have bold plans and my responses must be equally ruthless. Tell me, how many of your little friends will be ready?"

"Magister?"

"It's a simple enough question. My enemies are where I want them so I need everyone to deliver on their promise, or in some cases, lack thereof. My indulgence for those underperforming has come to at an end. They will be tested, they will be measured, and the chaff will be discarded."

"Like Fan and me?"

"The two of you perform adequately, though you have much to learn in order to deserve the opportunity I have gifted you. However, I am confident you will do so in your next missions. The others have not merited such faith."

Soraya's pulse thrilled of being included so intimately in his plans, and yet she couldn't help but fear the price he asked. She imagined a row of cold children's corpses. Lined up and awaiting new cairns at the foot of the cliff.

"But it'll be much more dangerous."

Zarbenus looked away, his brow creasing. "And yet so much more risky if I don't act; now and without mercy."

"They could die... Are they ready, Magister?"

"Sacrifices need to be made. It's all for Her glory, Her plan. What could be more important?"

Soraya rubbed her palms together, like they were already stained and she couldn't get them clean. "Is this Her will or yours?"

"There is no difference. For many years I have followed Her design, just as he tried before me. But unlike him, I will not fail Her. There is no price I will not pay. Can you say the same?"

The dreams were never clear instructions, never an inviolate mandate. They came as aspirations, swells of emotions, desires fiercer than hunger. They were the why and the because, never the how. That came later, in flashes of inspiration, sudden bursts of knowing absolutely and without doubt that she was on a divine path of righteousness.

Her breath was laboured as terror and zeal did battle in her chest. "Her will," said Soraya. "Always and forever."

Zarbenus stared at her, unblinking. Eyes that could tear away any lie, artifice or deception. She shivered in front of him. Naked and exposed as his eyes possessed her bare flesh. "You may go," he said.

She felt his attention move from her as if a physical weight had been lifted from her shoulders and so left him in the darkness and headed for the stairs, eager to start planning her next move. The light inside was golden and warm as the morning sun. Her joy was giddy, inescapable, and she laughed aloud. The others didn't have her faith. She knew the Magister's strategies were devious and impenetrable, but now she was to be given a chance to see beyond that veil. She swore that she would be worthy.

† † †

Zarbenus had seen her doubt fighting with her faith, and he knew she wanted to believe. Desperately needed to believe. Leaving the scrolls for her to discover had been a gamble, but what victory does not include the thrill of skirting failure? Her obedience would be absolute, and it mattered little whether she believed she acted for the love of her father, or for the will of the goddess he served. Assigning a domain for each Viper that proved sufficiently capable would determine once and for all their value. Encouraging their suspicions and conflicting loyalties simply ensured they would never combine those resources with enough cohesion to threaten his own plans. A soldier locked in mortal combat takes not a moment to ponder the distribution of an army, nor if an attack is but a feint or a ruse. What then is better than to keep both enemies and allies ensnared in action while the grand strategy unfolds?

CHAPTER 21:

CHILDREN OF HEKATE

"Come with me," said Fan, brushing woodchips from his sleeves as he entered the Nidus. He hung the felling axe on its peg by the door then paused to curl a finger at Ghost before heading up the stairs.

Ghost had never been in Fan's room before. The walls were draped with embroidered tapestries in vivid golds, greens and reds. Dragons fought with tigers and spear-wielding warriors wearing strange armour and fierce moustaches. His mattress was piled high with goat and sheep skins, with a turquoise and yellow Akkadian silk rug lying on the floor beside it. Over a dozen books nestled inside a cabinet beside the bed. On top sat three stumpy candles in front of a bronze statue of a shroud covered woman holding a key in one hand and a dagger in the other. The candles smelt of sweet beeswax, completing the air of almost wanton luxury compared to Ghost's quarters.

Soraya sat on the edge of the bed, fingering an ivory and silver scroll case in her lap. She looked up when Ghost walked in and nodded curtly. Cross-legged on the rug sat Crooked, Foul and Scab. Crooked, looking smug and amused, grinned at him.

"Good. We're all here. Now, I'd like to begin by calling to order this meeting of the Children of Hekate. Who wants to go first," asked Soraya.

"What's going on?" Ghost stood in the doorway, months of exclusion by the others leaving him wary and confused.

Fan eased his bulk down beside his bed and reclined back, hands behind his head. "I say the first order of business is to welcome Ghost and swear him in."

"Agreed," said Soraya. "For his actions, brave and selfless, in saving Scab's life, I propose he be permitted the rank of neophyte."

"I thought we said the whole ranks thing was too much," said Crooked. "None of us is in charge, we just agreed to work together. I understand that the whole thing was Temper's... sorry, Soraya's idea, but we never voted for her to be in charge."

"I'm not in charge," she said. "But someone needs to organise things or we'll never get anything done between all the bickering. This isn't a secret club for babies, we're here to honour the Night Mother and serve her will."

"As you see it," said Foul.

"Are you challenging me?" Soraya sprung to her feet. She stood tense in a combat stance, but Fan held up his hand.

"Enough," said Fan. "If I wanted to watch babies squabble I'd find an orphanage and steal their milk. We've got more important things to discuss here. Any of you who thinks otherwise is welcome do this without me. I've got better things to do with my time. Anyone?"

Foul glanced at Scab who shrugged and looked away. With a sigh, Foul stared at the ceiling. "Fine. You're in charge, Fan. Whatever you say."

Nodding his head Fan laid out pebbles on the rug. Six pebbles went together, two more off to one side. In the middle he placed a chunk of pink quartz that twinkled each time the candle flames moved.

"Six of us." He looked up at Ghost and beckoned him forward. "Yes, us. Sit down Ghost, this concerns you in particular. Six of us, two of them, and the Magister. As it stands the twins could never take us together, but they can easily pick us off, one by one. Until recently they never did anything serious that wasn't because Zarbenus told them to. Because of that, I've let things slide and didn't feel there was any need for me to get involved. For us to get involved." With the last statement, he turned his head to look at Soraya who gave a non-committal shrug.

Scab growled at Fan, then looked at Foul for support. "You get to choose when and if you get involved?"

"He does," said Soraya loudly. "He chooses what he does, I choose what I do, and you choose what you do. The question is; do we choose wisely, and then do we act appropriately? You are free to choose what you do, right?"

"Zarby would kill me if I didn't do what he wants," said Scab.

Soraya turned up her palms. "Would he? He never wavers from Hekate's Path, and we could all learn from that example. He says a lot of scary things, agreed, but that's just his way. I can't think of a time when he actually did anything really bad to any of us. Really bad, I mean."

"Timan," said Ghost.

She tilted her head as she looked at him; a model of composure if it weren't for the pale cheeks and parted lips. So much time had passed but everyone knew to be careful of mentioning his name around her. "What about him?"

"The Magister doesn't ever have to do anything if he can make someone else do it for him. Like Timan. He goes missing, and then Dogan mysteriously returns with Timan's knife, like some kind of trophy, and nothing is ever said?"

Soraya turned her head away so that no-one could see her expression. Fan slapped the ground beside him before any more questions could be asked.

"Ghost. Come in, shut the door and sit beside me. You'd been doing your own thing, and I thought it best to let you get on with it—while you weren't threatening anyone. What happened with Scab's poison changed my mind."

"They swapped his dosage! They were going to kill him and... I couldn't think of anything else to do."

Fan waved away Ghost's protestation. "I know. We were talking it over while you were out cold—there was plenty of time—and we reckon you've been building up your tolerances. Actually, that was Scab's guess; he's been taking a carbon purgative made from burned bread—an idea even Crooked was impressed with. We figured the twins didn't know that and somehow interfered with Zarbenus' dosages. How you knew is a separate question you can think about sharing with us. I won't push you on that, but you did save his life at the risk of your own. For that, for preserving one of the Night Mother's loyal subjects, we welcome you."

Did they have the dreams too? Is this why they followed Hekate? Ghost looked down at his hands still trembling faintly when he held them in a bad position. What did they think she would do for them? All she had done for him was to tempt him into danger and ruin his nights leaving him more tired in the morning than when he'd gone to sleep.

"Demir dreams about her too. He says she speaks to him. If that's right maybe she's on their side, not ours," said Ghost, changing the subject.

Soraya leaned forward. "She speaks to him in his dreams? Are you sure?"

"He said so, I heard him."

"And Dogan? Him too?"

"Nah. He was laughing at Demir when he heard about the dreams. If you are planning 'them and us' you might want to rethink if those two pebbles are actually as close as you think."

Soraya glared at Ghost. "You of all people are making excuses for that pair? After what they did to—"

Fan sighed and poked the pebbles with his finger. "None of us know what lies or half-truths he's fed them. There's still a chance they will come around. I think it would be best if everyone left those two for me to deal with. Especially you, Ghost."

"People say lots of things," said Foul. "It doesn't have to mean they'll actually do anything. Demir always—and I mean always—will take his brother's side. No question asked. When the time comes to fight they're going to do it together."

Fan covered his face. "Not this fight-to-the-death thing again. Why do you keep bringing it up?"

"Because Dogan always does," said Scab.

Soraya had recomposed herself and resumed her usual supercilious glare. "None of that is important. The Night Mother is. If we bring her glory she'll bestow her powers on us."

"The Magister says everything comes through him," said Ghost.

"Rubbish," said Soraya. "His powers come from her just the same. Anything he says different is only him trying to control you. And you don't need to believe him. Just try talking to her. I—"

"You have the dreams too?" Ghost felt the darkness open up inside him, the loneliness and isolation, reaching for something shared and comforting.

Soraya raised her chin, keeping her expression blank. "And that is why we are inviting you in. Your actions were inspiring. Pledge your soul to the Night Mother, swear it with your blood and we can begin."

Heat rose to Ghost's face. Everyone wanted him to be something they could use; a thief, a circus tumbler, an acolyte. Where were they when he was rejected by the world, again and again? His hands clenched. He managed on his own before them and certainly wasn't going to bow to anyone just because it was expected of him.

"No," he said, his lips a tight line. "I don't need her, I don't need you—I don't need anyone!"

His fists came up the second Soraya's feet hit the floor and the pair of them faced off tensely. Both held a hand hovering an inch away from their sheathed weapons; Ghost's burning rage setting flame to his cheeks; Soraya's face aglow with zealous fervour.

Fan rolled his eyes. "We don't have time for this. If you two don't sit down I'm going to start collecting loose teeth. And if none are loose I'm going to make them that way. You all ken?"

Ghost glanced at Fan long enough to realise that Soraya had already mastered her once-legendary anger, and that whatever else was happening, she actually listened to Fan. Slowly, cautiously, he lowered himself to the ground as Soraya sat back on the bed, ignoring him for the moment.

"Good," said Fan. "Now that's dealt with I think its time for our resident strategist to take things from here. Crooked?"

Ghost rocked back, blinking. Crooked, what?

"It started when the three of us were talking about how we might be tested. I thought we might be prepared by making a bag we could grab quickly that had everything we needed."

"That's a good idea," said Ghost.

Crooked nodded. "Yes, simple but useful. Then I thought, hey, we're good at different things. What if we helped prepare each others bags? So we did for Temper and it worked pretty well. My little key copier saved the day. It was just something I thought of when Fan was trying to help me charm faster. He kept explaining what he saw in his mind while he was working a lock, and I thought, hey, it would sure be easier if I could see the same things as him. In fact, it worked so well Fan did it too."

Chuckling at Ghost's consternation, Crooked produced a small flat box, small enough to fit in the palm of his hand. He laid it on the carpet and flipped it open. It resembled a wax pad that scribes used to take quick notes before transcribing to tablets or parchments; but the scraped wax held not impressions of a stylus, but of a key. He held out a hand to Fan who unbuckled his leather wristguard and passed it to him. The hidden knife fell out during the exchange so Crooked laid them side-by-side beside the flat box. Finally, he looked up at Scab who grinned maniacally as he produced from his pockets a dead mouse. He scowled, muttering to himself, then flourished a sharpened brass crescent for cutting purse strings. His subsequent curses were florid and creative, but not necessarily biologically probable, then he cheered. In the palm of his hand he held a tiny glass ampoule that appeared to contain wisps of smoke.

"Needs inhalation to work properly," said Scab, adding his contribution to Crooked's collection.

Crooked sat quietly, his fingertips stroking the strange objects in front of him. At length he looked up and winked at Ghost. "That's everything you should need," he said.

Confusion, frustration, and anger hit Ghost all at once. If they didn't stop smirking at him he was going to do something he'd regret. Something comfortingly violent.

"Need for what?"

Crooked beamed confidently. That wide toothy grin that Ghost was sorely tempted to stick his fist into.

"We didn't have much time to prepare for Soraya or Fan's big days, and we don't have much more now. Ghost, listen up. Soraya overheard a little about what the Magister is going to do with you next. And I have a plan."

CHAPTER 22:
RETURN TO THE GREY
MOUSE

"Wake up, boy, and come with me."

The Magister padded out the room while Ghost rolled out of bed, squinting at the early dawn light just catching the edge of the window frame. He tied on worn sandals, now so small that his toes hung over the soles, and pulled his cloak around his shoulders. He grabbed his tools, then just as he touched the door to leave, a recollection intruded his sleepy mind and he slid aside a loose panel in the wall, retrieving the bag of tricks within.

The Magister knelt in the living room, hunched over a pile of hemp ropes, jute cords, scratchy woollen blankets, and a pair of knapsacks.

"We are taking a trip, you and I. A week, maybe two. Are you prepared?"

Ghost stifled another yawn and held up his tool roll.

"Will this be like the trip you took Soraya on?"

"If you mean am I going to test you, and give you a name, then no. I could use an extra pair of hands, or possibly an extra pair of eyes. Or even an extra pair of ears. I really don't know until we get there."

"Why not take Soraya, as she is more experienced?"

The Magister threw up his hands. "Endless chatter. Do you not want to come?"

Ghost rushed to the Magister, cold panic shocking him into full wakefulness. He grabbed the backpack set out for him. "Yes, Magister! Desperately!"

The Magister grunted and returned to the packs. He tied off the smaller one and handed it to Ghost who pretended not to notice its weight as he struggled to get it on his back. Zarbenus slung his pack up onto a shoulder and walked out the door with Ghost trotting after him.

✝ ✝ ✝

The walk down the mountain filled Ghost with giddy excitement. Everything that had been strange and frightening when the Magister first brought him to the Nidus now seemed alive with endless possibilities. Each field, each copse and each brook seemed to offer a chance to spot a different singing bird, or a brightly coloured lizard, or an enticing new fruit, sweet-sticky scent from the rotting flesh beneath the trees in their orchards.

But the Magister strode on, never looking at the sights Ghost pointed at and questioned about. The Magister kept up the same steady pace as the mountain path flattened out to an undulating path over the hills and Ghost had to sigh and leave behind another new discovery and trot after him. They slept that night by bushes well back from the road. Making no fire until the time that dawn woke them, they rose stiffly from the lumpy terrain and took a brief meal of tea and dried figs. Even as Ghost still sipped the last of his tea the Magister crushed the last of the embers that warmed them on such an early morning. He took Ghost's cup and shook it out, then packed away their few things and resumed their journey down the road.

By late afternoon they reached the Grey Mouse taverna. As the Magister put his foot on the flagstone under the door, he took his hand off the door and placed it on Ghost's shoulder.

"If that old crow asks you about me you are to tell him nothing, do you understand?"

"I'm not to speak to him, Magister?"

The Magister shook his head. "Kanesh is a trafficker of information.

Talk with him if you will, but confine yourself to generalities. Never disclose the names of any of our students, nor share with him anything you have learned. Do you understand?"

"You want me to be... vague?"

The Magister squeezed Ghost's shoulder.

"Very good, boy. Yes, vague; an excellent word."

He chuckled to himself and pushed open the taverna door. The amber glow and flickering of candles mingled with the pipe-smoke and beer-belches, and the voluble babble of the tavern's patrons seemed just as palpable as the drinking jars they chinked together. Kanesh looked up from his station behind the bar as the door opened, then he shook his head at seeing the Magister walk in. He put down the mug he polished and crossed his arms over his chest, head to one side.

The Magister raised an arm in salute. "Well met, barkeep!"

"Where's my money?"

"Such a mercenary attitude from one who should be more patronly!"

"I'll not run your tab anymore. My arms are too short to handle a longer bill."

The Magister spread his arms wide as if he meant to embrace the old barkeeper. After a moment when the gesture was not reciprocated he sighed and spread his hands on the bar.

"I am on my way to pick up the money now. A drink and a meal, and within a week I will return to pay you all I owe you. What say you?"

Kanesh snorted and turned his back on the Magister, his attention returning to the mugs he was cleaning. The Magister placed his elbow against the bar and leaned forward, resting his chin on his fist, his voice dropping to a whisper.

"And with your money—and all your interest—I promise to bring you something of interest to you... something special."

Kanesh set the mug down on the bar in front of the Magister's face.

"How special?"

The Magister grinned roguishly. "For you, my dear old friend, something very special indeed."

"Hmpf. This is the very—and do I make myself completely clear—the very final time. After this, there will be no more favours, no more dear old friends. It will be over between us. A professional relationship is not meant to be as one-sided as ours has become."

"I agree completely! Too long have I over-relied on your boundless hospitality and your infinite patience. A new leaf is turned! Now, I'll take that table in the corner, and just pass me that jar up there on the shelf... no, no, the Parthian one, not the local slop. Good man. Now I'll take a hot plate of meat when you have a moment to bring it to me; but don't rush yourself, I don't want to be an imposition."

"As long as you promise me you aren't staying."

"Only a single night, I assure you. Then I must visit some friends," said Zarbenus.

"Will they be happy to see you coming I wonder?"

The Magister inclined his head. "They won't see me coming."

Kanesh growled, slung his wiping rag over his shoulder, but even as he raised his finger and opened his jaw the Magister had turned away. Zarbenus settled himself at the far table, working the wax from the stopper with his long knife and helping himself to a generous measure. The old taverna keeper sighed and shook his head.

"He'll never change, that one, and it will kill him in the end. We all need to change, as the world changes around us. Life is change, I remember someone saying. Who was it? Ah never mind. Let's take a look at you lad. Well! You've fairly sprouted up. Don't you look just like a wee model of himself, ha! You have a little cloak and hood too... and those eyes. You know, it didn't catch me last time you were here, but don't you really look just like him? Add in a scratchy beard and some inches to your height...

what a funny thing this is."

Ghost screwed up his face. "Don't make fun of me."

"No, no; not at all. You really are quite the image of him, but didn't you say you were an orphan when you last passed through?"

Ghost's gaze narrowed as he took in the relaxed smile of the old taverna keeper. He hunched forward to whisper. "I da ken I told you anything about where I came from last time."

Kanesh ran his fingers through his grey beard and looked into the distance. "Did you not? Huh. A funny thing memory is, when you get old. You forget where you heard things from. So, you're not an orphan then? You must be a relative of that scoundrel. That would explain how you look so much alike, you two."

"I... I've come from a different land."

"Have you now? Well that much was apparent from your mode of speech when we first met, but it doesn't really answer the question of whether you're an orphan or one of that lanky rat's family, does it?"

"Why do you want to ken? What's it to you?"

"To me? Well nothing at all, really. Just making simple conversation as you do when you meet a stranger, you know, to become better acquainted, so to speak. If you don't want to tell me, that's fine. You have a right to your privacy, I wouldn't want to force you to spill secrets you'd rather remain hidden," said Kanesh.

"It's not a secret!" Ghost flushed pink and looked around for the Magister, who appeared oblivious as he poured himself a second jar of wine.

Kanesh patted Ghost on his shoulder, and smiled as he stroked his moustache. "Hush now, young man. I'm sorry for prodding you, I was only having a bit of fun. I've no doubt that one has told you to keep quiet about anything and everything, but that's because he is a paranoid so-and-so and doesn't trust anyone; even if you'd been friends and partners since before you were born, lad."

"You were partners? You mean you *worked* with the Magister?" Ghost drew close to Kanesh as he whispered furtively, eyeing at the jeering and slurping patrons that decorated the bar to either side.

"Oh? You want to know about me now, do you? Well I thought you weren't much interested in becoming better acquainted, you know, just a moment ago."

"I want to ken more about the Magister. Please tell me?"

"The Magister, the Magister, well, well. He only started calling himself that these ten years past. Before that, there was another man called Magister, and this one here was his student. He called himself something different then too. Has he told you about those times or what his name used to be?"

Ghost looked down at his hands. "He hasn't really told me much about anything."

"Well, if he hasn't shared that with you, lad, then it isn't my place to say. But now, here I am opening up, what do you say, time to hear a jot about you?" Kanesh dragged a tall bar stool behind the bar and placed it by the wines. "Remember when I caught you at this exact spot? We entered into a deal then, or so I thought. What say you that we revisit that?"

Ghost nodded and hopped up onto the stool. Mug in hand, Kanesh waved at the barrels stacked around him.

"What will it take to wet your throat? I'd say that since you're tall enough—just about—to look me in the eye across the bar that you'd take a mug of beer?"

Ghost's eyes lit up. "Beer!"

A mug was drawn and Ghost sipped at the frothy bitter brew. He nearly gagged on the first swallow but under the scrutiny of Kanesh's arched eyebrow he managed a grin and smacked his lips noisily. Kanesh interrupted their conversation to fill up an empty pair of mugs being drummed on the bar top by two locals, then he returned to Ghost.

"It seems to me that just talking to people could get you all kinds of

264

information. You could learn all sorts of things, even different people's opinions of exactly the same events. Two men can watch a fight and come away with completely different stories about it. Maybe you are already old enough to make up your own opinions of how things happen, you know, after hearing different points of view? They say there are always two sides to a story and in my experience there's many more than that."

Ghost nodded, checking that the Magister still wasn't paying any attention to their conversation. Then he returned to choking down the vile amber liquid. Kanesh followed the glance and chuckled to himself.

"Tell you what; I'll start. I don't suppose he told you about trying to steal the jewels of a noblewoman from her country estate, did he?"

Ghost coughed and spluttered as he fixed his attention on Kanesh. "He never tells us stories like that!"

"Well, when you hear it you may understand why! You see, this noblewoman was famous for her taste in jewellery, but in the city there were too many guards at her townhouse, and more city guards around them. Anyway, we were in a taverna and, purely by luck you understand, her coachman was there. After a few drinks, he told us she had a lover and would sneak off to the country villa to meet with him, and all without her husband knowing. The lady, he said, would always fetch him a gold piece when he did the driving for these visits, on the understanding that if questioned by his lord he would faithfully swear that they had been to visit her sister in the neighbouring town."

Ghost grinned broadly as he hung on every word.

"So, being the young rogues that we were, and him a few years younger than me at that, we fed the coachman a few more drinks; then a few more after that. Eventually, we managed to wheedle out of him the location of the country estate, and the knowledge that the lady planned to go there the very next day; the coachman enjoying his cups on account of the expectation of that gold piece."

Kanesh paused in his tale and peered at the mostly full vessel in Ghost's lap. It was quickly returned to lips that welcomed it not, but still managed an approximation of an appreciative murmur.

"The next morning your master and I waited with horses ready in a street where we could watch the gates of the rich lady's house. Without much time passing the gates opened and her carriage rolled through; the coachman looking sour-faced and squinting against the morning sun. His hangover keeping his attention he never noticed us following at a discreet distance.

"The country villa was barely an hour away, but in the pastoral peacefulness the lady could meet her lover without being seen by the prying eyes of nosey neighbours and gossiping townsfolk. The carriage drew past a modest but well-maintained pleasure garden. Down a path collonaded with sculptures nymphs and sylphs and nereids. Ultimately it stopped at the villa, itself not much bigger than this inn but with a collection of roses running up its very fine stonework. Its smartly tiled roof in a rather better state of repair than mine, I'm sorry to say.

"A handsome and fashionably dressed young man emerged from the villa. He passionately greeted the noblewoman as she practically fell out of the carriage in her rush to get to him, and after that they retired inside. The coachman, no doubt from familiarity with the task, decided he had plenty of time to sleep off his sore head. He settled himself in the shade of his vehicle, pulled his cap over his eyes, and started snoring.

"Your master and I debated the next course of action. Eventually, bearing in mind that he was as he is now and remains my junior by a good ten years, decided that I would keep watch in case the house received any other visitors, and he would make a stealthy entrance alone.

"He was a brazen and bold youth, and inordinately proud of his skills. However, those skills were still in development, and he was not above making the occasional error. As I waited, diligently surveilling the road, I heard first your master cry out from within the villa, then a strong and angry shout. The next thing I saw was a wiry figure in black emerging from one of the upper windows and climbing along the rose-twined trellis. Seconds later at the same window appeared the face of the handsome young gentleman that we had seen welcome the noblewoman, save now his face a lurid red as he bellowed at your master. It appeared he was not some quailing fop, but a hale fellow fired by a furious temper. He swung himself out of the window and with reasonable grace—and bear in mind I was judging him in a professional capacity—clambered after your master.

"As this chase continued they soon disappeared around the side of the villa and I hurried to a new vantage point where I could see both the road as well as the two climbers, for now I was doubly concerned about anyone else arriving. The rear of the villa had lower outhouses attached to it, and in keeping with the rural surroundings, a small farm was in operation there. As your master dropped from the trellis to the flat roof of a stable, two farm workers spotted him and they raised, if I recall correctly, a pitchfork and a hoe. These they jabbed in his direction as he tried to find an edge of the building he could escape from.

"By now the young gentleman landed on the same outhouse and drew his definitely non-ceremonial sabre, advancing in well-drilled cross-steps. Your master, seeing no other escape, drew his own sword and they locked blades. Now your master, who is a decent hand on the hilt of a dagger, was never the greatest swordsman in the world. After only a few strokes the young gentleman had him disarmed and held captive with the tip of a blade to his chest. The gentleman still hollered furiously at your master, his face flushed and holding out the palm of his hand expecting something to be placed in it.

"I saw your master's shoulders droop and his head fall. He pulled a package from under his cloak and placed it in the young gentleman's hand, whose gaze fell to the object and the tip of his sword wavered. At that instant, your master turned and sprinted the length of the flat stable roof. He leapt off the end, his arms and legs flailing, then crashed through the shingles of a slope-roofed building beyond.

"I jumped onto my horse and trailing the other behind, rode for the farm buildings. I knew all chance of subterfuge or stealth was now lost to us and all that could be hoped for would be a quick escape. I burst through the bushes and pulled up as your master came running toward me; still chased not only by the young gentleman and the farmhands but also a mean-looking sow. She was a huge white thing nearer to the size of a short-legged horse, and was close on his heels all the while squealing a truly terrifying war cry. This presented a clear explanation of why he was covered from head to foot in pig slurry. The building whose roof he had demolished in his aerial escapade had evidently been a pig sty, and he had enraged its resident.

"Relief evident in his face, your master vaulted into the saddle of his horse. We wheeled away at full gallop, the angry cries of the gentlemen and the farmhands and the squealing of the sow fading from our ears. The danger passed, I took stock of the situation and despite his curses that I should be quiet, I laughed the whole hour ride back to the city!"

Ghost's damp-eyed laughter was cut short with a tumble of fear as he saw the Magister standing behind Kanesh, his face inscrutable.

"Telling your favourite story again, old man?"

Kanesh wiped his eyes as his laughter died down into quiet chuckling. "It took you days to get the smell out of your clothes..." He collapsed into another bout of laughter, struggling to breathe and slapping his thigh.

Ghost swallowed nervously and took the opportunity to slide his mug along the bar, hoping one of those that so freely guzzled would think it a gift and dispose of it on his behalf. The Magister's gaze was insistent.

"So Magister... I suppose I should learn that we can't always get the prize and sometimes running away is better, is that the lesson?"

A thin spider of a smile crawled across the Magister's face. "Oh, but I did get the prize. A pocketful of the noblewoman's best baubles; she wore only her prettiest to meet her lover. All he got from me in return was a pouch with a chunk of cheese and a hunk of dry goat that I'd been saving for lunch."

Kanesh's laugh faded into a dry wheezing. He held his hands at his ribs while he nodded. "Aye, that's true. You did get the jewels, but as I recollect you also found you urgently needed to leave the city and I never got my cut."

The Magister waved away the suggestion like a bad smell. "You did nothing for your share, and besides, that is old news."

Kanesh winked at Ghost, "What did I say? Never change this one, not even when he should be grateful. You know now lad, if it wasn't for me this master of yours would likely have met his end under the snout of an enraged pig."

Ghost started to laugh but received a clap to the side of his head from the Magister that shut him up.

"Hey," said Kanesh putting both sets on knuckles on the bar. "Easy on him."

"Easy?" The Magister tilted his head to look at Ghost. "You don't train a wild animal with kindness. It has to know the only thing in the world that matters is its master's demands. Right, Ghost?"

Under the squint of both opposed men, Ghost nodded, and the Magister huffed his approval.

"Time enough for bed, and my own fault for leaving you around this grey fool," he said. "We have an early start in the morning."

The Magister was even less talkative than normal as he roused Ghost before dawn. His hand poised to muffle any waking noises, but Ghost was becoming accustomed to rising silently and stretched his jaw while blinking the sleep away from his eyes. In the stables the Magister chose a tan palfrey for himself. He tied his pack to Ghost's and slung them across the horse's haunches before springing into the saddle. As Zarbenus walked the horse across the yard, leaning over its neck and whispering soothingly to it, Ghost selected a compliant looking donkey. It had no saddle to match so he folded two riding blankets over its back before jumping on and urging it after the Magister.

Ghost tried a few times to ask the Magister to tell him more about his days with Kanesh, but every time he started to say a few words it was greeted with swatting wave and an irritated grunt. Eventually, Ghost settled back on the patiently plodding donkey, the swaying of its round body vaguely soothing. The path led through thick woodland that covered the foothills, but as they crested one of the lower hills the trees gave way to open farmland. Far ahead of them, stars shone in the daytime with the golden capped towers of Byzantium twinkling their glory.

Ghost urged his donkey faster with jabs of his heels. Braying its protest it pulled up alongside the Magister's horse.

"Magister! Are we going to the city?"

The Magister grunted and looked down at Ghost. "Can I still trust you to be useful to me?"

Ghost's excited smile vanished as he frowned his annoyance. "I told Kanesh no secrets, just as you told me to. All I did was listen to his story. Maybe if you told me tales from your past I'd see your side of it."

"That sounds just like the old fool speaking. What did he tell you to do?"

"Nothing Magister. Just that I should make my own mind up about what I believe in."

"Quintessential Kanesh. That's him speaking alright," said Zarbenus.

"Is he so wrong, Magister?"

Zarbenus sighed and shook his head. "We were not so very different, he and I, all those years ago. I looked up to him at first, thinking an older man may know tricks that I did not, and the man... well let's say the man who first taught me was not always very forthcoming when I questioned him."

"That sounds familiar."

"Maybe I am more like him that I like to believe," said Zarbenus. He shrugged.

"Like Kanesh?"

"No, not him. I guess you could call him my master, although I never called him that. I may tell you that tale another day, but not today. I will tell you about Kanesh though, seeing as you're becoming such good friends. I was saying that when we first met, we were not so different. Despite him being older than me, we were enjoying every moment of our lives, taking what we wanted, and rushing from scrape to scandal without a single care. Those were good years, while it lasted. But all things come to an end. He began to question the very nature of what we did, and then, when he had the chance to take it all, he walked away."

"He stopped being a thief?"

"Everything. He walked away from stealing, killing, all of it. Coward. Then again, had he stayed in the game he would probably have gotten in my way. Maybe he knew that. Did Kanesh talk about my master?"

"No he didn't say anything like that," said Ghost.

"Nothing about how he died then?"

"He only told me the story about the noblewoman's jewels."

"Well, I suppose you would have to learn it someday, boy. My master passed a great power to me, a secret that I am the only man in the world who knows, but the very day he taught me it he was killed. Kanesh discovered his body and has accused me many times of doing it," said Zarbenus.

"But you didn't do it!"

"Why would I? He had already passed his power to me, why would I want him dead? If anything, the suspicion should fall on that grey dog's head. He was jealous of the power I had been given. Myself, I am convinced Kanesh killed him out of rage when he found out my master had favoured me and not him, and that by being my senior he should have had it by rights."

271

Ghost frowned and tried to imagine Kanesh so filled with rage that he would kill a feeble old man.

"I don't think that sounds like him."

Zarbenus looked away. "It was a long time ago. Maybe he is at peace with himself about it."

"I don't think I would forget killing someone as easily as that." The memory of the choking noise when he tightened his fingers around the child's throat.

"That old fart has killed plenty of men. Women too. Many more than I have. There was a reason why he was called the Death Crow. He never shared my preference for discretion over extinction."

Difficult memories Ghost had almost forgotten about pushed into his mind. He fell quiet as they carried on down the road, the towers of Byzantium growing taller on the horizon before the city walls themselves came into view.

Chapter 23:

A Victimless Crime

Zarbenus nudged his horse along as the path grew busy with traders on waggons and groups of haggard refugees in stained and tattered clothes. Water-sellers pushed their handcarts along the lines, tiny bells tinkling as they traded cool refreshment for coins worth less than beads. The merchants rested their plump bodies, nestled amongst the piles of goods for market on their vehicles; the refugees clutched worn limp sacks with all that they possessed. Working his way between them the Magister moved away from the route that led to the Lion Gate, heading for the squalid shanty town that festered like an unsightly growth outside the walls of the great city.

"You must excel in my eyes today, boy. If you are to surpass Fan or Soraya in my estimation," said Zarbenus.

Ghost sat up straight on his donkey and gave it a jab with his heels to keep up with his master. Finally, this was his chance.

"I will," he said.

"Good, then come along. We'll find a place to stay then enquire about the work I have been advised of." Zarbenus wheeled his horse around and urged it forward.

"Can we call on Raseyda and Bayezid?" Ghost wondered if they remembered him at all.

Zarbenus grunted noncommittally. "I asked after them last time I was here. Was told they'd picked up another boy and gone travelling with him."

Another boy. Ghost's head drooped. He'd been replaced so easily. The betrayal stung even as he tried to put them out his mind. Ghost scowled, then turned his thoughts to his master, and how he might make him proud beyond all others.

The lodging house was a squat and crumbling building on a narrow side street and Zarbenus tipped the stable-lad a few copper coins to take proper care of his horse and of the donkey. A few silver dinars and a room was secured, then the Magister spun on his heel and strode off into the city. Ghost jogged to keep the black cloak in sight as the crowds passed between them. Bitter sweaty bodies, sweetly scented bodies, the rustle of a hundred different cloths and the hum and hubbub of a hundred languages. The musical burble of the Parthians a melody for the percussive cadence of strident Spartans. He marvelled at how many words he could pick out of the different tongues, sometimes even catch the gist of a sentence before the speaker moved out of earshot.

Zarbenus nodded toward the sprawl of low buildings, warehouses, stables, gambling dens, inns and whorehouses that surrounded the gleaming blue walls of Byzantium.

"It's like the mud caked around the heel of a fine boot; you can never be so elevated that you don't still get some muck clinging to you." He smiled at the poetic allusion but his reverie was broken off by Ghost tapping him on the shoulder.

"Do I get to be lookout again?" Ghost's cheeks glowed as he followed alongside his master, walking over the strewn rubbish and stepping between dollops of horse manure.

A knot of women carrying reed baskets of grubby vegetables—shrilly immersed in their condemnation for the outrageously flirty eye colours the far-too-young daughter of the shoemaker had started wearing—blocked the path as they shuffled forward. Zarbenus took Ghost by the hand and forced his way through the crowd.

"Do I? Huh?"

Zarbenus squatted down by the corner of the road, pulled Ghost to his side and pointed through the stream of people and animals that choked the road. A solid stone building stood there, unassuming, but less looking like collapsing in a strong wind than most of its neighbours in the district simply known as the Shambles. On either side of the door a tall man stood erect, but with heads bowed, their full beards flowing down their chests. Each man wore a simple white sleeveless robe that hung past their knees, covering their armour. Their chain-mail sleeves and armoured boots were clean, polished, and glistened with fresh oil.

"Tell me what you think of them," said Zarbenus, inclining his head in their direction.

"Soldiers," said Ghost, scowling at them.

Zarbenus cuffed him across the back of his head. "Not what you feel about them. Look properly and tell me what you see. They call themselves the Athanatoi."

Ghost peered at them as he rubbed his head. The men's downcast eyes were closed and as he watched he saw that they were not completely motionless. Their lips moved, mumbling softly under their breath and he could not make out the words from their shapes.

"They cover their armour, but leave some of it for all to see. Not hiding very well, if that's what they intend."

"They aren't hiding at all. Why?"

"The building is plain, yet it has slit windows like a fortress. Do they want people to think that they are not soldiers?"

"In a manner. They think of themselves as different, but they are still soldiers. Their religion tells them to be humble, but it also tells them they have a holy purpose. A man who absolutely believes he is right will give his life for that belief."

"Don't all soldiers do that?"

Zarbenus spat viscously into the gutter. "Most soldiers think the money is easy, his food comes for free. As he marches to war he privately pities the man walking next to him who will most likely never come home again. All men think they are immortal, but these Athanatoi believe that falling in battle sends them to heaven, that is why they call themselves 'The Deathless'. They never retreat, never flee, even if they are slaughtered to the man."

Ghost screwed up his face. "I ken they're all stupid!"

"Then you are finally learning something after all. Now be silent and pay attention. This is what I have come to see."

A sonorous thrumming, at first only distantly felt rather than heard, grew and grew. Harmonious chanting of a double column of brown-robed monks drew near, heads bowed penitently like the Athanatoi. The monks' shaven tops of their heads bobbed in time with the chanting, their hoods turned back. At the front of the procession, a novice in a white tunic swung a perforated brass censer; cloying aromatic incense fuming from within. As he passed people in the crowd pulled wisps of smoke to their faces, touched their foreheads, muttered prayers and invocations.

Behind the novice strode a giant in monk's robes. He did not have their passive downturned faces and his noble countenance scanned the crowd with undisguised suspicion. Unlike his unarmed brethren, he bore a wooden club slung from his belt; a vicious-looking thing bound and studded with steel. His massive shoulders and neck were bound with heavy iron chains that lead to a large iron caged box. Though the cage was wrought of coarse metal, a box the size and shape of a hefty scholar's tome was encased within. Gold sheen and a rainbow coruscation hazed from between the bars, cast by the constellation of jewels embedded in it. Ghost had no doubt this was not a simple man of prayers and devotions. Each step he took had purpose, and the ground itself seemed cowed beneath his sandals. The crowd of onlookers took great pains to avoid his penetrating gaze.

After the giant came four monks bearing a platform on their shoulders, with a statue of a woman with one hand raised. In front of the statue sat a golden bowl with glittering red and blue gemstones inlaid around its rim.

Ghost giggled to himself. "I ken why this place is important to you, Magister. The bowl or the box?"

Zarbenus grabbed Ghost by the shoulder. "There are some things that are more dangerous than they are worth and that is one of them. The case will be empty and its journey merely ceremonial. It wouldn't be taken from the sanctum, not without a small army guarding it. It is the Arcasantos—holiest of holies—and wars have been fought over its ownership. It is probably the only thing in the world which can truly be described as priceless. Needless to say, you may learn a valuable lesson this afternoon. Some things will always—and should always—remain out of reach."

"Even from you?" asked Ghost in awed tones.

The God of Thieves grunted and resumed his oversight of the ceremony.

The Athanatoi raised their heads as the procession drew up to their doorway and stopped. The giant ignored them and gazed about, looking at the edges of rooftops, eyeing alleyways and sizing up strangers. Clearly spoken words in a language that Ghost did not know were exchanged with the monks. Then the Athanatoi took charge of the platform with the statue and bowl, and took it inside their building. The mission accomplished, the monks turned around. They resumed their chanting and returned the way they had come, led once more by the novice and the giant. A small crowd had already formed around the door murmuring in reverential tones until an Athanatoi warrior reappeared and bade them enter.

"Once a year the temple in the city sends the relic to spend the night at this place, the headquarters of the knights who liberated it from someone-or-other, in thanks for their sacrifice."

"Liberated?"

"Holy people never 'steal' things, boy. They 'liberate' them. May I continue?"

Ghost's cheeks flushed. "Sorry, I—"

"As I was saying—and despite the headquarters of these knights being so solidly constructed and without any apparently easy method of gaining access—there may be an opportunity to do some liberation of our own. Stay close, stay silent, and at least attempt to stay out of my way."

The stream of visitors continued throughout the afternoon, attracting the poorest worshippers unable to travel to the centre of the city; the lame, the sick, and the destitute. They all filed in, performed their acts of obeisance, their supplications, their offerings of gratitude. Then they filed back out, their faces a little less lined with worry, age or pressure, and Ghost wondered at the magic of it. Zarbenus browsed the stalls of cheap glass beads and rough peasant woven cloths until, eventually tiring of their lack of success in making a sale to him, the stalls packed away and their owners trundled off for the evening pushing the handcarts they had collapsed their enterprises into.

Lights flared and flickered on in the windows of the taverna and the conveniently located whorehouse facing it. Each establishment now fronted by a burly man in studded leather who nodded professionally at his counterpart as they took up station for the night. Zarbenus sauntered into the taverna and, with Ghost keeping out of the way under his table, slowly worked his way through first one, then another skin of sour wine. His increasingly bold and lecherous suggestions to a particular barmaid with curly coppery hair—which at first received nothing but a snort of derision— but when escalated to a pinch of her ample backside earned him a physical ejection from the establishment. Tossed by collar and belt into the street where he crawled on hands and knees; cursing the innkeeper, the innkeeper's parents and so forth back to some very hirsute progenitors. Finally, he collapsed on the opposite side of the street, and fell silent with the shroud of invisibility that can only be assumed when people wish to ignore you. Over the next few hours, occasional late-night wanderers passed close by. Each time Zarbenus mumbled incoherent slurred nothings and the passer-by rapidly found they preferred the other side of the street, trying very hard to pretend the old drunkard did not exist at all.

It wasn't until much later, when the last lights had gone out in the street and the only footsteps heard were the tiny scurrying of rat's claws on cobblestones, that Zarbenus lifted his head and yawned.

Ghost shook himself awake. "Magister, are you alright?"

Zarbenus belched stale wine and winced. "I created the opportunity to wait unnoticed. Now, after I have done all the hard work, and have the demon hammering a hundred drums inside my head to deal with, it's time for you to go to work." He indicated the Athanatoi bastion. "You know what to do."

Ghost looked at the bolted and iron-studded door, then at the slit windows, just dark slashes high in the solid walls. A proud standard hung from a lofty flagpole; its device and colours lost in the dusk. Broken teeth of crenellations marched around the edge of the roof, and though the door was no longer guarded, the silhouette of a man in a steel cap with a spear to his shoulder slowly paced behind the fortifications.

"Magister, I—"

"The door? You disappoint me each day, boy. When have I taught you to go as others do? Surely your mind must be accustomed to thinking in more creative routes? Smell the air, what does it tell you?"

The night's cool swept away the stale sweat from the streets that had been busy during the day. Smoke from log fires still lingered, and the dew settling on the hard-packed dirt gave off a loamy scent. Ghost wrinkled his nose. There was another note—a fresh stench with the ammonia of urine.

"The rabble here foul themselves in pits behind their houses, but the Athanatoi live disciplined lives. Their great buildings are made with the purpose of housing large numbers of men. What would be required?"

"A sewer?"

"And now you know why bringing a scrawny child with me was such a masterstroke."

"You want me to climb in through the sewer? That's disgusting—"

"This is not a discussion. Now, get to work."

Ghost reluctantly rose, surveyed the empty street, then crept over and circled the Athanatoi's mission house. Butting up against the giant slabs that formed the base of the great walls of Byzantium ran a dark passageway, half-obscured by detritus. At the far end of this slit alley, barely a few feet wide, a reeking metal grate was set into rough chiselled stones. The fresh stench threatened to overwhelm Ghost's stomach; even thinking about it made him shudder. He looked back to where Zarbenus lay in the shadows but could not make him out, yet he felt the Magister's watchful gaze.

The powdery mortar holding the grate crumbled under the probing of Ghost's lock pry. Slimy and rusted, it came away; frighteningly loud grinding in the still night air. After pausing for a moment and hearing nothing else he placed it beside the opening. The hole was barely wide enough for Ghost's shoulders. He first placed his feet inside, then worrying about not being able to turn around he clenched his eyes tight and went down head first.

The darkness was absolute and he could only proceed by feeling his way; the tunnel sloping away and down in one direction, then under the wall of the Athanatoi's mission in the other. Within moments the little light that had followed him down was lost. With knees and hands slopping through the mess he tried so hard not to think about, a fear grew inside that swept away all the worry about bad smells and choking breaths. He remembered another narrow stone place, one he could not escape despite his mortal terror. Memory of that dread—the cold dark stone all around, closing in—overwhelmed him. Every bit of light and warmth in the world leached away, all love, all family, freedom, joy. His shoulders shook, hands twitching beyond his control and his ribs growing tighter with each half-gasped breath knowing that nothing could help him down here. Worse, nothing would help him because he was all alone and would die alone. In the dark and in the cold, and no-one would even remember him.

He couldn't tell how long he crouched, remembering the little child trapped, listening to the screams outside from a world grown even darker and more horrific than his terrible cold tomb. But the splinter inside of him that didn't die that day—long ago—the splinter that grew cold and burned and scared him more than the dark. More than the cold. Because it was the part of him that would always be there. No matter if he was safe and happy. It could all be taken in an instant and he would be left worse than alone. He would be left with himself and that piece of him that would not die and would do anything, whatever had to be done to survive. That piece of him had no capacity for warmth, and no understanding of fear. As its chill spread through him it took control of his lungs, slowed his breathing. His hands stopped shaking and he began to crawl forward again, knowing with each hand going down and each knee following behind that the fear was still there. Of the walls pressing in, of being alone in the dark. Trapped never to get free, crushed beneath the weight. But it didn't matter. He could be scared, yet he would still keep moving.

A ruddy glow, waxing and waning intermittently from ahead, and Ghost realised the short sewer opened into a room lit with a candle. He shuffled toward it, then he was under the light. He peered up from a hole in the ground into a small chamber empty save a trickling tap. The smell grew unbearably strong and the squelching beneath his feet nauseated him. That was enough for him to climb out and take his chances with what he might find. He washed his hands and legs as best he could with the dribbles from the tap. He knew that the reprieve would only be temporary, that his clothes would be burned afterward, but felt a grim sense of satisfaction that he'd made it through. The door hung half-ajar and he listened before stepping through. There were two cots, one bearing a blanket-covered bulge that snored softly. A broad halberd rested against the wall and a pair of worn but highly polished boots stood side-by-side at the foot of the bed. Ghost watched for a moment, decided it was safe to proceed, took a step, then felt the blood in his veins congeal as the clatter and gurgle of a cistern echoed through the room. As loud as an alarm bell in the cool silence. The bulging blanket moved, a sleepy mumble from underneath, and a thick-fingered hand emerged, groping for his polearm.

Squinting despite the low light, the bearded Athanatoi night watchman thrust his head from beneath his blanket. Smeared his face with his palm, sniffed lugubriously at the empty room, the clatter in the washroom fading to a musical trickle. He exhaled noisily, tucked one arm under his head and pulled the blanket back over himself.

Under the bed, Ghost breathed as quietly as he could. When the moment above him ceased he peeked out. The watchman wore a gold chain around his neck, three keys strung through it. They swung over the edge and dangled in front of Ghost's vision. Two were basic, trivial almost. The third clearly an advanced design, hinting at Neapolitan origins, with three separate rows of bits and wards for engaging a triple-lock mechanism. Staring at this, his mind abstracted the movement of the levers as the shaft rotated. He recognised how long it would take him to charm open such a device without this very key, so he reached for the flat box of scraped wax.

Next, he passed through an archway on the far side of the room, which opened into a large central hall with stairs running up on either side. A plinth on the wall between the staircases faced the bolted and barred main door. Looking much like a birdcage, a steel enclosure squatted on the plinth. Ghost froze as he made out the hulking figures standing alert by the door. Only barely visible in the weak grey light that fell in pale streaks on the hall's floor.

Breathing as shallow as he could, he scanned the room, up the stairs and across to the silent sentinels; still motionless. He slipped to his knees, keeping his back to the wall so as not to create a moving shadow. Heading for the nearest stair until the change in angle abruptly scared him into realising that the inert guards were merely empty coats of armour hanging from stands. The relief so sudden that he had to bite his tongue as a giggle rose in him, sweeping away the memory of his terror just minutes before.

So the Athanatoi were safe behind their walls. So secure in the stark unfurnished room that they feared no thieves, yet here was one. An ornate padlock fastened the steel cage, wrought iron trimmed with brass. The keyhole a distinct 'T' shape and Ghost pulled out his tiny wax tray. Holding different sized picks and levers against the moulded impression until a vision of the internal mechanism formed in his mind; cogs and teeth turning, meshing, unlocking. A mechanism this complex would take many minutes to charm for one with the highest skill. Too many guards for such an exploit; could even the Magister have managed it? Ghost breathed a silent word of gratitude to Crooked and his prescient plans. With the pattern pressed into the box in his palm, it was as simple as if he'd held the key itself. A moment later the lock was defeated. Ghost examined the statue which though old wasn't wrought from anything more valuable than marble. The bowl in front had a collection of twisted and bent coins of the smallest denominations, copper and iron only. Each worth little more than a loaf of bread, but had been left by the poorest of visitors and represented a sizable donation in their lives. Did their goddess speak to them as well, or were these the offerings of the unloved?

Ghost lifted the golden bowl, then thought about the unfortunates who had left coins they could scarce afford. Muffling them with his hand and listening in case the noise disturbed anyone, he tipped them out in front of the statue. When he was done he still heard nought more than the sighing and grumbling of the sleeper in the antechamber. Tucking the surprisingly heavy bowl inside his tunic he turned to consider his escape but froze as footsteps creaked on floorboards above his head. Slow and measured treads of man of solid weight, either in soft shoes or bare feet, heading calmly for the top of the stairs.

Move now or be caught!

The footsteps carried on down the stairs, out into the antechamber. A small chuckle was heard from the snoring man, then a minute later a hissing stream before the footsteps retraced their path, treading methodically on each step of the stairs to disappear into the muffled silence at the top of the building. Then they stopped. A silence followed by a quizzical 'huh', then quick steps back down the stairs, running to the middle of the room. An alarm called, quickly answered by a groaned complaint from the antechamber and followed by more from upstairs.

Within moments torches burned, and four long-bearded men in white nightshirts stood in the central hall, arguing over the fate of the golden bowl, and puzzling over the untouched coins. Who would take gold, but not the money? The man who had slept in the antechamber blustered that no-one would have entered without instantly waking him to full combat alertness; a boast the discoverer of the burglary waved away angrily. They argued more, voices raised and heated words exchanged. Then to settle a point of contention two of them struggled to lift the solid beam that barred the door. They swung it open and all four surged out.

Save some cats fighting over a scrap of food the street was completely silent. The Athanatoi with the most strident voice bellowed his rage and charged toward an old beggar snoring in the gutter opposite; drunk no doubt, or in the embrace of poppy tears.

"Old man! Did you see aught?" The discoverer of the heinous crime took command as the others surrounded him. He grabbed the sleeping beggar by his neck and shook him awake; the beggar stammering and trembling at the rough awakening.

"Pity on a poor wretch, reverend fathers," he slurred thickly. The Athanatoi leader winced at the noxious breath and pushed the beggar back to the ground.

"No-one saw anything?" Recriminations and accusations flew harshly between the men, and they failed to notice a slim youth leaving the shelter of the suits of armour by their door, just as the final roof guard jogged past, breaking his vigil to discover what all the commotion was about.

Ghost ran up the stairs, finding sleeping quarters with rows of straw-filled pallets; boots and pieces of armour beside each. The furious voices continued from below, only a few moments did he have to act. He snatched up a long dagger as he made for the ladder at the far side. A cry from behind him. Ghost's chest tightened as he half-turned and saw a figure rise from one of the mattresses, unnoticed in the panicked sprint past. The soldier, naked save for his breechclout, pulled a shortsword from its sheath as he advanced. No time for a scrawny youth to brawl with a seasoned warrior as more men run to join the fray. The fine glass of Scab's ampoule cracked as it hit the Athanatoi in the face, his exclamation the only inhalation the poison needed to enter his body. He was a big man, toughened by seasons of war and hardship. The kind of man who would swap his sword to his left hand and carry on fighting, despite receiving wounds that would finish off another not as battle-born as he. The Athanatoi shook his head as he landed heavily on one knee. Trying to clear the fog that swept over his senses, stilling him, drawing in the long goodnight. A moment later he lay face down, unmoving.

At the top of the ladder, a hatch. Propped up by a single stick. Freedom clear in his mind as he clambered onto the flat roof, high above its neighbours. Quickly the dagger went to work. He slashed one, two, three of the guy ropes that secured the flagpole. Racing for the fourth he looped it around his left wrist with a practised acrobat's ease. The pole bent towards him, tension in the heavy rope dragging his feet across the roof. Shouts came from below, the ladder rattled as an armoured man mounted it. The top of a long-haired head appeared beneath the hatch door. Ghost slapped the leather band around his left wrist. The mechanism fired the hilt of Fan's throwing knife into his palm. He flung it underarm—a practised flick of the wrist—striking the supporting stick. The hatch crashed down followed immediately by a muffled cry of pain. Then with the other hand, his stolen dagger severed the final knot—and he jumped.

Arms spread like a bird he flew through the air arcing, not falling, as the flagpole bent and creaked, and reaching his apogee he let the rope slip. Ghost dropped the few feet to land in one of the empty barrels stacked by the tavern's side wall for collection the following morning. There he tucked up in stillness; alert and listening as the thrumming of the flagpole died away. Willing the slave-galley drum pounding in his temples to slow and still as his pulse returned to normal.

The arguing Athanatoi continued as they returned to their mission, and the door was closed once more. When he judged sufficient time had passed the old drunkard rose. The Magister straightened his back with a theatrical stretch before ambling over to the empty barrels and stacked amphorae. He tapped lightly on the edge of the nearest and Ghost's face appeared from within.

"Was such a dramatic performance necessary?" Zarbenus' face was stern, but one eye creased at his cheek.

"I was more silent than a ghost, Magister. I wanted it to be... magnificent."

"Well then. The bowl?"

Ghost produced it from inside his tunic and Zarbenus' smile completed itself, appraising the jewels briskly in the poor light and pleasing him with what he discovered.

"Well done boy. *Kudos.*" He stowed the bowl under his cloak and hooked a finger at Ghost to follow. Then he turned and took long, easy strides on the path out of the Shambles.

Ghost glowed from within. This was what he'd dreamed of. Together with the Magister; they were a team now.

"Magister... I da ken why you make us do some stuff. The others say you're a bit... batty sometimes. I don't but—"

The Magister stopped abruptly. He started to chuckle and placed his hand against the bulge the bowl made in his jerkin.

"You think a dancing man is mad because you cannot hear the music?"

He turned to face Ghost, squatted so their eyes were level and tapped a finger against his brow.

"What a wild and wonderful song I hear. Have faith little one. Have faith."

A desperate longing to hear the same music grew inside Ghost. A feeling of awe that his master was so clever to see a secret world beyond all others.

"Magister, it was magnificent, wasn't it?"

Zarbenus stood and drew his cloak about him. "Not nearly enough."

Ghost felt his heart sink. "But Soraya... and Fan... Don't I get a real name?"

The Magister turned with a cold stare that froze any other questions in Ghost's throat. It was so unfair he struggled to hold back the tears he swore he'd never shed again. His clothes were ruined and he smelt exactly like the latrine he'd just crawled through, but the sickness in his stomach was worse.

† † †

Later that night Zarbenus scaled the knotted ivy running down the back of the high temple to the Goddess. He gained entrance through a locked shutter that posed no challenge and into a private study filled with a vast collection of books, manuscripts, and engraved tablets.

He pushed aside the disarray of vellum and papyrus sheets that littered the central desk, laying the golden bowl in their place. Inside the bowl lay a folded note which read:

As I was making a bloody ruin of a nasty little snitch in my ranks
that I'd discovered was reporting to the Oculus Dei, he attempted to
win his life with the hidden whereabouts of this artifact I believe to
be yours. I care not a whit why your man—N—would be plotting
against you, but suggest that whilst I am cleaning my house, you
should consider doing the same to yours.

Z

Then he left the way he'd come, closing the shutters carefully behind him.
As he went he mused on the virtues of tactfully reminding those you dealt
with of your skill, your importance, and most of all your usefulness. What
was undoubtedly best though, was to have them think you are playing their
game, whilst unbeknownst to them, they are really playing yours.

† † †

Fan reclined by a window pretending to read a book on anatomy, his thumb
stroking the dark down that had started growing on his upper lip. Everyone
knew he couldn't read any more than any of the rest of the boys could, but
he looked at the pictures just the same while Foul and Scab napped nearby.
Soraya and Crooked sat cross-legged repairing climbing ropes, speaking to
each other in low tones. They took the chance to rest as often as they could
as the still and humid afternoons sapped their energy leaving them sleepy
and listless. As the evening drew in the brothers arrived back at the Nidus,
each carrying a sack over their shoulders. Crooked nudged Fan and pointed
at them.

"More loot for the Magister, I'd imagine," said Crooked.

Dogan and Demir sneered as they walked past. Puffing loudly they made
a show of how heavy their loads were, then dumped them at the bottom of
the stairs.

"A bit more to deposit on our account," said Dogan to no-one in
particular. When Fan raised an eyebrow Dogan continued. "If Ghost is in
the lead then it doesn't hurt to sway things in our direction."

"It's not a competition. You're acting like this is some big game," said Fan, shaking his head.

Dogan laughed at him. "Think what you like, you're already easy to beat. Ghost's winning for sure at the moment. He's definitely the Magister's favourite. For now, at least. Unless someone takes him out the game."

"Rubbish," said Soraya. "If anyone is winning then it's clearly me. He hasn't even been given a name yet."

Scab growled. "That means you should sleep with one eye open. And with a knife in your hand."

"Like any of you babies could take me in a fight." Soraya glared at Scab, who suddenly discovered an interesting place to scratch that prevented him from looking at her.

Crooked grinned. "You might get poisoned. Ghost has you on that one, he has all of us. If someone starts with poison he's going to make it for sure."

They all went quiet at that, fidgeting awkwardly. The brothers shared a glance, and after a pause, Dogan nodded to his brother.

"The way I see it only the best—say the top two or three—really need to worry about fighting it out. I mean who is going to bother killing Scab? He's more likely to kill himself." Demir chuckled.

"Thanks, weaker twin," said Scab. "You're just the slow and timid version of Dogan. No-one's scared of you."

He stood up, stretched out his arms with a yawn. Then he moved his sheathed knife to a more comfortable position on his belt.

"Shut up, runt!" Demir took a step towards Scab, but his brother's hand on a shoulder restrained him.

"In fact," said Scab as he leaned back and leered at Demir. "If the failures need to fight it out it'll come down to you and me. The shrimp versus the wimp."

Crooked guffawed watching the pair of them face off. "That would be like wagering on a battle between two slugs."

"An epic combat indeed," said Soraya. "One great sagas will be sung of!"

Scab scowled at her. "That's it. I'm poisoning all of you. No exceptions."

"Even me?" Foul clutched his chest, groaned and swooned to the ground.

"I'll do you last, but use hemlock so you don't feel anything. It's a good way to go. For Demir, I'll mix nightshade and ground bamboo."

Demir's head snapped around. "What does that do?"

"You're useless without your brother," said Scab with a feline grin. "Nightshade will paralyse you and the bamboo makes you bleed to death—"

"Doesn't sound terrifying," said Demir.

"—through your arse."

Snarling and swearing, Demir launched himself bodily across the room, knocking Scab from his feet. Both traded fists, elbows and knees as they rolled around.

Dogan—ignoring them—said, "The way I see it, even if the Magister says there isn't a competition, it won't matter if only one of us is left."

"Why would you think that?" Soraya took her familiar stance with hands on hips; the one she used when she felt like emphasising that she was the only adult trapped in a room with squabbling men-children. "Why does there have to be only one winner, or a winner at all?"

"You really believe that? I thought you'd memorised every twisted word Zarbs ever said. Like anything the mad fool ever makes any sense." Dogan mimed glugging from an invisible flask. "Haven't you been listening? It doesn't work like that. There is only ever one winner. And no survivors. That's the way it works. Like Timan. Thought he was the big man in charge, now he's dead."

Scab pushed Demir off him and looked up at them. "But the Magister said—"

Dogan helped his brother up off the floor. "He's dead, you imbecile!

Stop being such a godsdamned baby and grow up. We're what's left, and whether we're the pick of the crop or just a basket of rotten apples it won't matter if there is only one left standing. Not that a midget with a pea brain would get that."

Scab tumbled to his feet and pulled his blade in earnest. Dogan's kukuri knife came out a split-second later and they faced each other uneasily, the standoff interrupted when the front door opened and Zarbenus walked in with Ghost at his heels.

The Magister looked at the pair of combatants, sighed, then cleared his throat. "If you wish to fight amongst yourselves you'd be better off taking Ghost's example, and saving that enthusiasm for paying jobs." He looked down at the sacks and prodded them with his toe. "Some minor loot I assume. Soraya, attend me." Zarbenus turned away and loped up the stairs to his room.

Dogan arched an eyebrow at Soraya who looked concerned.

Ghost grinned widely. "We went on a proper job, but... well you know I can't talk about it." He continued to beam at the others even though no-one shared his enthusiasm.

The first knife to go back in its sheath was Dogan's kukuri. "Did he name you?"

"No," said Ghost and all the humour went out of his face.

Dogan's however brightened. "Third time's a charm, eh Ghost? Accidents always happen at the most unexpected times. You can rely on that." He chuckled then sauntered out of the door; apparently unconcerned at turning his back on Scab. Expressionless, Demir trailed after him.

"Infants," muttered Soraya disdainfully as the group began to break up, then she headed up after the Magister. Foul and Scab wandered off to the kitchen and Fan returned to his book by the window.

Ghost threw up his hands. "What's going on?"

Crooked headed for the stairs then looked back and beckoned for Ghost to follow him. He paused for a moment with his hand on Ghost's door to glance back down the hallway to the room he still shared with the twins. Ghost hadn't been inside since his beating, nor did he want to. If they entered his space then he'd make sure they'd regret it. He swept Crooked inside and closed the door behind them. There was scarcely enough room for Ghost on his own, and they faced off tensely. Crooked broke the stalemate first, holding up his palm and intoning *pax*. Ghost nodded, surprised by how much relief he felt from such a simple gesture. The smiles that rolled across their faces reminded them of simpler days, and without preamble they sat together on the floor, backs to the wall like they used to when they told each other jokes.

"They're going to keep coming for you until you break," said Crooked.

"Let them try. I'm ready for them."

Crooked scratched the back of his hand, looked around the room, anywhere but at Ghost. "If it's real, would you kill me? If you had to?"

Ghost punched him on the shoulder. "What do ya ken? No! Of course not."

Crooked sat quietly for a while. "Even Dogan?"

"He's just blustering so we're scared of him. Besides, Demir would stop him," said Ghost.

"Like the last time they went for you? What would you do if he went for me, or Soraya?"

Ghost stared at his hands, and they sat in silence until the awkwardness of being unable to speak grew too much. He sighed and crawled onto his cot, pulling his blanket around him. Still the tension grew between them, so Ghost rolled to face the wall so he wouldn't have to look at Crooked, until he took the hint and went back to his own room.

Why would he want to fight for any of the others—least of all Crooked—when no-one had stood up for him?

CHAPTER 24:

HEKATE'S NIGHT

Only in the small hours of the dark moon did the oppressive heat of the summer wane; a small relief for those gathered in Hekate's House to celebrate in her honour. The taverna at the crossroads that served as her temple in the city bore witness to an elite coven of worshippers.

Zarbenus slouched in his booth, his hood pulled back and his features clearly discernible in the flickering light of torches that replaced the lamps for the ritual. The silken noose slung around his neck intentionally conspicuous to all, as was the corpse of the scabrous dog that lay on the table; its blood pooling under the dagger and keys placed there. The fresh stench of entrails overwhelmed the familiar and less rank odours of such an insalubrious drinking establishment. Four cowled figures knelt in front of the table and Zarbenus leant forward to look them in the eyes.

"Begin," he said.

Two of the figures scuffled in an unseemly fashion as they got to their feet, the disturbance being brief as the corpulent man suddenly flashed a smile and gave way to the emaciated woman. She ignored him and bowed to the Magister.

"Doma Medea, you are welcome here," said Zarbenus, nodding to her.

Shrunken and hunched, Doma Medea brushed down the front of her gown with hands wrinkled like an old apple. She cleared her throat.

"As the leader of the most ancient and feared Oikos..."

"Second oldest," said Dom Scylla standing beside her, broad smile still writ large across his stout face.

Zarbenus drummed his fingers on the table. "Do any of you forget that not so many years ago I expunged the entire 'ancient and feared' Oikos Apion for their slavish addiction to trivialities?"

Doma Medea paused without comment, awaiting any further interruption. When it became clear there was none, she continued.

"Oikos Medea celebrates Her night with blood. Many years have we planned, with your guidance, Magister. Tonight the silk trade of Court Ertegun will fall under our most subtle control; joining that of their farming concerns."

"With blood..?" Zarbenus arched an eyebrow.

Doma Medea smiled toothlessly. It was not pleasant to behold. "Bloodshed can be subtle, my lord. A series of unconnected accidents; an asphyxiation due to choking on a fish bone; an unfortunately timed loss of a cartwheel on a particularly treacherous hillside path. The result of these events is that when the world awakens in just a few hours our agents will be in key positions and this oriental cow can be milked at our leisure."

Zarbenus bowed his head but before he could comment Dom Scylla had swept a courtly bow, brushing Doma Medea away at the same time.

"My lord. I apologise that you have to hear such actions described as 'subtle' on such a holy evening dedicated to the Night Mother. Oikos Scylla avoids such... theatrics. Quietly in the shadows has my family worked, our intrusions utterly invisible, and yet over the last year since we all last met, we have increased the gold and silver siphoned from the trade activities of Court Izmir. Our reserves are now," he glanced shrewdly at the two supplicants that yet knelt. "Significantly deeper."

"Give me a figure," said Zarbenus.

Dom Scylla's frown deepened as he tapped fingertips together, tallying his thoughts. He then smiled showing very white teeth. "More than 900 pounds of gold, in assorted coinage; 2400 pounds in silver."

Zarbenus stood and clapped three times. "Come sit beside me, Dom Scylla. Try the brandy, I recommend it."

Dom Scylla swept past Doma Medea, accepting the silver chalice Zarbenus handed him, quaffing it and offering his wholehearted appreciation of the vintage. As he settled himself in the booth he beamed with satisfaction and stretched out both of his arms along the back of the upholstered bench. Zarbenus walked around the table and stood in front of the two remaining figures, tugging lightly on the free end of the noose around his neck as he regarded them.

"Doma Vlastos, Doma Gavras. You have both managed your clans with discipline and efficiency. Despite the fact that your clan lineages lack the history of the other families, I am content that Oikos Vlastos and Oikos Gavras deserve places at this inner council. Do you wish this honour?"

The two women whispered their assent, keeping their heads lowered.

"Very well then. To Oikos Vlastos I give the Juventia Court. To Oikos Gavras, that of Yilmaz. I give you a year to operate in your own fashion and will see what you make of the opportunity. It may be not long from now that your families will be spoken of in the same hushed breath when fearful citizens mention Scylla and Medea."

Doma Vlastos and Doma Gavras began to rise but Zarbenus took each by the shoulder and forced them back to their knees.

"I have assigned you a territory. You will face no competition from your brethren. You and your loved ones will receive vast wealth, security and of course, your lives. I gift this to you and only I can take it away. Do you understand what you accept?"

His grip on each woman tightened like a vice, digging into their flesh and no doubt leaving his mark on them. To their credit, neither young woman flinched, and they both bowed their heads.

"Excellent," said Zarbenus turning his back on the women as they rose to their feet. "Our business is concluded and you may all go about whatever frivolities you have planned for the rest of the night."

The Magister stared at the almost recumbent leader of Oikos Scylla until the Dom spluttered his apologies. He drained the last of his brandy, set the chalice down and left, closely followed by Domas Gavras and Vlastos. Zarbenus returned to his bench and Doma Medea eased herself in beside him, declining his offer of a drink with a curt wave of her hand.

"The best thing that ever happened to those girls was the night you killed their husbands," she said.

"Will they succeed, in your opinion, Ariadne?"

Doma Medea plucked at the bristly white hairs on her chin. "Gavras for sure. Or very close to sure. But Vlastos? That family is trouble, always has been. I wouldn't think less of her if she failed, but it is by far the harder of the paths they face."

"A path we could smooth," said Zarbenus, placing his goblet back down.

"Never," said Doma Medea. "If she makes it she will become a weapon of unremitting terror. If she fails... then we'll simply switch to whoever is clever enough to bump her off."

"If you were fifty years younger I'd be madly in love with you. You know that?"

She laughed, a surprisingly sweet sound. "And I would use that weakness to murder and depose you. Be thankful things stand as they are."

Zarbenus nodded and topped up his brandy, swirling it and staring thoughtfully at the amber ripples.

"And what of the esteemed Dom Scylla?"

"He is an accountant," said Doma Medea. "An adept accountant to be sure, but he won't survive an hour if things turn to blood. And he makes such basic mistakes I shudder with embarrassment."

"Such as accepting a drink poured by me, for example?"

"Exactly so," she said, massaging her stiff knuckles.

Zarbenus stood, laid the noose on the table and walked to the door, drawing his hood back up. "Let's hope his son shows more promise tomorrow morning when he awakens to find himself the new Dom of Oikos Scylla. Goodnight, my dear Ariadne."

Zarbenus walked into the street, distant sounds of merry voices, then of breaking glass. Men chanting an anthem to the glory of the Greens cut off by screams from the Blues. Let the frivolities continue, he had much more to do before he slept. Curator Nicodemus had proven himself an efficient and intelligent man, yet he was neither brave not ambitious. He needed a man like Pallas to give him direction and purpose, and likewise, Pallas needed the rich flow of information that Nicodemus provided him. If their relationship were to schism then Pallas would instinctively lean on the next richest stream, and Nicodemus would seek a new mentor. The wily old Hierarch would be the hardest to turn which was why it was necessary to show some slight involvement with the unmasking of supposed treachery from the leader of the Oculus Dei.

To be involved in none of these critical events would have been as suspicious as being fingered for them all, so showing my hand but once hides all the other actions I have taken.

Things were unfolding as they should, the players performing their roles. It would just take some patience, and that he had.

† † †

Curator Nicodemus paused in the hallway as Hierius Laetoria, lean and wrinkled, led the plump and frowning Hierius Hertia from the office beyond. They murmured a greeting then continued their fiercely whispered debate as they walked away. The Athanatoi guard at the door glanced into the office, then motioned for Nicodemus to enter.

The clutter of scrolls on the great desk seemed to grow on every visit. Even now a few had fallen to the floor, and Hierarch Pallas was obscured by their jumbled mass. The holy man's withered ancient body seemed swallowed by his white robes of office. A hand that looked like bones wrapped in old parchment extended across the table, bearing a single ring on one finger. Nicodemus bowed across the table and kissed the ring with solemn deference.

"You are welcome, Nicodemus. It is so kind of you to visit a lonely old man. The Curator of the Oculus Dei is most generous to spare his valuable time. I'd love to hear some tales of the city; my legs tire so easily and I do not walk through our beautiful streets as once I did."

Now that I dwell upon such possibilities it occurs to me that the king's ransom of a bribe that went unaccountably missing and was supposed to discreetly be delivered to Court Ertegun for their compliance might not have been an unfortunate chance after all. It was ultimately under Nicodemus' command.

Nicodemus chuckled. "You have such a steady stream of informants and supplicants you can scarcely be lonely, sir, but it is always my pleasure to report to you. The gentleman in question has been sighted within the city again. Though it has been some time since he appears to have exerted his influence in person. Then again, like you sir, he is fully capable of controlling events within his sphere from a discrete distance."

"We are both discreet then, Nicodemus. I had not thought before of the similarities; however, my sphere—the heavenly one— encompasses his, and therefor I claim seniority!" The holy man laughed quietly before breaking off in a dry cough.

Similarly, months of arduous, painstaking work to retain the services of key warlords in the western armies of the Horde—an astronomical sum to be delivered under the care of my finest Han agents—can not be a bizarre misfortune. Nicodemus must have staggering resources hidden away by now.

The spymaster of the Oculus Dei smiled before continuing. "This week Zarbenus provided evidence that the noble Dacian family of which we recently spoke have indeed a strange habit for the bedchamber; the father shares his sheets with his eldest daughter, and the mother that with her youngest son. The information has already been used to assure their compliance when the war council votes on tithe allocations next month. This 'God of Thieves' strategy of stealing snippets of information for blackmail has proven to be much subtler, and much more effective than our original proposal of targeted assassinations. My spy also noticed another young apprentice following in the shadows."

Pallas shrugged. "My master, Diagoras, taught me that the wise man seeks out those most talented to serve him. It does not require great intelligence to follow such a simple precept."

The sacred bowl so fortuitously intercepted by Zarbenus is the third and most damning judgement against you, Nicodemus. I cannot confront you directly. Your position is too secure and I know not the furthest extent of your betrayal, nor with whom you conspire. It will take time to isolate and then replace you without incident.

"You are too humble, sir. None have your skill in persuading such men to work for you in the first place," said Nicodemus.

"Nicodemus, you always strike the correct balance between flattery, and reminding me of the acuity of your insights. I praise the Goddess you were sent to me. With the gentleman in question, I am reminded that a dog that is beaten will obey you when you appear powerful just as much as the dog you feed morsels; but only the spoiled dog serves you as well when you appear weak. Which approach then makes you the wiser master?" Pallas clasped his hands in a moment of prayer, his brow furrowed.

"Something is bothering you, I can tell," said Nicodemus.

Other than your treachery?

"Only I truly grasp the threat posed by the Horde. As long as the summer palaces of the nobles are not ravaged they belittle the danger. Most certainly they refuse to allow either an expansion of the Athanatoi forces, or to ally with our troops for decisive action. They perceive such as a strategy by the priesthood to claim a dominant role in power within the city—a role that once grasped would never be relinquished." Pallas shook his head. "The heathens will sweep away all we have built here, they worship only blood. Their blasphemy cannot go unchecked, or we are all doomed."

"Not all the noble courts are as oblivious as they appear, Hierarch. Many are quietly bolstering their defences and training militias that ignore the quotas allotted by the governing council."

"It is too little and it will come too late. Once the Horde fixes its hungry glare on us the attack will be irrepressible. Unless..."

"You have a strategy, Hierarch?"

Pallas steepled his fingers and regarded the spymaster over their tips. "Only that there must be some galvanising action, before all is lost. Something that shocks all the noble courts to their foundations, demands that they support us in what must be done. It has to happen soon, yet I admit, I cannot see what it can be."

If Nicodemus plots with Bey Izmir then I have gravely underestimated the power they jointly wield. That threat must be tempered ruthlessly, before it grows too great to forestall. Fortunately, I have a sufficiently controllable harbinger of death for exactly such a situation.

Nicodemus looked at the ceiling and breathed deeply. "Your gambit to manipulate the Oikos is proving effective just as they are becoming a credible faction."

Deception and misdirection, Nicodemus? You forget with whom you treat.

"Yes, but they are all under the sway of a single man. A man of enormous influence, whose weakness I have found and thus he is mine. For most men that weakness is a pretty face. Tempt them with a beautiful woman and they will follow her down dark paths that lead to their destruction; even if they are filled with doubt about her sincerity. But not so with this man. Zarbenus is in love with only Zarbenus. All he does serves only Zarbenus. Any act he performs in service of the Oikos is simply to further the burgeoning legend of Zarbenus. And what could one offer such a man? I tempt him with more Zarbenus. Eternal Zarbenus. You need not know the how, only that I lead him down a path of my choosing.

"The den of thieves he has built—his Vipers Nidus—well, let us simply say its purpose is anything but the education of a new generation of master thieves. However the manipulation of Zarbenus alone took years; time we do not have to break the myriad allegiances, treacheries, and bloodlines that knot the noble courts. They have battled each other for centuries, and alas I struggle to see what would unite such fractious parties." He shook his head as if to clear it. "Very well, send a message to our dear God of Thieves. Tell him it is time for him to climb the spire, and if he does not I will find another who will."

At least the motives and machinations of Zarbenus are clear to me. These are black days indeed when I trust a murderer more than any other.

"The spire..." Nicodemus tilted his head with the unasked question.

"He will know exactly what that means. While you are at it ensure gossip flows in the low town that the God of Thieves claims delight in his victorious atrocity. Never mind what, it will all make sense by the morrow. Now, go tend to things as you do so well, but permit me a boon and keep an eye on this new stripling Zarbenus favours. We must make sure that particular strategy remains on track. I will dwell on our other problems."

Nicodemus bowed low before quietly retiring and closing the door behind him. Pallas exhaled slowly, and his head rolled back against his chair as he gazed at the ceiling. In his mind's eye, the intersecting probabilities of actions and reactions of a thousand plots and schemes looped and spun around a central locus glowing with pure white light. He mentally nudged a vibrating pathway into a more favourable orbit, then he smiled.

Cautiously he eased himself up out of his chair and shuffled over to a plain wood-panelled wall, which he rapped with his knuckle before moving on. The panel opened and a beautiful young boy with pale golden hair emerged, lifting the hem of his long white robes as he stepped from the hidden alcove.

"What does the Goddess teach us about rebirth, Marius?" Hierarch Pallas perched himself on the window ledge in a somewhat precarious fashion for a man of his frail figure. He gazed at the gardens beyond as martins darted and swooped hunting for insects in the warm afternoon sunlight.

Marius cleared his throat and recited, "That, 'as all seasons pass, and winter must but change to the spring. So it is with wisdom and the greatest of which passes pure and unsullied yet burnished with experience from the old who become young again. Thus the cycle remains unbroken, and they that cherish this wisdom most dearly will never die.'"

"Your diction is wonderful lad! Now, what would be the demotic interpretation?"

Marius frowned for a moment then continued, "The people believe that if one's faith is strong enough they will be reborn."

Hierarch Pallas steepled his fingers. "Literally reborn. Or...?"

"A literal rebirth, and they have proof that their faith is justified with your—I mean your office's—eternal presence."

"And thus what would be the hieratic understanding?"

Marius' brow uncreased at the more comfortable question. "Rebirth of knowledge passes from the wise to the young. It is our sacred duty to faithfully pass on the teachings of the Goddess, and add the depth of wisdom that comes from years of service. The simple metaphor the common folk hold dear is quite sufficient for their menial lives and limited intellects. This is not so far from the truth to be considered misleading. Rather, that it is appropriate, and..."

"And convenient. Quite so."

Chapter 25:
Blood on the Spire

Zarbenus decoded the written message and scanned its contents. Then he crumpled the paper, threw it to the ground and crushed it into the dirt with his heel. They were supposed to be equals and it galled to be sent such explicit and curt instructions like some fettered lackey. Still, it suited his grander ambitions and that's why he stood in the crowds, allowing himself to be jostled and shoved like the common servant that Hierarch Pallas treated him as.

The Palace of Dreams; behind all the defences and guards 'tis a pleasure dome. An imperial *harîm's* court—a seraglio of exquisite taste and architectural marvels. A fortress it is not, but a fortress surrounds it. Its scale and grandeur separate it from the three concentric military fortifications that encircle it. The first manned by regular soldiers. The second policed by a contingent of hand-picked Basilisks. The innermost ring exclusively guarded by an elite unit of eunuchs chosen at birth and raised to a fanatical devotion for their calling. Beyond these gates, the only males that passed were the close family members and personal friends of the Pasha who, despite his retirement from the political scene some years previous, had remained the nominal head of Byzantium's most noble family. It was impossible for a man unknown to them to enter. Only female servants were permitted access, and a steady stream of them trundled carts filled with all the fruits and meats for the extensive kitchens. Veiled and discrete; more women carried baskets of eggs or bore yokes with wine caskets swinging at their shoulders.

The guards stood diligent and alert at each gate; questioning the female porters, rummaging through carts piled high with clucking chickens and belligerent geese. They didn't search everyone as the disruptions to the palace goings-on would have been too great. Not one of them noticed as a single porter—one the guards never felt drawn to examine in close quarters—detached herself from the procession and melted imperceptibly into the shadows at the base of the buttress wall of the palace. Veiled and elegant, walking past the final gate as cool breezes played within the irrigated pleasure gardens, the scents of jasmine and orange blossom wafting past.

Rolling behind an impeccably trimmed juniper hedge, Zarbenus made himself comfortable and dozed while he waited for night. Half-dreams came to him; visions of standing exultant upon the spire of the palace as a divine light infused his body. The years rolling away and an eternal strength filling every sinew of his frame. He could see to the far horizon, see all the people, great or common toiling at their labours. Just by listening he heard their hopes and dreams, their fears and terrible secrets, prayers and most private confessions. When he realised that the air had cooled and the skies were darkening the fantasies melted away, his attention sharpened and his senses sprung fully alert.

No-one passed through the garden as the evening settled in, though Zarbenus caught faint scents from a kitchen, murmuring voices and the clatter of dishes. Leaving his leafy nook he passed into the palace; pools of light where twisted silver candelabra cast their inviting glow, and deepest softest shadow where he slipped silently through the corridors. Was no-one ever still in this place? The chattering of the women formed a tapestry that lay across each floor of the palace, weaving itself from room to room. Zarbenus drifted between the strands leaving them undisturbed and his passage invisible to all.

✝ ✝ ✝

Stamos stood erect at his post, despite the long hours of boredom he was proud to be one of the elite eunuchs trusted by the Pasha to guard the most intimate family quarters. Nearly twenty years he had served, working his way through each promotion in rank through bloody-minded persistence. A man of modest height with wider girth than he'd have liked, so he couldn't compete on brute strength. Similarly, he wasn't the most quick-witted; he knew this and accepted it, for how can you overcome your faults if you deny them? Yes, grit was the attribute Stamos admired most in himself. Every shift he had ever served his back was straight, his senses alert, and he never snuck off for a quick nap or a sly cup of wine. Strict Stamos his compatriots called him, and in secret it pleased him enormously. Being strict for nearly twenty years had seen him to where he was now; a flawless, unblemished service record, with just a few months until he formally receiving his retirement and the excellent pension men of his level of sacrifice were used to receiving from a thankful Pasha. A little farm perhaps, maybe on the Aegean coast, a few vines, possibly try his hand at making some wine? These daydreams were all Stamos needed to keep his company on long, boring stints of lone guard duty where the safety of his post translated to an absolute minimum of interesting activity of any sort.

What was this? One of the *harîm* women strolled down the hall. As soon as she saw him she paused, then advanced swaying her hips and gazing at him over her veil. Dark, luxurious makeup around fascinating blue-grey eyes. So rare! Unusually tall and slim too.

Stamos liked tall and slim women—the taller and slimmer the better. Contrary to popular understanding, eunuchs were still men and they enjoyed the private company of a beautiful woman as much as any other; though a little creativity was required.

She was definitely giving him the eye. Tilting her head, turning her shoulders, and those rolling hips! Stamos ran the tip of his tongue across his dry lips. He surreptitiously sucked in his belly, stuck his chest out a bit more. Ladies love a man in uniform, he mused. Everyone knows that.

The *harîm* woman stopped in front of him, shyly peeking at him with those opal eyes; could he see a smile beneath her gauzy veil? She raised a pale finger and stroked the side of his face. He trembled, his throat tightened and he swallowed with difficulty. She leaned in close. Jasmine and rose perfume intoxicated him.

A whispered, husky voice; her lips so close he could feel her breath against his cheek. "So handsome... Maybe when I've finished with the Pasha I'll come back and get to know you."

Stamos liked a woman with a husky voice. It was one of the sexiest attributes he could imagine. He nodded, his heart thumping against his ribcage.

She exhaled, his spine shivered; she patted his chest, and his spear hand started trembling so hard he had to clench his grip to stop it rattling. Then she breezed past him, jasmine and rose in her wake, and she was gone.

Stamos took a long, deep lungful of air and a childish grin clambered up his face. Today promised to be one he'd never forget.

† † †

On the third floor a painted wooden spinning top lay in the corner of a room, fine gauzy silks hung from a single hook in the ceiling shrouding a crib beneath. Branching three-legged candlestands lit the room so the nursemaid might work on her embroidery as the little prince slumbered. Such strong lights cast deep shadows, and inside them Zarbenus worked unseen as he thrust a dark needle into the woman's neck; one gloved hand stifling her mouth for the brief moment before the poison stilled her for good.

He parted the silk and the child looked up, liquid dark eyes, and smiled. Zarbenus put his hand over the child's mouth and seconds later the poisoned needle had completed its work. He watched the life fade from those eyes, and what did he feel? It was a mercy to go out so quickly. Bey Izmir's son was lucky that it was Zarbenus to deliver the killing blow, t'would have been far worse and drawn out terror had someone less skilled than him be here tonight. The child's dead weight worse than a sack of rocks but Zarbenus slung the body over his shoulder, his mind consumed with the scene that was to follow.

The waxing moon wallowed behind thin wisps of cloud so he began his climb on the western wall. The heavily weathered mortar made for a fair ascent, even with his burden; the only challenge an awkward balustrade where the wall met the swelling tulip bulb of the spire itself. Breathing heavily he dragged the child's body up the slope, noticing in passing disappointment that what looked like gilding from afar was merely a bronze of some kind. Even base lead might have attracted thieves; this false wealth was worthless. The tip of the spire bore an iron shaft where once must have flown the emperor's standard. A fitting place for him to make his delivery. Swearing colourfully and sweating like a dog he half-pushed, half-dragged the corpse to the spike, pushed it up and impaled it there. He tilted his head to examine the macabre puppetry then with a knife from his boot slashed the femoral artery on each inner thigh. The blood flowed well enough then, rivulets trickling down the bronze dome and over the edge.

It was done. And now? The voices in his head taunted him, asking; what do you want, Zarbenus?

If I could, I would steal the sun and the moon from the sky! Why? Because they are there and no-one else could. In the brief span of life we are allotted, I want to take everything and when future generations look back, they see only me. Do you understand? No emperors or princeps or hierophants... only Zarbenus! Only me for all time!

A breath of wind the cadence of a woman's amorous sigh parted the clouds and bathed him in a milky light. Zarbenus spun to face the moon, grinning with bared teeth, and a hammering heartbeat that had nothing to do with the exertions of his hard climb. He held his breath, closing his eyes, feeling his cheeks flush, waiting for it to happen; for his gift to be bestowed.

A minute passed, then another, and then the moonlight faded as the clouds slid over once more.

Idiot.

What a fool he'd been to lap up tales of a magical prophecy like a gullible babe being told their bedtime stories. Zarbenus turned his back on the corpse of the mutilated child to climb back down the tower. But then, how was he to know, really? And why was it that Pallas always exuded such surety. It was more than just religious zeal, it went beyond faith—he knew things. Much as Zarbenus wanted to mock the Hierarch, it gnawed at him that all the preaching may actually have been right all along.

Chapter 26:

Heart of the Mountain

The Magister's absences at the Nidus frequently lasted several weeks, though he regularly took one of the Vipers on shorter expeditions. Despite Soraya and Ghost vying to be the first to rise in the morning and begin their forms, grumbling arose as the boredom spread amongst them. The twins had taken to practising together, away from the eyes of the others. Fan watched them walk down the path from the house, leading to whatever secret place they had chosen for their own purposes.

"Those two always gave me the creeps, now I don't trust them at all. Whatever they're planning."

Soraya paused her spiralling knife patterns and drew herself up before answering.

"The Magister teaches us not to rely on others, and that we should look to ourselves to accomplish things before looking to others."

"He says that a lot to me," said Ghost.

"Nonetheless," said Soraya, "You're just getting suspicious because you are bored."

"And we've eaten all the tasty stuff. There's only dry rice, and bits of meat so tough it's like chewing on leather. In fact, I think tonight I might try my shoe instead of any more of the stuff we had yesterday." Scab screwed up his face.

"Bleargh. I kept getting the taste coming up for hours afterward," said Foul as he chuckled.

"We could always visit the village tonight." Crooked didn't manage much excitement in his voice as he made his suggestion.

Ghost sighed and looked down the valley where the smoke of cooking fires and twinkles of light came through the leafy canopy below. "It's too easy. I want something new to do."

Soraya scratched the tip of her nose as she thought, something she would do when thinking about what evening tale she would spin. It was a gesture that filled the others with anticipation, and all conversations stilled as they turned to her.

"We could pack some food and blankets and just go away for a few days," she said.

"On our own?" Crooked looked to Ghost for support.

"Well, if you're still a baby you can stay here, Crookey," said Soraya. "But I think the rest of us can manage fine on our own."

Crooked puffed his chest out. "I'm not scared, I just meant we might not be best to go off when he doesn't know where we are."

"He comes and goes without telling us all the time. I don't see why this is any different," said Soraya.

"Fine then," said Fan. "Where will we go?"

"Anywhere. The Magister always tells us to take what we want," said Soraya.

Crooked sighed. "Yes, but we actually should have someplace in mind, if we just wander off we'll argue at every fork in the road."

Ghost looked out past the valley, to the white-capped mountain beyond. "I want to go there," he said, then as certainty rose he pointed at the taller of the two peaks. "I want to go there, I want to climb to the top and see the entire world."

But what he was thinking was: If I find my destiny I'll know who I am.

Soraya pursed her lips and looked at the mountain. "How far away do you ken it is?"

"No more than a couple of days. The Magister said he climbed to the top and back in a single day," said Ghost. "Why couldn't I climb it? And I think it stares back at me. I want to master it."

"I ken... it's too close to winter." Fan screwed up his face as he peered through the window. "It's a fine idea, but you know how quickly the weather can change. Besides, it looks like there is a lot of snow there already."

"But it always has snow on it, even in the middle of summer. This autumn's as warm as most summers and the snowline is as high as I've ever seen it. Come on... don't be scared!"

Fan rubbed the back of his neck as he pondered at the distant mountain, ignoring as Ghost tugged at his sleeve. "I'm not scared, just being careful. If you know your risks you can plan ahead."

"So you'll come?"

"Yes, I'll come, if only to make sure none of you do anything stupid. And I'm not going to walk the whole way there. We'll need some donkeys from the village. I'll have a word with Nuray's father and slip him a few coins." He tried to fend off Ghost trying to hug him, but after a few mock protestations he gave in.

Crooked winked at Fan. "Is that the girl in the village you've been sneaking out to meet?"

Fan sighed and patted Crooked on the head. "Woman. You'll understand when you're a couple of years older."

"I understand now!"

"Then be a man and learn discretion, or I'll teach it to you with my knuckles," said Fan.

Crooked laughed at that and headed back to the Nidus. In the house they began to pile up everything they thought would be useful. They rolled up blankets and oilskins and tied them with cord. Ghost threw ropes onto the pile in hopes of finding some exciting ascents, and Crooked made a separate pack with clean linen for bandages, adding a good selection of herbs and other remedies.

Soraya insisted they carry as much of dried goat meat from their stores as they could. "Better to have extra and have to carry it all the way back home than to run out and be hungry."

All the others agreed with that part of the plan. As they were making the final checks and tying up their packs Dogan and Demir came in. Their shining faces damp with sweat, cheerfully teasing each other. Their smiles faded when they saw the packs and bundles.

"What's going on here?"

"Are you going somewhere?"

"You seem not to have included us in your plans."

"It's not that—truly!" Soraya stood and smiled at the brothers. "You've been away all morning and we only thought of doing it a few hours ago, well Ghost thought of it and we all said it was a great idea."

"We're going to climb the big mountain. You coming?" Ghost hoped his casual attitude let everyone know he wasn't fearful of the twins.

The twins glanced at each other and grinned.

"Of course we want to do it!"

"We'll even race you to the top."

"Wouldn't want to come second to a runt like you."

Ghost bared his teeth. "We can do it now if that's what you want."

"We do," said Demir.

"When we get to the top we can put an end to—"

Fan patted Ghost on the forearm, steering him away from Dogan. "Settle down."

Ghost shrugged off Fan's hand, and returned to checking his pack. "You should pack your bags then. We're going to eat as much as we can tonight, and go to sleep early. Then we'll start off tomorrow at dawn."

The evening meal passed quickly, filled with excited chatting, and any differences between them were set aside with the anticipation of the coming adventure. The brothers seemed more relaxed than they had in months, and even chuckled at Crooked's jokes. Scolded upstairs by Soraya when they had finished, everyone retired. Crooked followed Ghost back to his quarters as they whispered together, then curled up under a blanket and slept there.

Ghost turned over restlessly in the night, unable to relax with the thrill of adrenaline in his veins. He dozed for some hours but as the night greyed into the hour before dawn he yawned and rolled off his cot.

"Just another hour..." Crooked grumbled with his eyes screwed tight. He rolled over, covering his head.

Ghost grabbed the edge of the blanket, and yanked it off him then held it up like a prize. "If you want it you'll have to come and get it, and that means wake up!"

Crooked squinted out from underneath his arm. "It's not even dawn!"

"It soon will be. Come on, we need to get up and get started," said Ghost.

"Remind me why I signed up for this?"

"Because it'll be fun. Now come on."

More grumbles rumbled from Crooked, but under his breath. He yawned and struggled to his feet. "I'm going to hold you to that. Any part of this that turns out not fun, and I'm going to blame you for everything."

"Where's your spirit of adventure?"

"In bed. Asleep," said Crooked.

Ghost laughed and slapped Crooked on the arm. "Let's get the others."

They knocked on the other doors and shouted encouragement, but when they got downstairs they found Soraya already awake and making a final check of their equipment and supplies.

"Eat quickly. I've laid out some food on the table. Once you're done you should each fill a waterskin, and then we can be on our way. Fan has arranged our transportation."

"Taking charge already, Soraya?" Ghost scowled. She looked at him like a cat watches a mouse.

"Don't worry, I'm not going to spoil your grand adventure. Just making sure we actually get out the door," said Soraya.

The twins pushed past both of them, mouths crammed with food, and went outside to wake up the donkeys. The indignant braying of the beasts flipped another wave of excitement in Ghost's stomach, and he hurried after Dogan and Demir.

The donkeys protested but were largely compliant once their bridles were on, a task which usually took two of the children acting as a team to accomplish. They nipped at the hands that tried to guide the bit between their teeth, irritable after their early waking. Once the animals had been bridled and their reins tied to a post they settled down, champing and drooling. Soraya tied two packs together and slung them over their haunches in a balanced fashion, then she tied her blanket roll over the top and jumped onto her donkey. Fan came out of the house last, carrying the remaining packs.

"I've left the Magister a note, telling him where we've gone and when we should be back."

"I don't think he'll worry," said Ghost. "As long as he thinks we're taking what we want because we can."

The dawn glowed coral and gold as they made their way down the mountainside. They broke away from the path that led to the village and veered toward the white mountains. As they rode they drifted apart, the brothers taking up the rear, whispering to each other and then snickering. Soraya kept her donkey ahead of the others, looking for the best path and whistling back to the others when she wanted to change their way.

"It's not like we're going to get lost, is it? We're not going to miss a massive mountain." Crooked kept his voice low.

"She's happier doing it. I say let her." Ghost shrugged. "Besides, if she is busy organising things and looking out for danger then she's less likely to find a reason to thump any of us."

314

"That is true," said Crooked, nodding.

By midday the mountain didn't look much closer, rather that it had grown in stature. They rested the donkeys at a lush sward that blanketed the sloping banks of a brook, and had their own lunch in the shade of a wild olive tree. Mosquitos and gnats swarmed them, but they slapped and swatted and muttered curses just for the chance to rest in the cool shade.

"That sun gets pretty hot beating down on your head." Fan was flushed and shiny from the morning's riding, a task he usually undertook with some reluctance. Despite no ill-feeling on his part, it seemed most animals did not take a liking to him, and he was as likely to get kicked as to mount up in safety.

"Mmm," said Ghost as he chewed a dried fig. "Should be good for the climb then."

They topped up their water skins and with a good deal of rein tugging managed to get the donkeys away from the patch they grazed. The low hilly ground they rode over was sparsely wooded, tiny autumn berries on thorny scrub flecking the landscape with colour. Riding without any shade the sweat trickled down their backs and ran down their faces.

"You call this fun?" Crooked fidgeted with his hood, his face pink and shiny. Wearing it up shielded him from the sun but it grew sticky and close after only a few minutes and it denied him relief from the heat any wisps of breeze brought.

Ghost beamed as he scanned the surrounding land. "Doesn't it feel amazing? Just to be able to go where we please?"

The conversation stilled as they almost rode into the back of Soraya's donkey. She was talking to an ogre of a man, a studded club resting on his shoulder and a very sour expression on his face. A fallen pine tree lay across the path, spikey branches snapped and broken, and the big man seated on the trunk.

"Think of it as a tax for using the road," said the big man.

"What I think is that you are a common brigand," said Soraya.

The big man laughed, but there was little humour in the sound he made.

"What a spirited child you are. Still, it ain't going to help you, I'm just a scout, but the rest of the boys are around near enough. Hand over your money and I'll let you pass. Give me any more trouble, and I'll take all your stuff, and those animals too." He grunted, stood up, and took a two-handed grip on his club.

The laughter of the twins trailed off as they came to a stop behind Fan.

"I'm not a spirited child, and I take offence at your tone," said Soraya.

She slid off her donkey and the others quickly followed. The twins parted and circled around the brigand. Fan and Ghost stood either side of Soraya, and Crooked walked quickly to stand a few paces behind the man.

"You're a scout for the Horde?" Ghost's face soured and he spat to the side.

Soraya drew her knife, and watching as the man's breathing quickened and grew shallow.

"Due to the degree of offence I take at your tone, the look in your eye, and even the way you smell, I have decided that we will instead be liberating you of your purse." She pointed her weapon at the limp pouch on his belt.

He laughed again, and this time there was even less humour in it. Maybe a tinge of nerves. "You can't rob me, brats. I'm not so soft that I won't beat a child."

The brigand lifted his club an inch off his shoulder. Five more knives whispered from their sheaths.

"Have you ever seen a lion killed by wolves?" Soraya's voice was so soft it seemed she was almost talking to herself. "I have. Oh, he roared and he snapped, but they were quicker than him. They nipped and tore at him, one after another. He bit at one, who leapt away as his brother attacked the lion's exposed flank, and so on. Took them half an hour to wear him down, near the end he just staggered and whimpered, blood dripping from a hundred wounds. Finally, the lion just lay down and bared its throat. There was no fight left in him. Spirit broken, overpowered and outmatched, he just wanted to die. We may be cubs to you, but we're wolf cubs.

"Each one of us here wouldn't even blink to draw a dagger across your throat even while you pleaded for mercy. Me? Personally, I won't even take the time to strike higher than your belt. Not when there are such easy, soft targets dangling in reach."

The big man's sweat ran down his face in sheets, and his eyes darted between their dispassionate expressions. The edges of their knives glittered, and not one of them pointed above his waist.

"Take it, damn you!"

He threw his purse at Soraya's feet. She caught it on her toe, flicked it up and tucked it into her belt.

"Our business is concluded."

She turned her back on him, goading him to act, but as she heard his soft exhalation she closed her eyes and smiled, knowing that she had beaten him. She mounted up and watched as the others got back onto their donkeys. They rode past without a word and it was not for another minute before they heard the faint voice shout from behind them.

"Damn you, devil spawn!"

It was too much, and all of them save for Soraya laughed.

"He was a discredit to vagabonds everywhere. Just a thug really, but I doubt he'll be standing there on our return," she said.

The incident remained the main topic of conversation that afternoon, each retelling giving rise to new fits of giggles. Soraya only laughed when in a moment of curiosity she checked the purse and found a very disappointing collection of copper pieces and two badly forged lead lumps masquerading as gold.

"I imagine he thinks we've walked away with a decent purse, but really there is only enough for a good meal here—excepting the chance that we'd find someone feeble-minded enough to accept these as gold."

Relief as the evening drew in made them eager to find a cool spot to sleep. A grove of almond trees proved a suitable place away from the road where they could make a small fire with little chance of being seen. Aware that the brigand or his friends could easily be trailing them, they decided to keep a watch. Ghost insisted he was still too excited to sleep and offered to sit awake for the first hour. He watched the stars come out and decided he liked them better than through a window. When his eyes grew heavy he shook Soraya by the shoulder. She woke without much reluctance to take her turn on watch, and so the night passed without incident.

The next day passed peacefully and the temperature cooled as they passed through cedar woodland and welcome shade. The Vipers made camp on a hillock beside a sparkling brook and spent a quiet night without interruption. The surprise at dawn was how much closer the mountain appeared, and how it dominated their whole view. The hills rose gently about its base then the craggy shoulders of the mountain forced themselves up out of the ground like a stone giant breaking free from a subterranean slumber. The lower slopes rough and rocky with sparse greenery visible at this distance, but above the snowline, it shone silver-white in the morning light with deep black slashes where deadly ravines cut through.

"We'll make it there by nightfall, then if the weather holds we'll go straight up tomorrow," said Ghost.

They soon found a proper trail heading in the direction they were going and picked up the pace. Riding past goats and sheep herded by a barefoot boy with curly brown hair, they waved at him. He smiled and waved back, then blew a kiss to Soraya. Her cheeks flushed pink.

"You have an admirer, Soraya," said Fan.

"Well at least we know that the locals are friendly," she said, ignoring any attempt to get her even more embarrassed.

Closer to the mountain, as they urged their donkeys up the increasingly steep slope, they saw roughly hewn animal enclosures and large drum-shaped tents. Nomadic Turan peoples lived in the area, though the grazing was better away from the mountain. Herds of dingy grey sheep foraged on the patches of grassland, with lone white goats chewing buds off the thorny bushes that sprouted from every crack in the ground. Boulders and broken rocks covered the area beneath the snowline and dark smears showed where landslides had scarred the slopes.

"We'll never get the donkeys up there. They'd stumble for sure and break their legs." Ghost tried to control his rising excitement but it seemed to him now that all his thoughts of climbing the mountain before this day were just dreams, here he was standing at its base, ready to take his first steps on it. Ready to claim his destiny.

So close to the base of the mountain they all agreed it best to press on to their final campsite. They ate as they rode, passing more friendly faces of men on horseback and the toothless smiles of old women bundled up in black shawls. The menfolk favoured bright scarves tied around their midsection, curved dagger thrust into their belt, the engraved hilts catching the sunlight. By late afternoon they stopped at a flat area between two piles of huge rocks. A Turanian family had pitched their tent there and Soraya spoke with them in a dialect none of the others understood. After some minutes she called the others over, and they shared their dried food with the family and received bowls of hot stew in return.

Soraya spoke at length with the father, a powerfully built man with a thick black moustache and keen dark eyes. His demeanour slowly changed from relaxed and happy to obvious alarm. The other Vipers did not need to understand his words to appreciate his intent.

"He calls it Sorrow and says that the mountain is very dangerous and hungers for death. That there is no reason to go there because all we will find is ice and... it is a place that should be left alone for the gods," she said after a moment's thought.

"I'm going even if I have to go alone," said Ghost. "He underestimates us, they all do."

"I've told him that, and that we are experienced climbers, but he begs us not to go," said Soraya.

"Thank him for his kindness, but tell him that we must."

Soraya spoke to the man again and he threw up his hands, looking to his wife for support who gave him a weary shrug. He spoke again with Soraya, first wagging his finger, and then with a sigh he leaned forward, speaking earnestly. The Turan pointed at places of note on the mountain's black silhouette, so tall that it blotted out almost half of the stars in the sky.

"He says he would not let his children go, and asks where our parents are. I told him that our father has made the ascent and he fears nothing for us. Then he said that the Turan call this the heavy mountain and that landslides are common; if you don't get out of the way you'll be crushed. The same can happen above the snowline, but with great chunks of ice breaking away and tumbling down. After I insisted, the only thing he said is that if we cannot be dissuaded then we should tackle it from the northwest, as the going is easier that way."

Ghost touched his hand to his forehead as he had seen the man do when they first met. The Turanian smiled and spoke again.

Soraya chuckled. "He says you are a clever young man and you learn fast. Maybe you will not die on the mountain."

"Ask him if he will keep watch over our donkeys tomorrow. We have those coins you took from the brigand," said Ghost.

Soraya spoke with the Turanian again, offering the pouch but he refused it. He grew close to anger with the force of his protestations, but lapsed back into easy humour as soon as she withdrew it. She too touched her forehead.

"He would not take it and says we are his guests. I'll accidentally drop it in his pocket the next time we pass," she said.

"What would the Magister say about such a reverse pickpocket," laughed

Crooked.

"He'll say nothing as he'll not hear about it? Am I understood?"

Whenever Soraya spoke like that the others would look away and nod in agreement. This was no exception.

To thank her host Soraya offered to tell a story that his children might enjoy, and after his encouragement, she began her tale. The Vipers could only snatch a word here and there but from the tone and her actions, they knew it was one they loved. They watched the faces of the nomad's daughters come alive in excitement. Even the man and his wife clapped their hands as the bold hero's bravery bested the irredeemable villain and avenged his lover's death.

The last of the apple tea was drunk, and the woman tidied the last of the coals into a small pile and covered them with stones. The man fiddled with the flaps of his tent until he restrapped it so that a long awning came down from the side and provided a sheltered area for his guests to sleep under.

They laid side-by-side on their blankets and soon fell asleep.

Chapter 27:

Dreams of Poppy Tears

The stench of stale sweat and the sweet-sickly aftertaste of opium smoke seeped around the ragged curtain that marked the entryway to the den where the dragon chasers went to lose themselves, to feed the coiled demon within. Even the refuse-strewn slit alley that led here was stilled and soporific. The distant tones of raised voices and clattering wheels from an industrious city seeming like ghostly memories—the pained cough from within, rattling with forced expectoration; the common language here.

Zarbenus paused, his hand unmoving on the curtain. Then he snarled, swept the soiled cloth aside, and dipping his head under the low beam he entered.

Coughing from the corner of the room stopped as he paused to let his eyes adjust to the gloom. No candles, just the twinkled red flares as supine figures on mats sucked at their pipes. To each side, sheets hung to partition off more private areas. An incomprehensible muttering from behind the one to the right, too low to make out more than the cadence of alternate pleading and disapproval; yet words from one throat in conversation with itself. An ancient Han woman raised herself from the only chair in the room, returning the pipe she had been wiping to a box of jumbled stems by her feet. She stared at Zarbenus with grim resentment, then untied the coin purse that hung from a loop around her neck.

Zarbenus stood up to his full height and with a curt chop of his hand stopped the woman's fumbling with the knotted leather cord. Her head tilted as she waited for his instruction, unsure what he could want other than his usual bribe. When he pointed at the box of pipes she leered at him showing her few remaining brown-stained teeth. He loped past her and pulled back the nearest sheet. The sole occupant of the alcove—a young man with the haggard skin of a crone—gaping up at him with unfocused eyes and clutching the carved rosewood stem to his chest lest it be snatched from him. He whined as Zarbenus hauled him to his feet, but offered no resistance and staggered away when prompted with a light push between his shoulder blades. Zarbenus' lip curled as he regarded the thin mat on the floor with its myriad stains and unidentifiable encrustations, but he drew his cloak about himself and settled down with his back to the wall.

The old woman brimmed with smugness as she drew near to him, chuckling to herself. He took the packed pipe she offered and brought the black resin to a smoulder against the coals of the brazier that dangled on a chain from her wrist. A dismissive flick of his head and she withdrew, pulling the curtain across as she did, leaving him in darkness. He watched the glow in the tiny bowl. Held it close as the smoke ran across his face. Sniffed it and stifled a cough as it caught in his throat. As the glow imperceptibly faded he thought of Pallas' words and weighed them for truth or trap.

But what do I risk, truly? The feeble-minded, cattle-folk, braying under their master's lash and straining not at all to break free from his leash. Surely those weaklings ensnare themselves. Leave the gate open at night and not one of them would dare venture outside, too safe in their herd, too scared to stand alone. The old man was right in that at least, scant few men stand above all others. Those that are reckoned leaders, heroes, villains... gods.

He rolled the pipe stem between his thumb and fingertips. Fear was for cattle. He put the mouthpiece to his lips and drew a steady breath, holding the smoke within his lungs and ignoring the burning as he would when lying in wait underwater. Exhaling in a slow, measured draft he felt the glow loosen his tense jaw, ease his shoulders and he let his head roll back to rest against the wall.

† † †

The golden light swelled as the grand curtains drew back to reveal the dapper figure on the stage and the audience murmured their approval. A faint round of clapping that petered off as the lone actor shaded his eyes, examining some distant vista and began his monologue. He pondered aloud what a strange fate to be thrust upon one so young. Whether he was at fault finding denial in his heart when his mentor—for an orphan like him, practically his father—requested a first and final boon from him.

A dark hooded figure now appears from the wings, unheeded by the young man who sinks to one knee and rests his forehead against his fist as he broods on his lot. The hooded figure, face wreathed in shadows, engages with the audience and tells them of his many years of sacrifice. That all he has cared for is the education and health of the young man they see before them. Is it not right, he asks them in tones reasonable and polite, that such a youth should feel some degree of debt and duty that ought to be repaid, with interest?

The young man awakens from his reverie, sees the hooded figure and cries out a happy greeting. Bounding across to meet each other they embrace warmly. The young man effusively declares his affection and affirms the rightness his filial bonds. The hooded figure takes a step back, an outstretched arm keeping some distance between them. He queries whether this outpouring of love means the youth is finally prepared to sacrifice his freedom for the heavenly path that lies before them both.

The young man turns away from the hooded figure and heart-wrenchingly agonises over his choices. The hooded man turns his back, calmly voicing that all is now in the hands of fate, but as he faces away the youth draws a dagger. The audience gasp, and with a loud plea for forgiveness the youth lunges in an unprovoked attack.

The hooded figure turns at the very last moment. He catches the wrist bearing the dagger and tearfully demands an explanation for such an unexpected betrayal from the one he held dearest in all the world. They wrestle, they fall, and both lie still. Then a sobbing is heard, a piteous wail as the hooded figure rises from the ground showing bloody palms to the audience who weep with him.

Now all is lost. The orphaned youth who was loved like a son. The ascension that they both could have shared, had only the youth been constant and true. Woe for the frailty of youth. Woe for the brief glimmer of hope, now extinguished.

The lights fade as the figures of the tragedy disappear from sight. As the audience murmur their laments at such a poignant ending, a glow appears gently on the edge of the stage revealing briefly the visage of a boy child; dirty-faced but of fierce countenance. That final light fades as well, and the scene is nothing but darkness.

ASCENSION, OR, THE PRICE OF IMMORTALITY

DRAMATIS PERSONAE

The Young Man, a youth

The Hooded Figure, adoptive father to the youth

A Ghost-child of mysterious provenance

A SINGLE ACT:

THE YOUNG MAN — How wonderful and strange is life! To be born with nothing; no parents, no roof over my head, nay not even a crust on which to chew, and then — Mystery! — a benevolent benefactor emerges from the shadows to cast mine weary child's body in warm cloth. To feed my soul and my mind, from his own fingers. [He wrings his hands] And yet... although I owe him my all, how doth I feel when in tones sweet and kind he asks that I repay that debt... and repay it in full...

[The Hooded Figure emerges, unseen by the Young Man]

HOODED FIGURE — Long have I toiled, fingers worn bare, all my coin purses emptied; all for this lad — my hopes! My dreams! ... my future... But does he love me, me who has raised him even as a father would? How would he shew his love? Should he not give anything I require... give everything I require?

[The Young Man finally sees the Hooded Figure, cries out a greeting and they embrace]

HOODED FIGURE — Beloved son! The warmth of your greeting gives me hope you will answer my bidding, make the great sacrifice, and honour your father in his time of need.

[The Young Man breaks away and turns his back on the Hooded Figure]

THE YOUNG MAN – What must I do? Betray my father who dost love me without question, or give my life for him and yet I have only come into my manhood — he has lived so many years already. Do the fates demand that I who've spent so few of my years should give them to one with

327

so many already cast in the dust?

HOODED FIGURE — 'Tis in the hands of the gods now... or rather, those that would be gods themselves?

THE YOUNG MAN — Forgive me, father! [He lunges with a knife at the Hooded Figure, they struggle and fall to the ground]

HOODED MAN — Cruel fate! Wickedest of endings! Years of toil lie in ruins, my son is dead, and with him go my dreams of eternal life, the godhead I was destined for slips from mine twitching grasp! All is ashes, pestilence and death...

[The lights fade until only the silhouette of the Hooded Man can be seen, his weeping growing fainter. Then a single candle is lit, illuminating a grim-visaged boy of some ten summers of age. The boy looks towards the Hooded Man, holds up the candle, then blows out the flame.

THE END

✝ ✝ ✝

Zarbenus lay in his stupor, his chin wet with his own drool. The boy... Ghost. Now he understood, understood what he had known all along and refused to accept. That was why Zarbenus denied the child a name, for one day the child would only be Zarbenus. He thought to himself, *anything I've ever wanted I've taken. What does it matter if some old man says its destiny or simply the whim of the gods? You act. Or, you do not act. What other choice is there?*

Then through all the fog in his mind—the rambling imaginations drifting through his dreams—his heart beat faster and chill spread through his sweaty palms. For the first time in his adult life, he felt terror.

Everything now depends on the boy.

Chapter 28:

Snowblind

Before dawn, the Turanian man rose and tied back the tent flaps as his wife nursed the fire back to life. The cool fresh air and the pale light woke the slumbering Vipers. After a hasty breakfast they shouldered their packs and strapped on their rolls, only then feeling the weight for sure. The Turan clapped Soraya on the shoulder and pointed out the path he recommended once again. He looked at the rest of the boys, and back at his daughters, helping their mother clean things away. He said something to Soraya and she laughed, holding her hand over her mouth. She shook her head and waved goodbye touching her forehead like the nomad man did.

They started walking, sharing smiles as the morning's golden glow bathed them. Briskly pacing themselves to cover as much ground as they could before the heat of the meridian came upon them.

"What was that last thing he said, Soraya?" Ghost listened hard to the dialect they had been using but could not understand more than a few words when the Turan spoke swiftly.

Soraya turned to him, grinning. "He wanted to know if any of you boys were ready to be married off to his daughters."

"What did you tell him?"

"That I might bring you back when you'd grown into men," she said.

"I'm a man already," protested Ghost.

Fan slapped him across the back of the head. "You'll be a man when you quit acting like a child. Now get moving."

It took less than an hour before the ground swelled upward. The pale yellow dawn rushed across the land, sweeping away the sharp shadows and picking out the swirls of dust that rose with each step they took. The mountain filled their horizon, and the wisping clouds that garlanded the greater peak seemed close enough to reach out and brush them away like cobwebs.

"Huh. That sure is a big pile of rocks," said Demir. The twins had moved a few steps ahead of the others, and were looking for a trail up the side of the mountain.

"What did you ken," said Ghost.

"Not sure, but the mountain back at the Nidus has a lot more trees on it. This looks more like someone just poured boulders out of the sky and left it there," said Demir gesturing widely.

"Maybe someone did." Ghost shrugged. "Come on let's keep moving."

"I'll be heading back down at midday, no matter how far we get or how close the summit is. I don't see any reason to take unnecessary risks." Soraya tugged on her pack's straps, made a small noise of satisfaction then started walking up the slope, the twins immediately following her.

Crooked turned to Ghost as they walked. "I thought being this far away from the Magister would loosen her up, but if anything I think she's getting worse."

"She's only looking out for us. You know she takes being the oldest seriously," said Ghost.

"Sure, but we aren't the lost and scared children that arrived at the Nidus. Plus, she isn't even the biggest anymore. Foul and me are both a squeak taller than her. You're almost the same size now," said Crooked.

"I don't think that was what made her the leader. She was the fiercest and that was enough."

"You never wanted to get back at her after she thumped you then?" Crooked bunched up his fists and made a playful jab.

Ghost laughed. "Nope. I just made sure to stay out of her reach."

A stream of small rocks tumbled down the slope and Crooked jumped to the side to avoid them. "Hey! Careful up there, you're causing a landslide!"

The brothers moved ahead of Soraya and scrambled over a large boulder. They looked back and laughed at Crooked, then carried on with their ascent.

"It looks like they'll make good on their promise to beat you to the top." Crooked dusted off his leggings and they started hiking again.

"I'm not competing with them, this is just something I want to do for myself." Ghost forced a nonchalant shrug.

"You don't mind? I thought you always tried to outdo them," said Crooked.

"This is different. I don't know why, but all these years I've tried to impress him, to make him proud of me, but whenever I think about this mountain I feel different." Ghost wasn't sure why he couldn't tell Crooked about the legend of finding a man's destiny at the top, he just felt he couldn't.

"What do you mean?"

"I don't know. It's just that... I need to know that there is something else out there, bigger than the Nidus, bigger than this life we have. I know I can never go home, and because I can't go back I have to go forward," said Ghost.

"But isn't us being with the Magister doing exactly that?"

Ghost wrinkled his nose. "The Magister says we all have our own paths to follow. I don't think he has a plan for each of us, it's more that he is watching us, waiting to see what we decide to do."

"Do you ever think about... well, why he brought us all together?"

"He told us. We're his children," said Ghost.

Crooked rolled his eyes. "I believed that, mostly, when he first said it, but the more I think it just doesn't make any sense. We don't look anything like

331

him—well you and Soraya do a bit—but me and the others don't."

"Maybe it's not him. Maybe it's us."

Crooked scratched his temple. "I suppose. But what could it be? We came from different places, and none of us were special."

"Except that we all had our families killed." *And now I can't even remember my own mother's face*, thought Ghost.

"True, but how many orphans would he have passed by to choose us? Hundreds, thousands maybe?" Crooked threw up his hands.

Ghost fell silent as they worked their way around a boulder surrounded by loose broken rocks, skittering smaller pieces down the mountainside. He looked back to make sure the others were keeping up. A few minutes behind them Fan lumbered along, his hands gripping the pack straps over his broad shoulders. Further back Foul helped Scab across a patch of loose gravel and up a steeper stretch of slope.

"I still believe him." Ghost's voice was soft but sure. "Everything he told me came true. Everything he said I would learn he has taught me. And I want to be just like him."

Crooked groaned. "Just like him—you mean moody and unpredictable?"

"He doesn't need to be watching us the whole time. He made us strong. You saw that highwayman. What other bunch of orphans could have handled that?"

"But why be like him? Why not a farmer or a shopkeeper?"

Ghost looked up the slope to see the brothers pulling further ahead. Her head down and plodding relentlessly, Soraya remained a few steps behind the twins.

"Come on, let's pick it up. I may not need to beat them, but I'm not having them leave us behind."

"You didn't answer my question," said Crooked.

"I know, I was thinking. Before the Magister came for me I thought the world had ended. I didn't see how I would recover from that or even survive.

Then he appeared with all sorts of strange rules and secrets, and as scared and confused as I was—he was always constant and in control. He's got no fear of anyone or anything, no matter how many times he tells us not to do dangerous things. I want to be like that; free from all fear and doubt."

Crooked squinted at Ghost. "For someone that doesn't talk much, you sure think a lot."

Ghost smiled, his cheek creasing. "Sometimes it feels like there is so much to see and do in the world I worry that I will miss it and then suddenly it will be too late."

"But we're still so young."

Ghost shrugged. "Yeah, I know, but sometimes I just can't wait and the need makes my chest go tight."

"Is it like that now?"

Ghost looked up the mountain, at the figures of the twins and Soraya above him, and he thought about how close he was to finding his destiny. "It was when I woke up, but now we're climbing I feel happier than I have for ages."

"Then let's catch them." Crooked started walking quicker, jumping over small rocks and resting his hands on larger ones as he clambered past. Ghost hurried after him.

The sun climbed higher, and the heat of the previous day returned with every degree it ascended. Ghost and Crooked caught up with the twins and Soraya as they paused for a drink of water in the lee of a house-sized boulder with scraps of yellow grass growing around its base.

"We thought we'd give you a sporting chance," said Dogan.

Demir grinned. "Seeing as you were going so slowly."

The brothers winked at each other as they passed their canteen back and forth. Soraya stoppered hers and wriggled to the side so that Ghost and Crooked could share the shade.

"I think we should wait for the others to catch up. Just give them a few minutes," she said.

"Agreed," said Ghost. He glanced at the twins as they whispered to each other. Planning something, probably unpleasant, but as the sun rose further he worried more about the wasted minutes spent talking. Probably not much more than four hours until midday. He couldn't waste any time, not with the risk that Soraya might call a halt to his adventure.

"We'll save the real race for when the summit is in sight," announced Dogan.

"How does that sound; fair?" Demir raised an eyebrow at the others.

Ghost nodded. "Fair enough, but just for fun. I don't care who gets there first."

Fan joined them, his face pink and glistening, and he sunk into the shadow of the boulder with a sigh and unstoppered his flask.

"I didn't think it would be this hard," he said after he had taken a long drink.

Soraya shook her head as she looked down at him. "This is the easy bit. It gets much harder further up. Do you think you can manage it?"

Fan grunted. "I can make it fine. I was thinking about those two." He pointed at Foul toiling toward them a short distance away, carrying a second pack in his arms. Even without his burden Scab staggered along red-faced and scowling.

"This isn't fun. The rocks are too big for me and my feet keep slipping." Scab crumpled to the ground beside Fan and lay there panting.

Dogan scowled at him. "Go home then, baby."

"And come back when you're bigger," said Demir. He flicked a pebble at Scab.

Scab growled as the pebbled bounced off his shoulder, and his hand moved to the hilt of his knife.

"Enough!" Soraya's glare swept across them all, locking eyes with them one at a time. "I said if we were going to do this we'd do it my way. If you carry on like this I'm going to smack you all and send you home. You ken?"

The rest of the boys grumbled their agreement, and the twins fell silent. Ghost glanced at the position of the sun for the hundredth time; more than enough time left, as long as they kept moving.

"Then we can continue," said Soraya. "Scab, pass out some of the heavy things from your pack, we'll each take a few of them and no-one will have to struggle."

Each of the boys accepted the bundles and flasks she passed their way. After staring at the items she held the twins grudgingly took them and stowed them in their packs.

"Everyone have another sip of water, then we'll be on our way. I'll lead and decide when we take breaks. No-one is to go ahead of me." She waited for any grumbles but none came so she shouldered her backpack and tightened the straps. "Let's go then."

The heat rose relentlessly as the morning went on. The gusts of wind that whistled down the ravines never enough to cool them as they sweated their way upward. After a little over an hour, they started to pass bigger boulders with dustings of snow on their caps, and the last of the parched grasses gave way to blue-edged lichens that clung to damp crevices.

Soraya glanced at the sky, then swung her pack to the ground. She wiped the sweat from her brow and smeared back her damp eyebrows as the boys gratefully found places to sit.

"A short break for a bit to eat and then we'll need to press on harder. We don't have many hours left before midday. Scab, how are you doing?"

He wiped away a trickle of mucus that reached his lips. "I'm fine. The pack isn't so heavy now."

"Good. See what we can do when we stick together?"

Dogan snorted. "He's just slowing us down, you know that."

"We should have left him behind," said his brother, but they both fell silent when Soraya stared at them.

The break was all too brief, but they rose without complaint and followed Soraya once again. The gusts of wind bore a fine sand that grated against their skin, and the eddies of snow that ran amongst the boulders and gullies grew deeper. Still the sun rose higher, and the punishing heat seemed incongruous against the chill rising through their feet. Off to the side they saw the lesser peak, though the summit they approached was lost in a vaporous mist.

Dry rivers of shattered stones left by landslides littered the mountain. Deep scars etched into the bedrock that bore witness to massive cascades that tore away everything in their path, leaving behind a treacherous steppe of loose shingle. Fine powdered snow covered the ground, piling in banks where the wind swirled across it. Each footstep gambled their lives and forcing them to crouch for balance. Worse were the natural gullies that crawled up the mountain, growing into deep ravines, narrow and dark. Fan eyed the crevasse as they trailed past, unable to see to the bottom of the treacherous depths. There would be nothing to recover if someone went down there. He had barely started tying a rope around Scab's waist when Foul took a step back to give him room, then slipped backward as his footing failed.

Foul cried out, arms flailing, Scab screamed. Fan turned, dropped to one knee, and lashed out with the free end of the rope he'd just secured. It whistled like a bull-whip, striking Foul across the shoulder. His yelp as the loose end burned his cheek turned Ghost and Crooked's heads in his direction, but by the time they saw what was happening Fan had grabbed the line with both hands. Great deep breaths and with a steady hand-over-hand action; Fan pulled him to safety with all the force and dignity of a portcullis chain.

Foul touched his face, winced, and looked at his fingers flecked with his own blood. His hands twitched involuntarily. "I guess thanks is in order. A second later, and I'd have been gone for good."

Fan finished knotting the rope to Foul so that he and Scab were secured. He peered at Foul's rope-burn, picked out some fibres then slapped a handful of snow against it. Satisfied, he grunted and looked away. "Handsome scar. Women will think you're dangerous and mysterious."

"Really?" Foul stood up straight, looking every inch the conquering hero. His near-death experience already transforming into an exciting anecdote inside him.

"Vapid, frivolous women, with no self-respect," said Soraya.

Foul shrugged. "But still, girls chasing me? Sounds like a clear improvement over none."

"Girls with no self-respect are my favourite," Scab chuckled at him.

"Enough about your imaginary women," said Soraya. "One day—when you're a big boy—you'll find out things are different. For now, save your breath for the mountain."

Soraya pushed the pace, checking the position of the sun every now and then. The group pressed on without chatter, their panting breaths coming harder as they ventured higher. Crooked tried to interest Soraya in sharing a rope tether, then looked baffled when she laughed at him. Her chuckles continued to drift back to him as she climbed ahead. After another hour she allowed them a short break of a few minutes to chew on some dried figs and a quick swig from their flasks, but soon had them on their feet and moving again. A broken shard of the mountain curved ahead of them, less boulder rubble and only a smattering of snow where the sun had melted the larger flows. At the base of the shard, dark openings of cave entrances watched them like empty eye sockets. A trickling brook ran down and across their path, slushy melt-water bobbing in the weak current. They squatted to drink with their hands and refill their flasks.

The sun still shone brightly and the white snow glared, but the air cooled quickly and the wind took a sharp edge that prickled their cheeks.

"My chest hurts." Scab panted, his hands on his knees, wincing with each

337

breath.

Soraya stopped and peered at him. "Can you continue, or do you need another break?"

"He'll be fine," said Foul quickly. "Once we eat lunch then all our packs will be lighter."

Crooked shivered. "Those caves give me the creeps. Bet there are wolves in there."

"Maybe in the winter," said Fan. "But if there were wolves you'd see cracked bones and other spoor in a midden up front. You can imagine monsters if you like, but save the spooky stories for night-time."

Soraya glanced at the sun, then up to the summit that still seemed a great distance away. "We don't have long before we will have to turn back. I don't think we're going to make it."

"No!"

Ghost rounded on her, hearing his heartbeat throb in his ears. The sun still had at least two hours until it reached its zenith. Behind them, the Turanian camp was lost behind the craggy foothills. Dust over the plains turned it into a milky sea, their mountain a lone island, adventurers on the lip of the world. All his problems, doubts, questions seemed to be from a different life. The cascading slope below stretched out endlessly; they'd come so far, so quickly. Above them the sharp ascent was crisp and clear, looking like it was only an arm's reach away. The pressure building behind his eyes, a throbbing headache, was probably just the exertion of the climb.

He pushed the thought away. "We can do it, it's not so far. Let's do what Foul said. We take just a few minutes of rest, then it'll be easy to make it to the top."

She crossed her arms and looked at him with a tilt to her head. "I'm not trying to spoil your fun. If we get into trouble further up there will be no-one to help us. Are you fine with that? Because I'm not."

Ghost raised his hands to her. "We're here to test ourselves, Soraya. To push ourselves into doing something we've never done before. It wouldn't be a challenge if it was easy, would it?"

She stared at him for a moment then looked away.

"No more than a quarter of an hour. Take your shoes off, stretch your toes, and fill your bellies. Then we'll push on and see if we can make it. But if we don't get there in time then we're heading back down—all of us together. Agreed?"

He nodded enthusiastically. "Agreed!"

There was a collective sigh as they settled down and unpacked their food, and for a short while they forgot their tiredness and chattered as they ate. The break did not last long, but they tied up their shoes without complaint and strapped on the comfortably lighter packs before setting off again.

The trail up the broken side of the summit soon became too steep to walk up and they followed a natural trail around the side leading back into deeper snow. Although more tiring to plough ankle-deep through the powder, they made quicker time without caring about loose scree slipping away on every step. The sun was just as bright around them and they squinted through the glare, but all the heat had gone out of it. The winds picked up, nipping at them as they unrolled their cloaks and pulled them close.

Scab struggled each time they forded a deeper drift. Steps ankle-deep to the others mired him to his knees, and despite his clenched jaw, his lips were pale. Twice Soraya looked back at him with a raised eyebrow, but each time Foul shook his head and put his hand on Scab's shoulder, nudging him along. The path petered out and a final stretch of bare rock, sharply harrowed by some ancient cataclysm, led upward to the very summit.

"It's too far," Soraya announced and pointed to the sky. "Midday already, and we'll need the rest of the time to get back down safely."

Ghost's stomach dropped as he heard her and he spun to face her.

"One hour! It can't even be that! Look, you can see the top, it can't even be a mile..."

"Distances can be deceptive, you don't know how much longer it will be, nor how hard the last stretch might be."

He sunk to his knees, his eyes darting between the top of the mountain and Soraya's stern glare.

"It never takes as long to go down as to climb up! Just one more hour, I promise, we can make it there—"

"We agree," said Dogan.

"We were promised a race so we're going to have one," said Demir, nodding.

Dogan tossed his head. "You babies can go down now if you want. But we're going to prove who the best is. Once and for all."

Soraya put her hands on her hips. "I forbid you to go any further. We're all heading back down. End of discussion."

The twins looked at each other and bawled with laughter.

"Forbid us?"

"You'll have to catch us!"

They dropped their packs and started running up the slope, reaching for each other's hand as they swung past the edge of a ravine, then off again and upward.

Ghost watched them go and his pulse quickened. "Sorry, Soraya...," then he was on his feet and charging after the twins, his backpack scattered beside theirs.

"Stupid children!" Soraya screamed and stamped her feet as the three figures raced away.

She turned to the remaining boys and they shuffled uneasily under the intensity of her exasperation. Glaring at them, she slammed her fist into the palm of her hand, three times, as if visualising each face that was disobeying her. Then she closed her eyes and breathed deeply.

"There isn't a choice now. We have to follow them."

"Really?" Foul blinked in surprise. "Can't we just leave them and go back down?"

"She's right," sighed Fan. "It's our fault that they aren't already at the top, I mean look at them. They're running, godsblast them. I can barely walk and those idiots are racing each other."

Scab groaned. "Can't we just follow them slowly? I don't think its that far. They won't be out of sight for long."

Soraya's hand wrapped around her fist as she ran her thumb over her knuckles. "Come on then. We'll sort this out later."

They clambered to their feet and wearily stumbled across the steepening slope. Soraya, Fan and Crooked each bearing an additional pack as well as their own. To the left, the ground fell away steeply to a sharp crevasse whose chthonian depths were lost in blackness. Scree and small stones thrown up by the rapid passage of Ghost and the twins spilled over the edge, rattled and then vanished in the silent abyss. Ahead of them, beginning to scale a nearly vertical section of cliff face that led to the summit, three small figures clung to the rock.

The twins pulled ahead, climbing as a team. One of them took a solid grip before supporting the other moving upward with his outstretched arm, and then following his brother up once his grip was certain. Ghost moved economically, testing each foothold and handgrip before drawing himself up. Not looking at the twins who paused to shout a jibe each time they increased their lead. They didn't try to dislodge the rocks above, but the unstable surface crumbled under the weight of toes and scrabbling fingers, showering Ghost in gravel.

Soraya stopped the rest of the boys at the edge of the cliff. "We'll wait here. It's too dangerous to climb after them. Damn it! I'm going to give them such a pounding when they get back here."

Fan eased his pack off and sat down. "You can give them each a thump from me while you're at it. I'm sick of all three."

Ghost followed a diagonal path, away from the twins and the falling stones. Along a fresh series of grips that he swung between, gaining height and drawing level with them. Only a few dozen yards remained to the top of the cliff, and the brothers cursed in unison. They climbed quicker, their path veering back toward Ghost as they chased him.

Soraya shrieked as she saw them heading toward the crevasse-riven edge of the cliff. "Not that way!" She waved her arms desperately but they didn't look down.

Crooked rose to his feet, his eyes widening as he saw the sheer drop that broke away from the mountainside. "Stop it! Stop!"

Shading his eyes, Fan squinted at the figures at the top of the cliff wall. "What do they think they're doing? I can barely see them."

Dogan reached for a higher grip and pulled himself up. He released his brother's hand as he clung to the rock, seeking a higher toehold, and the rock came away between his fingers. His body rocked backward as his other hand started to slip. Demir cried out, and stretched out his hand, leaning for his brother, his fingers spasming as he clutched the air. Dogan's foot slipped from the crack it had been wedged in as his fingertips touched his brother's. Surging with a final burst of energy, Ghost hauled himself up the last few yards, half-rolling onto a narrow ledge, out of sight of those beneath.

He looked up, for the first time seeing nothing but sky; an infinity of freedom. This was it. Finally, he was here. Hills rolling further away, and beyond that the broad clear curve of the horizon. So pure and beautiful, so free. She had said, *come climb me, then you will feel true glory.* Was that thrill, that elation, was this his destiny? He'd made it to the top of the white mountain; the impossible, distant spire of his dreams now conquered beneath him. If he could do this, then he could do anything, every desire would come to him. She would reward him, take him in her arms, and all the pain and loss and yearning. All of it would be gone, done forever, and in its place; everything he had ever dreamed. The glory hammered a pulse in his veins, a spinning lightness to his belly, a floating freedom from all his worries and doubts. His mouth opened wide in a silent cheer as the reality of the accomplishment started to settle in.

Grinning, he struggled to get to his knees, chest burning from the exertion in the thin air, and a hand closed about his ankle.

Ghost tried to pull away even as Dogan hauled himself onto the ledge. His face twisted and ugly, Dogan pulled out his kukuri knife. "So you made it to the top first. Shame you won't be getting back down, not breathing anyway. Imagine my tears when I tell your friends about your terrible accident."

Dogan's words came out slurred, his eyes unfocused. He swayed as he circled Ghost, the curved blade between them.

"Don't be stupid," said Ghost, willing himself to stay calm but the bottled-up rage inside him snarled for release.

Demir's head and shoulders appeared over the edge, and he clung there panting. Dogan slashed a wide arc. Ghost flinched back, reaching for his own dagger. Dogan stabbed straight and Ghost clumsily parried, his knife knocked out of his hand, clattering across the rocks. A drowsy lethargy dulled his fingers, feet heavy and sluggish. The mountain sickness had taken him, sapping his strength.

Ghost's heart flipped and Dogan chuckled. "I told you I'd kill you. Doesn't mean I'm going to do you quickly. You're going to scream just like Timan. He begged me, you know. Begged for his life like a terrified woman."

"Brother, stop," said Demir wheezing where he hung, too tired to pull himself up.

Dogan's eyes flicked in the direction of his brother's voice and in that moment Ghost hit him in the face.

Hard.

CHAPTER 29:

THE WRATH OF BEY IZMIR

Rose petals fell like snow, their perfume misting through the sacred basilica.
All around the hymns of the novitiates soared through the slender white
pillars and danced with the marble angels in the balustrade. Hierarch Pallas
stood tall and proud as he always did when delivering his sermons; the
power of the words rejuvenating his aged frame, if just for those few minutes.
He stood with one hand raised in benediction, the other resting on the small
damask-covered casket that lay on the great altar.

A casket that held the body of a murdered child.

Bey Izmir stood holding his wife's hand, his uncle Pasha Izmir to one
side, his closest confidant Bey Yilmaz standing on his left. All around him
his beloved family and his staunchest allies. He was utterly alone. His face a
mask of stone. The choir sounded like nothing more than a creaking door
opening onto an empty and abandoned room. The highest representatives
of each court filed past him, murmuring their regrets, whispering their
condolences; the young Bey Ertegun and his heavily pregnant wife, Celia;
those of lesser courts wearing too much jewellery for a funeral but trying to
impress with their seriousness. The Thracian ambassador, copper hair
falling about his shoulders, no words could express more than his puffy eyes
and clenched jaw. He'd built Yani a toy boat and showed him how to sail it
in the pond last summer. A memory comes—the child's cries of delight as
the wind caught the miniature sails. Then memories are forced from him as
another hand is thrust into his, they mumble words he cannot hear, he nods

then the next hand takes his. Even Bey Firat, hostilities between them abandoned at such an event, greeted him with sad politeness, clasped hands warmly. Nothing but formalities and platitudes from Curator Nicodemus of the Oculus Dei.

There were so many courts represented at these final rites that the cavernous cathedral felt more like a marketplace. So many families in their most expensive, yet demure, outfits, and supported by only the most indispensable of their retainers without whom they couldn't possibly function. Moving amongst Bey Firat's entourage, arranging chairs and smoothing laceworks, a frail and greasy fellow. His bloodshot eyes and trembling hands might signal the grief he'd suffered over the death of such an innocent, and not, for example, a recent opium binge.

Bey Izmir couldn't hear the words the Hierarch spoke, even when it appeared the windows themselves rattled at the thunderstorm of his impassioned oratory. Just dull echoes suffused with his pain and loss. Then it seemed to him that some time must have passed. Everything he saw was roughly rendered in shades of grey. Vision blurring as he swayed, not understanding how his legs still managed to hold him upright when all he wanted for the future was going into the ground; all too soon. Watching as his mind tremored, unable to accept the horror, reality fled from him. Faint echoes of distant voices against the stones. A shred of his sanity observing that any man's descent into madness must look very similar. He became aware that it seemed the grand temple stood empty. All of the votive candles burned down to stubs, just a flicker here and there, wisps of incense. He stood staring at an empty altar that had borne the body of his only son.

Baba! Baba!

The cries of his little boy. He should have heard them, felt them, somehow have known. Somehow should have saved him. He blinked away tears as firm hands took him by the shoulders and squeezed him into a hug.

"Bey Yilmaz, I'm sorry I didn't realise you were still here," said Bey

Izmir. His grief and isolation had made him imagine that everyone had already left, so alone he felt. The spell was broken and reality crashed back into existence around him. The voices surged chaotically around leaving him queasy and disoriented.

"I am always here for you, my friend. Always." Bey Yilmaz was not a tall or powerful man, but his eyes bore a frenetic energy; flickering between brilliant genius and sparkling geniality. He steadied Bey Izmir who swayed as he stood there. "Such a thing, ach! No parent should have to bear such a thing."

And he could still see it, every time he closed his eyes. The white spire, streaked with blood, the tiny shape on the flagpole, the one his guards gesticulated at with such urgency. The shape that was too far away for him to make out what it was, and yet he knew this was his only son, little Yani. Dead by the most brutal of violence. He could never unsee it.

"What will you do now? The whispers amongst the courts is that your spirit is broken, and it may be time for a new election," said Bey Yilmaz.

Bey Izmir glared at Bey Yilmaz, then his shoulders slumped and he nodded. "Thank you my friend, but the courts will have to wait. In the morning I'm leaving with all my household to our estate in Heraclea. We will grieve in private and wear the black there for a year before we return."

More nobles shuffled past, whispering words of sorrow and genuflecting. Bey Izmir didn't glance at them; gave no sign he even knew they were there.

"A year?" Bey Yilmaz ran his fingernails over the creases in his brow. "It will be difficult to maintain your position with such an absence, and besides, how would the courts be guided? The clerics or the Oikos will surely take advantage of this situation."

The altar lay cold and bare, a loose wreath of petals garlanding its pedestal. The body that had once borne the soul of his only son had been given to the sacred flame. All hopes for the future were now in the past. Were now ashes on the ground.

"They know me as I was. Izmir the Diplomat. Izmir the Negotiator. Everything I valued I built through words and reason. Guile and deception only when absolutely necessary, and only to foster peace. They think me broken? Then it is true. That Bey Izmir is gone. Crushed by his burdens and his failings. They will see that, and they will look away, return to other schemes and machinations. I will not be expected, nor will my actions."

Bey Yilmaz frowned. "Don't renounce all that you've achieved so quickly—"

"Achieved? Precious little. A broad consensus amongst the courts that our shared interests must be protected and that we should work together. Hardly a revolution. And all the while the world turns and we become less relevant by the hour. Tell me Bey Yilmaz, have you determined who killed my son, and why?"

"Multiple informants in the Shambles reports that Zarbenus brags of the act by his own hand," said Bey Yilmaz.

Bey Izmir covered his face with his hands. "He boasts? This makes no sense. What would that braggart gain by killing a child? Zarbenus must be put to death, but before he dies I must know for sure who he acts with."

"That... cannot be a very long list of suspects."

Bey Izmir stared at the altar Hierarch Pallas stood behind during his son's funeral. The man of the goddess; of charity, forgiveness, and of brotherhood. Even now Pallas intoned long verses from the Litanies of Faith, soothing words of comfort for those most in need of them.

"I need absolute proof and only then will I act. We require new associates. The kind I have long averred from involving myself with. Effective and efficient, and totally without remorse. Tell me, Yilmaz, can we find such people?"

"It is something I shall put into play during your absence. It will appear to observers that I am seeking to solidify my own foundations, building a power base from which I can assault your position. My thoughts however turn to an opportunity we may have at our disposal, given the events which have unfolded. I have information regarding the whereabouts of the legendary assassin known as the Death Crow. Furthermore, I understand that he is no supporter of Zarbenus."

"Then recruit him by whatever means necessary. Let all think I have been vanquished, let them scrabble for control over that which I cede. When I return I will purge this city with the blood of the unrighteous. Summon Nicodemus."

"Lord, you know he is the Hierarch's man?"

The Pasha's guards had already escorted the Curator of the Oculus Dei into the presence of Bey Izmir. Nicodemus briefly exchanged nods with Bey Yilmaz, then clearing his throat he swept a deep bow.

"My lord, my deepest condolences, if there is anything—"

"Kneel, spymaster. As is fitting before your masters," said Bey Izmir without preamble.

His cheeks reddening, Nicodemus carefully arranged his robes and did so.

"Lord, if I have offended..."

"Place your sword across his throat," said Bey Izmir to the nearest guard, whose blade answered immediately. "Speak now of Zarbenus. Make it useful enough that I will consider you to be similarly valuable."

The Hierarch paused his sermon and the entire crowd fell silent as they watched the scene before them. Undignified and unbecoming of a state funeral, yet impossible to ignore. Pallas' brow furrowed looking at the scene before them. Unimaginable for decades: the Curator of the Oculus Dei kneeling before the First Voice of the Council of Courts.

Nicodemus flapped his jaw, then swallowing hard said, "We have an informant amongst his apprentices, maybe..."

"Good," said Bey Izmir. "Find out which he loves the most, the one he prizes above all others... and punish them with a cruelty that will live for centuries in infamy. Now go, for I must be with my wife at this time."

The silence in the chapel was absolute. It was a credit to Nicodemus' courage that he spoke again.

"And Zarbenus?"

"I don't want him killed. I want everything he holds dear to be shattered and burned. To crumble in his hands as he weeps powerlessly for all time. I want him to live as long as possible with his mind and spirit destroyed. I do not ask this, Nicodemus. I do not even threaten you—I command it. Too long have I sought political expediency and diplomatic accord. Those days lie in the ground beneath my son's coffin."

With that Bey Izmir turned and left, Bey Yilmaz patting his shoulder and accompanying the retinue.

Chapter 30:
One Down

Dogan stumbled back, his foot skidded on loose stones. He staggered as he caught himself, stood upright. Unsteady lurching like a drunkard he brandished the kukuri as one knee wobbled beneath him. He touched his face, smeared the blood that flowed freely from his nose. He frowned, he swayed, and his ankle turned. Then he just seemed to lean backward.

"Oh," he said, frustration etching lines in his brow.

Ghost stopped breathing as ice ran through his veins, momentary clarity lifting the dull fog that wrapped his senses, muffled his thoughts. Dogan drifted away and fell from the cliff. Such a slight movement, an autumn leaf dropping, then he was past the edge of the ravine and gone. Ghost's knuckles had tensed and his fist had launched without any intervening thought. Blood demanded blood. Inside him, a voice roared its exultation; the vengeful voice he hated but never went away for long.

The moment's silence shattered by Demir. Screaming incessantly. It was the screaming that finally forced Ghost to look around. Demir clinging to the edge a few feet from the summit. Shaking. His face mottled white and red; pinprick pupils bathed in madness.

Watching from below, the battle hidden from view, all they saw was Dogan falling, his arms splayed wide. Fan fell to his knees as Crooked and Soraya ran to the edge of the crevasse. Nothing looked back but the endless darkness of the depths.

"He's gone," she whispered, then buried her face in Crooked's shoulder.

Ghost stood motionless and saw the wide expanse of the plains beneath the mountain. All the world for one moment, then the chilling knowledge of the price. A strange wetness on his cheeks. He tore himself away from his stricken paralysis and back to the edge of the cliff. Climbing down to Demir, still clinging to the same position—staring at the shadow of the crevasse and a tortured moan coming from deep inside of him.

"Take my hand," said Ghost.

He touched his fingers to Demir's wrist. There was no resistance as he tugged Demir's arm down to a lower hold, and moulded his fingers into a grip.

"Come on, grab it, we'll go down together. Demir... you can't tell anyone. Night Mother, I beg you. You know it wasn't my fault, but they'll blame me. Us. We'll both pay for it if you tell them. He tried to kill me, you know that."

Demir's moaning became a quiet sobbing, punctuated by great long gasps for air. He turned his head to gaze blankly at Ghost and the new grip he held, his eyes bloodshot and unfocused.

"We need to go down now." Ghost tested a foothold and tapped Demir on the ankle with his toe. "This foot now. I'm with you."

They moved down the cliff slowly. One grip at a time, then not another for long minutes as howls of grief suffused Demir. He shook even as Ghost rubbed his shoulder and tried to bear some of the burden of loss. By the time they made it to the base of the cliff Demir had fallen silent, his breathing shallow and irregular. Above them, the sun began the descent of early afternoon.

"We can't see where he... it's too deep." Soraya stared at the ground.

"I couldn't... he just fell—" Ghost looked her, then Fan, then Crooked. Meeting their eyes for a moment, then his cheeks burned. They couldn't know, he couldn't bear for them to know. He was a murderer. Again.

"I warned you," said Soraya, her mouth a tight line.

Demir's vacant gaze wandered to each of them, but none could bear to look at him. He sat on the ground, clutching his knees to his chest. Fan's face a stern mask as he glared at Ghost. Shame filling him, Ghost looked away.

"What do we do now?" Crooked's voice cracked as he spoke, still peering into the ravine.

"We have to head back," said Soraya. "There's nothing left to do." She picked up her pack and slung it on her back. "Ghost, can you keep Demir moving?"

Ghost nodded. Too drained to speak, too tired to think. They moved away from the cliff, Ghost glanced back over his shoulder with the feeling that he might see Dogan climbing over the edge; laughing at them for worrying. But there was no-one there. He felt inside his tunic and found the old silver denarius, worn at the edges, a secret he'd hidden for so long. He squeezed it in his palm, then threw it into the ravine, thinking that everyone deserves the ferryman. Then Ghost took his own pack over one shoulder, and Demir's over the other. He put an arm around his charge, tugging him after the others, and they followed with uncertain steps.

The wind turned colder and with it came flecks of snow. The sun grew paler as it slipped behind the foggy cloud that shrouded the summit, and the pallid light gave little comfort as they trudged downward. By the time they reached the snowfield the wind buffeted them from side to side powdering their clothes with snow. Scab stumbled with every step, his eyes tinged with a sickly jaundice. Foul asked him how he felt, but the words that came out in reply were slurred and unintelligible.

"Soraya, we need to rest," said Foul. "Something's badly wrong with Scab, and he's getting worse."

She shook her head. "The only thing that will help him is to get down this cliff. The mountain sickness isn't going to kill us. If the storm comes we won't survive the night."

Ghost looked around and as the skies darkened and swathes of snow

settled around them. He half-remembered stories from a lifetime ago. In a
mountain village that might have been his home.

"If the storm hits when we're out in the open none of us will make it
down. We need shelter."

"No!" Soraya shook her head vigorously. "Every step we take down is
closer to safety. You think any of us care what you think? Once we make it
to the snowline things will get better from there."

The mountain gave its answer as the last of the sunlight faded to the dull
hue of iron. Hateful winds surged and howled around them, ancient curses
in a language older than time. Scab tripped and fell, lay face-down and
motionless. Foul knelt by his side, tearing off his cloak and wrapping it
around the small shivering body.

"We're not going to make it. We have to get to the caves." Ghost pulled
on Soraya's sleeve, shouting to be heard.

She pinched the brow of her nose. "Fine. Do you remember where they
were?"

"Just beyond this snowfield, at the base of the broken shard. At least we'll
be out of this wind."

"Alright, lead on," said Soraya grimly.

Ghost guided Demir onward, holding him tight around the shoulders,
dragging him down the slope. Battering gusts of ice-flecked storm collided
with them in waves. Forcing them to a standstill, their heads bowed against
the onslaught. Foul carried Scab, draped in his arms; no longer shivering,
but hardly breathing. The snow drove at them in sheets and flurries,
intangible grey swirling worse than fog and only the total blackness of the
mountain to their backs permitting any sense of direction. Stumbling
through a drift that went past his knees, Ghost broke free and onto the loose
scatter of rocks at the base of the shard, disappearing under fresh powder.

"In here!" Ghost yelled.

He barely heard his own words and dragged Demir toward the cave mouth. Demir stood and stared into the darkness and Ghost put an arm around his waist to urge him forward. Fallen rocks half blocked the entrance to the cave, and sandy grit slipped underfoot as they clambered over. Crooked stumbled in, followed by Fan who waited by the cave mouth, calling into the storm for the others. A minute later Foul staggered in, Scab's cloak-wrapped body in his arms, Soraya clutching his shoulder so that they would not be separated. Ghost tugged on Demir's arm until he crumpled noiselessly onto the ground, and the others huddled up next to him. The cave only went back a few yards, little more than a fault in the rock face where elemental forces had shattered the mountain's shoulders. Sheltered from the force of the gale wind and the lacerating ice grit, they took a moment's relief of the shelter before the cold began to gnaw at them, creeping up through the rocks and biting through their clothes. Snow piled up at the entrance, their grey twilight drawing close and fading with each moment.

"He's hardly breathing." Foul's words slurred as he squatted over Scab.

"We all need to keep close together. We can wrap our blankets around us as well." Soraya fumbled in her pack, drawing out her sleeping roll and folding it around Scab before searching another pack for one to cover herself with.

"I'll be the one with my back to the cave mouth," said Ghost avoiding eye contact.

"We should all take turns." Crooked rose to swap places but Ghost pushed him back down.

"It is my fault. This whole thing was my idea," said Ghost.

"You didn't start the race after Soraya said we had to go down, it was..." Fan trailed off, looking at Demir who remained unmoving, and gave no indication he could hear anything being said. "I know some of you are thinking Dogan had some bad luck owed to him, and maybe he did." Fan and Soraya glared at each other. "But none of the rest of us would be here if it wasn't for you, Ghost. I told you to leave the twins to me. I warned you—"

"Stop it!" Even in the gloom of the cave, they knew the look that would be on Soraya's face when she spoke. "This is no time for blaming someone, even if someone was to blame. Some of us hated Dogan? Fine, I'll say it: I did. But we need to stick together and get through this; as the Vipers. Have some food. We have to keep warm and a full belly is the best way we can do that."

"What about a fire?" Crooked rattled his tinderbox. "My makings are dry."

"We don't have anything to burn except our blankets which we won't survive without, and our packs," said Soraya, her voice a forced monotone.

Crooked felt around inside his pack. "We've got a lot of rope as well."

Soraya snorted. "Burning rope and canvas packs won't keep us warm for long. Have your food and be quiet for a bit. I need to think."

Fan coughed. "Some of us should go for help. Scab and Demir are in trouble, but I reckon I could make it down the mountain and to the Turanian camp. They'd help us, wouldn't they?"

"No," said Ghost. "Soraya is right. We have to stay put. Our only chance is this cave."

"Why should we listen to you?" They jumped when Demir spoke, his voice racked with pain as he choked on the words. "After... after... this was all your idea...?" Tears filled his eyes and he rocked from side to side, gulping the air as his chest shook.

Ghost sat with his back to the entrance and the pale light that rose and fell with the ebb and swell of the storm. "Because it is still the right thing to do, whether you trust me or not. Any one of you can repeat the decision aloud and we'll say it's your idea, but going out there now is a death sentence."

In the silence that followed they fidgeted with their cloaks, tweaking hoods closer and tightening the blankets over their shoulders.

356

Fan cleared his throat, breaking the moment. "If this is how I die then I regret not making a last visit to the bakery in the village. I really could do with one of those honey-nut loaves about now."

Crooked giggled. "I don't want to die without tasting all the different cakes in the world."

"There are so many tales to learn, and I've learned so few," said Soraya as a smile uncreased her brow.

Ghost nodded, wiping his cheek with the edge of his hood and hoping they all thought he was merely tucking it closer. "If I die here I'll have never seen a jungle. Or a desert. Or the edge of the world. I don't want to die here."

Soraya touched his wrist and her warmth made him jerk away. She shook her head and tried again. "Are those your biggest regrets? Things you'll never get to do?"

Ghost remembered the night he strangled the child for its cloak—another cold night with lives on the line. He had two deaths on his hands now. Bloody hands. His throat closed up like spectral hands were throttling him. He thought of their faces and wondered if because of him the faces of all the others here today will be added to his memories. Maybe his punishment was to survive and carry the guilt with him wherever he went.

"I wish I hadn't made you all come out here."

The storm shifted direction and the gusting wind blew eddies of snow into the cave, clustering at the entrance and slowly piling higher. When it started to fall against Ghost's cloak he rose and swept it back with his hands, red and stiff from the cold, until the drift became a wall covering the entranceway to half height. Even when the wind turned in their direction the whistling chill went over their heads, and by measures they felt cold but their teeth stopped chattering. Scab stirred and mumbled. Yawning he allowed Fan to trickle some water between his lips and then feed him crumbled chunks of cheese. After chewing slowly and slurring his thanks his eyelids drooped again and he slid back into sleep, erratic whistles of breath his only sign of life. Foul curled around Scab and fell asleep, his normally pale skin tinged blue. Fan rocked back on his heels and his head dropped with a sigh.

Ghost felt the ache of the day's exertion in the clenching of his frozen back but refused to let his head slip or his eyes close. He held the image of Dogan falling away from the cliff edge in his mind. The sickness of shame that crushed his heart in iron fingers beat back the tendrils of sleep that wriggled at the back of his mind. He watched as one by one the others finished eating and put down their heads. Their breathing and snuffling whispered around the stone walls, the world outside the cave forgotten for a short while. By the time all the light from the cave entrance had gone the cold crept forward once again. The noise of the storm abated but the temperature dropped even further. Ghost rubbed ice crystals away from his eyelashes, willing himself to fight the fear even as it prowled in the dark, just out of sight. Death waited for all of them, but it watched him the closest, waiting for him to give up. Inch by inch it crawled toward him. Not so long ago he was counting the hours until the sun denied him his adventure on the mountain. Now the only thing he wanted was the daybreak; enough sun to keep his friends alive. The breathing from the sleeping bodies became softer and slower and his own thoughts evaporated like mist.

He shook his head and clapped his arms around his body. Slapped his arms and shoulders to bring some small glow of warmth back into them. The prowling death, just beyond his sight, padded around him. Smelling his weakness. Its hunger growing. Ghost's every movement took more effort than the last and warmed him less. All the while fighting the dull creeping desire to put his head down. To stop worrying. To sleep.

We will all die here tonight.

† † †

Damnation-burning-corpse-filth-dog-puke.

What a miserable hangover from hell. Zarbenus tugged his cowl so low he barely saw where he was going; just to protect his bloodshot eyes from any sunlight. His mouth sandy and sickly like he'd been licking a camel's arse all night. With each leaden step, his weary feet reminded him that with each year passing he was one closer to obscurity. As a miserable senile wretch that needed help to feed itself.

I'd rather die.

Easy to say but harder to act on when you've spent every hour of your life making sure that despite the adversities and enemies you so precociously court, you'll still make it to the next day.

And be one day older.

Which doesn't leave any alternatives, does it? Damn that Pallas—he was right all along. Him and his blasted sanctimonious Goddess. So that was what it feels like when she shoves her fist into your head and plays dice with your dreams. No wonder Pallas takes it all so seriously—and he gets these messages from her again and again? I almost feel sympathy for that shrivelled cadaver. Well, let's not go too far. Oh my head...

Zarbenus trudged the last few steps toward the Nidus, wrenched open the door and staggered in. Scratching idly at embers that floated under his skin. A dragon dwelt in his veins now, just as Pallas said it would. The house sulked in silence. Excellent. Those brats were off somewhere, and he could just crawl into his bed with a jar of wine and sup his problems away. His thoughts wandered, dull and aching somewhere in a skull that throbbed in rhythm with his pulse.

What did I want? Oh, yes. Wine.

He lurched to the kitchen, pouring himself a tankard of water from the pitcher by the door. He drained it in one go, and started a second which he sipped more sedately. On the high shelf two bulbous blue-glazed flasks from Butra. They made his tongue woolly but that would be an improvement over the reverberating headache that cloyed at him. He staggered out the kitchen with a flask in each hand. Making for the stairs, pausing by the big open window that looked to the north.

The great twin mountain peaks stood out clearly in the distance, burnished gold and red by the sun on the western slopes. The white-capped spire challenging the sky.

Zarbenus dropped both flasks, oblivious to the sound as they shattered; rich red splattering the floor and soaking into the tiles.

The white spire.

He roared inchoate demands for the Vipers to instantly appear before him. Ran up the stairs in three bounds, kicking open doors and snatching at abandoned bedsheets. His body slicked with icy sweat, claws in his bowels that threatened to give way, twitching shaking hands.

Where were they? Where was the boy?

A scrap of parchment lay the table, held in place by the little poison bottle. Zarbenus snatched it up, glanced at it, then slapped it back down. He slumped over the window ledge, staring at the mountain, willing himself to see tiny black figures against the snow. Everything his nightmares threatened coming to pass. What if Ghost ascended the white spire of the mountain? What if he slew the others there? Zarbenus' chest tightened, each breath a battle. He hadn't anticipated that the pampered Bey Izmir would seek such bloody retribution—and how was it even possible he suspected? This couldn't be true—it was he, Zarbenus who was destined to be greater than any before him.

He needed to find them. He needed to stop them. Before it was too late.

† † †

Blinking as he struggled against his own lolling head, twice as heavy as he could ever remember it. Ghost fumbled in his pack baffled by numb fingers, raw and chapped. He pulled out his tinderbox, dropping it twice before he managed to open it. The cold whispered to him. Telling him to lie down and sleep. Just for a few minutes. It wouldn't hurt to rest when he was so very sleepy.

Ghost spilled the straw and peelings of silver birch bark on top of his pack. Clumsily tried to form it into a mound with someone else's hands that refused to obey his commands. The hanked rope formed a loop but he knocked the mound aside with his trembling as he tried to encircle it. He swept the tinder up again, a small pile in the coil of climbing rope. His head nodding as he pushed complaining fingers into the loop of the firesteel and swung it at the flint in the tinderbox.

A single flare in the darkness. A pulsing spectral image that faded through shades of grey back into black again. He struck the stone again and the spark landed in the tinder. Glowing with desperate promise for a moment then dying away. The cold clawed his ribcage, a ghoulish grasp that pierced with each shallow breath. Eyelids so heavy he let them drift closed, just for a moment, his head nodded forward. The last weary movement, he struck the stone again.

A crackling noise on the edge of dreams. Dim red glow through his eyelids. Tarred rope, charring sulphurously, then burning with gusto. He coughed as thick smoke caught in his throat and small flames echoed on his cheeks, lapping against his clothing. Ghost flopped onto his side, no strength to raise himself, and dragged the first pack he could find closer. Searching it for food and water, and finding none, he tore it apart, driving his knife through the rough burlap. His fingers prickled with fresh blood flowing through them, but at least responded to his demands. He built the fire higher, setting aside the tarred portions of rope to be used carefully and putting the leather straps in the heart of the flames so they charred faster. The other packs held morsels of food and half-full canteens of water. He set the supplies aside and continued with his destruction of the rest of their gear. Watching the fire became a trance. Time ceased to have meaning outside of the tiny puddle of warmth. Knowing exactly how many pieces of rope and how many pieces of canvas remained. Knowing how long each would burn for. How fast. So much smoke—don't let it die away—don't burn the fuel too fast.

The last pieces went into the flames. A pale grey crept into the cave but Ghost didn't know whether he simply dreamed. He lay beside the cluster of bodies, spread his blanket across them. Then with nothing left within him to give, too weary to care, the cold finally took him down. Down to the still and the dark and the nothing.

Soraya shook him awake, pushing Ghost off her as she struggled out from under the pile of bodies and blankets. His head bumped on the floor and he screwed his eyes tight against the light that streamed into the cave. Muttering that he only wanted one more hour in bed.

"We made it..." Crooked sounded surprised. "I was so cold I didn't think I would wake up. I remember going to sleep and I don't remember any more than that."

"Mmm, I'm hungry. Is there any food?" Scab sat up. He stretched and yawned.

Fan kicked the ashes of the fire with his toe. "It looks like Ghost burned everything."

"He did what he had to," said Soraya. "I don't even remember going to sleep so I ken he probably saved us."

"I didn't do anything special." Ghost stifled a yawn and then got unsteadily to his feet.

"Nevertheless, thank you." Soraya smiled at him before picking through the last of the food and dividing it up between them. "Eat the last little bits and we'll get out of here."

Demir took the portion she passed him, looking at her with sad eyes and downturned lips before turning away to eat. Fan slapped her hand away when she passed him a dried apricot.

"This idiot nearly got us all killed on his precious adventure, and you're thanking him? How do you think *he* feels?" He pointed at Demir staring at

362

the ground between his feet.

"Wait a minute..." Ghost raised his hands, but Fan barged in front of him. Thrusting fingers jabbed him in the chest.

"Dogan is dead because of you, and it's only a freak chance that the rest of us survived. When the Magister hears about this then you're gone for certain. Just like Timan. Just like everyone who failed. And do you know what I say? Good riddance. You're dangerous and selfish, Don't even try to blame it on Demir; you want to be treated like a man then bear your part in it. We're better off without you."

Ghost's heart lurched at the thought. He turned to Soraya, jaw opening and closing as he struggled for words.

She shrugged. "He's right, you know. It was your plan, and we did say it was dangerous."

"But we all agreed to go!" Ghost's cheeks flushed.

"I da ken the Magister will think differently," said Crooked. "I mean... I don't blame you... sorry... but I ken he will. And probably us with you. I can't... have him throw us out."

Soraya reached out to comfort Ghost, but he flinched away from her touch. "I don't need your pity! I'll tell him that I made you follow me. He can do what he likes to me—"

"Settle down!" Her bark cut the argument short. "We aren't out of this yet and we aren't home yet. Bickering like babies won't help us nor will it answer what the Magister will do. If you've all finished eating then I suggest you wrap up in your blankets and we get moving. Scab, are you strong enough to walk?"

"A bit weak but I'll manage." He leaned over to Foul and nudged him. "I ken it'll get easier as we get onto the lower slopes."

"Fine. Pick up your things and let's get a move on," she said.

"He won't wake up," said Scab a moment later. He jostled Foul's shoulder, looked up at the others. Fan scooted Scab to the side and knelt beside them. He placed his hand on Foul's cheek, then his head bowed.

"He won't be waking up. He didn't make it."

Scab crumpled to the ground, burying his face in his arms.

"I know," said Fan. "He carried you in here through the storm. It took everything he had."

Ghost felt the ice drawing through his limbs all over again. "I—"

"Shut it," said Fan. "I'm this close to finishing you and burying the both of you here. Side by side. You speak a word to me ever again, and it'll be your epitaph." He faced away from the others as he collected their few remaining possessions. Even Soraya didn't raise her head or question him.

"We can't just leave him," wailed Scab.

Fan stood and turned his back on them. He swept Scab up over his shoulder and faced the snow wall that Ghost had made across the entrance to the cave. Overnight the packed snow had frozen solid, and Fan kicked it down. Snow covered the mountainside, and they squinted in the glare. Each footfall crunched as they followed the slope down, walking in terse contemplation of the day and the night that had passed before; the only sound Scab's sobbing. Fan's steady plodding pace led them on, his fury omnipresent. They walked within the storm of his wrath, despite the clear skies. Electric tension and a fearful anticipation of thunder.

The snow thinned as they walked lower, patchy drifts and sparkling rivulets of meltwater. After an hour they climbed down slopes where the snow nestled only in banks of shadow, and the rising sun caressed their foreheads. Passing over the rocks with the blue-tinged lichens, they left the last of the snow behind and moved between the tumbles of giant boulders strewn across the mid slopes of the mountain. Eventually when Scab fell silent Fan set him onto his feet and they walked together; Fan's hand on his shoulder. Climbing down came easier than scaling the mountain the previous day, though they skidded through the gravel streams. Scab and Demir both tumbled time and again, scraping their palms and knees as they went down, raising muttered curses from Scab but not a word from Demir. He lay on the ground, glassy eyes staring at nothing that was left in this world, then rose to his feet and resumed his silent progress. The sun eased higher through mid-morning, and with it the heat of the plains. Memories of the frozen night slowly baked out of their bones. Sweat streamed down their faces and more than one of them secretly wished for a handful of snow to cool their necks. As they walked the lower slopes the land levelled out until through the dust that hazed the horizon they spied the tents of the Turanian nomads.

The tents were still some way off when they saw a man running toward them. His cloak trailed out and his long black hair streamed behind him.

Ghost's palms grew damp. "He's come for us."

† † †

Zarbenus slowed when he saw them. From a breakneck sprint, to a loping run, a jog. Then long strides. Flanks heaving, he stood still as the children approached chewing their lips. The Magister pulled up his hood and his features disappeared into shadow.

"Where have you been? I arrived back yesterday only to find my house empty and cold. I followed your trail all night without sleep. And..."

Zarbenus paused, only glancing at each of them until he saw Ghost. He took a deep breath, then he frowned. "Where is Dogan? Where is Foul?"

Demir shrieked and jumped at Ghost. Fingers hooked, clawing for his face and knocking him to the ground.

"Stop this." Zarbenus picked up Demir by his belt, hauling him off Ghost who lay motionless on the ground. Staring at the sky, red welts running down his cheeks.

"Soraya, speak. What trouble have you gotten them into?"

"Magister it wasn't—"

Crooked stepped between the Magister and Soraya. His expression pained but resolute. "It was Ghost. On his own. Soraya did nothing wrong."

"Enough excuses! Tell me what has happened." Zarbenus dropped Demir on the ground and he lay still, head against the soil and breathing heavily.

"They were climbing, and Dogan..." said Soraya.

Demir screwed his eyes shut but did not move.

Fan swung a half-hearted kick at Ghost who barely flinched. "He did it. He took us up there and then he raced the twins. Dogan fell and we were caught in a storm that nearly killed us."

The Magister raised an eyebrow at Soraya, then knelt and swept his hands along Ghost's limbs. Turned his feet from side to side, rotated his hands, counted fingers. Apparently satisfied, he grunted.

"Nothing broken. What happened to Foul?"

Soraya sat down beside Demir and shook her head. "Ghost tried to stay awake the whole night to tend the fire. Without him, we would have gone to sleep and never woken up. I... I tried to stay awake but the cold was too bitter and I couldn't fight it. We thought Scab wouldn't make it, and Foul... he didn't. Magister, I don't know how Ghost was able to last so long."

"His people come from a cold land. Maybe their blood freezes slowly." Zarbenus stood up. "It is time for us to go. Demir. Stand up. Now."

Demir stared with damp eyes at the Magister and his mouth opened. No words came in his silent wail of pain, but after a few moments he rolled onto one elbow and then jerkily up onto his feet.

"Let this be a lesson to all of you," said Zarbenus. "If you trust someone else's judgement, you place your life in their hands. Look what happened next. Don't trust anyone. Make your own judgements. Stay alive and free."

"It was my fault, Magister. I should never have asked them to come." Ghost could not bring himself to face Demir, and just stared at the mountain in the distance. The Great Sadness.

Zarbenus turned to Ghost. "Did you climb the mountain?"

Ghost hung his head. "Yes, Magister."

"Were the others with you?"

"No, Magister. I... was racing the twins. I climbed down when I saw... him go."

The Magister faced the others. "You who remain. Do you blame him for this? If any of you would share his fate, speak now. "

They turned to Ghost who would not look up. One by one they nodded, all save Soraya who covered her face when Crooked touched her shoulder.

"Soraya, do you stand with Ghost or stay with us? You know what lies ahead. What needs to be be done; in Her name," said the Magister.

"Please..." Crooked took her by the hand, squeezed it. She turned her face to him, her eyelashes glistening, then she nodded.

"Then it is settled. Ghost is now dead to us. Do you hear me? We will never speak of him or Dogan or Foul again. Soraya, can you lead them home, without another unfortunate incident?"

Soraya took a deep breath. "Yes, Magister."

"Await me there. The horse I stole is being tended by your Turanian friends. Give it to them as payment. Events in Byzantium are unfolding at pace and the situation requires concerted intervention. The time for training is over and the time of the Vipers is at hand. I will be gone for some time, but I expect to see everything in readiness when I return. Soraya, you know what must be done."

"Thank you for trusting me, Magister." Soraya waved the others forward. "Let's go. We have a lot of ground to cover today and need to forage as we go."

Demir started walking first, without looking back; a disjointed puppet with tangled strings. After a moment the others moved to follow him. The Magister's hand fell on Ghost's shoulder, restraining him.

"Not you," said Zarbenus. "I cannot risk you within a thousand miles of me for what happens next."

Ghost's heart lurched as he watched the small figures walking away from him. Crooked looked back, mouthed the word 'sorry', then he too turned away.

It should have been me to die. I've failed the Magister.

The Magister's grip tightened as he guided Ghost to face the other way. "I warned you that no-one would stand with you if it placed them in peril. Now you know the truth, so put them from your mind. It is time to take you somewhere else, but I know not where."

"Where are we going, Magister?" Ghost felt the stinging scratches on his face for the first time and knew his cheeks were red; twin badges of shame.

Zarbenus pushed back his hood and sighed. Ghost stared at the Magister; recently shaved and looking so youthful. And familiar. He looked like a vision of Ghost's future. Kanesh had been right; the resemblance was uncanny.

Zarbenus met Ghost's gaze, frowned, then tugged his cowl back up. The Tahtakale would be too perilous this time, too close to his enemies, but it did lead to an interesting idea.

"Never ask questions if you aren't prepared for an answer you don't like, my boy. We take a different path now. You are never going back to the Nidus."

Zarbenus' plans for Byzantium lay in turmoil, the ascension promised by Pallas lay in peril, and the boy... Would he be saviour or adversary? Much remained to be done, and perhaps it was best that Ghost remained unaware of the true extent of his plans. His enemies had multiplied—something that would weaken the spine of a lesser man—but he knew that in itself presented a particular opportunity. With so many targets appearing in every direction it would be hard to miss any of them.

A war is coming. I have my lieutenants, now I need a general. A warrior none can oppose.

There would be time enough to devise his counter-measures on the long

368

journey ahead. Such things could not, and should not be rushed. Zarbenus smiled, for he knew that in the end, all things come to a patient man.

EPILOGUE

Rajputana. Many weeks later.

The path crested over a hill and from the top they saw small fields lined with crops, and simple mud-brick houses with thatched roofs. All about lay the dark jungle; lush and impenetrable. The alien calls of howling monkeys drowned out the strange song of the birds. Ghost started to run ahead but stopped and reluctantly returned to the Magister's side on hearing a rebuking whistle. He scuffed his heels as he plodded, muttering about their sedate progress toward such an exciting destination.

"There. The camp with the stone walls. That is our destination."

Ghost's face brightened, but as they drew close they saw a crowd gathered at the gates of the compound. A child of less than ten summers trying to break free of those restraining her, weeping the whole time. The folk around her red-eyed and their faces etched with anguish.

Zarbenus snapped his fingers to get their attention. "What has happened?"

"A tiger was prowling around near the fields for the last few days, and we knew it meant that there must be a shortage of prey for it to leave the woods. We warned everyone not to travel alone, but—"

"My sister!" The little girl shrieked uncontrollably as two women tried vainly to pacify her.

"We managed to drive it off when we heard her screams, but we were too late... her wounds were terrible."

"But why are you here?" Zarbenus gestured around them.

An old man barely taller than the girl drummed his cane against the ground as he spoke. "The Rai always protects the village. He has gone to slay the beast."

"Alone?" Ghost's eyes widened as the snarling mythical image of a tiger rose up in his mind.

"Rai Kasmir is the greatest warrior in the world. He will defeat it. He always does." The old man nodded as the other villagers murmured their agreement.

The Magister shrugged. "Seems like a pointless risk to take. Why didn't any of you craven cowards go with him?"

"The Rai said he cannot fight the beast and protect us at the same time."

The God of Thieves shrugged again and sat on the ground beside the gate. He pulled his hood down over his brow and closed his eyes. Within moments snoring emanated from him.

"There!" A skinny man with thinning hair shaded his eyes against the sun and pointed toward the fields. A huge figure walked slowly towards them, his head bowed and taurine shoulders slumped as if bearing a great sadness.

"The Rai has returned!"

As the huge figure drew closer Ghost saw the black-bearded man massaging his right shoulder. His pale brown tunic of the same coarse weave as the rest of the villagers bore dark stains around a gash in his shoulder, and another along his flank. The Rai's tight-lipped expression melted when he saw the villagers waving, and deep creases in his dark brown skin appeared above his cheeks. The villagers startled as they saw his lacerations, and they ran to him—the tallest of them not reaching his shoulder, and none of them with a chest thick enough to rival his massive thighs.

"Rai! You are wounded?" They fussed over him and tutted at his injuries.

"Rai, you must change into fresh clothes. Let me wash these in the river and stitch them for you." A hook-nosed old woman plucked at his bloodied tunic.

The Rai sighed and plucked at his flowing beard, pinching out a silver hair. "Be easy, my friends. It is not all my blood, but I fear I am showing my age. Ten years ago it would never have laid a claw on me."

Ghost stared at him and wondered how the Rai could seem so calm after battling such a beast. Surely this must be one of the legendary heroes straight out of Soraya's tales. "Did you truly kill that tiger on your own?"

Rai Kasmir nodded, but the smile went out of his eyes. "Sometimes such things are necessary, though I did not do it gladly. It takes courage, training... oh, and these." Rai Kasmir patted long triangular sheaths strapped to his massive thighs. Leather-bound crossbar handles straddled two vertical iron tangs that were bonded to the punch-daggers in their sheaths. "The kitara—the weapon of a master."

He looked down at the snoring God of Thieves.

"So this rascal is back."

Zarbenus pushed back the lip of his hood and grinned up at Rai Kasmir.

"I've brought you a new student. He is insolent, undisciplined and lazy. Think you can make something of him?"

The Rai knelt down and bowed his head to investigate. Ghost squared his shoulders, gritted his teeth and stared back up.

"Tell me young man; do you deserve all those bad things this scoundrel says about you?"

Ghost's eyes narrowed. "I'm not lazy."

Rai Kasmir laughed and stood up.

"Very well. We will try."

The adventure continues in God of Thieves: Injustice!

AFTERWORD

The fantasy world of The Craft of Shadows draws from hundreds of years' of history and legends of the lands that they visit. I've never let historical accuracy get in the way of the story, and I hope you have as much fun reading it as I did writing it.

BEFORE YOU GO!

I hope you enjoyed this book and are fired up by a burning desire to shout the author's name from any conveniently located rooftops. Emerging authors are deeply grateful for each and every reader they connect with. It would mean the world to me if you took a few moments to click/tap/poke your review online.

Thank you, and see you soon!

DB

About the Author

Diavosh has lived in lots of different places (currently Andalucía) and has one of those accents you think you almost recognise but just can't quite place. His favourite animal is the tapir, the reason being abundantly obvious to fellow tapir fans, and is a keen collector of those odd little books you find in adventure movies that ultimately lead to a white-knuckle ride through the mysteries of a long-lost legend.

Unlike the prevailing stereotype, he has no cats.

ALSO BY DIAVOSH BASSITI

The Jewel of Nineveh

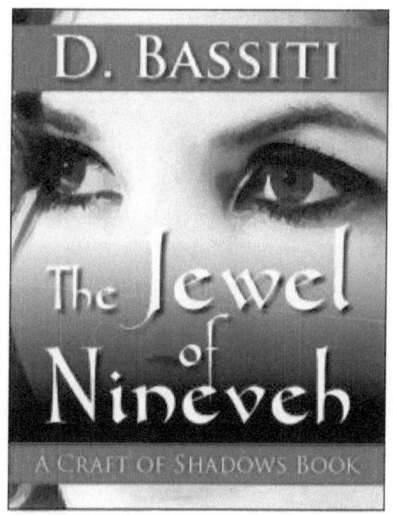

A lone thief fleeing conflict is trapped in a city being torn apart by intrigue, and finds his talents gain him the unwelcome attention of vying factions. His endurance and cunning are tested to breaking point as he struggles to stay alive and the spectre of war descends. As the stakes grow higher than his own problems he faces a dilemma; can one man make a difference?

—"A richly woven Persian rug of a story".

Amazon UK | Amazon US

Also From Vincto Publishing

Ten Little Lessons - Guided Lessons in Mindfulness by Louise Barker

If you don't believe in change then how can it occur?

My ego had to go. It was making my life a constant battle, but I've always seemed to learn the hard way. For my hard way to mindfulness, and for me to truly understand mindfulness, I needed to lose everything that was not within me.

The Little Book of Lessons are some of the tools that I have used throughout my own journey.

GLOSSARY

Athanatoi	"The Deathless Ones", fanatical warrior-priests in service of the Temple of the Goddess.
Basilisks	Byzantium armed forces under the control of the Noble Courts. Their name derives from "Basilikon telos" or the Royal Guards.
Bayezid	Rajput strongman in the Tahtakale performers, and guardian of Ghost during his time there.
Bey Ertegun	Leader of the Ertegun Court of nobles in Byzantium.
Bey Firat	Political rival of Bey Izmir, leader of the Firat Court of nobles.
Bey Izmir	Progressive First Voice of the Council of Courts, and heir apparent to the Pasha of Byzantium.
Bey Yilmaz	Highly intelligent and affable leader of the lesser Court Yilmaz. Supporter of Bey Izmir.
Captain Callista	Taciturn, one-eyed captain of the Failiana. Usually found working the route between the Black Sea and Byzantium.
Crooked	Freckly orphan rescued by Zarbenus to join the Vipers. Notable for his ingenious plans. Named after his limp.
Demir	Demir is the more reserved and cautious of twins rescued by Zarbenus. His brother is Dogan. The orphans, under the control of Zarbenus, form the group known as the Vipers.
Dogan	Dogan is the more outspoken and confrontational of twins rescued by Zarbenus. His brother is Demir. The orphans, under the control of Zarbenus, form the group known as the Vipers.
Doma Medea	Ancient and formidable matriarch of Oikos Medea.
Ertegun Court	Noble family of Byzantium.
Firat Court	Noble family of Byzantium. Once held the title of Pasha, still influential, rich and powerful.

Foul	Noisome orphan rescued by Zarbenus. The orphans, under the control of Zarbenus, form the group known as the Vipers.
Ghost	Ghost is a central character in God of Thieves, which broadly follows his life subsequent to his discovery as a feral orphan by Zarbenus, the Magister.
Hekate	Mistress of the Left-hand Path, Queen of the Night. Patron deity to Zarbenus and the thieves of Byzantium.
Hierius Hertia Hierius	Senior priest of the Temple of the Goddess.
Laetoria	Senior priest of the Temple of the Goddess.
Izmir Court	Noble family of Byzantium, that of the semi-retired Pasha and his influential son, Bey Izmir
Juventia Court	Noble family of Byzantium. Notable members include the great beauty, Celia.
Kanesh	Retired assassin and one-time conspirator of Zarbenus. Tavern keeper of the Grey Mouse in eastern Anatolia.
Kossak	Martial people of the mountainous regions to the west and north of the Black Sea.
Marius	Young protege of Hierarch Pallas.
Nicodemus	Virtuous and diligent Curator of the Oculus Dei; spymaster in service of the Temple of the Goddess.
Oculus Dei	"The Eye of God", espionage organisation in service of the Temple of the Goddess. Led by Curator Nicodemus.
Oikos Gavras	Thief-family of Byzantium.
Oikos Medea	One of the oldest surviving thief-families in Byzantium that control the underworld. Controlled by the crone Doma Medea.
Oikos Scylla	One of the oldest surviving thief-families in Byzantium that control the underworld.
Oikos Vlastos	Thief-family of Byzantium
Pallas	Scheming heirarch of the Temple of the Goddess.
Rai Kasmir	Noble Rajput warrior and master of the martial art of Gatka.
Raseyda	Acrobat in the Tahtakale performers, and guardian of Ghost during his time there.
Roach	Large and clumsy orphan rescued by Zarbenus to join the

Vipers.

Savarus	Grumpy ex-legionnaire and innkeeper of the 'Three Crows', close to the southeastern Lion Gate of Byzantium.
Scab	Scab is the diminutive and violent young orphan rescued by Zarbenus. The orphans, under the control of Zarbenus, form the group known as the Vipers.
Scab	Scab is the diminutive and violent young orphan rescued by Zarbenus. The orphans, under the control of Zarbenus, form the group known as the Vipers.
Tahtakale	Eastern district in Byzantium, near the Prosphorion Docks. Famed for its camp of acrobats and entertainers.
Temper	Fiery, orphaned Parthian girl rescued by Zarbenus to join the Vipers.
Temple of the Goddess	The dominant politico-religious force in Byzantium, based around the worship of a single Goddess figure.
The Vipers	A motley collection of orphans formed by Zarbenus for mysterious purposes
Timan	Apprentice to Zarbenus, occasional instructor to the younger Vipers.
Yilmaz Court	Noble family of Byzantium. Long-term allies and confidants of Izmir.
Zarbenus	Zarbenus is the eponymous anti-hero of God of Thieves. A mysterious master thief also known as, the Magister.